YOMI ADEGOKE is a multi-award-winning journalist and author. She is a columnist at the *Guardian* and British *Vogue* and co-wrote the bestselling non-fiction book *Slay In Your Lane*. In 2021, she featured on the *Forbes* 30 Under 30 list, and in 2023 was named one of the *Evening Standard*'s Leading Emerging Writers. *The List* is her debut novel and was an instant *Sunday Times* bestseller. It is being adapted for television by HBO, A24 and the BBC, for which she is writing and executive producing.

Praise for *The List*:

'One of the most anticipated books of the summer … It's obvious Adegoke's perspective is sorely needed in the culture'
Guardian

'One of the hottest books of the year … topical, thought-provoking and vital'
Marie Claire

'One of the most anticipated debuts of the year and with a perfectly manicured finger on the popular culture pulse, *The List* is a must-read … fans of *Yellowface* will love *The List*, too'
Red Magazine

'Thought-provoking and topical in its exploration of life both online and offline … it's written with sharp insight and is impossible to put down. The hype is real'
Independent

'This nuanced exploration of celebrity culture and online toxicity should win Adegoke new fans'　*Observer*

'Adegoke explores a tricky subject with enormous skill and delicacy, and the result is a brilliant, emotionally engaging novel, as taut as a thriller and just as compelling'　*Irish Times*

'Adegoke provides an acute and often chilling portrait of the power of social media, the online rush to judgement and the grey areas between guilt and innocence'　*Guardian*

'A deft exploration of sexual misconduct and cancel culture … Adegoke is operating right in publishing's red hot centre'
British GQ

'A blistering examination of the messy, knotted and contradictory intersection of social media and our private lives … a love story for our times'　*Harper's Bazaar*

'A great book … Such good reviews … So striking'
This Morning

'A topical, important and probing novel that thrashes out the moral issues around social media outrage and personal culpability. Adegoke captures an impressive array of voices and vernaculars with such supple verisimilitude, it feels as if her vividly realised characters are in the room with you'
BERNARDINE EVARISTO, author of *Girl, Woman, Other* in *Vogue*

'The kind of novel you can't stop talking or thinking about … powerfully irresistible'

SARA NISHA ADAMS, author of *The Reading List*

'Phenomenal. Brilliantly written, intricately plotted and incredibly clever … I'll be thinking about this book for a very long time'   ABI DARÉ, author of *The Girl with the Louding Voice*

'Cleverly constructed, utterly compelling, immersive and addictive'

SARA COLLINS, author of *The Confessions of Frannie Langton*

'An excellent novel by an excellent writer, full of sharp wit'

DIANA EVANS, author of *Ordinary People*

'A whip-smart and thought-provoking dissection of a terrifyingly plausible "what if" … a triumph'

RUTH WARE, author of *The It Girl*

'Beautifully written, bold and brave … A genius debut from a glorious emerging voice that must be heard'

DEBORAH FRANCES-WHITE, author of *The Guilty Feminist*

'An explosive and provocative critique. Adegoke asks: what does justice look like on the internet … impossible to put down'

SYMEON BROWN, author of *Get Rich or Lie Trying*

'A brilliant novel, every bit as entertaining as it is calmly, astutely condemning'   ANNIE LORD, author of *Notes on Heartbreak*

ALSO BY YOMI ADEGOKE
(with Elizabeth Uviebinené)

FICTION
The Offline Diaries

NON-FICTION
Slay In Your Lane: The Black Girl Bible
Slay In Your Lane: The Journal
Loud Black Girls

YOMI ADEGOKE

THE LIST

4th ESTATE • London

4th Estate
An imprint of HarperCollins*Publishers*
1 London Bridge Street
London SE1 9GF

www.4thEstate.co.uk

HarperCollins*Publishers*
Macken House, 39/40 Mayor Street Upper
Dublin 1, D01 C9W8, Ireland

First published in Great Britain in 2023 by 4th Estate
This 4th Estate paperback edition published in 2024

1

Set in Bembo Std
Printed and bound in the UK using 100%
renewable electricity at CPI Group (UK) Ltd

MIX
Paper | Supporting
responsible forestry
FSC™ C007454

In loving memory of my loving grandad

PART ONE

1

27 days to the wedding

They had been out celebrating the night before it happened. Their table, an unintended shrine to the schadenfreude gods, littered with emptied, gilded champagne flutes and bottles now upturned in their buckets. The happy couple unknowingly toasting the beginning of the end.

The room was dimly lit, the air salted by sweat from sticky-skinned revellers. It was after 9 p.m., so the bar area had morphed into a makeshift dance floor where London's shabbily dressed creative elite were slotting together like Tetris blocks. Michael surveyed the scene as he sat in the corner of an oxblood-coloured booth, his wife-to-be's long legs stretched out across his lap. He felt like the man. Sloppily drunk, Ola yawned jungle-cat wide under her mop of dark-blue braids. Then she stumbled slightly as she pulled herself upright to start their third fake fight of the night.

'But I CANNOT believe you,' Ola said faux-sulking, sticking out her bottom lip in a manner that took years off her. This was not helped by the fact that her dark plum lipstick was smeared at the corners of her mouth, making her baby-face resemble a toddler who'd raided her mum's make-up bag. 'You really can't say it?'

Michael reached over her lap for another glass. 'How am I supposed to know the answer, bruv!' he said. Though tipsy, he hadn't drunk that much and realised it would be some time before he caught up with her. They'd moved on to wine now and were sat in a private members' club whose name he couldn't remember; he wasn't even sure how'd they'd got in. Indiscriminate EDM was blaring from somewhere in the crowded room as he felt the Merlot mingle with his blood and warm him. It was all a happy blur: he wouldn't remember most of it the next day but the small details would stick with him. Ola's outfit – a black-lace bralette paired with a grey blazer and tapered trousers. Their stifled laughing at the wall-to-wall, off beat dad dancing. How her neck smelt, the softness of her skin and lips. They'd spent a good portion of the evening snogging in darkened corners like teenagers.

'It's a straightforward question, babe.' She pushed out her lip further still, in an unconvincing attempt to appear serious and slighted. 'You not answering is an answer, to be honest.' Ola clumsily untangled her legs from his and turned her back to him, arms crossed. Very obviously, she peered over her shoulder to see if he was still looking at her. 'If you're not gonna shed thug tears at the wedding, I don't even want it,' she slurred.

Michael feigned a pensive sigh, knowing it would rile her up. 'Aight, give me a minute to think.'

She whipped back around. 'A MINUTE? An entire sixty seconds to decide whether the 8th of June will be the happiest day of your life? The day you *yourself* said you've been waiting for since the first time you laid eyes on me? And then you wonder why I say men can lie!'

'I mean, I did see Thierry Henry at Gatwick that time in '08,' he offered wryly. 'And he nodded at me, I told you innit?'

'You're a prick …'

'Let me at least get to the church and see what it's saying,' Michael chuckled. 'You know I don't like weddings like that.'

Ola kissed her teeth. 'Yeah, well, at this rate there won't even be one. The fact you're saying you're not gonna be happy on our own wedding day—'

'Ola! When did I say that, please?'

'—is an absolute madness. What's currently ranking higher? Enlighten me.'

Michael stroked his beard.

'Do NOT say the first time I let you smash, Michael!' she said, jostling a glass in her right hand and punching his arm with the left.

He shot her a falsely incredulous look, eyebrows raised in mock shock.

'I mean it! Because I'm about to go full "Real Housewives of Streatham" and dash this at you.'

Laughing, Michael pulled her face towards him. He looked at her, taking her in for a moment with his eyes dopily half closed, and kissed her forehead.

Ola wriggled and wiped it, giggling hysterically. 'Move, man! You're trying to distract me and it won't work. I want answers, Michael. ANSWERS!'

She was raising her voice now, a few heads at the bar had turned and begun to look over. Michael could not believe how much he loved to indulge her, even when she was causing a scene. Today, he felt he could say without hesitation he loved every single thing about her. In fact, he was sure at this very moment, he loved her more than anything else in the world.

He couldn't remember a time they'd been happier. He never would. He would revisit this evening in the weeks after it happened, and think about all the things he would have said and done differently. That if he had known what the next day held, he wouldn't have dared to risk joking about their future together. He would have told her that he struggled to pinpoint the happiest day of his life because he couldn't decide between the day she agreed to marry him or the day she told him she loved him too. That he knew it would next be their wedding day, but one day that too would be overtaken by them having their first child.

He let a smirk slip, before kissing her forehead tenderly once more. 'When did we first smash again?' he asked, flinching as her fist missed his arm and landed on the seat cushion with a thud.

2

26 days to the wedding

Ola awoke at half past eight on a dreary May Monday, to the sound of her alarm accompanied by the concurrent pinging of WhatsApp messages. The high-pitched beeping did little to pull her out of her morning fog, made all the cloudier by bottles of champagne purchased for two (polished off primarily by one) the night before.

'Shit,' she heard herself whisper, nothing on her body moving but her lips. There was no way she could have had more than four hours of sleep. She lay there for a moment, savouring the last few seconds her face could remain sunken in her pillow before she was officially going to be late. Languidly, she stretched her arms above her head and turned towards the wall where an iPhone lay charging next to her like a neglected lover. She slid her finger, lengthened by a lime acrylic nail, across the cracked screen to silence it and squinted at the row of notifications.

139 flipping messages. Ola could guess who from and what about, too – the latest episode of *Game of Thrones* had aired the night before, and she could already picture the group chat's breathless commentary.

RUTH: Nah Im sorry guys but Dany is an icon. WE
HAVE NO CHOICE BUT TO STAN OUR KHALEESI 👑👑
👑🔥🔥🔥

CELIE: Erm, I have a choice. I do not stan.

Something, something, Lannister. Something, something 'The Wall'. Ruth in all caps lock with gifs and meandering paragraphs, Celie punctuating her friend's emphatic tirades with a solitary 'sis …' or just a silent string of question marks. The more rabidly they discussed it, the more certain Ola was that she wanted no part in what to her sounded like *The Lord of the Rings* with a dark sexual violence arc and a dash of casual ableism.

A couple of dozen messages would no doubt be from the florist, asking for the details of something or other that Ola had outlined the day before. She would feel less affronted by the continued enquiries about the peony to rose ratio in the bouquet if she hadn't spent so much money hoping to avoid being this hands-on. She wondered if the florist was simply doing her best to justify her extortionate rates by looking as busy as possible, or if she genuinely needed answers. Ola wasn't sure which was worse.

She winced as her phone buzzed twice more. It slowly occurred to her the likely source of most of the messages (which had now crept up to 141) was her boss, Frankie. Ola had promised to file the copy for a sponsored post by 7.30 a.m. that morning, 'at the very, very latest'. The deadline had been batted right to the back of her mind by the rental orders for the wedding: the special chairs, the high table, the linens, the draping, the lounge furniture, the portable dance floor, the lighting.

And then, calculating the costs of those things: currently more than her student debt. The week before, she had asked for an extension on the piece, as she was struggling to make the brief work. She'd been tasked with finding a seamless link between the male founders of Danish CBD-infused sex-toy brand 'Kalmte Kut' and body positivity. Ola had put it off partly in the vain hope that Frankie would foist it onto someone else at *Womxxxn* who was better at dressing up press releases from pseudo-feminist brands as actual articles. But she hadn't, and the piece remained unwritten.

Tooting to Victoria – Ola had less than twenty minutes to get ready. Bleary-eyed, she tapped the year of her father's birth into her phone. It shook in response:

> You are #BLOCKEDT till 9.30am (56 minutes)

Suddenly overwhelmed, she inhaled.

'Shit. *Shit.*'

Ola's iPhone was heavy with long-forgotten 'get-your-shit-together' apps. Unused apps for insomnia. Long-abandoned running apps, since she was sedentary for 80 per cent of the week. And, of course, #BLOCKEDT, the weapons-grade phone restriction app she'd recently installed to keep her off apps in the morning, since she was probably addicted to apps. She was tired of her Twitter feed being the first thing she saw when she woke up. Her screen time was close to six hours a day last time she checked – double the national average – and after three consecutively failed New Year's resolutions, it was either #BLOCKEDT or some sort of tech rehab. It did the job – a pop-up window would obscure her phone screen and stop her from accessing it at all until the block was lifted at 9.30 a.m. But as her phone continued to vibrate noisily, she felt its virtues were eclipsed by it being a total pain in the arse.

Ola sat up properly now. She drew back the curtains, bright orange against the dismal south London sky, and turned to survey her bedroom for damage. Not *too* bad. Last night's clothes were flung at the end of her bed. She avoided the gaze of the Maya Angelou line drawing she'd ordered from Etsy, with the words 'Still I Rise' written underneath in cursive script, and by her fishbone cactus, noted a star-spangled box marked 'Chicken Corner' filled with gnawed bones. A mug of wine without a coaster had marked her desk, but bar that, she'd got off lightly. Still, evidence of her night was laid out across the room like a crime scene, drunk Ola leaving clues and cues to fill in the evening's blanks.

She entered the bathroom, iPhone lodged under her chin, and carefully peeled off the oversized T-shirt that she wore as pyjamas, too hungover to pick up her pace. She scooped her endless navy braids into a large bun on top of her head, which she partially covered with a too-small shower cap. Placing the phone on the side of the sink, Ola stood naked in front of the bathroom mirror and stared. Her dark-brown eyes, now dark underneath. She bared her teeth, her gums and tongue blackened by Merlot. As she stepped into the shower, she smiled remembering the night before. It had been a good one. Not quite like old times, maybe better. The poor boy got the Uber back with her to put her to bed, bless him – she could still smell Michael's Tom Ford aftershave in the room – and though she couldn't recall the journey home, she could vaguely make out him removing her heels and her pulling at his face, saying his name in a sing-song voice as he bundled her under her duvet. Ola felt a pang of guilt – he'd had an early start this morning and she hoped her antics hadn't thrown him off on his first day.

———————

Ola and Michael had met at a media networking event for Black Brits three years ago in the summer of 2016, when charts were dominated by the Drake songs that launched a thousand situationships – 'Controlla', 'One Dance', his feature on Rihanna's 'Work'. They hit it off immediately. She'd been pleasantly surprised when he asked her out a week later, announcing her impending date to the group chat with the second-best picture of him she could find on his Facebook. In the first, he was at an Independence Day party with his shirt unbuttoned down nearly to his navel, sporting a small Ghanaian flag as a makeshift bandana. Ola wanted to avoid potential fuckboy accusations, so the one she chose was a black and white candid that made him look like a motivational speaker.

'Ngl, he's BUFF,' Ruth offered in the 'St Augustine's finest' WhatsApp group. 'But he looks like a fuckboy tbh LOOOL.'

'He looks like he played drums at church,' Celie added. 'And you know they're the worst of all.'

They admitted he was gorgeous, at least. Michael was even taller than Ola at six foot two, with almond-shaped eyes and flawless skin. Underneath a meticulously groomed beard lay a carved-from-black-marble face. He was well dressed, into details; never without a thin gold chain and a small hoop earring in his left ear that his mum hated and Ola adored. His looks were all her friends agreed on when it came to Michael. Celie and Ruth weren't ever sure anyone Ola liked was good enough for her, a reflection of their impossibly high standards (ones Ruth failed to maintain herself and perpetually celibate Celie didn't have to) rather than her bad taste. So, she barely batted an eyelid at their view of him. Ola liked the way she felt around Michael. Looser, less herself but more herself. He was street smart, funny and kind. And, although she didn't exactly like the fact that she always had to foot their restaurant bill, she liked even less what it said about her if she penalised him for it. 'With this gender pay gap you're constantly writing about, he really has no excuse,' Ruth said when they started dating.

'She's not wrong,' Celie concurred. 'The Bible says equally yoked, not, like, equally broke?' When Ola countered with by definition that would mean they *were* equally yoked, Ruth and Celie set their mouths in twin grim lines. They only seemed to be allied when they were disagreeing with her taste in men. At least the girls were hands-on with the wedding planning, helping Ola in every way they could, for which she was grateful. But she knew they still had reservations about him. Surely they would be satisfied now Michael would be out-earning her with his new job. Ola hadn't decided how she felt about that new reality yet – she'd put more money towards the wedding than he had, after all – but her happiness at his new role meant she hadn't needed to.

She lost her train of thought as her phone began to vibrate again, with what seemed like increased intensity. She blindly reached for it and, wiping vanilla scented cleanser from her face, slowly turned over the screen. The name FRANKIE W flashed furiously like a warning. Ola could see that alongside 148 messages, buried underneath a flurry of Instagram and Twitter notifications, she had 17 previously undisplayed missed calls. This confirmed it: she had seriously messed up. Defeated, Ola turned off the shower, wrapped herself in a fluffy turquoise towel and stared hard at the tiles of the bathroom floor.

Prior to this work hiccup, for the first time in a long time, she had felt at peace. Or however close she could get to that feeling. That real 'on top of all wedding admin, everything ticked off the Google calendar, all bills paid' peace was a sensation so foreign she could never quite lean into it, never fully trust it. She felt safer when the storm finally arrived than in the calm before it.

That morning, Ola thought the storm was going to come in the form of Frankie summoning her for a chastising disguised as a 'quick chat' when she got in. But it actually came minutes after she arrived in the office, at 9.30 a.m. on the dot, when her phone finally granted her access. She power-walked to her desk, eyes so low she wasn't even sure whether Frankie was in yet. She unlocked her phone and the first four messages were, as she suspected, from Celie and Ruth. Characteristically animated, Ruth's read:

EMERGENCY. PICK UP YOUR FUCKING PHONE!

FFS OLAIDE!!!!! U BEEN ON TWITTER???

CALL ME ASAP

HAVE U SEEN IT???1 HAVE U SEEN THE LIST?

Celie's message, short and direct like her, consisted of only four words:

R u okay, Ola?

3

26 days to the wedding

It was Michael Koranteng's first day in his new job at CuRated when 'The List' dropped online. He hated that those were the terms in which people discussed it, like it was a sneaker release or a Marvel movie trailer.

That morning, he had woken up before his alarm, first day jitters rousing him at 7.17 a.m. Michael was alert despite the late night – he hadn't gone anywhere near as hard as Ola, who he'd had to fireman-carry into an Uber home. When they arrived back, he managed to change her into an old shirt and get her into her bed, but it was another twenty minutes before she fell asleep. His battery had died so he couldn't order himself a cab and when he asked for Ola's password, she wouldn't give it to him unless he danced with her to their wedding song, Bracket's 'Yori Yori', and referred to her as 'Mrs Koranteng'. Thankfully, he managed to get the passcode from her right before she passed out, drool pooling on her pillow.

They had celebrated his new job by wandering through Soho, private members' club hopping, as they wondered aloud 'Who the fuck are we?' Michael could feel himself smiling at the thought of his soon-to-be wife. Ola was exceptionally pretty

– wide brown eyes, high cheekbones, with the wholesome, dimpled African beauty Afrobeats musicians dedicated entire discographies to. At five foot eleven she was tall and slender, in a way that she said hadn't served her well during her teenage years in Streatham, where her flat chest and slim hips had her at the bottom rung of 'fanciability'. By the time she arrived at university, what had once been deemed 'lankiness' was perceived as 'legginess' and had her mistaken for a model on occasion, as did her high forehead. Trademark waist-length braids that regularly changed colour made her all the more striking, as did a silver hoop in her button nose.

But she was not just a pretty face, oh no. Ola was smart and ambitious and supportive of him. She was also deeply principled and caring. Out of the few billion potential soulmates on the planet, he knew his could only be Ola Olajide. In twenty-six days they'd declare this in front of all the people they loved almost as much as each other. Almost. They had been through a lot, him and Ola, but today, Michael hoped, would be the first day of proving he deserved her – as much to himself as to anyone else.

As he opened his wardrobe, Michael reached for one of the few fitted, collared shirts he owned and a pair of smart black trousers, instead of his usual self-imposed uniform of a dark jumper, matching joggers and trainers. He knew he'd be a touch overdressed for the notoriously laid-back start-up but he couldn't shake the scornful voice of his mother, sarcastically enquiring why he wanted to give off the impression of unemployment on his first day. He was about to make his way down to the kitchen for some breakfast when he decided to check his phone. It had been left charging overnight, but the moment the screen lit up, he knew something was wrong. 21 missed calls. 59

WhatsApps. His stomach churned. Who had died? Michael
thought of his grandmother, who he didn't call anywhere near
enough. The last time they had spoken, over a week and a half
ago, she was just getting over minor surgery. He'd made sure to
text her every other day since the procedure and it had seemed
like all was well, but she was eighty-one years old. And patients
often died unexpectedly in Ghanaian hospitals, after less invasive
operations.

No messages from his mum, but several from miscellaneous
names he struggled to find a common connection between. The
first was from a man named Ryan, whose face he couldn't
conjure without looking at the contact picture and who he
vaguely remembered meeting at a podcast workshop a few
months before. Their last correspondence, a friendly exchange
about the date of the next event, couldn't have been more
different to his most recent message:

Is this shit true????

Was what 'shit' true? Michael wasn't sure he appreciated Ryan's
tone. He opened a second message then, this time from Ola's
best friend Celie, who had simply posted six question marks
followed by a link. Michael tapped it, launching his Twitter app,
which opened to an account with a greyed out avatar: '@_the_
list'. He frowned as he read the bio. 'Exposing the UK media's
most prolific abusers,' the text read. 'Live for 24 hours only.'
Michael's mood shifted from anxiety to confusion. What did
this have to do with him? The page was following no one, had
786 followers and had posted only two tweets. The first was
pinned to the top of the profile and captioned 'Our response',
with a screenshot of text attached:

Thank you to all who submitted. We created this
account as official channels continue to fail survivors of
abuse in the media and entertainment industries. We
have no choice but to do something ourselves.

In order to protect the safety and identities of those who
submitted, we are not going to be responding to DMs
about #TheList. This account will be deactivated after 24
hours.

Michael's mouth was dry. His phone was still buzzing with
messages but they were barely registering now. Surely, he
couldn't be … The second tweet showed a screenshot of a
spreadsheet, with two text-filled columns. He took a deep
breath before clicking on it and recognised his name immediately. There he was, number 42, wedged between a TV producer
accused of date rape and a journalist who preyed on teenage
girls. His first name was misspelt as 'Micheal', then 'CuRated'
was next to the words 'Harassment and threatening behaviour/
Physical assault at office Christmas party'. This was followed by
'Restraining order' in brackets. Under any other circumstances,
he would have been thrilled at the idea of being recognisable by
his first name alone, like he was a proper public figure. For a
moment, he wondered if he was panicking prematurely, since he
only officially started his new job today. Perhaps there was some
kind of mix-up; another Michael in production maybe, or in
accounts. It was one of the most common names going. This
train of thought lasted mere seconds, as he recalled the highly
retweeted announcement of his hiring last week. He exited The
List and looked at the tweet. 34 retweets. 203 likes. Posted at
6.30 a.m. He felt lightheaded and began to pace.

I'm going to lose my job, was his first thought. I'm going to lose the first job I've wanted, before I even start it. With quivering hands, he clicked the small flag icon below the tweet, next to the words 'Report an issue'. As he did, a menu popped up with options. 'It's spam.', 'It expresses intention of suicide.', 'I'm not interested in it.' No 'It's accusing me of assault' option, then. He chose 'It's abusive or harmful' and found himself even more frustrated at the next page. 'How is this tweet abusive or harmful?' Though he felt 'It encourages suicide or self-harm' was the closest, he opted for 'Includes targeted harassment' and pressed send.

He looked at the growing responses to the post, searching for names and faces he recognised among the likes. It was hard to keep track, the jurymen multiplying with each scroll. Each double tap felt to him like a conviction. There were now 217 likes; the last ever live show he'd done with the podcast had an audience of 210. He felt wobbly at the thought of what that number of people looked like in a room. And, those were just the accounts that had publicly interacted with the tweet – how many posts did he see, share and discuss without visibly engaging at all? He recalled Ryan's message from earlier: overfamiliar, accusatory. *Is this shit true????* Michael hardly knew the guy, and he had the confidence to message him like they were boys, throwing around allegations before 9 a.m. Nausea washed over him as he imagined the other messages piling up on his phone, from near strangers, from those he assumed should know him better.

He had woken up less than an hour ago as the newest presenter of *Tasted*, on the first day of the rest of his life. He was now going to work as a named industry abuser. The labels 'harasser', 'assaulter', 'abuser' hadn't been his long, yet he already felt permanently marked by them. He didn't know what to do.

Everything he had worked to build for the past six years was disintegrating around him. Michael wanted to disappear, for the ground to swallow him up. How on earth was he going to face his new colleagues? If they hadn't already seen it, it was surely only a matter of time. He was done for: he was in much more famous company on that list so, before long, it would go from being a thread on Twitter, to the gossip pages, to an article in the papers, to …

Ola. He needed to speak to Ola. He tapped her name in his contacts, knowing she probably wouldn't be able to answer till later because of the blocking app she had installed a few weeks back. He had warned her it was a stupid idea in case of an emergency, though he'd thought more along the lines of lost keys, not being anonymously accused of assault. After one ring, it disconnected. He tried once more; a few rings then this time voicemail. 'Yo, Ola, it's me,' he said, unsure what to say next. 'Can you call me as soon as you get this?' Ignoring the other messages, he began typing a reply to Celie.

This is not true. I need to talk to Ola ASAP

Celie's 'online' status changed to 'typing' instantly. He watched as her typing stopped and started repeatedly, before her avatar changed to the default stick man silhouette. She had blocked him.

The thumping in his chest was beginning to affect his breathing. He and Ola were getting married in a month. At least, they were supposed to be. He couldn't be sure what this meant for the wedding. Or for them, full stop. This list of abusers would turn any woman's stomach but Ola? This was the kind of thing she had spent her career documenting. The kind of thing that made her feel the world she was so desperately trying to change was simply beyond repair. Men like this. What did 'men like this' mean now his name was involved? Now he was the type of man she wrote about? He scoured The List again, trying to make sense of his place on it in the context of the others mentioned. I can't believe this is happening to me, Michael thought. But, deep down he had always wondered if something like this might, one day. Karma, perhaps. He held the power button on the side of his phone until the screen turned to black.

He sat on the edge of his bed to steady himself, his fingers on his temples. They were throbbing. After some time had passed, he slowly got to his feet, feeling his knees buckle as he did. He took another deep breath and ran to the bathroom where he was sick in the basin. Then he brushed his teeth a second time, buttoned up his shirt and left for work.

———

All eyes were on him as he stepped into the office – Michael couldn't pinpoint if it was because he was new, because he was Black, or because his new colleagues had already come across The List. The CuRated office space was like the platform's online presence come to life. Sleek, near algorithmic Instagram-chic; he was welcomed by neon yellow, green and blue signs that shouted slogans like 'Hustle' and 'Level Up'. There was a bus-red foosball table near the entrance and a set of glass-fronted mini-fridges at the end of each work area stocked with Evian, Diet Coke and Rekorderlig. At the back was a dimly lit recording booth.

'Michael!' He heard the booming voice of Beth Walker, CuRated's HR manager, before he saw her. Michael noted how sameish these London new media types often looked in their attempts to stand out – like two other women in the office, Beth donned a white-blonde pixie cut with black thick-rimmed glasses and silver hoop earrings of increasing sizes running along the rims of both ears. She was grinning at him toothily, her smile partially decorated with a near-neon shade of orange lipstick.

'We are sooo excited you are *finally* joining us!'

Excited. Okay. So, she hasn't seen it yet, Michael thought. 'Thanks, Beth. Can't wait to get started.' He was used to having to speak in two tongues, well versed in reserving one voice for his friends and the other for the workplace, but today he was even more self-conscious. He had expected Beth to be on the back foot when they met. Michael was well aware of how his hiring had come about. In late December last year, their now-sacked social media manager tweeted a photo of their Christmas party to CuRated's 656.4k followers. The image of their entirely white, twenty-six-person team quickly went viral, spurring on a #NotRated hashtag that trended on Twitter for two days straight. The men's digital content platform stood accused of 'gatekeeping' and 'white-washing'. Their case wasn't helped by how closely the site was affiliated with Black culture: videos counting down the most iconic rap music video vixens of all time, sponsored sound systems at Notting Hill carnival. Some months and two further hashtags later, Michael was join-ing the team to present their bi-weekly culture and lifestyle show *Tasted* on YouTube. His hiring had been announced to much fanfare online. And now he was sure it would cause more commentary, for all the wrong reasons.

'Such exciting times!' Beth exclaimed. 'So, before we go any further, I want to make sure I get this absolutely right. Your surname …' Her face was pre-emptively apologetic. 'Is it pronounced … Corn … Quran-ting?'

'Yeah, yeah,' Michael said, nodding enthusiastically at its butchering. 'That's it.'

'Amazing!' Beth clapped in celebration. 'I was so worried I'd mess it up! Now we've got that sorted, let's go and say hello to Seb, shall we?'

CuRated's CEO and editor, Sebastian Fraser, looked exactly as he did in his pictures; like a member of the Conservative Party's youth wing. Though he hadn't managed to find his age no matter how hard he searched on Google, Michael was certain that he could be no older than twenty-three. Clean-shaven and redheaded. He was a different, more corporate beast than his Hypebeast colleagues, wearing a pinstripe shirt underneath a grey suit jacket, with slim-fit trousers and very clean brown Oxford shoes. Sebastian was mid-conversation with someone about CuRated's social media strategy when Michael and Beth sidled over.

'Mike, mate!' he said, brown eyes darting towards him, hands outstretched to shake well before Michael reached him. 'Big, *big* fan of *Caught Slippin*. You and your mates are absolute lads! Hoping you can bring some of that banter to CuRated, yah?' He nodded for emphasis. 'Glad to have you on board.'

'Thanks,' Michael said, hoping Sebastian didn't notice the dampness of his hand as he shook it. 'Glad to be on board.'

'I'm sure Beth has told you already but we're one big family here at CuRated. All we care about is making things happen – *your* things. You guys are the brains. The bosses.' He continued to shake hands vigorously. Michael's wrist was beginning to get tired.

'I know I'm your "boss" technically, but that's all it is – a technicality. In the grand scheme of things, I'm bloody nobody, really. I just deal with the boring numbers stuff. Keep our little operation ticking over. *You* guys really make this what it is, so I hope you're ready!' Michael nodded and Sebastian finally let go of his hand, slapping him on the back.

'Jolly good! Now, mate …' he said, clapping his now slightly damper hands together. 'Let's introduce you to the rest of the gang!'

Michael was introduced to a stream of Jacks and Katies and Emmas and Toms whose faces and roles all began to blur. He was taken on a tour of the office that he couldn't recall by the time he was shown to his desk. He apologised for his standoff-ishness, blaming it on a headache, which was partly true, and spent most of his morning in a silence that he hoped they would put down to nerves. Once the clock reached 12 p.m., he turned his phone back on. Thirty-four missed calls, some from names he hadn't heard in years, others from numbers he didn't know. None of them from Ola.

Trying to think of anything other than The List was proving impossible; instead of getting to grips with the editing software he would be using, he was flicking through a mental Rolodex of every single girl he had ever met, moved to, dated, ghosted, cheated on – anything. The lack of context to the online claims had him frantically filling in the blanks, wondering if it was one of them who'd named him. Gabrielle King came to mind, a pious girl whose virginity he took in college on a course trip to Cyprus. They had shared a desk in a few lessons due to being next to each other in the class register and were friendly, then he'd heard through the grapevine that she *liked him* liked him. She wasn't his type – she had bad skin and worse clothes. But they had spooned in his bed on the first night of the trip and soon he was having unprotected sex with a girl he only ever really initiated conversation with when he needed to borrow a pen.

The whole thing was pretty wordless, and over before he knew it. Forgettable. He hooked up with her friend Martha, same trip, same bed, a few nights later and as they'd cuddled she told him that Gabrielle had regretted it and felt used. The morning after pill – which he'd crabbily paid for – had made her nauseous. At the time he'd merely grunted in response. Shit happens. Wasn't his fault she'd gone to an all-girls Catholic school when she was younger and was weird about sex. But maybe it had gone beyond simply being a shitty thing to do. Maybe it was something more serious. That wasn't possible, was it? It was absurd to even suggest … Though when he thought about it, he hadn't been great to Toyasi when they had been together. Efua, either. Or Tash. Or Jackie.

There had been others, too. Before he'd grown up and met Ola, he'd broken hearts. Dented women's self-esteem and then been turned off by their insecurity. He knew he could have treated the women he'd dated better when he was younger, dumber. He shuddered, aware that many exes left in his wake thought he was a dirtbag. But to what degree?

His phone was vibrating. 'OH LA LA' flashed across the screen. Ola was calling him.

Michael answered on the first ring. 'Ola,' he said, nearly breathless with relief.

'Hey.' Her voice was quiet.

'Hey, are you okay? Sorry if you've been trying to get hold of me. It's been … things have been a bit mad this morning. I guess you've seen—'

'Can we talk?'

Michael paused. Did he detect fear in her voice? 'Sure, yeah we can talk. We should talk.'

'In person?' If she was afraid, why would she ask to meet face to face? He wiped his damp brow with the sleeve of his shirt. This was Ola. He was being paranoid.

'Yeah, okay. That's calm. Is the Pret by Victoria Station all right? I can meet you there for lunch at twenty past twelve?'

'Okay. See you then.'

'Cool. Ay, Ola? I hope you know—'

She'd already hung up. Michael swallowed the lump in his throat. He got up and grabbed his backpack and jacket from the back of his chair, hurtling into Beth on his way out.

'Where are you off to in such a hurry?' she asked, grinning. 'Sick of us already?'

'Yeah, I mean no, sorry. Meeting my girl for lunch,'

'Ah.' She closed her eyes and held her hands to her chest in mock adoration. 'Don't you just love love?'

4

26 days to the wedding

Ola had slipped into work that morning and burrowed behind her desk, seemingly unnoticed. Frankie wasn't in yet and in a second stroke of luck, Sophie was in the kitchen area with her back to her as she poured boiling water into a mug of green tea. Kiran was hunched over her laptop, typing furiously and nodding her head rhythmically to whatever was coming out of her AirPods. Ola silently thanked the universe for these small mercies as she replied to Celie's message – *R u okay, Ola?* She was fine, thanks for asking, but what the fuck was going on? A minute hadn't passed before Celie tried to call her, twice. Ola quickly texted her back:

Can't talk, at work. Message me

Her friend's response came instantaneously – a link to a tweet followed by: 'Call me as soon as you can.'

Once she opened it, Ola squared her eyes at her phone to focus. Her head was spinning thanks to her hangover, so the significance of the post was slow to register as she read the text above the list of names.

This database will serve as a temporary tool to highlight
the severity of abuse in the UK entertainment and
creative scenes. We hope that this will lend a voice to
survivors and inspire those within the industry to be
more proactive in prevention. A * means that the
allegation was made by more than one individual.

As Ola read through The List, she felt a profound sense of dejection but also satisfaction. Fuck these men for what they'd done and fuck *yes* to these women for refusing to stay silent. Just a few lines in, there were so many different forms of abuse recorded that it made her feel sick: everything from unsolicited dick pictures, to sexual intimidation, to rape.

A feeling of foreboding came over her, her skin prickling at the familiarity of the allegations. Flashbacks to the handsy hug from *Womxxxn*'s director Martin Frost at the Netty Awards a while back. The same night, he'd made a bigoted quip about the Kama Sutra to Kiran and asked if, since she was pansexual, he was in with a better chance 'since they fancied everyone'. 'Is it just an excuse to have lots of orgies, then?' he'd breathed into her ear, his face reddening with drunkenness. 'Because if so, count me in!' And how could she forget her first ever internship? Why she had left two weeks earlier than she was supposed to, forfeiting a pay cheque she couldn't afford to pass up in the process …

Ola began to consider how she'd been made aware of The List this morning. Celie had sent it to her, frantically, asking if she was okay. Ruth had begged her to call, asking her in all caps if she'd seen it. But why? What did this have to do with Ola? What – or rather, *who* – had they seen on it? Her mind started racing. She scanned the names, over sixty of them, in search of someone she recognised. Was Martin on there? Had he finally been outed? Soon enough, a flicker of recognition sparked as she made her way down the spreadsheet: Papi Danks, Afroswing up-and-comer. She and Celie had attended a party thrown by his label a few years ago and though Ola remembered little about him, it was still a relative shock to see his name on The List. His family had gone to Celie's church.

Samson Mackay was on it too but she'd be lying if she said she hadn't expected that. Stories about him had swirled for years, older female journalists warning her to give him a wide berth. Next, she spotted Lewis Hale, football legend, regular on *The One Show*. Hadn't he been a runner-up on *Strictly Come Dancing* last year? Ola had no interest in sport but Lewis was a household name. He'd been a fixture in the public eye as a TV personality and pundit for as long as she could remember. The sort of guy you hoped was as nice in person as he came across on telly. He didn't seem the type. But she knew better than to think there was ever a 'type'.

She continued to read and then her stomach lurched violently as her eyes landed on entry number 42.

Micheal, CuRated, Harassment and threatening behaviour/Physical assault at office Christmas party (Restraining order)

Nothing could have prepared her. Her hands began to shake as her phone buzzed non-stop with messages. How could Michael be on there? *Her* Michael? She felt dizzy as she considered the words that followed his name. Harassment. Threatening behaviour. Physical assault; it was like she was dreaming. Head hot, she tried to process what she'd read but it made less and less sense with each second that passed.

The office walls began to cave in as she rose from her seat. As briskly as she had walked in, she turned around and walked out, running up the flight of stairs to the toilets of the vegan candle start-up above. Once inside, she nudged each cubicle door with a pointy elbow to ensure she was alone, sat on the lid of the toilet, took out her phone and scrolled.

The number of likes and retweets on the post crept up every time she tapped refresh but it was the multiplying comments that she couldn't take her eyes off. Shock and scepticism, anger and praise; all the messages screamed at her silently.

Who raised these people? Solidarity with those who were brave enough to speak their truth 🖤🙏

How has @_Matt_Plummer been able to keep his post at @ITVNews when he's been outed as a sex offender?

You guys know this is potentially libel, right?

#WeStandWithSurvivors #SilentNoMore #BelieveWomen #TheList

Some users went back and forth about the definition of defamation. Many eschewed words for raised fist emojis and multicoloured hearts. The majority were simply tagging other users, no doubt saving their commentary for private chats, setting her imagination ablaze with what else was being said. She returned to the original post, pinched her fingers together over The List text, then pulled them apart to zoom in until Michael's name filled the screen. She stared at it, as if by doing so it would miraculously start to shapeshift into someone else's. There it was in black and white, 'Micheal', sans the surname that would soon be hers. Small mercies, she supposed.

Ola felt embarrassed. And after a while, she felt more embarrassed that her initial, overriding reaction was one of embarrassment. It was such a self-centered response but she couldn't help it. Her eyes filled with tears and her ears flooded with the imagined sneers taking place behind her back, the fervent Twitter DMs being exchanged at her expense:

Ola's man's on here you know. Mad ting

As in Womxxxn Ola???

WOMXXXN OLA. CEO of "mxn are trxsh" twitter! She's with the "trxshest nxgga" of all

Sksksksssk! No fucking wayyyy … British Obama's are dun outchea!!!

Could she really blame anyone for thinking like that? That's pretty much what she'd have been saying if this had happened to anyone else. But she had dedicated the best part of a decade to rallying against patriarchy, rape culture and toxic masculinity. Ola had attended more protests, panels and demos for Women's Rights than she could count. She'd founded her university's Black Feminist Society when she was a fresher for goodness' sake, back when the conversation around feminism was unsexy and unInstagrammable. All the times she'd braved the backlash and trolling on her old Tumblr blog by sexists who hadn't liked what she was saying; it had been her beliefs that kept her going. She wasn't the type of person to miss the red flags and make the mistake of being with someone capable of that behaviour.

She thought to herself, Michael couldn't possibly be … but quickly pulled herself up. That's how it starts. 'He couldn't possibly' was exactly what was said about men who most certainly could and did. When her #MCsToo investigative piece went live at *Womxxxn*, exposing abuse allegations against men in the music industry, hundreds of fans suggested their 'fave' was incapable of the crimes she reported. Finding her voice among a chorus of deniers only a few years later was something she couldn't bear. All those women who had written to her after #MCsToo went viral, with their thanks, with their horror stories … what would they think of her?

It was hard to settle on one clear emotion from her overwhelming smorgasbord. She wanted to cry, that she knew, but wasn't sure if it was out of fear or anguish. She wasn't even sure what she was most afraid of, or for whom she was most upset. There was rage in there, for sure, a touch of pre-emptive regret. The only thing she knew for certain was that everything about her life had changed, in an instant. She felt herself doubling over as if sucker-punched in the gut, tears blurring her vision. She shook as she sobbed silently into her shirt, grieving both the blissful ignorance of moments ago and the future she had been planning with Michael. With a long exhalation, Ola tapped the direct message button on the account and shakily wrote a message.

I know someone on here … I don't know what to do.
Can you help me?

Send. Now what? Her legs felt like they would give way at any moment but she walked to the sink and opened the tap, cupping her hands beneath it. She splashed her face with the icy cold water, but still felt clammy. In a month's time, she was getting married to a man who she apparently didn't know. Her chest became tight. 'Ola, breathe,' she said aloud. She closed her eyes, searching her memory for the easiest of the breathing exercises Fola had shown her for anxiety. Suddenly, her sister's voice was in her ears. 'Exhale chaos; inhale peace.' She placed her thumb over her right nostril and breathed in slowly through the left. Then took her index finger and repeated on the other side, exhaling through the right. After three rounds, her breathing eased.

Ola shook herself. She checked her eyes weren't bloodshot in the mirror and then checked her phone for a response from the account. There wasn't one. She took a final deep breath and made her way back to the office.

As she reached her chair, still trembling, she noticed a notification in the corner of her screen on Slack, her workplace's messaging platform of choice. It was a message from Frankie, who was now in her office squinting at her computer. Ola's stomach did not sink – there wasn't much further it could go.

Can we have a quick chat? – FW xxx

Before, her morning bollocking courtesy of Frankie had felt like a life-or-death matter – now, it was merely something she needed to get out of the way.

Yeah I'll be down in five

She read back Frankie's message and glanced over her own once more. Eyes rolling, she signed off with 'xx' and clicked send.

The walls of Frankie's office were glass – representative of *Womxxxn*'s literal and figurative commitment to transparency, or something, she guessed. Ola felt that the by-product of surveillance was perhaps genuinely unintentional, since the team could see Frankie as well as she could see them: when she was reinstating crossed boundaries between gritted teeth to her ex-husband on a call, when she was wolfing down her first meal of the day at 3.30 p.m., Wasabi straight from the box.

Like the rest of *Womxxxn*, Frankie's office was various shades of pastel – peach walls, a baby-blue table light, lilac coasters. Her desk was in disarray, with papers strewn across it. On it stood a potted aloe vera plant, a framed photograph of her nuzzling a very blonde child and a rose-gold ceramic vulva in which she kept her stationery. On the wall behind there was a blown-up version of *Womxxxn*'s September 2017 digital cover. It showed American model and activist Jada Smalls breastfeeding her then one-month-old son; that year, *Elle* made history by featuring the magazine's first burns survivor cover girl, so Frankie booked Jada, the first person with albinism to be the cover star of any women's publication.

'Tell her to bring Zion – let's capture her breastfeeding,' she'd told Kiran at the time. 'Is Free The Nipple still a thing?'

'Pretty sure it hasn't been since 2014,' Kiran had replied.

'Well, pretty sure we can make it, if that nipple is an albino one? Black is the new white, is the new black, or something?'

Ola could see Frankie's furrowed brow over the top of her screen as she opened the door. In her late forties, Frankie looked amazing for her age, a prolific albeit private user of the non-invasive beauty treatments she often rallied against in op-eds. Even so, her commitment to ripping outfits directly off an Urban Outfitters mannequin – oversized boyfriend jeans, fisherman hats and chunky trainers – aged her. She reminded Ola of the mother in *Freaky Friday* post-body switch, dressed as her own teenage daughter. Something she felt was too ageist to articulate aloud but couldn't unsee. Today she was in a yellow denim boiler suit Ola had been eyeing online and a pair of white Vans.

'You wanted to see me?' Ola said in lieu of a greeting as she opened Frankie's office door. Her head poked around the corner as if she didn't actually intend to enter. Frankie forced the thin variety of smile someone gives to a naughty child that isn't theirs to discipline.

'Ah, Ola, yes, fab! I did want us to have a chat,' she said, tucking a strand of glossy, light-brown hair behind her ear. 'Take a seat. Were you having phone issues this morning?'

They had danced this dance many times before. Instead of saying 'Why are you late?' Frankie would say things like 'Was there traffic in Tooting today, then?' Instead of asking her why she still hadn't filed an article yet, she'd say something like 'Just checking how you're getting on? Do let me know if you're having trouble managing …' At first, Ola hadn't realised there were intended actionables behind the doublespeak, but she had quickly learned the steps to this routine. Sometimes, in a power play she'd never openly admit to, Ola would act like she couldn't read between the lines, forcing Frankie to spell things out plainly, which she failed to do without flushing a satisfying shade of maroon. Passive aggression was the lingua franca of the *Womxxxn* offices.

'Yeah, my bad,' Ola said, too fast, plonking herself in the chair opposite. 'I downloaded this app on my phone that locks me out of everything until nine-thirty, so I couldn't answer your calls.' She put her arms around herself, physically trying to stop floating away.

'I see! Clever clogs!' Frankie said, voice chirpy, face still tight. 'For future reference, can you make sure you loop me in with things like that? I do wish we didn't have to worry about work before nine and after five, but you know how it is with such a small team. It's really important *all* of us are on the same page.'

'Don't worry, I'm uninstalling it asap,' Ola said, trying to keep her voice even.

'Great!' Ola felt a 'but' coming. 'But I wouldn't necessarily say you should get rid of it altogether. Do you think it could be set for during work hours only? It's great you took the initiative to curb your time on your phone and I think it could be useful, you know, to make sure you're totally focused when you're in.'

'Noted,' said Ola. She adjusted herself in her seat and tried to guess the magic words to end this portion of their conversation. 'I'm not on my phone when I need to be, but I am on my phone quite a lot when I shouldn't be?'

Especially when I'm at home, sitting through your latest neurotic, bullshit, work-related crisis after hours, Ola thought. Frankie's smile finally began to creep into her green eyes. Her boss had won this battle with little resistance, a rarity that should have made her suspicious. Ola watched her shoulders finally drop, satisfied that the naughty child was now richer with a lesson learned. She was a cool boss, not a regular boss. A cool girl-boss.

She leaned forward. 'No worries, Ola. Listen, I get it. Striking a work–life balance is never easy. It takes time. I'm probably worse than you,' she said, half whispering. 'I'd have to download it myself, if I wasn't in charge!' She winked as she sat back again.

Frankie Webb was so casually audacious, you almost had to respect it. Ola begrudgingly found her scrappy, adaptable energy, her air of someone who'd just missed out on winning *The Apprentice* (making them all the more ambitious, vengeful even) weirdly admirable. Despite her moneyed background she could graft like a market trader on Petticoat Lane, had impeccable taste and a keen eye for branding. Her biggest rebrand project was herself; having edited a slew of women's magazines that peddled eating disorders for the best part of her career, she was an early adopter of 'brand feminism' online, when it became clear print was dying and self-loathing was becoming harder to shift. By the time half the women's magazine industry as she'd known it had collapsed, she was already preparing to launch the antidote to the disease she'd helped spread. This coincided with an uptick in the use of words like 'empowerment', 'intersectional' and constantly referring to white men as 'white men', a move that did little to distract readers from the fact that she herself was white.

In 2014, she launched *Womxxxn*, a women's sexual health platform turned lifestyle brand that released 'an agenda-setting digital issue' every quarter. Frankie hadn't even thought of how it would be pronounced offline, in real life – she chose the name after seeing 'women' spelt 'womxn' on Twitter and wrongly assuming the 'x' had been for aesthetic purposes. But even that oversight she managed to spin into insight, declaring it was pronounced 'Wo-minx' in a bid to encourage women to embrace their 'inner minx'. What *Womxxxn* offered thanks to a whip-smart team, was genuinely refreshing and purpose-driven, even if the flagrant hypocrisy often made Ola's head spin. For every ground-breaking story they broke on smear tests, there was an advertorial from a brand that had just made headlines for making a woman redundant four months into maternity leave.

'So,' Frankie said. 'You can probably guess why I've pulled you in for a chat this morning—'

'Yes, and again I'm really sorry about the delay,' Ola cut in and tried to adopt a more apologetic tone, desperate for the conversation to conclude. She shuffled in her chair. 'I promise I'll have it to you for tomorrow.'

Frankie looked confused for a moment, and then howled with sudden realisation.

'Kalmte Kut! Oh, no no *no*, that's a conversation for another day. As in, yesterday. Forget about the dutch dildos, woman – The List, we need to report on The List!'

Ola discovered the pit of her stomach was indeed lower than she had initially thought. She stared at Frankie dumbstruck, wondering how someone could look quite so upbeat about a feature that depressing, even without your fiancé being accused of physical assault in it.

'Ola!' Frankie clucked. She never did understand why her boss still pronounced her name *Oh-lah*, yet wittered on about her nephew 'Ollie' with no trouble. 'You mean to tell me you spend all that time on your phone instead of working and I'm *still* more in the know than you?' Ola simply gawked as Frankie continued, voice low as if gossiping.

'Okay, so, this thing called The List went live this morning. Apparently, it started out as a Google Doc, put together by loads of badass anonymous female journalists, activists, feminists et cetera – all the good kinds of 'ists'. And now it's a Twitter account that's put all these media bastards on blast. Rapists, sexists – the bad 'ists'. Sleazeballs and predators, all outed. I know this is very much up your street, so I'm putting you on it.'

Her boss continued to talk excitedly without pause, seemingly nonplussed by Ola's spooked expression. 'We need to go beyond the bare bones news story; we need women who are willing to go on the record. You did such a great job with MCs Too, I'm *sure* you'll have no problem with getting survivors to tell their stories. And we have to act fast – people are definitely expecting us to break this and we're best poised to! If you could send me a rough pitch by this afternoon, that would be ah-*mazing.*'

Frankie waited, finally thrown off by Ola's silence.

'Does that sound good to you, Ola?'

At times, Ola felt bad about how little she divulged about her personal life at work. She avoided after-work drinks politely, but like the plague, utilising her gift for storytelling to spin a line on some other, imagined post-work commitment she had. Other than with Kiran, she was evasive and vague about everything bar content, and when her colleagues attempted to segue from business into *her* business, aggressively beaming at the prospect of more than acquaintanceship, guilt would pool in the pit of her belly as she firmly declined. Even with her engagement, she wouldn't have broached it at work if Sophie from the Fashion and Beauty desk hadn't; she reluctantly showed off the small, marquise-cut diamond sat atop a thin platinum band for all of six minutes before snapping back to her usual reticence.

But in this moment, Ola was reassured that she had been right in maintaining her distance. Her lack of meaningful dialogue with *Womxxxn* staff combined with Frankie's inability to retain information that didn't directly affect her meant, Ola now realised, she didn't have a clue that Michael had been named. She probably didn't even remember the name of her fiancé, let alone know where he'd landed his new job. Shakily,

Ola found a smile for her. 'Sure thing,' she said, nodding. 'I'll send you an outline by two.'

As she left Frankie's office and made her way to her desk, Ola attempted to fix her expression into something less wounded. Her cheeks were prickling with heat but she managed to remain straight-faced. Darting past her distracted coworkers, she could slowly feel a sense of clarity cutting through her disorientation. She had to keep it together, just for now, and then she would call Michael. She needed to make sense of this. She needed to find out the truth.

5

26 days to the wedding

The post had climbed to 4,957 retweets and 8,003 likes by the time Michael arrived at Pret a Manger. Warmth enveloped him as he entered from the brisk breeze outside and he soon spotted Ola in a far corner, drumming her nails against the table. The straightening of her back assured Michael she'd seen him, but it was hard to read her face from the door. She was in all black – the only pop of colour aside from her hair and nails a pair of purple-rimmed reading glasses. This was his favourite Ola of many. Even more so than turned up, body-conned birthday girl Ola and turned on, brunch-drunk Ola – as clichéd as it was, brooding, bookish Ola with her frames and slightly too-big clothing (often faded black jumpers 'borrowed' from him) was his kryptonite.

Making his way over, he could see her phone was placed just out of reach, a pink KeepCup strategically barricading it from her tapping fingers. Michael knew she was avoiding it not because she didn't want to read what was being said about The List, but because she didn't want him to see her reading what was being said. A wave of humiliation washed over him that was so overwhelming he considered turning back.

It felt strange not kissing her hello, but he mustered a muffled 'hey' as he pulled out the chair to sit. Silently, he cursed himself for the choice of location. In hindsight, it felt off key to discuss something this serious in a chain coffee shop as commuters hurriedly ate chicken wraps and gossiped about their bosses. But what was the alternative? He wasn't sure if she'd feel safe coming to his flat or having him around hers. He wasn't sure if she would feel safe being completely alone with him. It was impossible to tell; she just sat looking at him, not saying a word.

'It's a bit packed in here, sorry,' he said, breaking the silence if not the ice. 'I don't know where people are supposed to have these conversations. You'd think some start-up would have sorted it by now. Some Airbnb ting for people trying to talk through their shit. Heartbreak hotels.' He laughed, uncomfortably. Ola continued to stare. They sat quietly for what felt like eons, his laugh hanging more awkwardly in the air with every passing second. He rubbed his arms.

'Ola, this is crazy man,' he began. 'I actually can't believe—'

'Stop. Please,' she said, cutting him off. She seemed to steel herself. 'Michael. I just want to know, honestly. Why is your name on there?'

Michael slumped forward over the small table, placing his head in his hands. Though he had prepared for this, he was surprised at how hurt he felt by her question. He knew she would have considered her phrasing, her tone – she was like that. Had emotion seen her abandon her first draft, or was this the least painful way to address it she had come up with?

'Try and put yourself in my shoes,' she said into his silence. 'I literally woke up this morning to see the man I'm meant to be marrying in less than four weeks named a potential predator alongside date rapists and domestic abusers.' Though her voice lowered on these last words, they rang in his ears. The uncertainty of 'meant to be marrying' and 'potential predator' cut through him in different ways, both equally brutal.

'You can't expect me not to ask. For my own sanity? My own safety?'

Michael coughed. 'Safety? Jesus, Ola …'

'Don't make this any more difficult. It's not exactly easy, having to ask you this.'

'You don't *have* to ask me anything. You're my fiancée. For you to accuse me of—'

'I haven't accused you of anything. But I can't even ask you about it? Something that's being shared by people I know, and that I'm being bombarded with messages about?'

'Messages?' Why hadn't it occurred to him she'd be getting them too?

Ola swallowed. 'People have been @-ing me on Twitter,' she said. 'Asking me if I know that I'm with an abuser, if I knew all along. The List was trending in London for fuck's sake.'

Michael realised his left foot was tapping violently against the lino floor and he moved his hand to steady his leg.

'Just tell me,' Ola said quietly. 'Who put you on there? Why?'

It was a simple question. One he was becoming increasingly sure he could answer after racking his brain and poring over his less than perfect past for the best part of the morning. Throughout the walk to Pret he'd planned what to tell her. Now nothing sounded quite right. How could it?

Michael looked at his wife-to-be, how her body was turned away from him. This was it. There was no going back. He was sure he had lost her and therefore uncertain if what he said next even mattered. Of course, he knew that he should tell her the truth. The whole truth. It's what she deserved, what she would want. But doing so would seal their fate entirely. And what about what he deserved? What he wanted? Though he didn't feel it at the moment, he was sure he was a good person. He would be good to her. He'd changed. He would never hurt her, in any way. And the truth hurts, doesn't it? So he lied.

'Listen to me,' Michael said, making the greatest effort he could to maintain eye contact. 'I swear to you, on both our lives – I don't know why I'm on there. I've been thinking all morning and I don't know who or why anyone would name me … I'm just as rattled as you are.'

He waited for her to respond. Ola was looking at him expectantly, as though this could not be all he had to say.

'I have never hit, threatened or harassed a woman in my life. I don't know what else to tell you,' he continued. 'I'm not abusive. You know this.' He hesitated, not sure if he should say what he knew she didn't want to hear, the exact words parroted by the various vicious men she documented denying allegations just like this. 'You know *me*, Ola.'

She was silent. He could feel his speech becoming garbled with desperation.

'If I'm being honest, I think someone is trying to get me out of my new job. Get me sacked. It's the only thing that makes sense.' The loud screech of a chair being pulled out from the table next to them made them both jump momentarily. After a while, Ola sighed and ran a hand through her braids.

'You're saying you have never hit a woman in your life?' she asked, her eyes studying his face. Her expression was so pained, Michael could barely stand to look at her.

'Never,' he said.

'But what about anything that could be seen as threatening? I mean, you do raise your voice in arguments sometimes. You've done that to me.'

'Come *on*, man,' he said, shaking his head, conscious of needing to sound as non-threatening as possible. 'That's when we've been in the middle of a fight. Not like—'

'And what about this assault at a Christmas party? When was that?'

'What office have I ever worked in to go to an "office Christmas party", Ola?' He was almost relieved she'd asked about this. Since graduation, he'd worked at the Apple store in Oxford Circus for three years, and then managed a Schuh in Stratford Westfield for another three years. His hiring at CuRated had been off the back of his side-hustle presenting gigs on popular YouTube channels and a podcast – *Caught Slippin* – he, Kwabz and Amani did that accrued a bit of a cult following. He wasn't 'famous famous' per se, but well known enough in certain parts to warrant a glance and a whisper.

'Okay, but weren't you let go by Schuh?' Ola pressed. 'Why?'

'I told you – I was made redundant and so were like five other people.'

'Well, is there anything you've done *anywhere* that could have been misinterpreted as pushy? Pressuring? Anything at all? I need to know. Right now.'

Before Ola, Michael had been a 'gyallis'; something he had probably regarded with a sort of smirking pride up until a few hours ago. As a teenager, if he saw a girl with a pretty face or a shapely behind 'on road', he called after her and expertly extricated a name, a smile and a number from her like a snake charmer. He'd follow them up the street sometimes, calling, sure, but not in a bad way. He knew girls who didn't feel attractive if they weren't chatted up at least once when they were out. Still, Ola had mentioned that as a teenager walking home, she'd more than once fearfully given out a fake number and prayed the guy didn't ring her phone then and there. When did it go from chatting up to catcalling? He had specifically gone after girls who were 'stush', too. No one wanted something *everyone* could have; you wanted what you had to work for. The girls who pushed back a little, crossed their arms and kissed their teeth before giving up kisses and opening their legs. Though now he thought about it like that, outside of the group chat, it sounded a lot like … harassment.

'I've never harassed anyone, no,' he said, firmly. 'I don't know how anything I've ever done could be interpreted as that.'

'It says someone has a restraining order against you.'

'I know, I've been reading about this. Someone can't have a restraining order against you without you knowing. I have never, ever had the court issue me one and I've been trying to find a way to prove it, but they only come up on standard or enhanced DBS checks, not a basic one or police records. And only companies can do those so—'

'So, you can't prove it,' Ola mumbled. 'Of course. Great.' She sagged back in her seat.

Michael stretched his hands out to place them on her shoulders by reflex, but caught himself. 'What's stopping you from believing me?' He was trying to be patient, but he was beginning to get frustrated. 'I would never hurt you in my life. You know that.'

'I don't!' she squeaked, her voice breaking. 'I'm … I'm honestly scared.' A chill went down his spine as she said it. 'It's scary, Michael, seeing those allegations about you. I don't want to be one of those women who thinks that just because you haven't hurt me, you couldn't hurt …' She stopped.

Michael cleared his throat, taken aback by her words. They stung, but he did his best to appear reasonable. 'I hear you. But it's not my word against someone else. It's my word against we don't know who. There is no way of knowing who submitted what, no checks. It was a Google Doc that anyone could edit. How could it not be taken advantage of in the wrong, fucked-up hands?'

She remained motionless for a moment and then nodded, though still stony-faced.

'Please, believe me,' he continued, encouraged by this small gain. 'Trust the man you are going to marry over an anonymous person on the internet. That's all I ask.'

Ola reached into her pocket for a tissue and dabbed at her eyes before nodding again.

It was only at this that he realised how tense his body had been. He fell back into his seat, deflating with relief. It was like an enormous boot – her chunky black Doc Marten – had been released from his windpipe. Ola believing him wasn't simply about the survival of their relationship, but his own sanity. He knew he was a good guy and most importantly Ola did too. He leaned over to place his hand on hers. She flinched.

Confused, he asked, 'What's wrong?'

Ola averted her gaze for the first time since they'd sat down. Her body language had bad news written all over it, her hands clasped together like they were holding on to each other for dear life.

'I'm going to … we're going to need some time.'

'Oh,' Michael said, her Doc Marten firmly back in position. 'When you say time …'

'I didn't say I'm calling off the wedding. It's in a month,' she said, clinically.

'That's the reason you're not calling it off? Because you don't want to lose the deposit on the marquee?'

'No.' Ola's jaw clenched as if biting back words she might regret. 'And I didn't say we can go ahead with it, either.' The floor beneath Michael gave way. A barista was shouting for someone to collect their order but the sounds of the coffee shop were swallowed by ringing in his ears.

'I want to believe you but I need time. And then there's work stuff too—'

'Work stuff?'

Silence. 'Frankie wants me to write a piece on The List,' she said, finally. Michael's jaw dropped. Ola still hadn't lifted her eyes.

'She doesn't know you're on there. I told her that I would do it but given your involvement I can't, obviously. I need to think about how to handle this.'

'You have got to be joking,' Michael said, fear catching in his throat. 'How about telling her The List is bullshit, and that the prick who put me on there is who you should be writing about, not me?' He'd lost his cool now, no longer concerned about raising his voice. The table next to them lowered theirs as if listening.

'I told you,' Ola said slowly. 'I'm not going to write it.'

'But you're going to allow a colleague to?'

'What do you mean "allow"? *Womxxxn* is a feminist magazine. We write about things like this.'

'Even if it's unverified, un-fact-checked bullshit that could ruin lives?' he hissed. 'You go on about ethics and shit in writing – how is this ethical?'

'There are nearly seventy people on there,' Ola said. 'Mostly high profile. Who knows how many survivors. I can't be responsible for silencing the voices of the women who contributed. I don't know about anyone else involved. I only know what you're telling me and what I want to believe about you.'

'What you *want* to believe about me,' he repeated, scoffing.

'Don't do that,' Ola snapped. 'It's not like you've always been honest with me, is it? Like you've made it easy for me to trust you?' Michael knew that was coming. It was only a matter of time until she broached it.

'I've made mistakes, I know,' he said, wary of further provoking her. 'Mistakes we agreed to move on from. But I'm not that guy any more. I'm definitely not *this* guy.'

Ola was picking at the corner of her acrylic. As she did, he glimpsed the engagement ring he'd spent months saving for and further months pestering Fola and Celie about, sending hundreds of potential choices via WhatsApp. He thought of how proud he had been at getting it right, her face when she'd seen it in Santorini, where he popped the question on a balcony overlooking the Pinterest-perfect views of the turquoise Aegean Sea. He tried to find comfort in the fact she still had it on.

'Does the fact I'm on there not make you think there are probably others being lied about too?' he asked.

'Michael. Statistically—'

'Don't chat to me about stats, man,' he cut her off, losing it at that word. 'This isn't a Twitter thread. Talk to me as a person. Your partner. People are out here spreading lies and you don't give a fuck. You know Celie has blocked me, right?'

'Can you try to calm down?' Ola hissed. 'I know this is hard for you, but this is hard for me too. And shouting at me isn't exactly helping to prove that you're not who these people say you are.'

'You're not the one having their name dragged through the mud. By your own girl as well. For richer or poorer, in sickness and in health – but fuck him if he's falsely accused of assault though, yeah?'

'What do you want from me?' Ola spat. 'For me to resign? Or should I email Frankie and tell her I can't write the article because my fucking fiancé is named? Yeah? I can draft that now.' She reached for her phone and unlocked it, then paused before her next sentence. Her brow unfurrowed, her face contorted with confusion. 'Shit,' she said.

'What now?'

'The List. It's gone. It's been taken down from Twitter.'

'Oh. Shit.'

They fell silent again. Michael watched Ola refresh the page until she placed her phone face down in front of her. She held her empty KeepCup, as if in need of something to do with her hands. The look of concern had eased, but her body was still rigid.

'Well. Hopefully that's the end of it, then?' Michael said after a beat. 'Now it's gone, maybe that's it?'

He tentatively placed his hand around hers once more. She let him this time, but dropped her gaze again as she spoke.

'If you can't prove to me that none of this happened, Michael, the wedding is off.'

6

25 days to the wedding

'You look like an *angel*!' beamed the bridal shop assistant as she smoothly zipped up Ola's dress. 'And what a waist! You were tiny when I last saw you, but it's ever so slightly looser in the middle than before. *Lucky*. I'll get some more pins to see if it's worth us taking in.'

Had she managed to lose weight in one day? Maybe Ruth had been right when she said she was looking even thinner than usual. It wasn't impossible; she hadn't eaten a single thing since The List had been posted.

'Are you sure you're all right?' Celie said, once the door of the boutique clicked shut. 'You look exhausted.'

'Because I *am* exhausted,' said Ola, shaking her head, sending her veil swaying. They hadn't been there for more than half an hour and she was already desperate to leave. She stood in her heels on a podium in the centre of the room, making her appear even taller. On the rails behind her were an army of wedding dresses in differing shades of white (egg shell, bone, porcelain) and fabric (satin, crepe, chiffon). It was as if she was their commander, illuminated by the garish chandelier overhead and the fairy lights strewn along the large baroque mirror's edges.

She certainly felt as though she were heading for a battle she was unprepared for, jittery and skittish no matter how much she tried to settle.

'You been eating?' Ruth asked. Ola gave an abrupt nod and her friend sighed. 'I'm not gonna lie, I'm rattled,' said Ruth. 'Some anonymous enemy of progress said some shit about Michael that no one can prove and now you guys are on the rocks? Whose jaw do I have to rock, for real?'

This was no time for jokes, but that was Ruth for you. Ola's reluctant smile – the first she'd cracked in twenty-four hours – wasn't visible from behind her veil, but Celie shook her head hard enough for the both of them. 'On a level, though,' Ruth went on, her voice serious. 'I'm worried about you, man. This is so fucked up. I mean, a month before the wedding?'

Ola shook her head. 'I have no idea whether it can even go ahead.'

'But you said yourself there's no evidence,' said Ruth. 'I don't see why you should call off your whole wedding because of one troll. They're the ones who've done something wrong, not Michael.'

'She doesn't know that,' Celie cut in. 'She can't know for sure. No one can.'

Ola had kept the veil on to shield herself from the room's excessive brightness. The suite seemed engineered to make her feel like she was in a bizarrely fancy police interrogation room; candelabras on every conceivable surface, cheap LED lights that said 'Love' and 'Mr & Mrs' on the walls. Her forehead beaded with sweat underneath the lights, as if she was in custody.

She had been waiting for the final fitting ever since she'd first tried on her wedding dress – an ivory, backless floor-length silk slip, with an intricate pearl, white-gold and diamond headpiece attached to a veil so long it nearly reached the hem of the gown. When she'd sent Fola the pictures, her sister had compared her to Yemoja, the Yoruba deity, then claimed she was 'channelling her Divine Feminine', which was her go-to compliment whenever Ola wore anything other than trousers. It was more understated than her mother had wanted, calling it 'plain', but it was the only dress she'd tried on that made her feel like 'her', as opposed to a pantomime fairy godmother. Plus, her second and third outfits more than made up for its restraint in the spectacle stakes. She'd been looking forward to feeling as effortlessly beautiful in it as she had the first time, but after the events of the past twenty-four hours, she could barely stand her own reflection. Since yesterday, Ola had been desperate to see Ruth and Celie face to face for some sort of guidance. She loved them dearly, but quickly realised how naive she had been to think they would be able to help.

Ruth Nnadi was, as the Jamaican men who frequented the bookies on her high street called after her on her way home, a 'fluffy'. Thick not just at the hips like the lyrics of her favourite rappers but everywhere, and proud of it. A tattooed constellation sat on her back that she'd had done in 2008 after seeing the same design on Rihanna. These days, she was thankful it was covered by inches of sleek, shiny hair. Ruth never stepped out in less than birthday girl make-up, doubling up as a mobile advert for her services as a part-time MUA and lash technician; matte foundation covering her walnut-brown skin without a pore peeking through, lips glazed in a Fenty gloss. Like today, her eyes were usually heavy with lashes from her line 'Cashmere Lash Doll' that she sold through her Instagram. She bought synthetic ones from Chinese vendors, repackaged them in luxe black and gold-bowed boxes marked 'Siberian mink', hiked up the prices by 400 per cent, and thanked her customers kindly for doing their bit to support Black business. Ruth was the kind of girl African mothers-in-law would accuse of strangling them in a 'prophetic' dream.

Celestina 'Celie' Tembe meanwhile was the manifestation of their fasting for the perfect daughter-in-law. A 'Proverbs 31' woman. Her formative years had been spent bashing Bibles, and though less zealous now, the piety never left her. Flowing floral dresses and skirts crowded her slight, five-foot-two frame, worn with opaque tights, whatever the weather, whatever the hem length (though it was without fail below the knee). Celie exuded the energy of a supply teacher – pursed lips and passive-aggressive positive affirmations (or when her patience was really being tested, scripture) muttered when she had nothing nice to say, incapable of saying nothing at all. A fan of Christian rock and theatre, her first and foremost love was books. She worked at a plucky indie publishing house as an editor. A few days into the job, it occurred to Celie that there were more people named Helen at her imprint than minorities. The figure trebled if you included those called Helena.

Ola's best friends sat on the lilac chaise longue, trying their best not to make her fitting day any worse by falling out. It was hard to say if Ruth and Celie would be friends if they met today. Though they'd known each other for over twenty years, they judged each other for the same things they had at the beginning of their friendship: their life choices, dress sense, general opinions. Celie thought Ruth was ratchet and Ruth suspected Celie only thought she was ratchet because she was suspended in the 'Sunken Place' (she wagered that Celie secretly got a kick out of being the 'brown girl in the ring' at work, too).

Ola lifted the lace from her eyes and threw a scornful look that Celie pretended not to catch. 'Yes, I know no one can know for sure,' she said, sounding more defensive than she hoped. She couldn't tell who she was trying to convince, herself or her friend. 'But it's complicated.'

'I don't see how,' Celie said stiffly. 'If this was one of us, you'd be the first with your placard out, shouting about "complicity" and "internalised misogyny". What's the difference? Other than, say, the twenty-odd grand you've put down for the wedding.'

Ola's face remained unfazed, but that barb hit her where it hurt. 'First of all, it's not about the money,' Ola said, while not entirely confident that was true. 'Secondly, I told you – he has to prove that he didn't do anything. I haven't said the wedding is definitely going ahead.'

'Then why are we here?'

Ola didn't know the answer to that. Why she was standing in front of her glum reflection, a modern-day Miss Havisham dismayed at an upcoming jilting of her own. At Pret yesterday she'd meant her ultimatum and ignored the messages Michael had sent afterwards. But here she was, back prickling with pins and sweat as she tried on her wedding dress for what might be either her penultimate or final time wearing it.

'Because if I cancel it, it's cancelled,' Ola said. 'That can't be undone.' The only thing that freaked her out more than going ahead with the wedding was calling it off. 'I need some time to think.'

'You don't have time. It's literally in a month …'

Ruth turned towards Celie so she could properly scowl at her. 'You think she doesn't know that?' she said. 'Things are bad enough with all them feminists up in her mentions and now she can't even catch a break from her bestie, Jesus!'

She decided to disregard Ruth's disparaging use of the F word that suggested Ola was not one herself and nodded. Ola's survival strategy online was silence. Deactivation would be too dramatic, she thought, so she deleted Instagram and Twitter from her phone and handed her accounts over to Fola, who changed her password. Thankfully, this wouldn't appear suspicious: her followers rarely realised how much time she spent online since she was more of a lurker than a poster. Even though Ola tried not to look at Twitter, it was impossible not to. In an alternative timeline where Michael's name wasn't mentioned, she would have been among the first to retweet The List. She was tempted to archive the handful of pictures she had of her and Michael on Instagram but decided it would read as suspect. As would turning off the comments function, but that meant the odd rogue comment got through. Fola was fast at deleting, but not fast enough – within the first hour or so of handing over, Ola came across over twenty comments of varying degrees of accusation and anger.

'You know how social media is,' Fola's voice had crackled over Skype from Panama when Ola rang in a flap. 'They'll be on someone else's ass by next week. Consider this the universe giving you the time to finally get your shit together. Meditate. Detox. Drink some damn water.'

This wasn't to say her sister wasn't worried. Her usual Zen had been deeply disturbed by what Ola had told her. Fola would message her about the situation every few hours; what was happening now? Had Michael explained himself? She had suggested he contact his former employers for written confirmation that he never attended any Christmas parties. This initially made Ola feel better. But when she sent her sister what he had forwarded – emails from the Apple and Schuh stores stating that they didn't host Christmas parties – Fola asked if he could perhaps provide a signed letter with a printed letterhead, in case of forgery.

'Listen, if there's one thing Dad taught us – God rest his soul – it's to never underestimate the lengths men will go to maintain a lie,' she'd said. 'It's the only time they can multitask!'

He should be here, Ola thought. Not just because his little 'Bíntín' was supposed to be getting married, but because her dad would know how to make her feel like she might make it through this. She found herself thinking of him more and more as the wedding approached, hearing his oft-said proverbs when she was alone: 'A man accused of stealing a goat should not entertain visitors with goat stew'; or 'ears that do not hear advice accompany the head when it's cut off'. As a child, whenever she asked him 'why' about anything he'd respond with 'Y has a tail and two branches', much to her frustration. His inability to be direct used to drive her and her mother crazy. But Ola would give anything in the world to hear him say one of his cryptic maxims today.

Celie was standing behind her now. She reached upward and gave Ola's shoulder a gentle squeeze as they both gazed mournfully at her reflection.

'I'm going to say something you might not want to hear,' she said. Ruth's eyes rolled back in the mirror till only the whites were visible.

'You're like a sister to me. I know your heart. But that doesn't mean I understand what you're doing. I'm here because I love you, but also because someone needs to tell you this. What Michael has been accused of is serious – staying with him could be dangerous ...'

Ola felt a twinge in her stomach. 'I'm not saying this to defend him but he's never been violent with me, Celie. Not even close.'

'Does that mean he never could be?' her friend said. 'And even if he never is, a lot of women, survivors, will be disappointed that you of all people are choosing to stand by someone like that.'

This stung. Ola was not standing by a guilty man, as she reassured herself hourly. She was simply trying to get to the truth. But no matter how she sliced it, she felt she was becoming one of the women she wrote scathing columns about; the wife of the football player who called a woman too drunk to consent a slag. The girlfriend of the musician who helped bring underage fans up to hotel rooms after the show. The fiancée trying to shut down a story because it implicated a man she loved.

Ola tried to remain level-headed but she was devastated, especially because she knew she couldn't rule out that Celie might be right. But, even so, they'd been friends long enough for her to give Ola the benefit of the doubt. They had known each other long before jokingly referring to the slowly gentrifying Streatham as 'Saint Reatham' became a self-fulfilling prophecy, when their lives were a blur of Just Do It bags and *My Wife and Kids* reruns. Hanging out at the ice rink when it wasn't cordoned off by police tape, and sitting on the back of the bus when it wasn't occupied by older, harder kids. Then Ola and Celie both went to study English literature at university – Celie at York and Ola at Durham – and would often visit each other's campuses. Ruth rarely went up to see them, abhorring the long journey to 'the sticks' and everything about it when she got there ('You lot said you had Black nights up here?' she'd say, each time they went clubbing. 'Playing Sean Paul twice then going back to "oonts oonts" music don't make it a Black night!'). Neither university had many Black students, even fewer from state schools, so Celie's visits made Ola feel she had a little slice of home with her.

The three of them had their traditions. Ones that now more than ever, as they got older and their diaries fuller, ensured they still saw each other. Like their annual outing to Notting Hill Carnival, though they skipped the after-parties now and the 'pum pum shorts' and 'batty riders' were swapped for bottoms that actually covered theirs. But it was increasingly rare they were all together, and this wasn't how Ola had envisaged their most recent reunion.

'I haven't "chosen" to do anything,' she said, jerking her shoulder away from Celie's hand. 'Obviously I know women don't just throw around allegations. But The List is anonymous and crowd-sourced — and this is the internet. I thought we'd all accepted that people on the internet make things up? Or are we pretending that we didn't watch *Catfish* now?' In a world where she could leave a Tripadvisor review of a restaurant she'd never been to, anything could happen.

'So you're saying a bunch of women got bored and decided to wreak havoc on random men's lives?'

'This is the thing though — we don't even know if they *are* women,' Ola mumbled, without conviction. She hated defending Michael when she didn't know what she thought herself. 'It could have been hijacked for revenge or some agenda.'

'I've never heard that one before,' Celie scoffed, stepping back. 'Very convenient.'

'Come on, Celie. That isn't fair.' She shuddered. 'Let's change the subject. Please? I just want to be fitted and get out of here, okay? I don't like talking about it like this. It's coming out all wrong and making me sound like an apologist.'

Celie shrugged and looked at her shoes. 'Well if it walks like an apologist and talks like an apologist—'

'Then usually it's an apologist, but in this case it's our best friend trying to do the right thing?' Ruth interrupted, voice raised. 'Low her man, it's *Ola*! The biggest SJW we know! And you know I'm not Michael's number one fan, but doesn't he deserve a chance to prove himself? It's innocent before proven guilty – whoever put him on The List didn't even spell his name right!'

The three of them heard the click of the door as the bridal shop assistant pushed it open cautiously, as though she had been listening in and waiting for the end of a sentence to make her sheepish entrance. She maintained eye contact with no one but Mirror Ola and began adding more pins to the back of the dress.

'Looks amazing, doesn't it?' she said under her breath, to no one in particular.

Ola cleared her throat awkwardly. 'Thanks.' She turned to Ruth and volunteered a feeble smile. 'I appreciate you. And I do understand what you're saying, Celie. Believe me.'

'This is why I don't tell her shit,' Ruth said, unperturbed by their new audience. 'She acts like hers don't stink.'

'I didn't say that,' Celie half whispered. 'I said that this approach, acting like nothing has happened, is insane.'

'Celie, the invites have already gone out!' Ola spluttered. 'The church is booked. The reception venue, booked. The flights from Nigeria *and* Ghana, booked. The £979.99 dress is fucking paid for in full,' she said pulling at its sides wildly. The sales assistant's bright-blue eyes bulged.

'You helped me pick the fucking thing. The caterers, the photographers, videographers, the DJ, the live band all paid for

…' As Ola listed them, she became overwhelmed. Nigerian weddings were big; Nigerian–Ghanaian hybrid weddings for sort of Insta-famous, accidental influencer couples were *huge*. For weeks she had been fretting about how much there was left to do; now she couldn't believe how much she had already spent.

She hesitated, almost embarrassed to say what she felt.

'At the end of the day, this is the man I love. I have to be sure of what I'm doing to him. To us. If this was either of you, you know I'd give you the benefit of the doubt. You do understand that if I call it off, that's essentially me saying that I think he's guilty?'

'And if you go ahead with it, that's you saying that he's innocent,' said Celie.

At that moment, Ola's phone began vibrating on the plush velvet footstool and she swung around with such ferocity that the hovering bridal assistant let out a panicked yelp. 'NOW WHAT?' Ola shrieked, ruching her dress up to her knees and stomping towards it.

'I'll just get some more pins …' the assistant said uselessly, hurrying out of the room. Ola jerked her phone up towards her face.

Heya Ola! How are you getting on with piece? Any
updates on interviewees? – FW xx

'On my fucking day off?' Ola raged. 'During my final fitting? Really?' She threw her phone down onto the footstool where it landed with an anticlimactic bounce. Infuriated, she kicked the stool's side. Celie and Ruth exchanged worried glances.

The List's disappearance had only raised more questions for Frankie, who began to bound after any tweet or back-alley blog post about it like a bloodhound. The resurfacing of racist tweets by Wellness influencer Morgan Briggs from 2012 saw it drop in relevance but screenshots of screenshots were still floating around in group chats and Facebook groups. So far, The List had only been reported on gossip sites or as a straight news story, with names, professions and allegations redacted. Frankie was after an in-depth investigation and was petrified that someone else would beat them to it, a worry Ola shared for entirely different reasons.

Even after it had stopped dominating the timeline, The List continued to drive the day's discourse. Women with public accounts admitted submitting names to it and their reasons why. Others spoke of how they recognised men who had abused them. 'Hi friends. I can't believe I'm writing this but my rapist is on The List' read one tweet, seared onto Ola's brain. 'For the first time in 9 years, I felt able to name him to my partner.' Then came the backlash, swift and inevitable. The mix of allegations led to criticism: men described as 'creepy' being named next to serial drink spikers. 'How was "belligerent sexism" quantified, and should it really be next to grooming and attempted kidnap?' a journalist asked on Twitter. Ola had never felt so conflicted – she wanted it all to go away, but remained disgusted that so many wanted these claims dismissed.

Aside from Frankie, no one else at *Womxxxn* raised The List with her, not in a work or water-cooler gossip context, yet she knew it was being spoken about. 'Can you believe Matthew's on it?' Ola heard Sophie telling Lucy in the corridor yesterday, when she'd arrived back from seeing Michael, her colleague, twirling her fork in something squiggly from Itsu. 'He was in my DMs a couple of years ago despite the big ol' rainbow flag and "Lesbian" in my bio …'

'It's Lewis Hale I can't get over,' Lucy had whispered back. 'He seemed so nice! I voted for him on *Strictly*, and everything. I know my dad's going to be devastated, bless him – he loves him!'

No awkwardness towards Ola, however. Even Kiran hadn't mentioned it, though in her typically direct way she had asked Ola why she looked like she was on the brink of mental collapse. The wedding was the last thing she wanted to talk about but it was a convenient alibi. However, the omission began to feel intentional. Had her colleagues put two and two together about the identity of the misspelt Michael? Why weren't they bringing it up? Ignorance? Embarrassment? Or good old-fashioned British feigned ignorance to avoid embarrassment? She sincerely wished she hadn't spent all her time alienating herself from every single person she worked with.

The line of argument she'd overheard most in the office was one she had made before: there is no smoke without fire. You didn't simply end up on a list like that, if you hadn't done *something* in the first place. When they'd been sat across from each other in Pret, Michael had glared at her like she was a traitor, huffed with disappointment at the fact that she hadn't shrugged off the allegations and gone back to discussing the wedding running order. But he was good at rationalising wrongs to himself and others around him, which worried Ola. He blurred lines, overstepped boundaries then acted perplexed by people's upset. Rarely did Michael tell Ola bold-faced lies, but he did have a tendency to decorate; he would deceive through embellishment or the omission of some facts altogether. Take, for instance, 'the incident', right at the start of their relationship. What if he was hiding some similarly awful truth?

There had been hiccups in their relationship where she'd thought of calling it quits. In their early years, she had avoided asking for a break because she knew he'd consider it a ready-baked excuse to fuck someone else. Michael was a habitual line-stepper when it came to other women, often pushing the boundaries of what was appropriate within their relationship. She wouldn't roll loaded dice. Years had gone into building their relationship, building him, and the idea it could be for nothing – or worse, for someone else who hadn't had to lift a finger – rocked her to the core.

Ruth huffed with exertion as she got up from her seat, pulling Ola out of her thoughts. She picked up Ola's phone and held it out to her.

'Password.'

'Why?'

'Because I'm about to message Sheryl Sandberg and tell her not to holla you on your days off, that's why,' she said. 'The pressure is real. From Michael and your fam and all them Twitter activists, but then work too? Not to mention the whole of Black Britain is gonna be shaking if you lot split up. You're couple goals for real. You know one girl at work has you guys' engagement picture as her lock screen?'

Ola groaned. 'I never asked to be some ambassador for Black love.'

'Yeah, well, with great cheekbones comes great responsibility.'

The joke didn't even register. It gave Ola whiplash, the swiftness with which the internet gods gaveth and the swiftness with which they tooketh away. In days, she had gone from one half of a power couple to a pariah. They were ruined as a unit and as individuals, social capital accrued both separately, and as one, gone.

'I'm trying to do right by everyone,' Ola said, voice glum. 'There isn't really anything that stands up yet, except that Michael has never been to an office Christmas party, which both his jobs confirmed.'

'One potential hole in an accusation renders the whole thing obsolete, right?' Celie said, snorting in disbelief.

At this, Ola almost blurted out that it was precisely her aversion to this logic that had seen her hire a private investigator with the remainder of her obliterated savings. That it was costing her £85 an hour she didn't have. That she hadn't even told Fola she'd done this.

Ola had needed to do *something*. And that something ended up being adding a shifty, gruff-voiced guy called Luke to her WhatsApp after finding his details on a forum and asking him to gather any information he could on Michael. He'd explained that for the agreed flat rate, he could follow him, stage stakeouts, send her access to all his public records ('That includes some criminal records and court documents, if you'll be needing that, love,' he'd clarified, in the casual tone of a cashier informing you that the kitchen roll was half price this week.), perform basic background checks, look into his social media and a whole range of activity that she was currently too stressed out to remember. While he couldn't legally tap his phone or bug his flat, for an additional sum that Ola couldn't stump up, he could 'see what was possible'. Celie thinking she was weak was one thing, but she'd rather she thought that of her than knew about this. If she told Celie the truth, she'd confirm what Ola already knew to be true: this was no way to start a marriage.

'I'm not saying that!' Ola shouted, finally at the end of her tether. 'I'm saying why not wait until we have more information before blocking him on WhatsApp?'

'Because I have all the information I need,' Celie said, without hesitation. 'Because I believe women.'

The 'and so should you' was practically audible. How clear the right answer was to her. It made Ola shrivel under the spotlight of the chandelier.

'Believe women,' Ruth tutted. 'What about when women are chatting shit? Isn't feminism about equality? Men and women are both dickheads. And listen yeah, these people always find a way to try and bring Black men down.'

'And what about all the white men who were on there?' Celie said, the irritation in her voice clear. 'How do they fit into your conspiracy? It's not every day be a pick-me, Ruth.'

'Nah, nah, nah, HOLD THE FUCK UP,' Ruth said, pointing a knife-sharp nail towards Celie as if challenging her to a duel. 'Nobody is a pick-me over here, sis. I just *get* picked. You're pressed because you haven't been picked in a minute. Come like a Bounty bar in the Celebrations tin. And not just because no one is checking for you, with your white on the inside self. You only discovered your Blackness in 2013 because of Tumblr and you want to talk about Black men?'

'Because you caping for them has worked out *so* well for you, right?' Celie spat, gloves well and truly off. 'I guess Troy finally stopped ghosting you then?'

Ruth's bottom lip quivered as if she was searching for a response, and then as if she was about to cry. She kissed her teeth and sat back down, the chaise longue letting out a small creak as she did.

It was almost comical how dreadful today had been. How Ola's preparation for the best day of her life had been among the worst she had experienced. Stood in her wedding dress, in front of the judgemental and pitying eyes of her maid of honour and chief bridesmaid, Ola was at breaking point. Plagued by a two-day stomach ache and shattered nerves, she tried one last time to regain her composure.

'I'm not asking for either of you to understand,' Ola said. 'I just need you to not make me feel any worse than I already do.'

'I hear you,' Ruth replied, pulling her into a hug. 'And people who have never had real relationships are not in the best position to be running their mouths about yours.' Still smarting from Celie's comment about her last failed romantic encounter, Ruth was determined to land a blow. Celie's sharp inhale served as proof that she hadn't missed this time. She muttered something inaudible and then shook her head.

'I don't see why someone would choose to accuse Michael out of the blue,' Celie said after a while. 'He's got no money to extort, no real clout to chase. What's the point?'

This point had eluded Ola ever since she'd seen The List. A motive for why someone would do this to him. As much as she avoided it, it was still there: doubt. The possibilities troubled her. That he was innocent in his own eyes, but genuinely guilty in those of his accuser. That he was innocent, but had done something heinous enough for this to be revenge. Or that he was guilty.

From the moment they met she'd known that Michael was flawed and hoped her blind eye to it wasn't indicative of a character flaw of her own, a manifestation of her 'daddy issues'. Michael meant well but had been 'laddish', problematic. Ola took pride, whether she admitted it or not, in the idea that she had tamed him. She thought she had, anyway. He was capable of lying, that was certain. But was he capable of this? And if he was, what did that say about her, her choices, her judgement, her morals? The familiar hot sting of resentment began to rise in her chest. Michael was not the only one who was at times dishonest with Ola in their relationship. She was as guilty of lying to herself as he was. As the anxious rumbling inside her grew, she reassured herself it could be settled with a hearty plate, a large glass of red and a message from a man named Luke.

7

19 days to the wedding

Michael and Ola sat next to each other in the lawyer's office, their bodies close but not touching. His arm hovered right by hers, stopped by a line he couldn't cross, invisible to all but them.

'Okay, so what you're saying is we …' Ola corrected herself quickly. '*He* wouldn't be suing Twitter for this?'

'That's right,' the lawyer Gary said, with an enthusiastic nod. 'See, section 5 of the 2013 Defamation Act states that if website operators act quickly to take down a third-party defamatory statement, they won't be held responsible. In layman's terms, websites are just intermediaries for free speech, as long as they are not aware that the published content is harmful.'

'But you reported the tweet immediately, didn't you?' Ola said, turning to Michael. He gave a non-committal tip of his head.

'Yes, but there lies the perversity of the defence,' Gary said, resting his elbows on his desk and interlacing his fingers in front of his chin. 'Sites are discouraged from actively monitoring content in case it *is* defamatory – they're essentially told to ignore it unless it's pointed out to them. You said The List was down a few hours after Michael flagged it, correct? They hadn't even responded to his report yet. Since it came down before they were aware of it, there's no offence. At least not in Twitter's case.'

Ola's phone flickered for a moment next to her. She studied the notification, and then nodded back at him.

'Got it. And since Michael doesn't know who posted it …'

'… Mr Koranteng would have to obtain a Norwich Pharmacal order, which would compel a third party – Twitter, in this case – to provide information relating to the individual who posted it; their registrant information, their IP address et cetera.'

Michael began to zone out. It wasn't that he didn't care, he was simply numb. As they huddled in the lawyer's office, the only indication that Ola was 'with him' was where she was seated. Gary Deakins, a portly, pink-faced man, was showing more warmth towards him than his fiancée. Perhaps because he hoped to bleed him of money he didn't have. Ola, meanwhile, had made it clear to Michael in every conceivable way that she wasn't there for support.

It had been seven days since their sit-down in Pret and he had struggled to work out what to do. He wasn't entitled to legal aid and the Citizens Advice Bureau were no help, but when he told Ola he'd found someone willing to give him thirty minutes of pro-bono legal advice, he thought she'd at least be happy. It was Ola who suggested she come with him to the preliminary chat in a business-like reply, to make sure she 'was privy to everything said'. He hadn't exactly expected congratulations but he hadn't anticipated this degree of coldness. It was as though she felt she was the only person suffering in this – or suffering undeservedly, anyway. Couldn't Ola show a bit of confidence in her husband-to-be? Michael didn't understand why she was so ready to think the worst of him. He hadn't always been an angel, but he'd never laid a finger on her, never so much as shouted at her. Yet she was willing to take the word of a total stranger over his, all because it was supposedly the 'right thing to do'.

The not knowing was what drove Michael mad. An all-consuming need to decode what was or was not being said, at any given time. Not just with Ola, but with everyone else too, particularly at CuRated. Was Sebastian usually this hands off with staff or was he avoiding him? Was the perma-forced smile that stretched across Beth's face daily – but didn't reach her eyes – on account of a general unease around men of colour or men she believed capable of hitting women? Yesterday, the manager of a budding Black British actor who'd landed a starring role in a *Paid in Full* reboot had called to pull him out of their interview at the last minute. No explanation, no apologies. Celebrities were finicky to deal with but when Michael asked to reschedule, it was ignored.

A lot of people were disappearing on him: people on the periphery of his life that he noticed more clearly now because they were gone. Not many had made their disgust with him as plain as Celie, which had hurt although they were never close. But something had shifted and it was difficult to explain without sounding crazy. He was invited to fewer events. His gaze was avoided. However, nothing was quite concrete; he couldn't know for certain if he was being rational or teetering on the precipice of full-blown paranoia.

Getting named on The List felt like being held in a constant state of waiting. Like receiving a broad but terminal diagnosis – he had unknown weeks or months left to live but the fact that this condition would one day ravage him was irrefutable. When it had first happened, Michael thought that even if people had seen The List, he would rather they never mentioned it to him. He'd archived every conversation asking him about it, blocked and deleted contacts who had enquired. At this point however, over a week down the line and without a full night's sleep since it had been published, he wanted to know exactly where he stood with everyone – even if they'd rather it was several miles away.

He heard Gary's muffled voice say something and Ola's repeat it, and then suddenly they were both looking at him expectantly.

'Michael?' she said.

'Hmm?'

'Gary asked if The List account has reappeared on Twitter since?'

'No, no. I mean, not that I've seen. I know it's been shared other places though.'

'Okay, well, I'd suggest with any other sites you may be aware of that are hosting the defamatory content, you contact them and request that it be removed,' Gary said with a nod.

'Ah. Okay.'

'As for the original, it's incredibly hard to trace a posting to a particular individual,' Gary continued. 'That being said, it's usually possible to trace it to a particular computer and then we can use circumstantial evidence to establish the identity. Though, given the nature of this list, the poster in question might not be the individual who actually made the offending claim.'

'Right,' Michael said, barely comprehending.

'It's not a quick or easy process.'

'No?'

Gary adjusted his tie. 'It's not a cheap one either.'

The words hung in the air. Michael could hear Ola's measured breathing, her shifting her weight on the couch cushion, crossing and uncrossing her legs. Head clouded by static, he glanced at her out of the corner of his eye and saw she was picking at the cuticle of her now bare ring finger.

'The least you could do is concentrate,' Ola seethed as they left the office, rummaging through her bag to retrieve her iPhone.

'I was.'

'You weren't. I was the one asking all the questions,' she said, peering down at it.

'Ola, I let you ask the questions because you wanted to ask questions.' Ola didn't reply.

'You keep checking your phone,' Michael said.

At that, she looked up. 'No, I don't.'

'Yes, you do.'

She huffed. 'Okay, and so what if I do? I have a job and concerned friends and Twitter trolls and a wedding that may or may not be happening, so yes, my phone is a bit busier than usual. Is that really the biggest issue at hand, Michael?'

He paused. 'You're right. I'm sorry.' Ola pursed her lips and went back to squinting at the screen.

When Michael proposed ten months ago, he had captioned the image of them – sunkissed and kissing against a sunset – #BlackLove, not only for discoverability, but as a declaration. She was a *good* Black woman™ and he a *good* Black man™ and it was undoubtedly a *good* thing they had found each other. And, it was nice to see complete strangers agreed – nearly 30,000 of them, if the likes on that post were anything to go by. Next thing he knew, he and Ola's faces were plastered on Instagram pages named things like @melaninmarriages and @blackluvdontcrack, sandwiched between pictures of Beyoncé and Jay-Z and the Obamas. Over the course of that surreal two-week period, they gained 47,000 followers between them. Since then, he had posted pictures of them regularly, to further adoration from strangers. He had no idea that one day he'd do anything he could to feel less visible. Or that one day his relationship with Ola would remind him of his parents, with their picking at each other and bickering.

'Are you still going to the police station?' Ola said, eyes still glued to her phone.

Michael jerked a shoulder upward. 'I'm not sure. The more I think about it, the more I'm not sure if they can do anything.'

Going to the police wasn't something Michael would normally do, no matter what. It had been 'fuck the feds, fuck the pigs, fuck the jakes, fuck the boydem' for as long as he could remember. But time and his options were running out. When he'd floated the idea to Ola earlier in the day, hoping it might appease her, she'd seemed receptive. In the cold light of day, however, he wasn't sure if he could go through with it.

Ola raised her head, confused. 'Well, you can't afford to take this to court,' she said. 'So if not the police, then what?'

'I don't know, Ola. But the police? They're not exactly well known for having Black men's best interests at heart, are they?'

'Yeah well, you'd probably only be worse off if you were a woman trying to report a rape,' she snapped.

Michael shrunk back and Ola's voice and eyes softened slightly.

'I get what you're saying,' she offered. 'But if you haven't done what you've been accused of, then maybe they can be some small help?'

He nodded reluctantly. 'I guess, if you think it's worth it?'

'I mean, it can't hurt.' A pause. 'Do you need me to come with you?' Ola was asking because she felt she had to, he could tell.

'I'm good, it won't be long. Unless you want to …'

'Nah, nah, don't worry. I'll leave you to it.' She jutted her chin out at him as a sort of goodbye and walked away, crouched over her phone. It was better this way, he thought. He wanted support she wasn't able to give. And on his own, he'd feel less like he was trying to convince two people of his innocence as opposed to one.

It took all of his resolve to get himself to the station. The walk was agony, the stress making his joints ache. The last time he'd felt anywhere close to this hollow, so tired he could sleep and never wake up again, was after Schuh let him go and he struggled to get a new job. By then, the podcast had made Michael something of a micro-celebrity, and his presumed success online, versus the shitshow of his professional life, only made him feel worse. Throughout their relationship, he'd celebrated Ola's wins as his own; he was thrilled when she announced her blog had landed her an interview at *Womxxxn*. But her promotion to Current Affairs Editor was harder to get excited about as it coincided with his redundancy. His self-esteem, already rocked by unemployment, had to suffer the blow of being her 'scrub' boyfriend.

Before that, he had struggled with his mental health during his first year at De Montfort University. He missed his mother's cooking and his friends and everything that made home, home. He started smoking too much weed and drinking more than ever. When he started missing lectures and then deadlines, he was pulled to one side by his course tutor, then ordered to see the student services team who ordered him to see the campus therapist. He went to three appointments and said exactly what he thought they wanted to hear each visit: yes, he missed home and he felt lonely some days and overwhelmed by his new surroundings, but it wasn't too bad – everyone experienced changing 'mental health' after all, and some days it was better or worse than others, just like your bodily health. Yes, he did have friends he felt he could talk to, thanks, he and his roommate Kwabz got on famously. A visit home would definitely help and he was going at the end of the month. After that, Michael managed these feelings through university with the help of lots of alcohol and lots of women but the idea of them overtaking him once again, as a big man, scared him.

From the outside Plaistow police station was an old red-brick building that sort of looked unthreatening, like a school. But when Michael got inside and saw the missing persons posters and ballistic glass at reception, he couldn't believe it had come to this. Michael was where his mother had prayed her son would never end up. He'd dodged the dodgy yutes at school and the policemen that picked fights all his life. Yet here he was, trying to stop his teeth from chattering in an overly air-conditioned interview room.

'And where were these messages posted?' the policeman said, having trouble following. He was sat behind a large, flat-screen computer monitor that had looked futuristic in the noughties and now looked entirely antiquated. The laminate was peeling on the top of the old desk and most things in the room were a shade of blue; the navy blinds, the generic cobalt desk chair, the grubby blue-grey carpet, speckled with black, flattened chewing gum.

'On Twitter,' Michael replied. He heard the policeman begin typing.

'What exactly did the messages say?'

'It was a post, saying that I was guilty of harassment and there was a restraining order against me for physical assault.'

The policeman pulled a questioning face.

'Which is not true,' Michael added, for the second time. 'But obviously before it was deleted, it was screenshotted and is still spreading.'

'So the post in question has been taken down?'

'Well, yeah it has,' Michael said, panic starting to rise in his voice. 'But the damage is done.'

The policeman scratched his head. 'I'm very sorry, Mr Koranteng, but this appears to be a civil matter, not a police one.'

'Please man, is there nothing you guys can do? I'm supposed to be getting married in two and a half weeks. We're meant to be writing the seating plan tomorrow and my girl can't even look at me.'

'Have you tried contacting Twitter directly?'

'I already did. Like, I sent a message but they don't have a number you can call, innit.'

The policeman tutted and stopped typing. He placed his hands on his thighs, then sighed.

'I'm not sure what we can do. There isn't a named accuser. There is nothing material other than what was written in that tweet, which no longer exists.'

Michael's foot began to tap. 'There's been other stuff too.'

'Other stuff?'

'Yeah.' He cleared his throat. 'I'm being harassed online.' Saying it made him feel stupid. It didn't sound serious. It had started with one or two comments from the same account – @ mirrorissa92. A number small enough that the social media manager at CuRated, flannel-shirt-wearing, sandy-haired Simon, was able to delete them as they came in, without bothering to alert Sebastian.

> @mirrorissa92: Micheal Koranteng's actions towards myself and countless other women can't be ignored #SackMichealKoranteng #TheList

> @mirrorissa92: Platforming woman beaters are we, CuRated? Still #NotRated it looks like. You hate to see it

> @mirrorissa92: Micheal Koranteng is an abusive piece of shit. CuRated have to do the right thing by women and sack him. NOW.

Simon assumed it was one, slightly unstable basement dweller who had developed a fixation on their handsome new hire. It happened from time to time – people said all sorts from burner accounts. Then, a few hours later, came another comment. And another. Simon blocked the account the next day but what he assumed was the same poster returned immediately, under the moniker of @mirrorissa90210. He blocked that account too, and within minutes another popped up – @mirror_issa. Each time he deleted an account, it reincarnated under a variation of the same screen name – @mirrorissa29, @mirrorissa_92, @mirrorissa93 and so on. Simon decided to flag it to Michael, who had clocked them coming in as soon as they started. He knew it wouldn't stop, though he couldn't tell Simon why. On his second day at CuRated, Michael saw @mirrorissa92 calling for his sacking and then the release of his home address. He felt that familiar sinking feeling that had made him sick a week before. He'd been trolled mercilessly since The List went up but @mirrorissa92 was different, relentless. They made reference to Michael's personal life. They claimed he had abused them.

'And this "mirrorissa92" account – do you have any idea who's behind it?'

'It's anonymous,' Michael said. Then he gathered himself. 'But I think I might know who it is. I think it's the same person who put me on The List.'

He felt glad Ola wasn't there but in a way he also wished she was. One more fallout with her and he'd probably confess everything. All of it. Because a big part of him wanted her to know. That he had lied when he said he didn't know who'd named him. That despite his professions, he was indeed a shitty person. He was not an abuser. He wasn't a woman beater or violent. But he was dishonest. He'd made promises he hadn't intended to keep. And now he was certain it was this that had landed him in this mess.

Michael would never cheat on Ola. Sleeping with someone else while he was with her – that was a line he'd never cross again. But he never told her about the messages. The phone calls. The sexts. The Facetimes. What Kwabz had called an 'emotional affair', which Michael still thought sounded like a made-up term. When he and Ola fell out or he felt rejected – which was more often than he cared to admit – he and Jackie would exchange messages they probably shouldn't have. Messages he prayed Ola would never see. Michael had never meant what he'd said to Jackie. But he was now certain that Jackie wanted to show him just how much words can mean – and the damage they can do.

PART TWO

8

15 days to the wedding

> So, what you're telling me, yet AGAIN, is that you still
> have nothing to show me???

Frankie's eyes were narrow and her mouth a line as her fingers
tapped the keyboard. Though Ola couldn't hear her irate typing
from her office, she could see it through the glass walls from her
desk.

> You've wasted enough of my time on this, so can we get
> straight to the point for once: what the hell is going
> on???

Ola's fingers hovered over the keyboard as she thought carefully
about her next choice of words. Holding her nerve was crucial
– she had an audience, after all – but so was ensuring she didn't
piss Frankie off any further. That morning on Slack, Frankie had
enquired whether Ola had finally made progress on her
write-up about The List. Her boss had purposely done this in
the main Slack chat where all staff could see the exchange.
When Ola replied that she hadn't, Frankie continued the chat-

turned-drag publicly, on the same medium. As Ola's dressing-down commenced, her colleagues were as stiff and silent as shop mannequins, drained of colour and comment by this desperately awkward scenario. Only the hum of the laptop fans could be heard across the stillness of the office. Ola started to type:

OLA: I'm really sorry Frankie. It's taken me a lot longer than I anticipated and I admit my planning has been poor

FRANKIE: Poor? It's been a SHITSHOW. Will you at least do me the honour of an excuse? Or am I supposed to put this down to you being 'busy' with the wedding again, despite me SPECIFICALLY telling you this was a priority???

Caps lock. Her patience was wearing thinner than Ola had ever seen; not a mitigating 'lovely' or 'fabulous' in sight. This wasn't passive-aggressive, this was aggressive-aggressive. Ola kept her sights fixed firmly on her screen.

OLA: I don't want to submit something subpar, so just need a little bit more time

FRANKIE: Subpar at this point would be better than nothing at all. Don't you have ANYTHING to show me? Not a single interviewee name or lead?

OLA: I'm sorry. It's been a lot harder than I thought

This was true. It had been almost a fortnight since Frankie had commissioned her for a deep dive on The List, a commission Ola planned on forfeiting to someone else on the team. But she realised she didn't want it to be written by someone else – she didn't want it written at all. Not until she was satisfied Michael was guilty. Had she believed he was, she assured herself, she'd be more than happy to feed him to the wolves. Perhaps 'more than happy' was an overstatement, but even so. She needed time for Luke to investigate. Prove or disprove it, for her own sanity, and then maybe later, for the article. She was talking to Luke more regularly than the wedding caterers, fishing for updates, but so far all he'd sent was the world's most boring background check and some blurry pictures of Michael on his lunch break. She felt terrible; wracked with guilt every time he reported back to her with nothing, but never truly relieved because neither of them knew exactly what he might find.

Ola's lacklustre excuses were starting to look like an affront to her boss's authority, so it was only a matter of time before Frankie hit breaking point. Now, she was having a full-blown meltdown on their Slack. Tearing Ola a new one as her staff-turned-murder-witnesses wondered what to do with themselves.

> FRANKIE: This is SO disappointing. You've always been disorganised but it is striking me as outright incompetence at this point!1!!

> OLA: I'm sorry I don't have a better excuse. I promise you I'll get you something by tomorrow. This won't happen again

> FRANKIE: That's right, it won't because Kiran's taking over.

Ola could have sworn the room began to tilt. She jumped out of her seat – she and the wheels of her chair squeaking simultaneously as she did – and made her way to Frankie's office, knocking on her transparent door and entering before she answered.

'But I've already started it, Frankie,' she said, shutting it behind her. 'I've done loads of research so—'

'Tough tits – and I'm using that term in a reclamatory sense so don't start – it's too little, too late,' Frankie huffed. 'You've been a shambles recently and I'm sick of it. You're not the first person who's ever had to plan a wedding, you know. I'm not sure what's going on, but the moment it starts affecting your ability to do your job, it's a problem.'

Ola didn't dare move.

'Now, we've got a lovely feature coming up on a plus-sized cam girl turned sports bra entrepreneur, and I know you'll do it *fabulously*,' Frankie said, the sweetness seeping back into her voice. 'Be a darling and get the fuck on with it, yeah?'

Of all the people at work Ola had wanted to avoid this topic with, Kiran was top of the list. Kiran was the only person she considered a friend at *Womxxxn*, where they'd both worked from its inception. Their colleague Sophie Chambers had been the first hire of the original, core 'woke-force' of three (which Frankie had since quadrupled). Sophie was a stylish, social media savvy journalist who had accrued a thriving online presence of over 80,000 followers on Twitter courtesy of

#CastrateTheStraights. She would use the hashtag when quote tweeting 'stomach-churning examples of cis-heteronormativity' – gender reveals, promposals – and eventually it saw her banned from the site, until she was reinstated in a blaze of glory after a petition labelling the move homophobic went viral.

Sophie was the most extreme edition of 'social media vs reality' Ola had come across. She looked just as she did in her pictures online, with her cotton-candy pink hair and clear grey eyes, but she couldn't behave more differently in person. Online, she was all sassy clapbacks and call-outs. Offline, she was so conflict averse that when Jada Smalls misheard her name as 'Sophia' on the cover shoot she hadn't corrected her, spending the whole five hours rechristened.

Kiran Ranaut had been brought in a few months later to write for both Culture and Lifestyle and Ola was drafted in last as a senior writer. Today, Ola headed up the Current Affairs desk but back then she struggled to make ends meet as a freelancer, doing six months maternity cover at a now-defunct digital news site while writing about sex and relationships on her now-defunct blog, CumTheFckThru.com. The three of them made up *Womxxxn*'s team of senior editors (alongside their unofficial titles as writers, subeditors, commissioners, office cleaners and therapists).

At times Ola felt conscious about her role as 'the Black one', but imagined Kiran and Sophie felt the same about their obvious roles as the Asian and the gay one, too. After Kiran came out, Frankie began to joke that she could have single-handedly filled *Womxxxn*'s diversity quota, since Kiran was pansexual, British-Indian and dyspraxic. 'If I'd have known, I wouldn't have bothered with Sophie or Ola – I got a handful of the letters in both LGBT and BAME in one go with Kiran! It's like I'm on bloody *Countdown*!' She repeated a version of this gag at every staff party once she'd had a few, as if she wasn't sure that they'd heard it the last time because they hadn't laughed.

Kiran was in the kitchen area when Ola found her, AirPods in, filling her sustainable water bottle. Her thick black hair was undercut halfway up the back of her head and the rest tied in a topknot, with ash-blonde ends from grown-out bleach culminating in an unintended ombré effect. That was Kiran in a nutshell – effortlessly achieving cool. She wore a large white shirt with dogtooth trousers, socks starting just below the hem and disappearing into black Wallabees. From her left ear hung an oversized earring, shaped like a safety pin. Ola tapped her shoulder and she gasped, dropping the bottle in the sink. She spun around accusatorily, then sighed with relief.

'Aunty! Thank fuck it's you,' she said, placing her hand on her chest. The nickname was one of the many ways she'd rib Ola about their age gap; she had her number saved under the grandma emoji.

'Sophie keeps trying to get me in some sponsored video they're pulling together for L'Oréal's new eye serum launch, that "#UnderEyesSoWoke" campaign.' She fake-gagged as she pocketed her AirPods. 'She's freaking out that the reality of our white as fuck office will be revealed, a la CuRated. It's about to be 2019's very own Kendall Jenner Pepsi ad, just watch.'

'Shit,' said Ola. 'How are you gonna get out of that one?'

'I told her it was against my religious beliefs, but someone's clearly snitched on me, because now Sophie's probing me for details.'

'Like?'

'Er, like what religion I am! I've never mentioned it before, so she's making out like she's prying to "avoid any future confusion". I said it was offensive to ask.' She burst out laughing at this, hearing Ola's reply in the silence and raised eyebrow.

'Oh, come *on*. It actually is!' she said with a grin. 'That's literally why they have the "prefer not to say" option on those forms. Or, as it is for me, the "I'm assumed religious because I'm brown but am not going to confirm or deny it" option. Let me utilise one of the few forms of Asian privilege there is!' She waited again for Ola's laughter, but it never came. Kiran wrinkled her nose.

'Okay, what's up? And *don't* say the wedding because if you're going to look this miserable about it every day then you probably shouldn't be getting married.' She nudged Ola lightly in the ribs.

Ola held her face in her hands. 'I don't know what to do, Kiran.'

'About what?'

'About …' she stopped. There was no elegant entry point to the conversation. 'About The List.'

'Oh, that? I just got a message from Frankie saying that she wants me to cover it,' Kiran said. 'What's happened?'

What had happened indeed. Ola searched for the least alarming way to sum up the situation for Kiran. It was actually a very short story: the context however, was miles long. Ola wanted to answer every question she knew would come before Kiran asked.

Wise beyond her years, Kiran was a formidable journalist and one of the few people in the office who treated their profession as more than a means to free press tickets. When she'd first met the wunderkind, Ola had admittedly been a bit jealous of her, which was unfashionable and unfeminist to admit. Kiran was the type of person who would make the

Forbes 30 under 30 list (she still had a whole five years to do so), but only post about it to decry it as ageist, capitalist and the epitome of everything that was wrong with the prevalence of 'millennial hustle culture'. She also put her money where her feminist morals were: volunteering at women's shelters on weekends and donating a large portion of the money she made from a popular Patreon. Ola couldn't bear the thought of Kiran thinking badly of her.

'Ola?' Kiran probed.

'I don't think anyone should write anything on The List yet.' Kiran tipped her head back in confusion. 'Why not?'

Ola took a deep breath. 'I don't think it's the right thing to do, before we know all the facts.'

'Um, we're not going to be reporting it as "all the facts" though? It's a developing story.'

'Well, should we really be giving column inches to an anonymous list that anybody could have contributed to?' She cringed even as she said it. She was finding herself arguing the opposing viewpoint depending on who she was with, a turncoat in every context.

'Yes, because if these men did do what they're accused of, we owe it to the survivors, Ola. To our readers,' Kiran said with slow precision, as if explaining times tables to a child. 'What's got into you? It's not like it isn't already out there. The *Guardian* did a short piece, *Vice* too. Buzzfeed's write-up went live today and I'll be damned if those quiz shitting twats—'

'If they did, though,' Ola cut her off. '*If*. And if they didn't?'

'Then they can clear their names. We're not accusing them of anything. There will be plenty of "allegedly"s thrown in.' Kiran took a small step back. 'You're sounding a bit like a Jordan Peterson plant right now.'

'I know one of the men accused,' Ola said, surprising herself. Silence. 'Okay …'

'It's Michael. He's been accused of physical violence, threatening behaviour and harassment.'

'Woah,' Kiran said after a moment. 'I don't understand. Frankie sent it to me and didn't say anything.'

'She doesn't know.'

'Oh my God. It couldn't be some other Michael?'

'Nope.'

'Fuck. Are you okay?'

'Nope.'

Kiran paused a beat as Sophie and Lucy brushed past them to grab brightly coloured Joe & The Juice shakes from the communal fridge. She edged closer to Ola once they were alone, her voice lowered. 'What the fuck, man.'

Ola sighed. 'Every day I wake up and feel sick. Like I'm a traitor to the entire female population, as well as my fiancé. I've never been so confused.'

'Right. Okay …' Kiran said. She was quiet for a moment. 'But I really hope this isn't you telling me you're standing by an abuser?'

'Kiran …' Ola looked at her with pleading eyes. 'I can't say he is an abuser.'

'Oh my days,' Kiran said, sounding more disappointed than annoyed. 'Seriously?'

Ola felt her face burn with shame.

'It's not like I've just taken his word for it,' she said. 'But some of the allegations don't add up. Like they said he assaulted someone at an office Christmas party – he sent me evidence from his past jobs that prove he's never even been to one.'

'What if it was at someone else's Christmas party?'

At that, Ola went cold. She hadn't thought of it. She looked down at the vinyl flooring, defeated. 'I'm not saying we never write about it, I'm asking we hold off.'

'Straight women are at it again,' Kiran muttered under her breath. 'Weakest links.'

'Oh, for fuck's sake, Kiran.'

'It's just interesting that you've been more than happy to talk about the importance of "believing women" until the one time it actually requires personal sacrifice. And by "interesting" I mean "total hypocritical fuckery".'

'You're not being fair,' Ola said. Her voice was cracking; she couldn't be bothered to pretend it wasn't. Kiran's eyes scanned their surroundings to check they weren't being listened to.

'None of this is fair,' she said. 'Not on you, not on the women he may have harmed. What if he doesn't even realise he's guilty? What if what he thinks is consensual, is actually harassment? Given what we know about the stats and—'

'So, what if with the stats a woman has decided to lie?' Ola jumped in. 'If, say, 99.9 per cent of women are telling the truth, there are 0.1 per cent that aren't, right?'

'Ola, I don't feel comfortable with where this conversation is going ...'

'Neither do I,' Ola said, her eyes prickling. 'But is it so hard to conceive of? I could accuse you of assault on a burner account right now.'

'Okay, so potentially one could be lying,' Kiran shot back. 'Should the stories of all the other women be discarded? Realistically most of the men probably did something to end up on there.'

'I don't see why we can't aim for an outcome where no one is needlessly hurt ...'

'When has that ever been the case, Ola? When women do exactly what they're asked by the system and are routinely failed? Of course we'll take matters into our own hands. Women have been collateral damage for years – I'm sorry that this time it *might* be Michael, but there are always stray bullets. That doesn't change because you share a John Lewis gift list with someone on the end of one.'

'Those stray bullets are hitting me too.'

'I mean, that never bothered you when it was others. What is the difference between this and the Gully TV thing?'

She had been waiting for the comparison to be drawn and should have known Kiran, with her encyclopaedic knowledge of every online 'cancellation', would be the one to make it. In 2017, an anonymous blog post had gone viral, accusing at least three affiliates of the then culturally defining Grime platform Gully TV of harassment. It gained traction from music journalists and artists, and Ola had done a viral piece a few weeks later, #MCsToo, that looked at its downfall and the silence around abuse within the UK music scene. Gully TV shut down permanently three months later.

Had that been irresponsible? She had tried to be rigorous: getting texts and emails where she could, double-checking the dates, flagging discrepancies. But these ethical questions around reporting on The List were ones she hadn't grappled with when writing #MCsToo. If someone had been falsely named on #MCsToo, did it invalidate the whole piece? She couldn't honestly say she thought it did: a further four women came forward about one of the men in question and he was eventually charged with kidnap and aggravated assault. Another was arrested after inappropriate texts and pictures to a fourteen-year-old fan were leaked. He had been a producer and recently, she'd found out he was also named on The List. Ola knew he was guilty of what he was accused of, and yet her fiancé who claimed to be innocent was named alongside him. Defending Michael felt like defending them both, and all the other named men.

'I'm not sure there is a difference,' Ola offered after some time. 'All I can say is I did it because I truly believed what I was being told was true. When it comes to Michael, I guess I don't know what's true. So, I'm doing my best to find out. He's been to the police, he went to get legal advice—'

'The police? A lawyer? He's moving like he's the victim here!'

'But if it's not true, Kiran, he kind of *is*, isn't he? If he does nothing, he looks guilty. If he does something, he looks guilty. He's fucked either way.' Ola paused and bit her lip. 'I hired a private investigator, you know.'

Kiran's eyes and mouth became wide at once. 'What?'

Ola glanced about the room. She glimpsed Frankie now up from her desk, pacing her office on a phone call and felt a chill travel up her spine.

'He's been doing background checks, following Michael,' she said quietly. 'He's not found anything but I can't have him stop, can I? I'm getting bombarded with messages. Fola's had to take over my accounts. He might or might not have done this but I'm paying for it either way.'

It was becoming a battle to get her words out. Ola squeezed her face hard to shut herself off like a tap but before she knew it she was sobbing uncontrollably, tears streaming. Kiran pulled two sheets of kitchen roll from the counter and handed it to her, rocking Ola's shoulder with her free hand.

'Don't get upset. They'll start asking questions and I know you hate people being in your business.' Ola laughed brittlely as she blew her nose.

'Okay, what is it you actually want from me?' Kiran said, her face screwed up with distress.

'I just want some more time, before the piece goes out. We still don't know the truth. Please.' Ola realised she was shaking.

'Let me at least see what else Luke comes back with,' she continued. 'I'm asking for me, not Michael. But Kiran – I'm worried about him. I'm scared of where his head is at, and what he might do.'

Kiran's eyes widened again. 'Not to *me*,' Ola said wearily. It was a constant battle, balancing her fears for Michael's wellbeing with the dread that he might be guilty of what he had been accused of. But as much as she attempted to smother her feelings of concern, she couldn't help it. Where would all this love for him go, if she found out he was guilty? She couldn't just make it disappear, as hard as she tried. 'Look, I know I've put you in a fucked-up situation and I'm sorry. But I didn't know what else to do—'

'I'll speak to Frankie,' Kiran said firmly. 'I am not going to stop it, but I will hold it off, until we do some more digging and can really get some concrete information. But don't thank me for this,' she said as Ola's lips began to part. 'I don't feel good about it.'

'Okay. Well, I appreciate this. A lot.'

Kiran threw a glance over her shoulder and watched their boss pacing her office. She gave a light shake of her head as she turned back around to face Ola, a few strands of hair coming loose from her bun.

'I don't trust cis men, Aunty,' she said. 'But I do trust you. Whatever god I apparently worship is gonna send me to hell for this, though. So you better be right. Michael better be telling the truth. And he better be able to prove it.'

9

13 days to the wedding

It took longer than Michael expected to get the email he'd been dreading. The List had gone up and come down two weeks ago, but it was clear that it had since reached his CuRated colleagues. He'd noticed conversations petering out when he entered the kitchen, rigid smiles that erred on grimaces whenever he greeted someone. The atmosphere was frosty, but more painfully, it seemed fearful. It had only been a matter of time until his inbox finally pinged with a message from Beth that afternoon, subject line: The List.

'The truth is, we were notified about your presence on it the day you arrived,' she said, after a sip of tea. She had summoned him to Sebastian's office, and he wondered how many more mortifying chats like this were to come. 'We've had some concerned emails. But we don't do gossip at CuRated – we do enhanced DBS checks.' She laughed, awkwardly.

'We did one as standard before you got here, which would have outlined any cautions, spent or unspent convictions, and anything else held on police records that's relevant. There was no restraining order. Nothing.'

In an instant, every single interaction they'd had was reframed.

Every 'how was your weekend?' chat by the fridge, every cup of tea offered.

'Right. I see,' Michael said finally. He was trying to stay present but everything was starting to go fuzzy. Beth sounded like she was being beamed in from another dimension, her words barely cutting through the cloud of his thoughts.

'I did make some calls to your past jobs for good measure, too,' she said. 'It was the second time they'd been asked about a Christmas party apparently and they said they don't even have them! And so we assumed that nothing came up because the allegations aren't true ... correct?' She scanned his face.

'Correct.'

'Of course.' She sipped her tea again. 'We did hope to discuss it directly with you at one time or another. Seb was going to broach it, but you seemed ...' She squared her eyes at him. '... fragile.'

Michael squirmed in his seat.

'We hoped it would die down eventually. But with these comments under your videos, some of your colleagues have expressed discomfort. And that puts us in a ... more compromised position.'

'Right ...' Michael said. 'So, what does that actually mean?'

The silence that followed felt endless, broken only by the ticking of the clock on the wall. 'We just don't know, Mike,' Beth breathed at last, her voice sounding foreign and unnerving without its usual buoyancy.

He nodded. 'I'm fired.'

'I didn't say that,' she said, nervously. 'We value you as a member of the CuRated team and that's exactly why we're sat here. To work out how to navigate this.'

Beth was by this point clutching her mug for dear life. His thoughts went to Ola, in Pret two weeks ago, fiddling with her

KeepCup and looking as defeated as Beth did now. All because of his mess. Briefly, he forgot how sorry he was feeling for himself and felt a wave of pity wash over him. Beth wasn't a bad person. Neither was Ola.

'Okay,' Michael said, sitting up. 'What happens now?'

He could see the cogs whirring, almost hear the ticking of her entire thought process. How could she resolve this in a way that appeared the least problematic online? He knew it didn't help CuRated that he was Black, which for once, was useful to him. Ousting their only Black employee months after a corporate race scandal was a bad look. But on the other hand, so was housing an alleged abuser. So rudimentary was this game of Top Trumps she was playing. Who would Black Twitter back? Blue tick Twitter? Black Feminist Twitter? They're Black too, but they're women, and Michael, well, was apparently not great to women …

'How about you take some time off?' she said, her voice sounding nearly level again at the possibility of a temporary fix.

'Some time off …' Michael repeated.

'Just until we're able to work out how to move forward. Could be worth us talking to a PR? Anyway – get some rest in the meantime. You do look like you could do with the break …'

Her eyes scanned over him again and her face crumpled into a look of pity.

'All right. So I'm not sacked?'

'You're not sacked. We're putting you on temporary leave till we know how to move forward. Paid, don't worry.'

With just under three months left of probation, he was incredibly worried. But instead he said, 'Okay. Cool. Thanks, Beth.'

'You're welcome, Mike. This must be extremely tough and we'll do whatever we can to support you.' He hadn't been expecting some form of condolence since no one was supposed to feel sorry for him, and it didn't comfort him when it came. Beth had bundled up her tote bag under her arm as they prepared to leave, but hesitated midway as she rose and remained in a sort of perching position.

'I hope you don't mind if I ask you something?'

'Nah, ask away.'

'Do you have any idea who put you on there? Or why?'

He swallowed. 'No idea.'

Beth shook her head. 'Bloody hell. There are some nutters out there, aren't there! I suppose that's the internet for you, isn't it?'

———————

Michael left work straight after, and once he got home he went to the kitchen to pour himself a very large glass of Jack Daniel's. He'd been smoking more weed than usual recently but had avoided day drinking since university. Today it was necessary; he could feel that old weight in the pit of his stomach pinning him to his couch, the tightness in his chest that he knew so well. His aura darkening, a cloud of smoke making his mind foggy. He'd been here before and he needed to stave off the creeping despair.

Once he felt calm enough, he texted Ola about the meeting with Beth. They hadn't spoken properly since their visit to the lawyer's last week; the few conversations they'd had in-between felt more stilted by the day. The guilt about Jackie, about the position he'd put Ola in, was eating him alive. Was the wedding even going ahead? He had no idea. When he raised it, she repeated what she'd said a fortnight ago: he needed to prove to her that he was innocent. But every time he thought he'd come close to doing so, he realised he was at a dead end. He rang the police four times before giving up, reciting his case number to a different officer each time.

'There haven't been any threats made,' the last one had repeated matter-of-factly. 'Unfortunately, unless it's proven that what they're saying isn't true, it's very difficult to move forward.'

'How do I disprove what a person I can't identify is saying? I don't have any evidence that Jackie's behind these messages. What do you guys want me to do?'

'I'm sorry, Mr Koranteng.'

When Ola eventually replied to Michael's message about work some hours later, her response was tepid. She didn't seem to think much of it. He followed up with a text about what Beth had told him about his DBS and how it revealed no restraining order, but it was as if the news proved nothing at all. If anything, she had more questions.

His fiancée clearly felt this was a battle between them as opposed to one they were fighting together. The only person showing any real concern for him was his mum, who didn't even know about The List, thank God, but was bombarding him with worried calls about both the wedding and his wellbeing. She had even pushed his dad into sending him a stock message of concern. He knew that would have taken some doing – Michael's dad had never been particularly hands-on, for which his mother overcompensated by never loosening her grip on her only child, her 'miracle Michael'. It was disconcerting, how growing up he had felt both smothered and overlooked in the same household.

He was desperate. It passed three o'clock and home alone, whiskey coursing through his bloodstream and blood rushing to his head after a large spliff, Michael decided he was going to tell his friends about The List.

He had been mulling over doing it for some time, as the comments under videos became messages to his leaked work email. His anxiety skyrocketed each time he monitored what was being said online, each time he lost another mass of followers. But it was equally high when he was off his phone and in the dark. Maybe when it came to his friends, he had some control.

For days, the group chat had continued as normal and he'd missed hundreds of notifications. Nobody had asked why he'd been AWOL, likely assuming he was tied up with wedding planning. Michael's friends, his actual friends, hadn't mentioned The List and he knew it was because they hadn't seen it. It had gone viral in a section of the internet they didn't frequent. It existed in a world they weren't part of, another dimension, but the horror was unfolding all the same. At times he thought of raising it with Kwabz, but he wasn't sure how to drop it into conversation – they only saw each other in person these days at birthdays, for a last-minute drink-up at Amani's. It was weird raising it by message, especially as he'd spoken in nothing other than emojis for more than two weeks. But who else could he speak to?

He opened the group chat, currently named NOT GONNA GET YOU THAT ASS, KWABZ – the guys were in the process of rinsing his best man about something. Instead of offering up a preamble, Michael simply sent a screenshot of The List, with the words 'Someone's put me on this'.

'What is it?' Kwabz wrote back. There were four of them in the chat, including Michael. He and Amani had gone to the same secondary school in Canning Town and met Seun (or Sean, depending on who he was talking to) and Kwabz at university. It had been right after graduation that they'd started *Caught Slippin* on a whim – there was disagreement on whether it had been Amani or Michael's idea, but all agreed the podcast had got bigger than any of them expected. Amani was a part-time PT, whose most committed relationship was with the gym he ran. With light-brown eyes and hair that touched the top of his shoulders when in plaits, he had been the heartthrob of their year, spending most of his tweens and teens compared to Omarion, Bow Wow, Lil' Romeo and whatever other baby-faced light-skinned crush covered Black music magazines then.

Kwabz served as the group's moral compass, forever scandal-ised by his friends' behaviour, which frequently made him the butt of their jokes. He had a way with words, which he utilised at Waldegrave Manor teaching Year 9 English and for three years on *Caught Slippin*, before he landed the job and came offline entirely to avoid being surveilled by his students. Michael had been the everyman, Amani the funny one, Kwabz the one who stopped the show from being pulled from streaming services altogether. While he didn't have Amani or Michael's looks, what he lacked in that department, he made up for with charm, banter and having dreads.

Seun/Sean meanwhile, like many men in the corporate world of Canary Wharf, had the arrogance of someone far better-looking and his USP was having 'no filter'. A man who managed to wear a blazer and smart trousers in every conceiva-ble context, whether it be to a christening or the cinema. That his gorgeous, on-off, long-suffering girlfriend Rachel had stuck with him baffled the entire group, which they let him know any moment they could. He used to come on the show as a guest sometimes, usually for the 'cakes of the quarter' segment where they'd ranked celebrity and civilian buttocks. But he never committed to it full time, reminding them that he lived in the real world where he had to 'rise and grind'.

'Read it,' Michael wrote back. He felt too ashamed to type out what had happened to him.

AMANI: Oi c'mon man. Ain't noone tryna read all dat lol

MICHAEL: Its a list of abusers in media

The typing notifications came to a halt, all at once. Seun was the first to reply.

SEUN: Fam whattttt???

AMANI: ?????

AMANI: Whats goin on??? Why you on this??

MICHAEL: I dont know. Never threatened/harassed/assaulted anyone in my life, and definitely not any women

AMANI: Obviously not. You don't have to tell me dat. But this is bonkers bro

SEUN: Yo is this meant to be someones idea of a joke or???

MICHAEL: Nope. Woke up on my first day of work and saw it

SEUN: Ola must be losing her shit

AMANI: I dont know how anyone could put you down
on some nonce list, are they fucking nuts?

'Not a nonce list,' Michael wrote back quickly, feeling his head become hot. He was too high for this. He wasn't proud of what he was being accused of, but he felt the distinction was important and often lost.

MICHAEL: Nothin to do with kids or sexual abuse.
Says I'm a harasser/physically assaulted someone.
Which I havent

SEUN: Gotta get a lawyer involved bruv

MICHAEL: Already tried. Even went to the feds, they
can't do nothin

SEUN: Well obviously the feds weren't gonna do
nothing! But it's defamation I swear? U got to take them
to court. I know a couple guys who could back u

MICHAEL: Take who to court? It was posted on an
anonymous account, by an anonymous person. Who
am I gonna sue, Twitter?

SEUN: They cant track IP addresses?

MICHAEL: Everything you say I will have already tried,
trust. I was thinking of writing a statement

AMANI: Nahhh fuck dat man. That's what people do when they did that shit. Am I lyin Seun?

SEUN: Facts. You'll end up getting dragged even more

AMANI: Yoooo, they got my nigga Danks on here! Now I know this shit aint real. Look at the timing, right after his mixtape dropped smh

SEUN: Bruv, I'm seeing Lewis Hale on ere. That Guy Abe too! Its all mad. This is lookin like one set up, I cant lie. Evil eye ain't no joke

AMANI: No joke. Did I tell you man about dat one Dagenham ting that try say I emotionally abused her, cos I said her sister was buffer than her? 💀💀💀

SEUN: I swear u did try to move her sister tho 👀

AMANI: Sjgdfdfff 😂 yeah but the way they try it with these made up words. As soon as she started telling me I was 'gaslighting' her I had to hit block real quick. Using medical terms for common lies

SEUN: How the fuck they got Mike on there and not Amani tho, real talk. The guys a menace looool

The conversation erupted with dozens of lols with dozens of o's. Then Amani began telling them an urban legend he'd heard from a friend of a friend, about a girl from Finsbury Park who apparently poked a hole in three of his boys' condoms a few years apart, kept all of the subsequent babies and has them all paying child support to this day. 'Where was the consent?' he wrote. 'Where's The List for the gyal that do that shit?' Then Seun chimed in that even when Black men were guilty, they weren't allowed to make mistakes and move on like everyone else and that Chris Brown had paid his dues. Plus, hadn't Rihanna hit him first? Before long, they descended into crying laughing emojis and it was all over, like Michael hadn't disclosed anything at all.

A separate WhatsApp notification popped up from Kwabz.

'Bro,' it simply said.

'I know,' Michael replied.

KWABZ: This is all a bit mad

MICHAEL: Yh. I know

KWABZ: Listen. You know your my darg. But man has to ask. Is there any truth to it? The allegations?

MICHAEL: Kwabz, I have never hit or harassed a woman in my whole life. Or threatened. Mum's life

KWABZ: Okay. You know how mad this looks tho?

MICHAEL: I know. I understand if you dont know what to think, cos I probably wouldn't either. It's not exactly like I've been a saint

Kwabz knew this better than anyone. In fact, at De Montfort a begrudging Kwabz had turned away girls from their halls in hysterics, reluctantly covering for Michael who couldn't come to the door and deal with it himself as he was usually out fucking someone else. He had often felt shitty at uni and though it shamed him to admit it, women often made him feel better about life, about himself. During one of their more dramatic fights, a friend with benefits on his course had said he was a 'user'. But what did that even mean, a 'user'? He never asked her for anything, was never intentionally cruel. What was the line between a user and, well, an emotional abuser? Between an emotional abuser and an immature teenage boy or man in his early twenties? Perhaps there wasn't one and that was the problem?

> MICHAEL: But whoever put me on there said they have a restraining order against me – fam, that is not true, doesn't even show up on my DBS

> MICHAEL: You've known me for a minute bro. I'm just hoping you know I'm not capable of these things

> KWABZ: Cool. I didn't think that what I read matched up with the guy I know. Would be a bit mad not to ask tho

> MICHAEL: Nah I hear that still. Tbh I'm kinda glad you did. Dem man aint even thought to ask me nothin, talking about Chris Brown and all sorts

Kwabz bothering to ask suggested that had he not believed Michael's answer, there would have been a severing of ties. Seun and Amani's unquestioning support, however, gave credence to what Ola had long said; that men only have issues with abusive men outside of their immediate circle. The closer to home, the blinder their eye becomes. She was probably right. Though he'd matured over the years (and potentially, even faster over the past two weeks) he had been as bad as Amani and Seun, if not worse. Those times they put nudes they'd been sent by the *Caught Slippin* listeners into the group chat a few years back. The women couldn't have known they would do that – and he would never do it now – but he'd been a part of it. He was never asked by his fans if he wanted them, mind, they sent them unprovoked. Still, the nonchalance of Amani and Seun today made him feel a bit ill. As did the fact that Kwabz's enquiring, as direct as it had been, didn't stir up the same disappointment and anger that he had felt when Ola had.

KWABZ: Yh I can't lie they're not serious guys. But anyway. Do you think this could be the work of you know who?

MICHAEL: J?

KWABZ: Yep

MICHAEL: I didnt even want to mention but I'm ngl, I know its her. Who else?

KWABZ: Bruv … This is why I told you to lock that shit off. None of this was worth it

Amani and Seun would make jokes about him and Jackie since she started turning up at their live shows, but only Kwabz knew what had been happening. 'Ay big bum Jackie is here for Michael again!' they'd cackle whenever they spotted her. He'd laugh it off each time. The boys had big mouths and he couldn't risk anything getting back to Ola. Kwabz, on the other hand, was the one he knew would approve of it the least but also most likely to keep it quiet. Michael swallowed another sip from his glass before typing as the whiskey burnt his throat.

> MICHAEL: I know. And I did, as soon as the messages started goin left, I told you. Before me and Ola got engaged I had her blocked across everything. I knew she was upset but not to the point where she'd do this

> MICHAEL: I feel like if I holla her, shes gonna start saying I'm harassing her or some shit. I dont know how far she wants to go with it

It had been a DM slide that started it with him and Jackie. He and Ola hadn't been together long, or at all depending on who you asked. Conversations around their murky, six-month 'talk-ing stage' were hard to navigate. In his mind, the first rule of a 'situationship' was that there weren't any. It was back when he was working in retail; finding his feet in presenting took much longer than either of them cared to remember. She hadn't said it, but he knew Ola thought she could do better. Sometimes he wasn't sure if Ola liked him, even if she loved him. It was as though she was more in love with the idea of who he could be, as opposed to who he was. She'd speak about his 'potential', rather than his present state. But Jackie was different. She thought he was smart. Funny. Somebody.

Jackie had sent him the 'eyes' emoji, with no words but late enough at night that the message was received loud and clear. She'd been an early *Caught Slippin* listener, someone he recognised from the comments section on their YouTube videos. He'd followed her back immediately on Instagram after receiving a few dozen like notifications from her, on pictures stretching back all the way to 2014. @jackie_ayyx – they didn't call her 'big bum Jackie' for nothing. But he was cautious. Responded to her thirst traps in private DMs: flame emojis for her eyes only.

If Ola had seen the initial Instagram messages they exchanged, there would have been no trouble. It was obvious Jackie fancied him and he was courteous, but never encouraged it. But that all changed when he gave her his WhatsApp. Despite what he told himself, he knew he was crossing a line when he invited her to chill with him and the boys after a live show. The point of no return was reached when they first slept together, hours after he had been simpering over bubble teas with Ola at the Boxpark in Shoreditch. Jackie dug her nails deep into his back that night and hadn't taken her claws out of him since.

Jackie was, in Kwabz's words, 'ready to risk it all'. Michael could treat her how he wanted. It was like she existed purely for his use, like a kettle or a toaster. He knew how she felt about him, and yet he'd ignore her for days at a time. And when he felt like talking to her again, she'd be right where he left her. Ready and waiting. After Ola found out and it all blew up, Jackie still wound her way back, eventually. Even after she got serious with the guy she had been seeing, a man who seemed to give her the consistency and emotional availability she had begged Michael for. After a year of no contact, Jackie texted Michael 'Merry

Christmas' out of the blue. He'd been made redundant a week before. She was just in time. When he replied, their dynamic was as it had always been. It was his feelings, not hers, that he had been responding to.

It had lasted just over three months the first time, and nearly two months the second. When Jackie started getting serious about leaving her boyfriend, Michael began to slowly ice her out. Taken longer to reply to texts, sent lukewarm responses to her nudes. He knew it was an asshole thing to do, there was no excuse. And this time, she didn't take it lying down. She'd text repeatedly. Call him non-stop, leaving hysterical voice notes and voicemails shrieking about Mikey this, Mikey that. She even showed up at a *Caught Slippin* show with her new guy, thinking it would make Michael jealous. Instead, he looked right through her on the front row, then made sure he didn't mingle afterwards and went straight home. When he arrived back, she'd sent an essay on WhatsApp, bullet-pointing all the ways in which he'd hurt her. He thought that was the end of it.

Then, a few weeks later, a missed call at 2 a.m. followed by a rambling message, drunkenly typed he'd assumed. It was different from the others. Scary in places. Something in her must have snapped. She said his life was over, that he should die, his mother should too. There was a vague threat of an acid attack; if he hadn't deleted all their correspondence so Ola wouldn't see it, he'd have shown the police. It was too much. Even Kwabz, who usually shook his locs with Aslan-like pious disapproval at Michael's behaviour, had read and reread the messages, baffled by the sheer force of her response. But all of this, more than a year later? Adding him to The List? It was hard to believe she hated him this much. As thoughts about Jackie continued to swirl in his head, Michael's phone vibrated with a new message.

KWABZ: I feel for you man. Dunno what I'd do

KWABZ: Just wait for it to pass tho. Keep your head up but a low profile. Whats Ola sayin? Her head must be gone

MICHAEL: She said if I cant prove I didn't do anything then she's not going ahead with the wedding

KWABZ: Fucking hell bro. Hopefully she knows you well enough by now to know you aint no abuser

KWABZ: You alright tho?

Michael paused before typing his reply:

MICHAEL: Not really

KWABZ: Talk to me

He wanted to. To tell him that he couldn't sleep at night. That sometimes he'd smoke his way through entire days until they blurred in a haze of smoke and Netflix. That he'd find himself googling (and then deleting from his search history) what a longing, not to die exactly, but to 'not exist' any more, meant. That the first few results were suicide hotlines. He could promise him, truthfully, that he didn't want to die. More, it was almost like he wished he'd never been born in the first place, which he knew sounded frightening but not as frightening as his future seemed. He hoped Kwabz would understand, because if he didn't, maybe Michael wasn't well after all? He was having trouble envisaging an outcome that didn't see him marked as a predator for life – and he wasn't certain a life like that was worth living. Michael reached for his drink with his free hand and started to type with the other:

>MICHAEL: Its just mad stressful

KWABZ: Listen bro, this is just online shit. If you never dropped it in the GC, I wouldn't even know it existed. In the real world, you still have your job. Your boys. Your girl. People will be dragging someone else in a few days

>MICHAEL: I hope so man

KWABZ: You need to stop thinking the worst, my brother. God's got you and so have we. You know Im here if you need to talk yh?

>MICHAEL: Yh man. Appreciate you bro

Michael pulled up the screenshot of The List in the group chat. He studied it daily without fail, measuring the perceived likelihood of his guilt against the others named. Some of them he hadn't recognised initially, which in his mind was damning – if people had been named for blackmail or clout or 'hating', why choose nobodies? Others he knew well; even if he hadn't been on The List himself, Michael would have still been troubled by it since it included Lewis Hale, one of his all-time favourite footballers. By the end of the first week, however, he was familiar with all of the names on there. Where surnames had been included, he perused their LinkedIn accounts, read and reread their tweets. Carefully examined their Instagrams, in the hopes he'd find something, anything that proved they were good men, and therefore he was a good man too. There had to be others like him. Men who were on there for being a different type of dickhead. Some hadn't posted since The List went up, but most of them continued unchanged with their updates as if everything was fine. Though The List occupied his every waking moment, many of them seemed to be getting on with it and getting away with it. If they were guilty, they'd got off scot free. So why did he feel so relentlessly punished?

In the corner of the kitchen, Michael glimpsed the dozens of empty gift bags waiting for party favours and felt his eyes fill. He turned off his phone. A mental anguish, so strong that it was physical, gripped him. As he took another swig from his glass, he stared at the beige bricks of his kitchen wall, imagining hitting his face against them until his lip split and his nose broke. His eyes began to mist over and he drew back his left fist, punching the wall as hard as he could. Then again and again. The pain coursed through his hand each time it made impact and a sense of calm shot through him, like he was being injected with morphine. When he eventually exhausted himself, the wounds on his knuckles were obscured by blood. He watched it as it pooled on the floor.

10

11 days to the wedding

By the fourth time she hobbled up Romilly Street, Ola was thoroughly regretting her shoe choice. Her feet would have fared much better in boots than in the pointed-toe heels she was wearing, which felt like they were squashing all five of her toes into one large one.

She hadn't anticipated this much walking. Neither had Google Maps. Ola pushed up her glasses, the tip of her nose nearly touching the screen as she peered at the app, perturbed. It claimed she had reached her destination eleven minutes ago. The more she walked, the more she was reminded of how much she felt like a tourist in Soho. It was an area she felt she should wear nice shoes to, even if she was often dodging various yellowish fluids kerbside – piss, or beer that tasted like it. Today her mind was distracted, preoccupied with how this afternoon's conversation might go and whether her CV was up to date, in case Frankie found out about it.

Despite failing to find incriminating evidence about Michael, Luke had finally come good. Not on what she'd asked for but on a side project he took up when it became clear he'd exhausted every avenue regarding her fiancé. By way of some sort of dark web dark magic Ola didn't understand, Luke had traced the creator of The List. And in good time too: Michael had made it clear he knew something was up when she last saw him at the lawyer's. They'd messaged a few times since then, almost formal in their exchanges, but they hadn't spoken in days. The only possible points of conversation between them were The List or The Wedding, and there was no sense discussing either until they could establish the truth. The lack of communication with her fiancé wasn't practical, she knew that, but nothing about the situation was.

It was getting harder, too, to turn a blind eye to the wedding admin piling up. Ola was yet to confirm it or call it off, with a week and a half to go. Currently, Luke's were the only texts guaranteed a response; Celie was messaging about whether she should give the printers the go-ahead on place cards and Ruth was incessantly nudging about the shot list, badgering her in the group chat that morning:

OI. Whats the plan man??? Photographer is on my dick
and Bella Naija asking if they have permission to share
the pics on their insta

'No Bella Naija' Ola had simply replied, her first response in days. As far as almost everyone invited was concerned, nothing had changed regarding the 8th of June. Every day Ola wondered how long she could hold off making phone calls. But today would force an answer. Luke had confirmed the identity of The List's creator as Rhian Mcintosh, deputy political editor at the *Observer*, and when Ola and Kiran did some digging, they realised it was an open secret. The truth had started drifting to the more dangerous parts of the internet, rumblings among men's rights activists that it was either Rhian or a BBC alum, Louisa Meade. There was talk that Masc On, a blog run by pick-up artists, was planning to run a piece outing one or both of them.

It hadn't been easy to get in touch with Rhian, who seemed to keep a low profile online even before alt-right websites were threatening to dox her. She had no Instagram, Facebook or LinkedIn that were public, and her Twitter had been inactive since 2015. But after much pestering from Kiran through mutual acquaintances, and assurance that this was only a provisional chat, she'd agreed to an anonymous interview with *Womxxxn*. Rhian seemed surprisingly willing to talk, in order to avoid Louisa getting caught in the crosshairs and to control an already out-of-hand narrative.

The interview was, of course, not real. If Frankie ever found out they had not only set up a fake interview but one with a subject she would quite happily kill to get hold of, there was no doubt she wouldn't hesitate in killing them. Kiran had already put her neck on the line by getting Frankie to hold off on publishing the article. She'd told her boss, not entirely untruthfully, that she had vague connections to The List's creator and then flat-out lied that she could secure an exclusive on-camera video chat. 'I think I saw her wipe drool from her bottom lip,' Kiran told Ola. 'She told me to put all my energy into that and gave me an extra fortnight!'

When Ola reached the women's-only members club Venus, fifteen minutes late, she saw it was an inconspicuous black door she had walked past multiple times. She pressed the barely there buzzer and a voice worthy of an ASMR video came from the speaker. 'Afternoon, Venus,' it husked.

'Hi. I'm here to see Rhian Mcintosh?'

There was the click of the intercom followed by the click of the door and Ola was transported to what felt like the product of a marketing agency brainstorm on girl – no, *woman* – heaven. Pink marble floor, mirrored walls, a white reception desk punctuated with white orchid-filled vases. On the terracotta-hued feature wall behind it hung line art featuring breasts of differing sizes, shades and degrees of suppleness. Above was a sign in big pink neon letters: 'Venus: A home for the home girls', with the goddess of love sat atop a planet, looking into a shell-shaped mirror at the end of her outstretched arm. A kiosk on the left was selling babies' bibs, water bottles, T-shirts and tote bags plastered with the same image and next to it, a sign outlining what was on each floor in fancy rose-gold lettering. The fifth was home to a make-up room called the Dollhouse next to the gym, Im/Perfect. It was funny, Ola thought briefly, how feminism had swung to now meet patriarchy in the middle, seemingly agreeing that what women wanted was everything to be pink and focused on making them look good.

She was directed to the bar and restaurant 'Sirenum Scopuli' on the first floor to meet Rhian. Ola made her way determinedly to the lifts, mentally flicking through her questions. 'Who put Michael on The List?' was a great place to start. With a sinking feeling, Ola realised that whatever Rhian said would seal their fate, one way or another.

Rhian was sat at the bar in a coral-coloured chair shaped like a seashell, in front of a glass of sparkling water. Had she not been obsessively googling her beforehand, Ola would never have noticed her. She was an entirely nondescript brunette – paper-pale with her hair scraped into a low bun, thin-lipped and thin-eyebrowed in a long-sleeved striped tee and a well-worn pair of white Converses. As she approached, Ola felt a faint bitterness towards her, this woman who had ruined her life in a way too abstract for her anger to be fully realised. When they exchanged curt 'hellos' as she sat down, Ola caught the remnants of a northern accent that took her by surprise. Rhian was so soft-spoken, she had to strain to hear her. She didn't seem at all taken aback that it was Ola greeting her instead of Kiran.

'I hope you don't mind me bringing you here,' said Rhian, as they shook hands. 'It's not really my cup of tea, it's a bit ...' her voice trailed off. 'Anyway, it's empty around this time, so ...' she shrugged. 'Plus, the fettuccine is decent.'

Ola surveyed the restaurant. Mermaid motifs lined the bottom of the wallpaper and a portrait of Rosie the Riveter reimagined as a sailor hung behind the bar. Except for a waitress, and some disembodied brown boobs she'd peeped in reception, Ola was the only non-white woman in there.

She tried to sound as conversational as possible. 'I think I get what you mean about it being ...' Ola didn't finish her sentence either.

Rhian was looking past Ola's head, appraising the space like an estate agent.

'More of a Soho House girl yourself?'

Ola let out a small, clipped laugh. 'That obvious?'

'No judgement,' Rhian smirked through a sip and put a hand up. 'Card-carrying Venus member who lost her Geordie accent way too long ago to talk. And too quickly.'

Ola let out another laugh, a real one this time. Michael would tease her when she said membership to one private members' club or another in her line of work was a 'necessary evil'. It was a running joke, her encroaching 'boujieness', with her penchant for jackfruit 'pulled pork' and turmeric lattes. When she referred to herself as working class, he would take the mick, calling her the 'voice of streets she no longer lives on'. When she pointed out she lived in Tooting, he would say she was just like the area itself, steadily getting posher.

She glanced at the clock on the wall. 'I don't want to take up too much of your afternoon …' Ola started.

'Yes, of course.' Rhian opened up a small menu shaped like a clam. 'This is on *Womxxxn*, right? Because I'm definitely getting a thirteen quid gin and tonic.' She grimaced as she read. '… with "Reclaiming my time" lime.' Ola nodded.

'Nice one.' Rhian scanned the menu. 'So, what do you want to talk about? The List more generally, or specifically, your fiancé?'

Ola must have looked like she was about to keel over. Rhian put the menu back down and placed her hands flatly on the table as if steadying it. 'That wasn't some kind of trick question, by the way,' she said. 'But yes, I know who you're engaged to.'

A familiar apprehension began to rise in her chest. Who else knew? Did Frankie? Was this all part of a plan to call her out on Twitter? Rhian didn't use Twitter though. Or did she? Maybe she was live-streaming this on Facebook as they spoke?

'You know?' Ola spluttered. 'But why didn't—'

'Look. There are people who want to do me serious harm. Mainly MRAs, but I have to vet anyone before I meet them. Thoroughly.'

'I'm a researcher by trade – it wasn't exactly hard,' Rhian continued, coolly. 'You've deleted most of them, but your "baecation" snaps come up on fan pages once you've been through enough results. Congratulations, by the way. When's the big day?' Her eyes wandered towards Ola's unadorned ring finger.

It had been stupid of her to think Rhian wouldn't work it out. She was a journalist after all. But it threw Ola, as it usually did when anyone outside of the other 'dark web' – Black Twitter, the #BlackLove Instagram hashtag – was aware of her relationship and surreal online fame. Another running joke between Michael and Ola was that she was the fuckboy of their union, since he regularly posted pictures of them with gushing captions while she appeared single from a glance at her profiles.

Ola didn't like attention, good or bad. It was a miracle that she had survived the aftermath of their engagement post. While she cringed at the never-ending stream of heart emojis under the odd pictures she posted of them, she understood the mania. She was half of a smart, attractive, Black '#CoupleGoals' couple – a rare sight when you reached a certain status, especially in Britain. She knew that it had meaning in a world where it was assumed a man like Michael – fine, upwardly mobile, Black – would be with a lighter or whiter woman. But the endless notifications that followed overwhelmed her. The anxious feeling she'd get when she stumbled across her brown bikinied body in that precious, personal moment highlighted for strangers to see on the Instagram explore page. The comments asking after Michael when she hadn't posted him in a while, demanding to know if they were still together, sis, and if not, what was his number? Or did he have an older brother, sis? Or a younger one? The constant projecting of others' expectations, all because they took a cute picture together once. She had never wanted the visibility to start with, hardly considered herself 'an influencer'. And now, despite all her care, her coyness, Fola's eventual deletion and archiving, Rhian was sat across from her, confirming Ola's fear that once you fed something to the internet it was never truly yours again.

'Eighth of June. But I'm not 100 per cent sure what's happening with that,' Ola said shortly, obscuring her fingers with her sleeves.

Rhian's eyebrows shot up and she blew a long, drawn-out whistle. 'You're cutting it fine, aren't you man?' Her accent came as quickly as it went. 'When do you plan on making your mind up? The altar?'

'I don't have a plan, if I'm honest,' Ola said. 'And, again being honest, that's why I'm here.'

Rhian cleared her throat. 'I did assume there might be more to this than the interview.'

'I'm surprised you were still happy to meet me.'

Rhian gave a nearly imperceptible shrug. 'Willing, more than happy. But I did a bit of digging, read some of your stuff. You seemed sane. You're not the first person that's reached out but you're the first I've met with.'

'Well, I'm glad. Thank you. I guess there's no point in me beating around the bush.' Ola inhaled deeply. 'I need you to tell me who put Michael's name on The List. Please.' She quickly raised both hands to stop a sentence Rhian didn't get to start.

'I read the disclaimer on the post, and I get it. I know there's a need to safeguard. But I also need to know if the man I'm supposed to be marrying next week is someone who abuses women.'

Rhian took a small, deliberate sip from her sparkling water and clicked her tongue once she'd swallowed. 'I can't do that, I'm afraid.'

The anger Ola felt was sharp. This woman had made the past two and a half weeks of her life unbearable, no matter how noble her motives, and now she was refusing to help her? She could feel her nostrils flaring, reason leaving her body with each exhale.

'Okay,' Ola said, attempting to keep her cool. 'Why?'

'Because I don't know who put him on there,' Rhian replied. 'I wouldn't know how to go about getting anyone's names.'

'You have no way of accessing anything that could be helpful? Even though it would only be used by me, to understand whether what's being said is true or not? For my safety?'

Rhian shook her head. 'Even if I did have that information, I can't say that it would be right to give it to you. I have to consider the safety of the survivors, too.' She paused. 'I'm assuming you believe he's innocent? Michael?'

Ola chewed at the inside of her cheek. She wanted to leave since it was clear Rhian would be no help. But she remained seated.

'I'm not sure,' Ola said. 'That's why I'm here.'

She wasn't sure, though according to Michael she should be by now. Apparently, CuRated had confirmed there was no evidence of a restraining order found on his DBS – he was getting them to put it in writing. Too bad that didn't account for the allegations of harassment or physical assault. With Michael's history of lying, she needed irrefutable proof. It was something, but not enough.

'I imagine you do,' said Rhian, sounding almost bored, like they'd already had this conversation. 'Or you wouldn't be here …' She paused again. 'Am I right in thinking you've written about this kind of thing before? MCs Too was you, right?'

'Yeah.' Ola felt self-conscious as she said it. It was startling to think how differently she would have approached this situation if it wasn't for Michael. She had been so proud of #MCsToo. Now it felt like evidence of her own duplicity.

'It was and still is important,' she hurriedly clarified. 'But even outside of Michael, you know as well as I do how important fact-checking is, verification, sources.' The change in her tone was subtle but there, now less conversational and more akin to a reporter. 'As a journalist, this conversation matters.'

Rhian looked unmoved, curling her lip slightly. 'Well, we have that belief in common,' she said. 'That's why I made The List in the first place.'

She'd been thinking about doing it for years, she said, since 2017 to be precise. October that year, when the rug had been pulled from under Harvey Weinstein and stories of systemic abuse were coming out in sickening waves; first from Hollywood, then the music industry, then fashion, then everywhere else. Across the world. #MeToo saw men named via press, summoned to court or held to account online. Female writers across time zones were in Facebook and WhatsApp groups, sharing their experiences, warning each other of the most prolific offenders. They'd done this interpersonally for years, but the power of the digitised whisper network was truly a sight to behold.

Rhian had been in Washington covering the first year of the Trump presidency, and was being sent Google Docs naming men whose work she read religiously, men she'd worked *with*. They'd stealthed women, threatened them, assaulted them, raped them. It was particularly painful since Rhian herself had once been in an abusive relationship with a former colleague. They'd dated for seven months before he first laid his hands on her. The first time she named him it was via an anonymous Google Doc.

Women continued to share stories for many months, even after #MeToo began to disappear from the headlines. A tipping point for Rhian was when that same journalist ex of hers was brought up in a Facebook group – the victim posted photos of her bruises. That evening, she created a spreadsheet for women in the UK media to populate.

'I only sent it to nine people,' she said. 'All of them in the industry, all of them trustworthy. They're the only contributors I know by name. We agreed that they should only send it to people they trusted. And then those people sent it to people they trusted. It just got bigger and bigger, and harder to control.'

'Well, it would,' Ola said, sounding more snide than she'd intended. 'Since you put it on Twitter.'

'I didn't,' Rhian said. 'Some women decided to go public with it. I said no, but they rightly argued we were potentially leaving women outside of our network at risk. Either way, I deleted it but of course copies were floating around by that point. You can't really "own" something like that,' she said, making air quotes with her fingers.

It was only live for two days. But soon it was no longer just listing male journalists; there were actors, musicians, podcasters, influencers. The more people it went out to, the more names added, the more Rhian said she started to panic. The spreadsheet wasn't password-protected; she hadn't thought it needed to be. By the time it had reached Twitter and she saw it being casually referred to as a 'rape list' she started having trouble sleeping. A man she'd worked with was said to have tried to kiss a colleague without consent – he tweeted that they'd been on a date and he had genuinely, albeit drunkenly, misjudged the moment.

Ola pulled a sceptical face. 'How could you have not foreseen the obvious risk of it being manipulated?' She felt like a charlatan for asking, given #MCsToo, but that was different. Wasn't it?

'Of course I knew there were risks,' Rhian said, sounding unmistakably defensive. For the first time she looked uneasy, as she fiddled with the end of her sleeve. 'The usual slut-shaming and gaslighting. Most who read it were too scared to even contribute. They were afraid of accused men finding out who put them on there and retaliating.'

'Well, I was scared too,' Ola said. She stopped for a moment, uncomfortable with how dismissive she was sounding. 'I know it's different. But if you see your brother or dad on something like this without explanation, without evidence … what are you expected to do?' It occurred to Ola that this was why she hadn't left earlier. Who else could she ask?

'I know it's hard.' Rhian was stoic again, back on form. 'But I don't think that pain necessarily trumps the pain of survivors. The vast majority of these types of allegations are true. We know th—'

'At a police station, yes,' Ola cut in. 'In court, yes. But online? Would you be okay with other crimes being handled via the court of Twitter?'

'I'm saying these crimes should be dealt with in the first place,' said Rhian.

'Look, I believe women,' Ola said. 'But false allegations being rare doesn't make them impossible. Like, there was an entire historical period where Black men were getting jailed and lynched because white women were lying that they'd attacked them. Emmett Till? The Scottsboro Boys? If I told you it might be a racist who put Michael on there, would he be deserving of white, liberal sympathy then?'

Rhian began to squirm. It was clear she was thinking very carefully about what to say.

'I understand your point,' she offered eventually. 'The List was supposed to be a space where women could speak their truth without being accused of lying. But that's what is happening anyway.' She shook her head. 'All I can say is that I didn't do it maliciously. Or lightly. A lot of these men have money. The worst that could happen isn't them walking free – it's them suing their accusers. And since I made it, I'd be number one on that list.'

Ola thought of Kiran, what she'd said when she mentioned that Michael had spoken to a lawyer. She felt grimy all over. Rhian shouldn't be sued for trying to create an outlet, by men she hadn't even accused herself. Ola's aims had been the same when she wrote #MCsToo. She couldn't help but think again of the shell of a person she'd sat next to at the law firm that day, however. That was the last time she'd seen Michael. An entirely broken man. Two weeks ago she told him if he couldn't prove his innocence, it was over. And what had he done? Ola hadn't said it would be easy, but the difference was, she'd hired a bloody PI and was sat across from The List's creator a fortnight after it went up. When she should be off being a Bridezilla about something, breaking in her wedding shoes.

Michael meanwhile had stopped texting, stopped talking. Gone into himself. Was that how an innocent man behaved? But that was Michael: when he'd been out of work, had it not been Ola scouring job sites? Nights spent helping edit his show-reel, proofreading his covering letter. In his CuRated application, she referred to him as 'sedulous' – she was sure he hadn't even bothered to check what it meant. And now, she was so tired, couldn't remember the last time she'd had a full night's sleep or a day without tears.

She coughed, feeling a tingle in her tear ducts. 'Don't you regret any of it?'

Rhian said she regretted feeling as though she had let down those she sought to help. Before long came the panicked emails from women who had contributed in the belief The List would only be shared privately. Although the claims weren't linked to them, they felt humiliated. They'd read comment after comment poking holes in their stories, calling them attention-seekers. She mentioned a YouTuber sharing a now-viral video of his poly-graph and its subsequent racking up of over 70,000 views. It was inconclusive, yet enough to cast doubt on the other stories, which so many were already eager to disprove.

'If one woman is proven to be lying, we all become liars,' Rhian sighed. 'If some bloke decides to off himself or shoot up a cinema because of this, then it becomes about how feminism is killing innocent men, despite the countless innocent women who've lost their lives at the hands of abuse. That's why I might regret parts of it, but I don't regret *it* itself.'

Ola, increasingly accustomed to being lost for words, said nothing. It was as though she were debating a version of herself from a universe in which this hadn't happened to her fiancé. She'd hoped a troll or some other bad faith actor had created The List to stoke up the culture wars. Not someone who, in another life, she would have enjoyed a liquid lunch with as they self-flag-ellated over their well-intended champagne socialism. Since the beginning Ola had attested that The List had been made with good intentions. She was heartbroken to realise she was right.

'I have to get back to the office,' Ola said, after a few seconds of silence. She rose to leave and they both nodded at each other in sombre recognition.

'All right. Sorry I couldn't be more help.'

There was a tension in the air that made Ola hang back, something Rhian clearly wanted to say. 'You know, before my ex hit me, I would have never believed he could,' Rhian said. 'Just … look after yourself, yeah?'

Ola returned a feeble smile and a nod, before making her way out of the restaurant.

As she stepped into the Venus foyer, Ola's iPhone let out the fleeting vibration of a text. She took it out, already mentally drafting her response to Luke to tell him that his work wasn't done yet when she saw it was from a withheld number.

I don't know who submitted Michael. But they did it under the name mirrorissa92. Not sure if that means anything to you. Whatever you choose to do, I hope you choose you.

Turning on her aching heels as fast as she could, Ola frantically bashed at the lift button before racing back up the stairs to the first floor. She arrived at Sirenum Scopuli no more than a few seconds later, with a beaded brow and a heaving chest, but it was too late. Rhian Mcintosh was nowhere to be seen.

11

7 *days to the wedding*

Normally, Michael could think of nothing worse than when the departures board at the bus stop did that *thing*. That exasperating thing, where it said clear as day in orange text luminous against black, that the bus was coming and proceeded to count down till it said 'due'. Then, just as you readied yourself, the countdown started over again, even though the bus hadn't shown up. It happened all the time at the Aintree Avenue stop and used to be the worst part of Michael's week. How lucky he had been.

The bus delay would usually have enraged him, but today he felt nothing. He hadn't even bothered putting his hood up in the drizzle, though his uncut hair was now sodden and his nose had begun to run. It was like he was sleepwalking. Trudging through the endless slop of his life, something pushing him onward begrudgingly.

Today, that 'something' was seeing Ola. She'd sent him a curt text last night to say that the wedding cloth she'd helped his mum order had arrived at her flat, and he quickly offered to pick it up. It was an excuse to see her; she'd still been avoiding him, only reaching out when absolutely necessary. This would be the first time they'd been face to face in almost a fortnight and he hadn't been to her flat in almost a month. He missed her kaleidoscopic, bric-a-brac bedroom that seemed plucked from a far more chaotic Pinterest board than her diametrically opposite Wednesday Addams wardrobe aesthetic.

It'd been ages since he'd been to the office, too, and it really was beginning to feel like he was off sick. Wedding nerves had evolved into full-blown wedding nausea. It was in a week – too close for them to do anything other than go ahead with it, surely, but there was still enough time for Ola to pull the plug. Maybe that would be for the best?

By the time the 115 arrived, Michael was soaked through to his skin. He trudged upstairs and folded himself into a corner at the back, pulling his hood over his head as the bus's bright lights made him self-conscious. His hands and face felt tight as the rain dried off and he chewed at the dead skin on his bottom lip that was too painful to peel.

A text from his mum temporarily distracted him from how nasty he felt. Every day, she would send messages into the ether that Michael routinely ignored, practically talking to herself. When he didn't answer her calls, she left pleading voicemails that she must have known would receive no response. He'd eventually reply with a limp 'I'm fine' every now and then, but that only ever made her more rabid, asking where he'd been and why he was so determined to give his own mother a heart attack. His lack of communication with her wasn't personal. Messages in the group chat had piled up too. Seun had tried to ring him a handful of times and Amani's bi-weekly invitations to train with him at his gym were disregarded. Kwabz had threatened to come round to visit but Michael had thankfully managed to convince him it wasn't necessary. If Kwabz had made it to his flat, he'd only have been more concerned. He would see the drained bottles of alcohol that revealed the true extent of his friend's drinking. The dirty plates and crockery that lay across the floor, litter that hadn't made it to the bin of his normally spotless home.

As he did every time he found his phone in his hand, Michael clicked on the teacup icon among his most visited sites in his web browser. He held his breath. Relief flooded through him as it opened. No new posts about him on 'All Tea, No Crumpet' since he'd last checked in the morning. The spotlight was now on a YouTuber called 'That Guy Abe', who took a polygraph test he claimed would prove his innocence in relation to The List allegations. He documented the results in a monetised video and when they came back as 'inconclusive', he was let go by his agency. His lucrative Boohoo Man partnership remained intact, however, much to the annoyance of those on All Tea. Users vowed he would lose that too, if they had anything to do with it.

Michael closed the tab and unclenched his jaw. He lay his head against the bus window as the rain drummed therapeutically against it. He was grateful the latest post wasn't about him, though it would be again soon enough. All Tea, No Crumpet (or @AllT_NoCrumpet as it was styled on its social media pages) was Britain's biggest Black gossip forum and boasted tens of thousands of subscribers and hundreds of thousands of followers on Instagram. Their currency was scandal: everything from leaking private DMs to bad selfies with baiting captions.

The assumption was that All Tea was populated by people without friends, or jobs, or lives but Michael wasn't so sure. He was taken aback by how normal the commenters seemed. Especially on the page about The List; many of them clearly felt they were doing the right thing. The other day they'd targeted the production company that owned an accused podcaster's

show. They spammed their comments section with the allegations and got it suspended indefinitely. The forum had been
thrilled and it had made Michael's blood run cold. Every day he
read its members monitoring his movements online, speculating
about his moves offline. They'd call him every name under the
sun. They'd talk tactically about how to get him out of his job,
how to find and release his address. They even kept track of the
'blue ticks' that had unfollowed, or more alarmingly, refollowed
him, which he realised with horror late one night last week
while reading a conversation between users:

@Poison_Ivy_Carterrr: The Jays are following M!chael K
again 🌱

@incog_negro: Both of them?

@Poison_Ivy_Carterrr: Boy one and their couple account
🌍 Not her personal one yet

The Jays were acquaintances Michael knew from his podcasting
days – both pretty, hazel-eyed with toffee-coloured skin and
loose curly hair. The girl was a haircare influencer and the guy
had been a runner-up on *The Voice UK*. They were better
known together on their channel 'Jay and Jay 4 Life'. After The
List went live, they unfollowed him across every social media
platform. A few days ago, he'd seen them outside the big
Topshop in Oxford Circus. Once it became clear eye contact
was unavoidable, the boy Jay had bounded towards him like a
Labrador.

  'What's good man, long time!' He'd grinned, revealing a set
of perfectly arranged teeth. Michael remembered an Instagram

story of him and the girl Jay biting onto a peculiar LED mouth-piece and their teeth had glowed fluorescent white ever since.

'Saw the announcement about CuRated,' he continued, before Michael had time to respond. 'Congrats! Big boy moves!'

'Ay, I'm just tryna be like you, bro,' Michael offered, unconvincingly.

'And we can't wait to see the wedding pics!' the girl Jay piped up, curls bouncing as she did.

'Thanks,' Michael said. 'Not gonna lie, when you lot came over my heart nearly beat out my chest. Not all the announcements about me recently have been good. Or true.'

The Jays shifted their weight from side to side simultaneously, laughing feebly. 'Yeah, well,' said the boy Jay, after a moment. 'I don't know what everyone else is saying but I never believed it, bro. You can't believe everything you read online, can you?'

The girl Jay nodded. 'The amount of times I've heard I'm pregnant after a big lunch? People are mad!'

When he got home, he had opened Instagram for the first time in days; sure enough, their joint account was following him again, leaving a trail of love-heart likes behind them. But he couldn't stop thinking about the fact that the girl Jay hadn't refollowed him on hers.

All Tea users clocked everything – someone had once posted that they'd spotted Ola without her ring. Neither of them were famous enough for this, were they? He didn't think so. But the more famous men seemed much harder for them to take down. One well-known columnist for a men's magazine was dogged by abuse allegations for decades and despite endless emails to his editors, it had been business as usual for him.

'Canning Town Station,' the automated voice of the 115 suddenly announced.

Michael lurched forward as the bus pulled up to the stop and made his way to the train station. It had stopped raining again, but the sky remained grey and churlish. He was relieved he had reached the underground; soon the internet would cut out and he wouldn't be able to read All Tea any more. Vince Staples would accompany him on the Jubilee Line to London Bridge, J Hus for the Northern Line to Tooting Broadway.

Ola's neck of the woods was normally a sensory overload once you left the station; fruit sellers and fishmongers and fabric shops and flower stalls, all battling for increasingly limited space in SW17. But Michael was anxious and distracted, spending the entire walk to her place in a daze and doing his best to drown out intrusive thoughts with music. When she opened the cream-coloured uPVC door to her flat, he was taken aback. She was naturally skinny, but looked emaciated in an enormous black hoodie of his, eyes taking up half of her face. They were blood-shot at the corners. Still no ring on her finger, but no nails either, her usual brightly coloured claws gone.

'Hey,' Michael said softly.

She nodded in response. He wanted to hug her so badly, but Ola was stony-faced and silent, arms across her chest as she stood thin in the door frame. Her eyes widened at his appear-ance momentarily and Michael looked down at his unwashed T-shirt, searching for a wine or blood stain. Everything about him looked worn and crinkled: his trainers, his uncharacteristi-cally dry skin, greyish and ashen. She didn't ask him to come in and Michael didn't offer to. Instead, she stood aside and reached around behind her. As she turned her back, Michael peered over her shoulder inside her flat and felt a pang of nostalgic grief. Unopened packages were stacked up in the hallway and the various framed posters and prints left little wall space in the living room. The intentionally clashing pillows, the patchwork throw that had revived her Gumtree couch; it felt like he hadn't been there in years. The last time he had, they had been wasted and in love and excited about their future together. There had been so much to look forward to, with the wedding, his new job starting the next day. Michael coughed, hoping to dislodge the growing lump in his throat.

Ola wordlessly passed him the Sainsbury's Bag For Life with his mum's wedding cloth in it, and in doing so her hand grazed the scab forming across the front of his knuckles, making him hiss in pain. Instantly, likely without thinking, she pulled it towards her.

'What did you do to your hand?'

The scar wasn't obvious against his cacao skin. He didn't want her to see it, but he let her trace it with her fingers just so he could feel her. For a moment he considered holding her hand but thought better of it.

'Ahh, that,' Michael said. 'I buckled on my way to the corner shop the other day. Fucking embarrassing.'

She looked at him quizzically, unable to hide her worry. Michael felt a twinge in his chest. As much as he hated seeing the concern in her face, it was a welcome reminder that she still cared about him. That she loved him.

'How's work though?' he said, gently setting down the bag on her welcome mat. He didn't know what else to ask but needed to fill the silence to keep her on the doorstep. It had been so long since they'd talked properly. Everything was small talk these days. At this, she dropped his hand and placed her arms back across her chest.

'It's fine. Thanks.' She hesitated. 'We're not doing The List article by the way, if that's what you're wondering.'

'Oh. Is it?' Something inside him slowly uncoiled.

'Yeah,' Ola murmured. 'Frankie wanted Kiran to write it instead but we decided it was best to wait. There are still a lot of questions.'

'Rah, swear down?' He blew out of his mouth and puffed out his cheeks. 'Boy. I can't lie, I'm surprised. I'm happy you lot did the right thing though.'

Ola bristled at 'the right thing'. 'Yeah, well. It's not like Frankie said it's never going to happen.'

'Well, let's hope it doesn't come to that.'

She took a small step backward. 'You hope we aren't able to warn people about abusers in the industry?'

'Ola. That's not what I'm saying.' He placed his hands on her shoulders, forgetting himself. He was surprised that she let him do so. The bones of her shoulders poked into his palms in a way that alarmed him. She had lost even more weight than he had.

'I don't know how to talk about this to you,' Michael said. 'I feel like I'm always saying the wrong thing.'

Ola looked up at him with softness he hadn't seen in weeks. 'Same. It's impossible.'

They stared at each other, and for the first time in a long time, even if only briefly, Michael felt Ola could see him. See the Michael she'd said yes to, not the supposed abuser he'd been sullied as. He could feel her idea of who he was becoming more distorted by the day. That she was forgetting why they were together. It was hard to believe now, but they had made each other happy once. Michael had been living in his childhood bedroom when they'd first met, still trying to catch a break. He'd recognised her from Twitter at the networking event where they crossed paths, and was taken aback by how she looked exactly like her avatar yet completely different. There was a playfulness to the ever-present dimpled smirk that appeared smug online.

Their first date took place near the month's end and he was broke, so they wandered around the Southbank Centre, arguing over who was the best Grime artist of all time, without ever truly disagreeing (oscillating between Kano and Ghetts, fighting the opposing corner interchangeably). Then, she got them dinner at a tapas restaurant nearby, where she asked him which biblical parable shaped his adulthood anxieties. He replied with the Prodigal Son and returned the question. 'That one with the greedy guy who saves up all his crops and dies with a barn full of shit he can't use,' Ola said between bites of the fried baby squid.

Seeing her in the flesh had been weird, as before then they'd already debated in his mind several times. Long before they met, the odd blog post of hers would be floated into the group chat, punctuated with a solitary 'Thoughts?' next to the eyes emoji. Amani and Seun's commentary usually started and stopped at the headline, bemoaning 'feminist agendas' and concluding most of her problems, if not women's worldwide, could be fixed with 'pipe'. Now and then, Michael found himself retrospectively livid at how they used to speak about the woman he intended to marry. Once they started dating, his friends stopped the jokes. But remembering made him pissed off, at himself, at them. They weren't bad boys, his boys. But wasn't that the issue? Why was 'not bad' so often good enough?

A light rumbling from the sky interrupted them and Michael looked up to see the clouds beginning to gather again. He wouldn't risk asking, but the relaxing of Ola's jaw and shoulders made him dare to hope she might ask him to come in. He sighed deeply. 'What are we going to do, man?'

'I don't know, Michael. I don't know.'

He tutted. 'I really thought the biggest challenge we'd face at this wedding was which jollof to serve.'

Ola rolled her eyes and smiled. 'You're so dumb.'

They both laughed weakly. Michael kept his hands on her shoulders and gave them a light squeeze, before readying himself to say it. He knew he shouldn't, it would spoil the moment. But he did anyway.

'You know I wouldn't do those things, Ola. Right? I know you're a good person, and that's why you're trying to do the right thing. But please tell me you know ... You know that I'm not a bad one.'

Her large eyes shone almost immediately. And as her lips parted, he heard her phone vibrate in her tracksuit pocket. She reached for it as she writhed out of his grip, studied the screen intently for a moment. Then turned her attention back to him, her face now grave.

'I have to go.'

'Oh ...' – he couldn't hide his disappointment – 'right now?'

'Yep.' She looked at her phone screen again. 'But I'll see you later, yeah? Tell your mum I said hi.'

Next thing he knew, Michael was facing the front door of her flat. It all happened so quickly, the exchange over before it began. But he'd felt it, that shift in the atmosphere after she read her phone. Her exterior hardening, the drawbridge going back up. That message had changed something. Suddenly, she was secretive, evasive. Like when she thought he hadn't noticed her angling her phone screen away from him at the lawyer's. He shook his head. He couldn't entertain those thoughts right now. It was too dangerous. But as he walked away from her flat, he couldn't stop thinking about what that change in her might mean. When he had behaved like that, it only ever meant one thing. He was texting someone he shouldn't be.

He put his hands in his pockets and began walking briskly back to Tooting Broadway Station, hoping to avoid the imminent downpour. Just thinking about Ola betraying him made Michael feel sick, but then remembering that was exactly what he'd done to her made him feel worse. His thoughts soon turned to Jackie. What was going through her head? It still made no sense to him. Was it possible that she truly believed he'd been abusive towards her? Did she genuinely think he had been harassing her when he … he couldn't think what, no matter how hard he tried. If anyone had made threats, it had been her. He couldn't predict what she might do next. A recurring nightmare within this nightmare was that if he and Ola did make it down the aisle, Jackie would be at the end of it, waiting to interject when the pastor asked their guests to speak now or forever hold their peace.

Michael pulled his hood more tightly over his head as he walked, and fished his phone from his pocket with his other hand. He opened the page concerning The List on All Tea. The account @mirrorissa92 – the very same Jackie – would comment on All Tea now and then, chiming in with the abuse and calls for action. 'Mirror Issa' – it was a reference to *Insecure*. Ola watched it religiously. Had Jackie? He was pretty sure she was born in 1992, as referenced in the screen name.

Part of his hourly ritual involved looking at her page on the forum, never sure of what he hoped to find there. Perhaps she'd slip up and mistakenly reveal her first name or accidentally tag her location. The thread on The List had reached seventy-three pages now, so he went back a few and scrolled, till he found her last comment.

'That gap tooth narcissist M!icheal K needs to be got all the way up out of here,' @mirrorissa92 had written one day ago. 'He must be held accountable for his treatment of women. RIP M!cheal K – the evil that you have done is enough!'

Maybe he was evil? Still, he had defended himself against that charge. 'How about you tell us all what apparently happened,' he'd replied when he'd first come across it. 'Or can you not, because nothing actually did??' Today, he tapped the 'thumbs down' icon on the comment, feeling useless as he did, and went to her profile.

mirrorissa92
Active Member
From: Outer space
Member Since: May 10, 2019
Posts: 34
Last seen: viewing this thread, 2 minutes ago

As he read the last line of her profile, Michael stopped walking then and there in the street. Two minutes ago. Jackie was probably still online. It had started spitting now, and his phone screen was dotted with tiny water droplets. He hurried as he tapped the message icon, wondering what approach to take. What could he try that he hadn't already?

'I know who you are,' he typed slowly, passers-by groaning and shaking their heads as he blocked their path. 'I know you put Michael Koranteng on The List.'

He'd avoided mentioning his name up to this point but fuck it, he thought. He knew it was Jackie; she likely knew it was him, too.

'Why are you doing this?'

Send. He exited the site, and picked up his pace.

As he reached Tooting Broadway Station his phone trembled in his hand with another message from his mother. Michael thought of her. Of Aunty Abena happening upon The List somehow and sending it to her. Articles on The List still hadn't mentioned anyone by name. Yet. They'd begun alluding to professions, referring to 'former athletes' and 'reality TV stars'. At any moment, however, it felt like his name would tip from the backstreets of the internet into the news, the real news. To remind himself that the allegations about him only circled on gossip pages and blogs, he'd relentlessly refresh a separate tab he'd keep open, where he'd typed his full name into the search bar. Each time he tapped: nothing. No headlines, no updates. A few links to a press release about his CuRated hiring. His name was only tarnished in certain corners of the internet. As Kwabz said: he still sort of had his job. Ola hadn't left him just yet. And yet on All Tea, No Crumpet there was a deluge of fresh hate every few hours. How could a minority of people be talking about The List and yet it seemed as though the whole world was whispering about him? In a way it was a world, *his* world. Michael turned off his phone and put it away, vainly hoping to feel as though everything had stopped for a moment. He pushed his earbuds into his ears and made his way through the under-ground entrance, as the skies opened up outside.

12

5 days to the wedding

Kiran was nodding diligently, her blonde topknot bobbing up and down as Abi gushed with thanks. She was talking a mile a minute, round cheeks framed by dozens of tiny, snake-like braids.

'We weren't expecting such an amazing turn-out,' Abi was saying. 'And the donations made separately from the tickets? I think we've raised over seven hundred pounds, altogether!'

'That's incredible! Isn't it, Ola?' Kiran gave her upper arm a gentle squeeze. Ola's eyes darted sheepishly behind her glasses, taking in the rammed room. Tonight's event had taken place in a small community centre and they were standing right in the thick of the forty-odd person throng. The space was fit for purpose but worse for wear. Flyers for events dated as far back as 2011 hung faded and wrinkled on the walls, while the white markings of a badminton court were faint against the scuffed maple floor. Ola's eyes settled on the fire exit peeking through the chattering crowd. She had made it clear earlier she didn't want to stay for the networking segment and was keen to get out of there as quickly as possible.

'Seven hundred pounds,' she repeated, still watching the door. 'Yeah. That's sick.'

Ola was distracted. For days, she hadn't been able to shake the image of Michael at her door. He'd looked terrible, as though everything in him had been obliterated by an aggressive illness. Eyes hollowed, cheeks gaunt, shoulders so tight to his body. Through his matted beard, his lips were withered and dark like the bark of a tree. He reeked of alcohol, plus there was that nasty cut to his hand. He was obviously lying when he said he'd tripped. So, what had he really done to it?

Her care, however, was almost instantly smothered by defensiveness when he had asked her about work. Had he been being facetious? They'd avoided all mention of *Womxxxn* up until yesterday. They didn't talk about anything properly any more; he'd even stopped asking about the wedding. Once upon a time she had told him the most boring minutiae of her day, down to what flavour crisps she ate at lunch. But now every sentence they exchanged was loaded, a word away from their next fight. And arguing felt like it was for increasingly higher stakes. Their relationship was hanging by a thread, and there on her doorstep she could see Michael was too. She'd seen him down before. But that bad patch when he'd lost his job paled in comparison to how he was at the moment. An argument at the wrong time could tip him over the edge. She was scared for him.

She was scared for herself, too. Fearful of what might happen if they did argue. Maybe she'd been lucky in the past, hadn't pushed him far enough. If she asked him whether the name 'mirrorissa92' meant anything to him, would he fly off the handle? Who knows what he'd say if he knew she'd met with Rhian, let alone if he found out about Luke. What he'd do. The lies were piling up and her guilt over them was too. When he'd begged her to tell him that she believed him, she hadn't been able to answer. But she couldn't ignore how much she wished she could tell him what he wanted to hear.

'How are you girls getting back?' Ola could hear Abi asking Kiran. 'Have we booked a cab or are you getting an Uber?'

'That won't be necessary,' Ola interjected. 'It's not that far.'

Kiran furrowed her brow at this. 'We're in Islington? You live in Tooting ...'

'It's still London, isn't it?' Ola said, quickly. 'Can't be more than thirty quid for an Uber. Don't worry about it, Abi.'

Kiran bared her teeth in what was supposed to be a convincing fake smile but concluded in a confused grimace. 'They're obviously going to claim it back on expenses, babe. What you're doing literally makes no difference,' she said through her teeth.

A none-the-wiser Abi was tapping at Citymapper on her phone. 'All right, well let me know and I can get that sort— oh!' She clicked her fingers in remembrance. 'Before you get going, I must intro you to our admin assistant, Nour. She's an aspiring writer and wants to get into journalism once she graduates – massive fan of both of you. Do you mind?'

Kiran shook her head and before Ola could protest, Abi had disappeared into the crowd. Her friend inched closer to tug her by the bottom of her shirt.

'Aunty. Stop it.'

'Stop what?' Ola responded. The room was brimming with a mixture of journalists, influencers and activists, some she recognised from her Twitter feed, others from the 'accounts you should follow' tab that she'd never bothered to. They were all huddled in groups, chattering among themselves as they picked at the complimentary finger food of samosas and prawn fingers. She couldn't help but wonder if she was being avoided.

'*This*,' Kiran hissed in her ear. 'All of it.'

Ola could tell her attempts at proving that she wasn't a piece of shit were beginning to grate on Kiran. And to make matters worse, her efforts were having the opposite effect.

Rhian's text message after their meeting had shaken her. She clearly had her suspicions about Michael. Ola had known everything Rhian said about The List in theory but talking to her made it all unbearably real. The women who contributed to it dominated her thoughts while she was awake and as she lay in bed drifting off into fitful sleep. She saw their faces in her dreams. So Ola had become committed to showing – herself and the world – that she was indeed a good person. As soon as she got back into the office that day, she cornered Kiran about her volunteer work at a women's shelter in Tower Hamlets and offered to accompany her. She trawled GoFundMe for causes and donated £200 to a single mother in Clapton who'd had her lease terminated early by her landlord. Then she smashed the 'more like this' button and gave to another eight crowdfunds in a row, being sure to tick the 'make my donation public' button each time. The gnawing sensation in the pit of her stomach remained.

That gnawing anxiety had brought her to this community centre, the location of the *Womxxxn*-sponsored panel Kiran was moderating. Kiran had helped organise it to raise funds for the Iwosan Group, a charity offering counselling to refugee women. Days before it took place, Ola had contacted Abi directly about getting involved with their small planned talk and had quickly commandeered it entirely. She'd acquired free booze, a high-profile activist panellist and merch-filled tote bags. Ola had even emailed a small Instagram bakery asking them to support with branded cupcakes. They declined in an abrupt email stating they 'weren't in the habit of working with individuals complicit in the very type of abuse they claim they want eradicated'.

Initially, Kiran had been incredibly supportive of her attempts to make amends but the exchange with Abi had rubbed her the wrong way. Ola turned to look at her.

'I don't know what you're on about.'

'You do,' Kiran shout-whispered over the chatter. 'And I promise you, saving the Iwosan Group thirty quid isn't going to stop Tory cuts to women's services. Or help you in wrestling with your guilt over all this.'

Kiran wasn't wrong. Ola slowly trying to bankrupt herself by footing transport fees was just her weird way of paying a penance. 'I was just having a bit of a wobble,' she said flimsily.

'Ola. You are wobbling. You are jelly. I get it. But can you try and act like a human being? Not this ... feminist fembot trying so hard to do and say the right thing that she looks like she might short-circuit.'

'Easier said than done. Especially here. Like, I swear I saw that girl from the *New Statesman* looking over earlier and whispering?'

Kiran glanced surreptitiously in the direction Ola signalled. 'What, the fit brunette with the fringe?' she said. 'Actually, now you mention it, she is ... but how do you know she's not looking at me?' She shot a wide smile towards the woman in question, who offered her a small wave.

'Kiran, I'm serious!'

'So am I!'

Ola let out a huff and Kiran rolled her eyes.

'I don't know, I just feel off,' said Ola. 'Like I shouldn't stay. The longer I'm here, sooner or later, someone is going to bring up The List.'

'Are you guys talking about The List?' Nour was by her side suddenly, inches away from her and sans Abi. She couldn't have been more than twenty and had a biblical sort of beauty – the type that made you think of milk and honey and our daily bread. Dewy-skinned, with full angular eyebrows and a fan of naturally thick, dark lashes that made Ruth's sets seem sparse and wiry.

'Nour?' Kiran asked, offering her the opportunity to introduce herself.

'Yes, and I'm not going to pretend I'm not hugely fangirling right now! Your questions on tonight's panel were just – ugh, perfection.' She turned to Ola. 'I've actually been reading your stuff since "Cum The Fuck Through", wayyy before I should have been,' she said with a laugh. 'You nearly got me sent to Lebanon! I sent my mate your interview with that mindful masturbation instructor yesterday – still one of the funniest things I've ever read. You're gifted!'

Dad had called her that. His 'gifted gift'. He'd spotted her writing talent as a child. Her name, he'd said, was always destined to be in print – 'Olaide Olajide'.

She cringed at the speed with which Nour's fawning made her warm to her. She didn't deserve it, but she needed it. At the prospect of being stanned, she felt herself standing with her back somewhat straighter, slipping into her 'proper person' costume and prepping to say something equal parts sage and nonchalant. At *Womxxxn* Ola wrote often about women, especially women of colour, suffering from imposter syndrome. But now, with this Gen Z mentee hanging on her every word as if it were the transcript of a holy book, she had never felt like such a fraud.

'Oh, cool,' was all she could muster. 'Thank you.'

'Thank *you*,' Nour said, placing the palms of her hands together and mock bowing.

'Anyway, were you guys talking about The List?' Ola felt her body go cold.

'We were. It's definitely caused a stir,' Kiran offered tepidly. 'Well, a much-needed, overdue table-shake, more than a stir.'

'For sure. There were a few guys I'd heard stuff about on it.' Nour hesitated, then lowered her voice. 'Someone I had a run-in with, too.'

'Really?' Ola piped up.

Nour nodded. 'Do you guys know Matthew Plummer? Sports journalist?' Ola recognised the name from Twitter, where it was accessorised with a blue tick. She'd only ever seen him from the shoulders upward – half-smile poking through a thick blond beard in a byline photo.

'It rings a bell,' Kiran said. 'What happened?' Nour scanned the room and stepped closer. 'Much worse things have happened to people, of course,' she said. 'But when I was in my last year of secondary school, I went to an event he spoke at. Afterwards he approached me and said we should go outside and chat.' She swallowed.

'Once we're outside, he's all over me. I thought I was probably reading too much into it. But then he kissed me. Afterwards he messaged saying that he would give me some one-on-one advice if I wanted, over a drink. I told him it wasn't legal for me to drink yet and he said we could smoke instead, snort something if I wanted.'

Ola suppressed a gasp. Matthew Plummer had to be approaching his fifties. The thought of a pubescent Nour, basically still a baby now, giggling and sneak-reading her old blog as Justin Bieber played in the background, all while dodging kisses from a fully grown man … she felt a chill run down her spine.

Kiran's face was a picture of abject horror. 'What the entire fuck. I'm so sorry that happened to you, Nour. What a cunt. Did you—'

'I didn't go, no,' she said. 'He sent me a dick pic and I blocked him. But I beat myself up over that for years, like "maybe it's just how things are in the media? Maybe I've messed up my chances?"' Nour sighed. 'Makes me shudder, thinking about what could have happened,' she said, closing her eyes tightly and shaking her head, as if doing her best to scramble the image of what might have been.

What would Ola have done if the words by Michael's name on the spreadsheet had been 'groped underage girl'? If they had been sexual assault or sexual battery or grooming or rape? Would she have left him immediately, or would she be right where she was now, with the wedding not yet cancelled as she tried to ascertain his innocence? She was sure she would have ended it, no questions asked. But if that was the case with those kinds of allegations, what made the current situation so different?

'It was obviously common knowledge about Matthew,' Nour continued. 'On The List he had six asterisks by his name!'

Ola's throat had closed up. Message well and truly received, universe, she thought. You can't possibly make me feel any worse than I already do.

'I hate how the focus is back on men, already: their needs,' Nour went on. 'Instead of talking about how we got to the point of needing The List, or what we do now so we don't have to do it again. At the end of the day, this is the most I've ever heard the industry talk about the abuse that happens inside of it. That matters.'

But of course I can feel worse, Ola thought. Much worse. This was all too on the nose. Was Nour a plant? That or Ola's guilt had become so acute that she had started suffering from literal hallucinations, her conscience manifesting as her very own Tyler Durden SOAS student with amazing hair.

Kiran shrugged. 'Patriarchy's gonna patriarch.'

'Right?' said Nour. 'It makes me feel terrible, thinking about how many girls Matthew would have reached out to after me. And how many less he would have been able to if I'd said something.' Nour rubbed at her eyes.

At this, Kiran's tone shifted sharply from sisterly to teacherly. She was becoming emotional too, Ola could tell.

'None of that was your fault, Nour. Do not blame yourself for a grown man's actions – you were a kid.'

'I was,' she said, her voice catching. 'But I'm not now.' She dabbed at the outer corners of her dark eyes with her wrist and gave a sad smile.

After saying their goodbyes, they made their way to the car park and Kiran linked Ola's arm. They walked through the warm evening air in part silence, the distant sound of drum 'n' bass and strangled mewling of a nearby street cat providing an oddly comforting sort of ambience.

Ola slowed her pace. 'I left my first ever internship two weeks early,' she said. 'One of the writers who was supposed to be looking after me on the news desk tried to put his hand up my top, at after-work drinks.'

She felt Kiran's arm stiffen inside hers. 'Fucking hell.'

'I'm scared, Kiran,' Ola admitted. 'That I'm part of the problem. That I'm helping make this cesspit of an industry worse for her. For all of us.'

Ola desperately waited for her friend's assurances to fill the quiet and the void inside her. For Kiran to tell her that a piece of shit would never care so deeply about doing the right thing by everyone involved. But the echoes of the faraway revellers and the distressed cat, her kindred spirit and wretched familiar, only grew louder, as did the silence between them.

13

3 days to the wedding

As Michael reached Arrivals at Heathrow Airport, he made a last-ditch attempt to freshen up, patting at his unkempt trim, hastily rubbing Vaseline on his chapped lips. He rummaged for a piece of gum, hoping it might mask the alcohol on his breath and silently wished he'd brought a pair of sunglasses. Everything inside the terminal was too bright. He squinted at the arrivals board. British Airways. Accra. BA078. Landed 10.47.

She was here but Michael couldn't see her in the commotion of Terminal 5. He waded through the backpacks and bouquets, edged past the queues for coffee and chauffeurs holding up laminated signs or illuminated phones with passenger names on. All about him he could hear the gentle scraping of wheels on the terrazzo floor; suitcases, baggage carts, children sat atop fluorescent ride-on luggage. He pulled back the cuff of his sleeve so he could check the time on his watch. The urge to do so on his phone was overwhelming, but he was trying to wean himself off his obsessive trawling of All Tea. He'd even considered downloading #BLOCKEDT at one point, it was getting so bad. He realised he'd been checking it a few times an hour, on a good day. Michael fidgeted with the drawstrings of his hoodie, unable to keep still. Maybe a quick look couldn't hurt, just to see what was—

'Kweku!' His grandmother's voice was unmistakable from across the concourse, standing outside the WHSmith next to a legion of suitcases only slightly smaller than she was. She was in a large, overlong wrapper and matching head-tie, blue with orange polka dots, interspersed with bigger purple tie-dyed blobs. Her hands were a blur of frenetic energy as she waved with the vigour of someone half her age. He would have run to her if he'd had the energy.

'Mafe wo!' she cried, as she enveloped him in the bear hug that was once the bane of his adolescence. The skin on his bottom lip split slightly as he smiled.

'I've missed you too,' Michael said, momentarily forgetting everything else.

He was overcome by how happy he was to see her well. She was still recovering from her surgery and it had been touch and go as to whether she'd be able to fly out. Michael squeezed her back, savouring the seconds before she'd step aside, taking him in as her eyes welled with happiness and worry, and ask her youngest grandchild 'Biribiara bɔkɔɔ deɛ?'

Thankfully, she slept all the way from Heathrow to Enfield. It had been a long journey from Ghana and by the time the cabbie had loaded the last of her luggage into the boot, she was out like a light in the backseat. They'd chatted on the way to the taxi rank – about her abdominal pain, the wedding, Ola. But he'd known her line of questioning would have changed once they got inside the car. She'd been eyeing his blackening knuckles the entire walk down, but sleep got to her before she could get to him. Had she managed to stay awake, the ride would have been unbearable. She only spoke to him in Twi and he could only answer in English, which would have made his assurances that he was fine even less convincing.

As they pulled up to his parents' – a yellow-brick, two-bed terraced Enfield home – he placed another stick of chewing gum between his teeth and lightly sprayed himself with a cheap deodorant, his groggy grandmother squaring her eyes at him. His mum was out on the doorstep in her dressing gown before he'd even knocked on the door, the women's greeting a flurry of back pats and swaying hugs. They looked so alike, with their short, plump bodies and round eyes, though his grandmother's skin now sagged gently at her neck and her left pupil was clouded by what looked like the beginning of a cataract. She pulled away from their embrace eventually, and gestured her hands at Michael's.

'Yaa,' she said, his mother's name, 'ɛdeyɛbɛn na ayɛ me nana yi?'

He stuffed them into his pockets but his mum was eyeing him cautiously, as if only now really seeing him. She said nothing and pulled him into a tight hug, then ushered them inside.

That was a conversation they'd be having later, no doubt. He'd prepared for it, even before his grandmother voiced her concerns. His mum noticed everything about him; when he gained or lost a few pounds, when he was due a trim and whenever something was wrong. But what was wrong with him simply wasn't a discussion they could have. Michael could categorically say that he worried more about the potential effects of the allegations on his mother than on him. She didn't really understand the internet, the idea that people could publish whatever they wanted. The number of chain letters she'd forward to him daily, claiming a pastor had brought a man back to life who had been dead for twelve days in Obuasi, or that

Nana Akufo-Addo had been hospitalised with a mystery illness; he'd stopped bothering to debate their veracity with her.

'If it's not true, why would Aunty Abena send it, eh?' she used to protest. 'Is she not a woman of God?' If he began to explain what was happening to him, he imagined it might finish her off. He could see it clearly: her writhing on the floor in tears, as she shouted in Twi that they were trying to kill her only son.

Michael quietly dragged his grandmother's bags into the living room, where his dad was sitting in his armchair, his right hand on the remote and his left around a malt drink.

'Hey, Dad.'

His father grunted in response and nodded, eyes not moving from CNN. By now, Michael had learned not to take it personally, though as a child it had been a different story. Back then, his dad worked long days and was out most evenings doing what any reasonable adult would assume with God knows who. The little time his father was at home, he spent it as he did now: silently splayed in front of the television. Michael realised long ago that his mother's prying into his own life partly stemmed from her loneliness. This was the brutal truth of why Michael couldn't let anything happen to himself – he was all she had. Recently, he'd only found the strength to get out of bed because of the guilt that engulfed him when envisaging his mother's hysterics at the police informing her that they'd identified his body. He knew he had to keep it together for her. But how much longer could he maintain this charade? Masquerading as a happy groom about to start the rest of his life, when at night all he could think about was ending it. He didn't know how much longer he could hold on.

He had promised himself he'd never be like his father. Never be the man who made his wife's life difficult, made her feel alone by virtue of being with him. He'd tried with Ola, so hard. But he couldn't help the creeping feeling that the failure was genetic. Inside his DNA and out of his hands. As a child, he heard pastors speak of the 'curse of Eve' but it was men who were truly doomed, he thought, by nature or nurture or both. It sounded like an excuse, but Michael didn't have rational reasons for why he acted so selfishly. The person he loved most was in pain because of his actions, and it wasn't the first time. He had never felt about anyone the way he did about Ola, but he worried he treated her with the same disdain. Michael was led purely by emotions, like an animal. And yet his dad, who appeared to have none, was the same.

Michael looked around the living room. The decor was identical from when he was a child. It smelled the same, too: the faint but ever-present aroma of bell peppers and garlic. The signs of age were undeniable, the once-beige couch now browning, the curtains frayed at the edges. A poster of a grinning, kente-wearing girl underneath the word 'Akwaaba' had suffered water damage over the years. Framed photos of Michael from various life stages grinned out at him from the walls and mantelpiece: him in reception class, bearing a gummy, gappy smile, all the way to him in his mortarboard and gown at graduation. Soon wedding photos were supposed to join the gallery, though he couldn't imagine them there.

His mother sidled up beside him and placed a small hand around his waist. He turned to pass her the Sainsbury's bag he'd brought from Ola's, and it's heavy weight made him shake his head. The extra-ness of Africans was something to behold. Two outfit changes for their mums, three for him and Ola. Their mothers had campaigned for merging their cultures in a mish-mash of a Nigerian–Ghanaian wedding, complete with aso-oke, kente, two types of competing jollof and hundreds of distant relatives on both sides. Ola and Michael had wanted something smaller but eventually they 'met in the middle', meaning they did exactly what their mothers had wanted. The wedding would be quite the spectacle, if it went ahead.

'Hello, Mummy,' he said as cheerily as possible, placing his hand over hers. 'ɛte sɛn?'

He tried not to think of how thin her skin felt, how veiny her hands were. He hated how much his parents changed each time he saw them. Although he'd been AWOL, it couldn't have been more than a fortnight since he'd last Facetimed his mum. She held her phone in a way that made her look like a brown egg when she answered: cut off at the chin and filming directly up nostrils that were already flared in anger at not knowing how to work video calls. Her sorrel skin was taut and youthful, but lined around her brown, bug eyes. His dad's hair, what was left of it, was grey, peeking out from his ears and nostrils. It was nice to see them outside of the small square they resided in on his phone.

His mother stared at him, pausing with pursed lips before making a clucking noise.

'I'm okay, Kweku,' she said, voice laboured as if returning from a shift at a coal mine, despite it being her day off from Boots pharmacy. Suddenly, she pointed her finger upwards dramatically. 'Even if my son wants to drive me to an early grave with stress. How many messages must I send for you to reply me?'

And we're off, Michael thought.

'I'm sorry. I got distracted with work stuff.'

She blew air from her nose in something resembling a laugh. 'It's okay oo.' The tone of her voice said it most certainly wasn't.

'Mum, come on man. I said I'm sorry.'

'I'm not your "man",' she said dryly. 'I said it's okay. It's my own fault. Was it not me and your father that decided to bring you here? You have come to England and been raised among *obronis*, so why won't you do as the *obronis* do?' She shook her head from left to right. 'One day you'll throw me in retirement home, like they do.'

At the start of their relationship, Ola had warned him she knew all about 'Ghanaian mothers and their sons'. In their mum's eyes, she'd said, they could do no wrong; they coddled them, flattered them. They washed their clothes well into adult-hood and would probably still wash their asses if they could. This was only partly true. As her only child, her perfect 'boy born on Wednesday', Michael's mother doted on him and remained certain that no one was good enough for her son. But she spent the rest of her time acting like he was the bane of her existence.

'I should have texted you back, Mummy.' Michael was suddenly six years old again as his mum muttered to herself in Twi. He'd stretched his knowledge of the language to its limits but was certain he was being insulted. 'I'm sorry for worrying you.'

His mother shook her head. 'It's not just today, Kweku. Every day, when I text you, it's showing one tick. When I call you, voicemail. I have been worried sick! I am *still* worried!'

'*Kafra, wai*,' he groaned. How could he explain that his phone gave him anxiety, that every time it vibrated, panic rippled through his body?

'Anyway, I'm here now. Do you want us to spend the entire time I'm here talking about when I was busy?'

She peered at him over her reading glasses a while longer and let out a small tut.

'How is work?'

'It's all right,' he said, not exactly wanting to discuss CuRated but glad that was over with. 'A video I did went viral. Got over a million views.' He tried to sound enthusiastic about it, though he hadn't even responded when Simon had excitedly alerted him over email.

As he'd suspected it would, his mum's face opened out into a wide smile, displaying their shared tooth gap. 'We thank God!' she said, clasping her hands together. 'Where can we watch it?'

'I'll send you the link later.'

'Okay, son. Praise God. We are proud of you.'

The drama of the interrogation just moments before had dissipated. He knew that later that evening, she'd regale her friends from church on WhatsApp with an exaggerated spiel about his job that he'd later have to deny. Once, he'd been a talking head on a *BBC Breakfast* panel discussing the representation of Black men in the media: she told her friends he was working there.

Tension diffused, she looked towards his grandmother's bags. 'Let's take *nanabaa's* luggage upstairs, yes?'

Michael glanced at his watch. There was still time. 'Cool.'

He gathered the bags and wondered how his grandmother had managed to lug them through the airport alone. They shuffled past her as she lay on the couch, whistling through her nose as she slept, and made their way to Michael's childhood bedroom. This was the only part of the house that had really changed. An exercise bike was now collecting dust in the corner where he used to play his PS2 as a kid, and then his PS4 when he'd had to move back after university. Binders brimming with papers were stacked high on the desk by the window. A broken television sat at the end of the bed, surrounded by bin liner after bin liner of clothes. It served mainly as a guest room and a place to put the things they promised they'd send back to Ghana one day and never did. He dropped the bags by the bed and turned to see his mother watching him.

'You look sick, Kweku. Very sick. Your face looks too skinny. Has Ola been making sure you're eating?'

She and his grandmother were the only ones who ever called him by his Ghanaian name. Ola too, when she was taking the piss out of his mum. He tried to smile.

'Mum, I'm okay. I'm just stressed with work, wedding stuff.'

She closed the door gently. 'Okay then. So what did you do to your hand? Hm?'

'I tripped over. It's fine.'

'I don't know why you don't like to talk to me,' she huffed. 'I didn't want to ask in front of your father, but you and Ola – you people are fine? All is okay?' She kneaded her hands together for a moment.

'Kweku, no marriage is perfect, but if you put God at the centre of it, you cannot fail, okay? Through Him, we can do all things. Your dad and I are proof of that. We've had our problems, but we manage.'

They weren't even married, yet Ola and Michael's union was already struggling more than his parents' loveless marriage. He was gasping for a drink to take the edge off this conversation. After university, he hadn't been a big drinker – that was Ola – rather, he was the type whose tongue loosened just the right amount when he'd had a few. Right now, he was desperate for a sip to give him something to say.

'We're fine. It's just been a bit hectic.'

His mother's forehead puckered with concern. 'You're sure? I know I'm your mum, but you can talk to me.'

Michael almost laughed aloud. He was sure in other households it was 'I'm your mum – you can talk to me.' After twenty-nine years of everyone in the Koranteng family pretending they had no emotions other than anger, he was supposed to start talking about his feelings? He loved his mother dearly – she had sacrificed everything for her son, her family. But that didn't mean he could confide in her.

'Trust me,' Michael said. 'Everything's calm.'

She sighed. 'Kweku, when was the last time you went to church?'

'MUM!' he said, voice raised. 'I'm fine!'

'Okay oo, okay,' she said, shushing him. 'If you say so,' she sniffed. 'My daughter-in-law – she is well?'

Michael thought back to the last time he'd seen her. How frail she'd looked, her demeanour. At her door, he'd felt the tension in Ola's stillness. Seen the strain in her committed yet unconvincing attempts to appear comfortable. He couldn't help but notice her hesitancy, her second-guessing before she committed to saying things that made him feel like an axe murderer. She'd looked like a goldfish, her lips parting and coming together as she thought about what she could say. He was sure he scared her, or at least how he might react to stuff did. That like a hostage in a thriller, she was simply biding her time. Serenading her stalker with sweet nothings so that, once distracted, she could knife him in the back and escape.

'She's good. We're good.'

'Good,' his mother said with a nod. 'Even though she doesn't seem to mind that her husband is wasting away.'

It appeared he hadn't got off as easily as he thought. His mother had several bones to pick; now she'd finished cleaning her teeth with his, she was sharpening them ready for his fiancée.

'I'm not wasting away,' he said calmly, avoiding the plainly laid verbal booby traps as best he could. 'And Ola, like me, has work to do.'

'You mean that website of hers, writing about toy penises?'

Now she'd really started. He gritted his teeth.

'Mum.'

'What?' she asked innocently. 'She writes about toy penises, at that sex shop, yes? And multicoloured condoms?'

For his mother, the fact you could order vibrators from the *Womxxxn* site had set its status as a sex shop in stone. A year into their relationship, she had been sent Ola's review of a 3D-printed dildo by Aunty Abena. After the tantrum she threw, it surprised him that she was attending the wedding. 'When there are so many nice Ashanti girls at church, without metal in their nose,' she'd lamented. Eventually, Ola grew on her. She liked her as much as she could a Nigerian daughter-in-law. But, of course, she had notes.

'Please tell your wife to put them down. For me, eh?' she continued. 'No more toy penises, no more condoms. Not when I don't yet have grandchildren.'

When Michael eventually popped the question to Ola, his mother celebrated more than they did. She was one of five sisters, all of whom had three children or more, and she had struggled to conceive before and after Michael, a shame she continued to make his problem. As traditional as she was, her desire for grandchildren superseded her conservatism. If Ola got pregnant out of wedlock, she assured them, she could organise a quick turnaround traditional wedding ceremony, complete with a high-waist kente skirt fortified by an obscuring wrap-around.

Michael felt his stomach drop. Whenever he thought about his future with Ola, he thought first of their kids. How many girls they wanted versus boys. Rubbing her swollen feet and belly as they debated whether the children would have Ashanti or Yoruba first names.

He curled his lip. 'Can you low it? Please?'

'You must start trying for children as soon as possible,' his mother pleaded. 'When I was her age, I was already raising a four-year-old!'

'Cool. Thanks.'

'You know, women's eggs and breast milk, they're like any other. They can expire, Kweku.'

'Okay, Mum, I've heard.'

'Is that what you people want? For it to be sour, bitter for the baby? It's not nice!'

A baby. They hadn't held hands, let alone cuddled in nearly a month. Sex was off the table, obviously – the elephant in bedroom of a couple that had once been so regular in that department. He couldn't have managed it even if he wanted to. He was far too depressed. But Ola worked at *Womxxxn* for goodness' sake; she was sent Willy-Wonka-esque lubes and remote-controlled cock rings from brands by the boxload. Trying them out together was once a tri-weekly occurrence at the minimum. The other day, they'd awkwardly ignored the unopened press packages from Ann Summers and Lovehoney in her hallway.

In bed, they'd been experimental. But a hand on her throat, a paddle against her bum, binding her, biting her … it felt like the sex life he once boasted about to his boys could now be used as evidence of deviancy. While the allegations hadn't mentioned sexual assault, his name being on The List meant they may as well have. Who remembered the specifics? He wondered how Ola saw it now in hindsight, with this new context. That's if she was thinking about her sex life 'in hindsight'. She could, of course, be getting it from somewhere else. He could hardly blame her. Michael was becoming increasingly convinced that was the secret she was hiding from him. Would he ever be able to forgive her if it was? What did it say about him that he wasn't certain he could, after all he had done?

The one other time they'd stopped having sex was because of him, too. When he and Jackie initially started hooking up in his early days of seeing Ola, Ola had found out. From his perspective, there was debate about whether they were 'official official' at the time. Ola felt they had been, and she'd seen the messages, the pictures. However you looked at it, Michael had been underhand: he'd been sleeping with them both and told Ola he hadn't been seeing anyone else.

To this day, he maintained he hadn't been 'seeing' Jackie. Not properly, not like he was dating Ola. Yes, he'd sweet-talked her, declared feelings he didn't necessarily have between face strokes and shoulder kisses. But that had been in the moment, when they'd been in bed. Still, Jackie had been hysterical after he ended it. Messaging Michael non stop, DMing Kwabz with pleas. Michael had ignored them all and, on reflection, wasn't proud of his behaviour. He was even less proud that when Ola confronted him about Jackie, he'd lied and denied it at first. And, once he couldn't hold that line any more, he'd become defensive. His refusal to take responsibility had hurt her even more than the dishonesty. To this day it amazed him that he'd managed to convince Ola to take him back.

When it became clear that he and Ola were patching things up, Jackie had turned her sights on his girlfriend. She bombarded Ola with harassing messages, pictures and screenshots of messages from him that nearly broke them up for a second time. How he managed to pull it back, he still didn't know. Kwabz somehow got Ola on the phone: they talked it out, then worked it out. She'd made Michael swear on both their lives that he'd never speak to Jackie again, and he had meant it when he did. But when he lost his job, slowly the insecurities seeped in again. The temptations. It wasn't as hard as he hoped it would be to reply when Jackie sent him that text the following year. It would have been better if he'd loved Jackie. Liked her, even. But it wasn't about her. It was about him.

Of course, he'd considered coming clean with Ola the second time it happened. Had he done so, the lingering questions she had about The List could have been answered more directly. Maybe, he thought, if he clarified he and Jackie hadn't had sex when they reconnected, Ola could see a way to move past the infidelity. He and Jackie rekindled things, yes, but he never touched her. It sounded ridiculous – they'd Facetimed, sent each other nudes, described in explicit detail what they would do to each other if they got the chance, but she had a boyfriend by then too, and they both agreed that was a line they wouldn't cross.

The more he thought of telling Ola, the more he felt their brittle union couldn't bear the weight of another betrayal. It had been so hard to win her back the first time. Today, they weren't technically back on track but on a kind of path through this nonetheless: he didn't want his admission of a second dalliance with Jackie to risk them coming off the rails for good. Besides, confessing only guaranteed Ola leaving him, not her definitive dismissal of the allegations. Nobility was great, but he'd rather be a ratbag with his relationship.

The rumble of Michael's stomach caught the attention of both him and his mother.

She tutted again. 'You this boy will say you're not wasting away,' she said. 'At least stay for dinner. There's waakye.'

He was never going to turn down waakye, even at his lowest ebb. She knew that.

Michael checked his watch again. 'Okay, fine. But I can't stay long.'

'Can Ola make waakye now?' his mum asked rhetorically.

Michael ignored the jab and made his way down the stairs, where his father remained frozen in the same position, like no time had passed at all. As Michael gripped the banister, he felt dust gather underneath his fingertips and he noticed small specks of it catching the light in the air. He looked at the clutter crowding the living room, mentally drawing a direct line between his mother's habit of hoarding and his minimalist approach to his own flat. His dad used to joke, when he used to make jokes, that Michael's mum deserved a cut of his tab at the Wotaa Ba Ha bar (where 'uncles' of a certain age accosted women that were a long way off from theirs), since her nagging drove him there constantly. Michael almost preferred it then, when his parents made digs at each other. Now they hardly interacted. The success of their marriage wasn't determined by its happiness, but by the fact it was still going.

Was this his future? Ola despising the man that she'd married. Him too dejected to care. All this time, he'd feared her calling it off when it was clear that in three days' time they were going to get married and that would only be the beginning of their troubles.

Michael followed his mother into the kitchen and began to help her plate up the evening's meal. A quick dinner, a bit more wedding talk and then he was out of there. He had to be fast. He couldn't keep the former Crystal Palace centre forward, Lewis Hale MBE, waiting any longer.

14

1 day to the wedding

The washcloth warmed with the heat of her stinging skin, so Ola turned it over to the cooler side. She winced. It wasn't working. The beauty therapist promised her that after paracetamol and a cold compress she'd be 'right as rain', but she was struggling to make the short walk to her laptop.

She applied light pressure to the cloth as she stood, examining her nails as she did. Long, square and pearlescent, with a rhinestone rim. That morning she'd had her toes painted the same shade, had her lash extensions put in, too. The grooming had taken six hours in total, travel excluded. The bikini wax had been the biggest time drain, even longer than styling her hair, which was now slicked back and black. Her neck was beginning to ache, head heavy with the weight of the matching long, kinky ponytail the hairdresser had attached.

The wax took so long partly because of the twenty-minute break Ola had insisted upon. The volume of her screams, guttural and piercing, had shocked her as much as they had the beauty therapist. 'Do you normally go this long without a wax, hun?' the therapist had asked, wrinkling her nose. She smothered aloe vera onto Ola's groin with gloved hands. The burning quickly turned into a more tempered throbbing along her bikini line.

'No,' Ola said hoarsely, blinking away tears of agony. Surveying her assailant's blonde hair and dark roots, she imagined a scenario in which she asked her if she usually went so long without a touch-up, hun. 'I've been busy. I'm getting married tomorrow.'

'Awwwww, congratulations!' the beauty therapist said, swirling wax that resembled honey around the end of her wooden spatula. She wiped the warm wax on the left side of Ola's outer labia and placed a white strip on the last tuft of hair. 'Okay, m'love, on three. One … two …'

She pulled and once again Ola's skin was lit like a match.

'All done!' the therapist cooed, showing her a thick patch of congealed hair on the back of the strip.

'Don't worry about the tenderness, it will go down in a few days,' she said, squeezing the aloe vera onto her palms to smear along Ola's vulva. 'You might still be a bit sore on your wedding night, but for other reasons, ey?' She giggled.

Ola couldn't bring herself to force a smile. Thinking too long about any aspect of her and Michael's relationship was difficult, but sex most of all. It was hard not to reframe his tastes as something sinister. The bruises on her thighs and bite marks on her collarbones she had begged him for. What had his willingness to hurt her said about him? About her? About them?

Limping with the cold compress between her legs, she pulled her laptop from under the debris of her desk. The rehearsal was in a few hours and she had no idea how she could face it. Playing dress-up as a functional woman, in a functional couple.

She opened Skype. Fola answered after one ring, blurred by the bad connection but unmistakably grinning, the screen made up of the squares of her pixelated image and her shining teeth.

'What's good, twin!'

It was fuzzy, but Ola could see that she was in the back of a car. Relief shot through her instantly; seeing Fola's face always made her feel calmer. Had the line been better, she would have seen an only slightly different version of her own staring back at her, minus the dimples, plus a snub nose. Aside from their noses and height (Fola was statuesque at five foot ten but smaller than her big sister, as Ola loved to remind her), their physical differences were minimal. Fola's head had been shaved since the age of seventeen, which she compensated for with inordinate amounts of jewellery: huge jade earrings weighing down her lobes, rings made of quartz from knuckle to nail cuticle – each piece attracting one energy or warding off another. Ola would periodically receive pretty crystals in the post, with a scrawled note from her sister detailing how to 'activate' them, though she only ever used them as bookends. Today, a speckled pink stone and smooth cloudy crystal hung from two separate necklaces.

Ola slid her laptop backwards, hoping it would improve the connection.

'Hey! Are you almost here?'

'Just touched down in London town. En route to yours, bitch!' Fola paused. 'You good?'

'Sis. Today's been mad. Got my nails and hair done. Nearly lost a lip in a freak waxing accident.'

'The hair's cute! But I do *not* know how you do that bikini wax shit,' her sister said. 'Only place any hair is coming off on my body is my head, àṣẹ.' She clasped her hands together at the front of her forehead as if in prayer.

'I don't know why I bothered,' Ola agreed. 'It's not like anyone's going to see it.'

'So you just didn't want to get hitched with a bush, huh?' Fola tutted. 'I know Audre Lorde is side-eyeing your ass from heaven.'

Ola laughed. Her sister would have had a point a month ago, but Ola felt like such a constant contradiction these days that she wasn't even sure if it counted as hypocrisy. It was difficult to pinpoint who she was any more, whose 'side' she was on, though she abhorred that simplistic framing. But it was the truth: Rhian's words played in her mind on a loop daily, and when she wasn't thinking about her, she was haunted by Nour. That girl had looked up to her but would be dismayed if she knew the truth. At work, neither she nor Kiran had spoken about what Nour had told them since, and Ola felt more ashamed each day. She let out a tired exhale.

'Fola,' she said after a moment. 'I feel really off, man.'

'Listen. I knew it!'

Ola felt her mouth curl up into a smirk. 'The ancestors alerted you, girl?' she said with a mock Canadian twang, enjoying what she knew were the last fleeting moments of light-hearted chatter between them.

'No, not this time, even though they usually *do*,' Fola chided her. 'Did I or did I not say that *Love and Hip Hop* would come to Miami next? Out of all the fifty states!' Even through the bad connection, Ola could see her sister's eyes widening with wonder at her 'gift'.

'But it was my twin senses,' she went on. 'My twin senses were *sensing*.'

Ola and Fola were not twins. They looked more alike than some identical sets and were the same age, but Fola was seven months younger and had a different mother. She also had a different accent, being raised in Ontario, Canada. The only thing they shared was a father, though they hadn't been aware of that or each other until they were fourteen. Their dad travelled, flying back and forth between Lagos and London regularly on 'business' that extended beyond his work, as eventually became plain. He travelled to North America a great deal too, promising Ola that he'd take her to see the Statue of Liberty and the Lincoln Memorial. As a child she had been convinced the statues were boyfriend and girlfriend – Dad promised he'd take her to officiate their wedding. He'd also once convinced her on his return from Adelaide that the Australian city had a Yoruba name, just because it looked a bit like hers. He was goofy like that. Like Fola.

Did Ola ever suspect his secret? Were there signs? These were the questions she was asked on the rare occasion it came up with someone she didn't know well. The truth was, Ola couldn't say she had any inkling that her father had another family. She hadn't thought of him as what she'd describe as a 'love rat' if it were another man. Her mother, however, hadn't suspected – she'd known. Although Ola loved her mum, she struggled to respect her because of this. She had always been more of a daddy's girl – she saw the same charisma, humour and generosity in Michael that she missed so desperately in her father. Her mother meanwhile had been traditional, submissive, a doormat; the supportive 'neck' to her father as head of the household – everything Ola rejected, even back then. Sometimes she worried her mum's passivity was her heirloom and she fought against it, hard. And while intellectually she knew her father was to blame for his indiscretions, she couldn't help but feel someone could only disrespect you if you allowed them to.

Her dad passed away from prostate cancer in 2002 and the first time she and Fola were introduced was just days before the funeral.

'This is your sister, Folake,' her mum murmured once they were all seated in their family's damp-ridden, cramped living room in Streatham, flanked by family portraits that Fola's eyes continued to wander towards. 'She's from Canada.'

Apparently, they'd been referred to as 'the twins' within the family long before they'd met. Through Fola's face Ola realised how much she resembled her dad. Alongside leaving them in the dark, he'd left them his smooth, dark skin and dark, doe eyes. Their dad's indiscretion was written all over both of his daughters' faces.

That he had accidentally called both of them each other's names became something they laughed about as adults. As did the discovery that they had both watched the sitcom *Sister, Sister* as lonely only children in the 90s, wishing they too would find a long lost twin. They'd half joke about inevitable siblings scattered across the world, eventually coming out of the woodwork. A 'Bola' in Kentucky, a 'Lola' in New Zealand.

'And the *audacity* to give us rhyming names?' Fola would cackle. 'The nerve of Nigerian men!'

'How many times – Olaide and Folake do not rhyme!' Ola would rebut.

'You know full well what I mean. Dad really was a mess.'

'Yeah,' Ola would laugh along. 'I miss him.'

'Me too.'

After a while, Fola stopped reminding Ola of their dad in a way that was painful. Ola's mum grew to be very fond of her, the assumption that the girls were her twin daughters on visits becoming less burdensome. It was hard not to: Fola was the very embodiment of a sunny Sunday morning, bringing the same light their dad had. Ola didn't see her as much as she'd like – Fola inherited the travel bug from their father and was currently teaching English in Panama – but she spoke to her more often than she did most people with whom she shared a city.

'So what's going on?' Fola said, placing a hand under her chin and leaning into her phone as if she were sitting across from her in a Costa. 'The rehearsal is at five-thirty, right? Do you know how to pronounce your new surname yet? Because I sure as hell don't!'

Ola was half expecting to taste blood. Her teeth were pressing into her bottom lip so hard she felt she might mistakenly slice it open like a satsuma segment.

'I'm not sure if I can do it.'

The bad picture quality worsened and became out of sync as her sister jolted backwards.

'Wait,' Fola said. 'Hold up. You can't do what. Tonight? *Tomorrow?*'

Ola nodded silently.

Her sister raised her eyebrows. 'Girl, I'm in an Uber from—'

'Do you remember when you told me I should pay someone to track down whoever was behind The List?' she cut in. 'So I could ask them questions and stuff?'

Fola thought for a moment. 'Yeah, kind of. I mean, I was kidding but sure.'

'Well, I did, but for Michael. A private investigator has been following him for a month.'

Fola's eyes bugged and her mouth hung open, hands squashing the sides of her face. She became an eerily accurate re-enactment of Edvard Munch's *The Scream*, with her bald head and cartoonishly spooked expression.

'He hasn't found anything,' Ola quickly asserted. 'But I feel like that's the problem. I'm never going to know what happened, am I, Fola? I'm never going to know the truth. How can I ever trust him? How can he ever trust *me*, when I've been spying on him?' And just like that, she was crying.

Fola placed her hand on her thighs and bowed her head wearily, a facsimile of her bedraggled sister. 'Well shit. I – I don't even know what to say,' she stammered. 'I thought you were okay now, after the emails from his old job? I just assumed that's why you stopped bringing it up, you know? With the wedding being tomorrow, and all? Shit. Fuck.'

As if hearing the hysteria rise in her own voice, Fola slowed her breathing to calm herself and shut her eyes. She stroked the pink stone dangling from her neck. Probably summoning strength for the pair of us, Ola thought, from her stones or their ancestors or both.

'Okay.' With a suck of wind Fola was back in the room, slipping into problem-solving mode as per usual. 'Do not cry. You are going to be okay, okay? Okay. Who do I need to call? What do you need me to do?'

What Ola needed her sister to do was exactly this. To take control of what was entirely out of control. To occupy the space in reality that Ola had long vacated. She needed her sister to step in, step up. But what Ola *wanted* was different. That was for her sister to hear her scattered thoughts. To not necessarily help her make sense of them, but acknowledge them so she wasn't talking to herself. No cheering up, just a non-partisan guest at her pity party.

'I don't know. Man. I'm so fucking dumb.'

'You are *not* dumb,' Fola snapped at her. Her sister was ever ready to fight Ola's enemies, even if they were Ola herself.

Ola shook her head. 'Maybe I should have just ended this when I saw The List. But I can't drop him without knowing. I love him, Fola. Too much. It sounds stupid, but I do.'

'That doesn't make you stupid. That makes you human,' Fola said. Her voice was an audible hug. 'Imagine the choices we'd make without love fucking up our faculties? Life would be perfect. Except we wouldn't have got *Lemonade*. Or *Ctrl*. Or, like, any Adele. Okay, we'd be missing some heartbreak bops, but you know what I mean!' She went quiet, the low hum of Kiss FM muffled in the background.

'But sis, whatever you choose to do, you have to do *something*. And fast.'

She had to. She knew that. But Ola felt faint thinking about the individual phone calls she'd have to make to each and every guest if she called it off, never able to explain the real reason she'd walked away. The crushing debt from unfulfilled deposits. The shame. Marrying Michael was the only path that made sense at this point. She had no evidence he was innocent, but none that he was guilty either. And logistical nightmare and cash loss aside, imagining life without Michael was like trying to imagine what it felt like to not exist – pitch-black, nothingness. He was the love of her life, whether she liked it or not.

Before all this, they had been looking at where they wanted to buy a house together. They'd discussed the timeline of when they planned to start trying for kids. Could she really end this here, start again? Install the apps, present a version of herself that was a precursor to the real her, make the small talk, have the big talks only to be ghosted and uninstall until next time? It made her tired even thinking about it, as it did just hearing about it from Ruth.

Of all the gendered 'gaps' she wrote about at *Womxxxn* – the pay gap, the orgasm gap – it was the time gap that disgruntled her most. Not simply in the relation to the comparable hours of leisure time men had on average compared to women. She bristled at the idea of 'girls growing up faster than boys' but Michael's twenty-nine and her thirty-one were light years apart. Their age gap was so small, but so big. He had another decade, maybe more before he seriously had to worry about kids. His thirty-one would be what her early twenties were: an age of exploration, years he could afford to waste. Theoretically, she believed in the perks of singledom: women lived longer, were found to be happier statistically. But perhaps she was more like Frankie than she thought. The gap between who she was and who she thought she was, was wide. The gap between who she thought she was and who *people* thought she was the widest of them all. Even she was taken aback by how much a white wedding clearly meant to her.

'I just don't know, Fola.'

Her sister straightened up. 'Do you trust him?'

Silence. 'Sometimes. Most times. Do I think he's capable of what he's been accused of? I don't, but that doesn't mean anything, does it?' Ola could barely trust herself; she wasn't sure how much love might be clouding her judgement. Abusive men are all innocent in the eyes of someone, wrongly persecuted to a loved one. But it was impossible to outrun this feeling that this had all been a terrible mistake. And at times it was even harder to think what it would mean if that were true and Michael was innocent, what he had endured.

Fola nodded as if taking notes. 'Does he make you happy?'

Michael did make her happy. But he made her sad, too. Not in equal measure; he'd hurt her with his lies before, battered her confidence. But he also made her feel like she could do anything. Like she *should* do anything. When they'd visited Santorini, she insisted they hike the volcanic crater, only to realise that Havaianas weren't the best choice of footwear. He carried her on his back for most of the way, never uttering a self-satisfied 'I told you so' as she would have. Michael loved her, flaws and all. And that was why there was a side to her that no one else saw but him, that only he could coax out. Perhaps he created it? He encouraged her to be carefree and silly. He made her 'smiley', a word that even in childhood would never have been used to describe her.

Michael made her both weak at the knees and just weak, generally; she had so little resolve when it came to him. The apple doesn't fall far from the tree, Ola thought, as her mother's relationship with her dad came to mind.

'He doesn't make me as sad as I'd be without him,' she said, truthfully. As soon as the admission left her lips, the decision was made, they both knew it. Fola's face looked like she'd just bitten into an onion she had mistaken for an apple. She remained cool, tracing the outline of her pink stone again.

'Listen, I'll support you whatever, okay? That's what I'm here for. Unless you're still trying to have me sitting next to Michael's crazy-ass cousin. That's different.'

Ola rolled her eyes. 'Okay, let's not casually stigmatise mental health, please.'

'There she is!' her sister said with a clap, tension leaving her voice. 'She's back!'

Ola gave a light chuckle. 'Gifty's not crazy. She just has big Patience Ozokwor, Nollywood witch energy.' She nodded at the screen. 'No offence to the supernatural community.'

'None taken,' Fola deadpanned.

'Thank you,' Ola said seriously once their giggles had subsided.

'Yeah yeah, I'm the greatest, we been knew,' Fola laughed. And then her face became serious too. 'I'm here for you, though. Always. You know that?'

'I do,' Ola said tearfully, longing to hold both her sister and father at once. 'Thanks, twin.'

15

1 day to the wedding

Michael hastily texted Ola as he made his way up the gravel path to Lewis's home in leafy Orpington, unconsciously noting his peripheral vision becoming viridescent.

> Left order of ceremony booklets at mine. Can you bring pls? They're in bag on kitchen counter

He'd come straight to Lewis's house from the barbershop and been in such a hurry he'd forgotten them. In the time it would take for him to get back, pick them up and then make his way to the rehearsal, he would have missed the whole event.

Michael was sure that meeting Crystal Palace legend Lewis Hale this afternoon, even under these circumstances, would still be the least surreal part of his day. Everyone would be at the rehearsal this evening: Kwabz, Amani, Seun. Celie, Ruth, Fola. Ola's mum, his mum and dad, Pastor Oyedepo. Split into teams of either the none the wiser or the unwilling abetters, upholding the facade out of loyalty. He half expected to arrive to an empty church. Ever since that fateful day The List went live, he hadn't heard a single update from Ola about the wedding prep. He wondered if she would even reply to his text. If she did, it was acknowledgement that they were really doing this.

As he reached the driveway, Michael noted two Range Rovers parked out the front, one black, one silver. The gravel underfoot began to get finer, and soon enough he was stood outside a property reminiscent of a BBC Sunday evening period drama. He knew Lewis was extremely wealthy, but it didn't stop him from being bowled over. This wasn't a house; it was a manor, endlessly sprawling and surrounded by acres of lush foliage.

Originally, they'd meant to meet two days ago at the Walworth Arms, a Beckton-based pub that looked like it had been ripped off the set of a Midlands-based soap. Lewis texted him the day before they were due to meet:

Michael m8, I'll b in a black baker boy cap at the bar when u get there :)

Michael knew, that Lewis knew, that Michael knew exactly what he looked like. He was a very famous man, even to those who didn't watch football. It was clear that Lewis hadn't sent it because he was worried Michael wouldn't spot him; it was because he was worried he wouldn't turn up.

In the end he hadn't made it, but not for lack of trying. Getting out of his parents' house was a lot more difficult than getting in. After stuffing him with waakye, shito and boiled eggs, his mum troubled over how tired he looked and assured him a quick nap would do no harm – she'd wake him up in half an hour. He hadn't taken much convincing and woke up at 1 a.m. with nine missed calls, a blanket over him and imprints on his cheeks from the couch pillows. It was the best rest he'd had in weeks.

This time, they agreed to meet at Lewis's house. He and Lewis's brief conversations were only ever about The List and meeting up to discuss it, but Lewis ended all texts with a colon-eyed and bracket-mouthed smiley, as if emojis and the gravity of the situation eluded him. Michael wasn't entirely sure how he had got his number – he imagined Lewis was famous enough that it wouldn't have been too hard for him, or whoever a retired footballer gets to arrange that type of thing. It had been early in the morning when he'd messaged:

> Hi, Lewis Hale here. This the correct number 4
> Michael Koranteng? Hope u don't mind me gettin in
> touch :)

Obviously, Michael assumed it wasn't really him. He imagined it was a troll who'd hurl abuse about The List when he replied. It was only when Lewis's agent reached out that he realised it was legitimate. The agent told Michael that Lewis preferred speaking on the phone and Lewis rang him later that day to explain that he wanted to have a pint with him and 'a talk'.

'When you say "a talk", do you mean about The List?' Michael had asked, trying to get his head around the madness of the present scenario.

'Correct,' said Lewis. The sound of his voice felt like a time capsule. Only Black British men of a certain age spoke with this pseudo-cockney, 'h'-dropping accent that segued so effortlessly into a Caribbean lilt.

'You want to talk to *me* about it?' Michael repeated.

'No flies on you, son.'

'Can I ask why? Like, no disrespect, but you don't know anything about me.'

'You're right, I don't really,' Lewis conceded. 'But I do know a bit about your girlfriend. Gave her a google.' He had said it as if it was the most normal thing in the world.

'Well, my PA did anyway, after she looked up everyone else. When she got to you, she found her. Ola the journalist, right? One of the good ones by the looks of it. She writes about some … *interesting* stuff!' Lewis started to laugh and Michael waited for him to get to the point. 'Anyway, I assumed if she vouched for you, being a feminist and that, it might be for good reason.'

Michael's stomach rolled over as he said it. Ola's presence was a sponge, either cleaning up his mess or absorbing the vitriol aimed at him. People viewed him as a better person because she was with him, and judged her more poorly because of it. He knew that if she left him, she would inadvertently be confirming his guilt, but this was the first time it had been acknowledged so plainly. It was probably for the best that she didn't know he was meeting Lewis. How could he rationalise associating with someone accused of 'violent homophobia' and 'abuse' to her when he struggled to justify it to himself? At this point, what was one more secret?

What Michael couldn't put his finger on was why Lewis wanted to get in touch in the first place. Lewis wasn't like him; he'd been in the papers for all sorts of things before. The List was only circulating in certain sectors and hadn't yet reached your average *Strictly* viewer. They weren't in the same boat by any means.

Lewis was standing at the bottom of large stone steps leading to the front door as Michael arrived. The first thing Michael noticed was his posture. He stood bolt upright with shoulders back, holding himself like a lawyer giving an opening statement in court, anxiety only apparent on his face. Michael had nearly a foot on him, but Lewis looked as strong and stocky in his forties as Michael remembered him being when he'd watched him play as a kid. He was clean-shaven and bald – not a hair in sight on his head – but his barely there stubble was dotted salt-and-pepper grey. A fair-skinned man with a fair amount of freckles, the colour of a cashew nut. Crow's feet perched at the edges of his kind eyes and fine laughter lines framed a wide mouth in which sat slightly too large veneers.

'Michael; what's 'appening, son,' Lewis said as he made his way over to him, his face flooding with relief. He extended a hand. 'Lewis.'

Michael thought how strange it was, watching someone introduce themselves when they knew you knew who they were. Michael didn't know Lewis from The List. He knew him from football cards and Black History Month posters at primary school, smiling wide between a badly drawn Mary Seacole and Richard Blackwood. Michael and Amani had both worn his number 9 shirt on mufti day. He knew him from 116 goals from 263 appearances for Crystal Palace. His fourteen hat-tricks. Palace's second highest goalscorer of all time. Commentator on *Match of the Day*. His mum loved him on *The One Show*.

'I know you are, man.' Michael couldn't help but be a bit starstruck. 'You're a legend.'

Lewis gave a nervy smile. ''Preciate that, mate,' he said, walking up the stairs towards stone pillars that led through to an enormous, solid-oak front door. 'Come in.'

Michael noted how high the ceilings were in the entrance hall, the sweeping arches too. A gargantuan crystal chandelier hung at the centre, and to the left was a sweeping staircase with the original antique wooden banister. On every wall was a selection of black and white, over-the-shoulder portraits of his wife Samantha, who Michael recognised from the *Daily Mail* sidebar and one of those reality shows, 'Celebrities Do Something'.

Lewis watched as Michael gawped. 'You want the grand tour?'

There had been whispers in the press over the years of Lewis's diminishing fortune, but one look at his house put those rumours to bed immediately. Despite its classic exterior, the interior was the height of modernity. Most of the walls were off-white against grey oak flooring. Each room looked airlifted from a luxury hotel – the gym, the indoor swimming pool, the TV room – and smelled of sandalwood. This was the case even in the kitchen, which didn't smell like anyone cooked in it. Michael was intimidated by the geometric taps in the sink, which resembled the Tesla logo and looked like they had been designed by one of its engineers. In the living room were more tasteful pseudo-nudes of Samantha. Thin and largely expression-less, she was practically part of the furniture, like the talking appliances in *Beauty and the Beast*. It was as if she'd once been an anthropomorphic ironing board until true love's kiss trans-formed her into a very lean Lithuanian woman with glassy grey eyes, jet-black hair and snowy skin, who almost exclusively dressed in tawny brown athleisure.

Like every other communal area, the kitchen was all sharp corners, shades of cream and susceptible to staining. Samantha wasn't in but even the things that did prove her existence – her fanned fashion magazines on the coffee table, her Louboutins in the hallway – felt purely ornamental. Michael felt hesitant about leaving any mark of his presence, so out of step with the sterile aesthetic.

He was thankful when his phone went, giving him somewhere to put his hands. It was Ola. She'd replied to his message with a 'thumbs up' emoji. That was it then. The wedding was happening.

'Everythin' good?' asked Lewis, noting Michael's perturbed expression.

'Uh, yeah, I'm fine. Ola's gone to pick up the order of ceremony booklets. It's the rehearsal tonight. Wedding tomorrow.'

'*Tomorrow?*'

Michael nodded, hardly believing it himself. Lewis made a noise halfway between the sucking of his teeth and a tut. 'Jesus. You need a drink more than me,' he said, glancing towards the wine-filled glass cabinet lining the wall.

He asked Michael what he'd like and then pulled two bottles of Guinness from a fridge as tall and wide as a wardrobe. It was covered with photo magnets featuring two smiling tweens with frizzy hair. He set them down on glass coasters on the large quartz coffee table in the living room.

'Thanks for this, mate.' He lowered himself onto the couch. 'I know it's not your neck of the woods.'

'It's calm,' Michael said.

Lewis mentioned he had grown up in Elephant and Castle. He was a 'Souf London boy' at heart. 'Though I'd rather The Glades than the Elephant and Castle shopping centre, any day,' he said with a laugh. 'Know I'm not allowed to say that.'

He had been made aware of the allegations – accusations of him being 'violently homophobic and abusive' – by his team the day The List was published. It was something his agent, manager and publicist were monitoring, as they did with all press stories about him. It gathered little traction initially – Lewis being older and largely offline. But he was also one of the most famous men in the country.

'Only a matter of time before they start publishing names,' he said. 'The papers do a front-page story on a tweet made by a parody account, then wonder where all the fake news is coming from. Them! It's coming from fackin' them! I never thought it could get worse than in my heyday – every other week I was accused of a nightcap with some hooker or a three-some with a bunch of WAGs, but now? Now every paper is a tabloid and their sources? Twitter,' he said, heaving a sigh. 'I'm going on. Not like you've had it any easier, is it?' He paused for a moment.

'What's your story? How'd a nice lad like you end up on there? Or are you a nasty piece of work like the rest of 'em?'

Michael fixed his eyes on his bottle.

'Some girl I was talking to,' he said, knowing how it must have sounded. 'A fan of my old podcast. We were involved for a bit when I was with my girl. I wasn't great to her, but nothing like what's on The List. When I took a step back, she started making threats about how she'd "ruin my life". She was serious, I guess. But yeah. I fucked up.'

Lewis gave a knowing look. 'Let he who is without sin and all that.' He paused. 'Does she know? Your missus?'

'Nope.'

'*Bloodclarrrrt.*' He drew out the r's and then sipped his Guinness, as if attempting to obscure whatever face he couldn't help but pull.

'It wasn't physical,' Michael felt the need to say. 'Between me and this girl. We weren't sleeping together.'

He winced, hearing himself. Straightforward infidelity prob-ably made more sense to this former Premier League footballer.

The more gallant he attempted to present himself, the more absurd he sounded. Like he'd thrown away his entire relationship for sexts. Lewis nodded anyway.

'It happens,' he said, scratching at the nape of his neck. 'So what's the latest, then?'

'Well, we're apparently getting married tomorrow, even though Ola pretty much said she won't ever trust me again unless I can prove my innocence. Which I can't do without telling her about Jackie.'

'Sorry to hear that, mate. Proper catch-22.' Lewis took another sad swig. He set his mouth in a sorrowful frown once the bottle left his lips. '*Ah suh it guh.*'

Seeing Lewis so cowed made Michael feel uncomfortable. It was like watching his dad lose a fight; a part of his childhood was being bludgeoned to death in front of him. He shifted in his seat, and the cream leather upholstery squeaked lightly.

'You know the worst bit for me?' Lewis continued. 'Can't even bloody defend myself, my agent says. If I do an interview saying "I'm not homophobic and abusive" most people will be like "Who said you were?"' He shook his head in disbelief. 'Brings more attention to it.'

'It's not true though, is it?' Michael said, almost by reflex.

Lewis looked up from the table. 'Is it true about you?'

'No.'

'Well then,' he snapped. 'Do you think we'd be sat here if it was true about me?' He took another sip from his bottle. 'You sound like every other knobhead on the internet, asking me that.'

Michael raised his hands in defence. He'd only asked a question. Is this how unreasonable he had been with Ola? Lewis closed his eyes and sat back in his chair.

'Sorry. Didn't mean to get the hump.' He eyed his drink. 'You don't know me from Adam – who says I didn't punch up some poor fairy?' He took a cigarette and a stainless-steel Zippo lighter from inside his blazer pocket, and lifted it towards the cigarette's end. 'You mind?' Michael shook his head and Lewis flicked the lighter upward. He took a long drag and closed his eyes again.

'When my girl asked me if the claims about me were true, I was pissed,' Michael confessed, after a moment. 'That she thought I could do that shit … It still gets me sometimes. Like I know I'm not perfect. Not at all, but I'm not …'

His voice trailed off and Lewis nodded. 'You seem a decent lad, Michael,' he said. 'Sounds like you've found yourself in a situation you shouldn't really be in. I'm sure she knows that.'

'I'm not sure any more, man. And it's not like the truth is much better. I've done her dirty.'

'I feel you,' Lewis said. 'The truth hurts.' He brought the cigarette back to his lips and really looked at Michael then, taking stock of him. He suddenly appeared pained. 'Can I tell you something, mate?'

Michael shrugged. 'Go ahead.'

Lewis cast his gaze downward before he spoke and furrowed his brow, his forehead crumpling into wrinkles. 'You got mad at your missus for askin' because you didn't do those things, right?' Michael gave a quick nod.

'But see, just now when I got pissed off at you for askin' me, it's because I did.'

Michael fell back into his armchair, dumbstruck. Had he misheard him? Or was Lewis trying to ruffle his feathers with a sick joke? Michael didn't have time for this.

'I was being defensive,' Lewis said. 'Because it's complicated.'

Only the clink of Lewis's Guinness against the glass coasters could be heard in the room. As Michael looked on, he was gripped by a sudden sense of uneasiness. Lewis seemed more serious in this moment than he had in their entire conversation and Michael feared where this was now going. Who had he been talking to, confiding in?

'So you—' Michael started.

'Are abusive?' Lewis chipped in, putting his cigarette out in the ashtray. 'Nah, son. Definitely not. Homophobic? That could be said, yeah. I've been known to be. I've used some language I shouldn't have. Called people names during fights. Like most blokes my age. But I'm also gay, which probably makes things a bit less straightforward.'

Michael sat and waited for the punchline. He waited for the sarcastic follow-up or wry grin. But it never came. Lewis simply took yet another casual sip of his drink. Michael did everything in his power to avoid any expression that would betray how much what he'd just heard had floored him. There was more silence.

'Don't worry, mate, you're not my type,' Lewis eventually said. 'More into blondes.'

Michael coughed, trying to loosen words from his throat as well as muster a similarly casual tone to Lewis's. Eventually, he narrowed his eyes, sarcastically.

'So even when it comes to guys, swirling continues among Black footballers,' he said, cocking his head. 'What do they put in you mans' bottles at the training ground?'

Lewis guffawed and the tension in the air, in their bodies, dissipated. He told Michael that he'd been gay – not bisexual, he stressed – for as long as he could remember. In the closet for the entirety of his upbringing in his Seventh-Day Adventist household and his seventeen-year marriage to Samantha, who he loved dearly. It was risky for him to have boyfriends; he had slept around a lot in his prime but discreetly.

'I wasn't even sure if I was into blokes more than, you know, physically,' he told Michael sheepishly. 'I kept tellin' myself it was just sex and I loved Sam.'

Lewis almost managed to convince himself of this until Cris. But when they met, he fell for him in an instant. They'd happily seen each other in private for a year and a half. Cris was the only serious partner he'd ever had aside from Samantha. They'd eventually broken things off, after Lewis had refused to leave her.

'We fought about it. I said some very fucked-up things. But there was never any fackin' abuse, on either side.'

Michael's chest was heavy. 'And now he's put you on The List for revenge?'

'No, no, no,' Lewis said, prodding absentmindedly at the corner of his drink label with his nail.

'Cris would never do that. His junkie sister, on the other hand? Jo wanted £50k to keep her mouth shut. I paid her off ages ago and hoped I'd seen the last of her. But now she wants double and she's trying to goad me, take the piss. It's mind games, accusing me of homophobia when she knows …' Lewis's voice trailed off and he started again after a pause. 'I don't think she just wants money any more, the sick fuck, but she knows I'll give it if I 'ave to. And Sam's not stupid. She's been asking questions I can't answer. I know she thinks I have a mistress. This though? She'd never forgive me. And Sienna and Melanie, to hear that their old man …' Lewis coughed to clear his throat.

'I'm desperate. So desperate that I've outed myself to a near stranger, who could blackmail me too.' He let out a gruff laugh.

'But I don't know what else to do at this point. You'd think carrying this shit around with me forty-odd years would mean it gets easier. It don't.'

'Boy,' Michael said, lost for words. He'd only just met the man and they were having a conversation deeper than Michael usually had with his own friends. It was clear Lewis was eager to get this off his chest to someone, anyone. 'I don't even know what to say.' Michael was quiet for a moment. 'Have you thought of threatening her back? Taking her to court?'

'I 'ave. But if it went to court, I'd need to prove it was Jo. And that would mean going public with the fact I've been unfaithful to Sam. With a geezer.'

A deep dread began to weigh Michael down. The helplessness of Lewis's situation reminded him of the helplessness of his own. The smoke from Lewis's dimming cigarette had blended with the scent of the diffuser, making the air in the room feel thick.

'I went to the police,' Michael said. 'Tried a lawyer, too. Waste of time.'

'No point in me going to the police either. Me being "violently homophobic" – it could technically be deemed true, with my past. But you need more than a tweet and a box on an Excel sheet for the context of Lewis Hale, mate.'

'Have you thought of …' Michael broke off momentarily. '… providing that context?'

'You mean coming out?' Lewis said. 'Thought about it, during a moment of madness. Cris has said a million times that he'd come forward and make it clear I was never violent. But that would do more damage to my career than if I was a homophobe. It was before your time, but I'm sure you know about Justin Fashanu, in the nineties? John's brother?' Michael nodded but Lewis continued as if he hadn't.

'Britain's first openly gay footballer. Black boy, too. Imagine that, back then. Before he came out, he was the first Black player to get a £1 million transfer fee, in '81. Should have been a legend. You would have still been in primary school when news of his suicide broke. My friends spoke about it like he deserved to die.'

Lewis also said he remembered the professional football player John Fashanu's damning comments about his own brother in the press, his vehement disowning of him. John's words had made Lewis burn with the imagined licks of hellfire. He couldn't imagine his own siblings, who he was close to, responding much differently if he had come out. Or his parents. They were God-fearing, proud Jamaican people who had arrived in England in the Windrush generation, instilling in their four children Christian values and a strong sense of their culture. But this sometimes meant if it wasn't a pastor at church condemning Lewis to hell, it was Buju Banton on 'Boom Bye Bye', calling for his death from the car speaker. Or watching his siblings nod in agreement when Shabba Ranks said men like him should be crucified, live on Friday night TV. On the day Justin Fashanu's death was announced, Lewis overheard his father's disgust as he discussed Justin's 'lifestyle' with his beloved mother in the kitchen. He heard her pity for what she saw as a lost soul with an affliction, a perversion. No other professional player in the UK had come out as gay since.

'And why would they?' Lewis was saying. 'What for? When I was a kid, it was all HIV jokes. I'd be a liar if I said I never pointed the finger, to keep the heat off me. And it only got worse when I started playing. The nineties was peak football hooliganism, lad culture, all that. Jo can do her worst – it will never be as bad as me going public.'

Michael avoided Lewis's eyes as he spoke. 'I hear you, trust,' he said. 'It's fucked, man. But if Cris's sister ain't going nowhere … maybe it's better coming from you? She could blackmail you forever. Or just out you anyway, when she feels like it.' Michael felt his throat become tighter as he began thinking about Jackie; he was doling out advice he should take himself.

'I mean, I'm not saying it would be easy, not at all. But would it really be worse than all this? You're retired and TV's more …' He searched for the right word. 'Liberal, than football. There's still a lot that ain't right in the world but it's not the nineties. It's different now.'

'Yeah, now it's all about "pride" and being "born this way",' Lewis said, with a mirthless chuckle. 'Shovin' it in people's faces.' He lowered his voice, as if they had company. 'If people knew, I wouldn't be me any more. It would be like I'd changed, even though I ain't changed, you know? I just want a normal, peaceful life. With Sam and the kids. I'd lose everythin'.'

'You're *you* though, man,' Michael stressed. 'Yeah, dickheads would chat shit, no doubt. But I'm not sure *everyone* would turn their backs on you. You're a legend; that won't ever change. Like, I don't think any less of you, now I know.'

'Really?' Lewis said. He looked unconvinced. 'How do you and your mates talk about "batty boys" normally then, ey?'

'I'm not on that,' said Michael. 'Not my business what a grown man does in his personal life.'

'All right.' Lewis took another sip from his drink. 'Your mates, then. What do you do, when they're making the usual gay-bashing jokes? You tell 'em it ain't right?'

Michael thought of Amani and Seun. Their coded remarks on the podcast about men who they deemed 'fruity', their flagrant comments in the group chat. And like he had done in those scenarios, Michael said nothing as he sat across from Lewis. Lewis gave a curt nod in response. 'Exactly,' he sighed. 'And that's not me blaming you, by the way. I don't say nothin' either. But all this talk of how different things are these days … well, it feels a lot like it always did to me.'

Michael's chest began to feel restricted. 'But what's the alternative? Leave shit as it is?'

Lewis watched him dispassionately before giving a light shrug.

'Nah man,' Michael said, his voice was trembling. 'This ain't right. I don't give a fuck what anyone says. Suffering in silence because what, dickheads online say we deserve it? And not just us. How many other innocent men could be on The List? How many other lives might these people decide to ruin?'

Lewis looked uneasy, raising his thick steepled fingers to his lips. 'Careful, lad,' he said. 'Don't get ahead of yourself.'

Michael grimaced. 'What do you mean? You reached out to me about my situation – there could be other guys on there in a similar one.'

'Already told you – if it hadn't been for your missus, I wouldn't 'ave,' Lewis said. 'Wasn't exactly evidence, either; loads of women stay with cunts, don't they? So don't get confused; plenty of horrible bastards on that list. I heard about that rapper, Papi Danks, way before this all came out. I got added to a WhatsApp group a few days ago, right, filled with lads on The List all claiming they've been framed. If anything, it just made it clear that they deserve to be on there. Bunch of woman haters, the lot of 'em. What's it my Sienna says … incels. That's the one. Bunch of incels.'

No one spoke for a moment, Lewis's nails against the bottle, picking at the label again, filling the silence. Then Michael banged his hand hard on the table, making Lewis jump.

'Fuck!' he exclaimed. His hand began to throb as soon as it made contact with the surface, numbing his fingers. 'What are we supposed to do?'

Lewis placed the bottle to his lips and tilted his head all the way back as he swigged the remainder, patting the bottom for the dregs. He looked at Michael.

'That's why I asked you here today,' Lewis said with a serenity that worried him. 'See, I have an idea. But you probably ain't gonna like it.'

16

1 day to the wedding

Michael kept the spare key taped underneath the plant pot on the left. Or was it the right one? Ola forgot which each time and ended up having to lift both. This was harder than it sounded, as they were large, cast-iron monstrosities reaching her shins and required her to kneel on the ground to tip them backwards. She crouched to lean the left pot against the wall and scanned the base. No luck. She moved across to the second and did the same. Jackpot. Ola dusted the debris of Michael's porch from her knees and opened his front door.

Entering his hallway, her underarms were moist with exertion and apprehension. She felt thankful the sweat wasn't visible through her shirt, a black, 90s-style graphic tee with Louis Theroux on the front, paired with distressed dark denim shorts. The casual clothes looked at odds with her extravagant, extra-long wedding hair, nails and lashes, reminders that the wedding was just around the corner. Ola wasn't sure how she had managed to let a whole month fly by with no answers or direction on what to do about the wedding. How could she focus on the order of the procession, the pace of her walk, when she didn't feel she should be there at all? But when Michael texted, asking her to pick up the order of ceremony booklets from his flat, she took it as a sign. It was an opportunity to be alone in his house, with his laptop. An opportunity to dig as deep as she possibly could. As guilty as she felt, what choice did she have? Rationality had long left the equation, ever since she'd got Luke involved in this mess weeks ago. The wedding was tomorrow and her total confusion was presently overriding her feelings of regret. This was the eleventh hour. If she didn't find anything on his computer, she'd take it as the universe saying she'd done all she humanly could. If she did … she'd cross that bridge when it came.

Ola raced up to Michael's bedroom. The air inside was smoky and stale. Stacked plates with congealed foods lined the floor and too many bottles of whiskey sat empty on his side table. It was difficult not to be affected by the tragedy of his surroundings. Cracking open a window, she bent over the open MacBook on his bed. Her heart rate quickened as she typed in the password, certain he wouldn't have changed it. Then she was in.

Sat on his bed, illicitly logged in to his laptop, Ola realised that she had no idea what it was she hoped to find. A neatly outlined log of his harassment activities was unlikely. And, anything that might even hint at abusive behaviour was probably deleted by now. She clicked her way through his Gmail inbox anyway and a grubby feeling came over her. Though her gut feeling was hard to ascertain through the dread, something told her she was searching for an answer she already had. Deep down, she believed that Michael hadn't done anything wrong. If that was indeed the case, then it appeared that the only person who couldn't be trusted in their relationship was her. She sifted her way through the digital pile as swiftly as she could: through job applications and trainer orders, all the way to exchanges with his university landlord. She typed in 'restraining order' and 'harassment' and 'Christmas party' in case she'd missed an electronic copy that the police had sent to him of his summons. She typed in 'mirrorissa92'. Nothing.

Annoyingly, his desktop wasn't any more illuminating; Michael hated clutter, throwing around the diagnosis 'OCD' in reference to himself as so many tidy people did, much to Ola's chagrin. Aside from a handful of work-related documents, there wasn't anything at all. She opened his browser and manoeuvred up to 'recently closed tabs' – it immediately opened up to three. One was a countdown video on beard oils fronted by him, which currently stood at 1,020,843 views. When she moved on to the next, a niggling at her conscience saw her freeze; he'd been browsing The White Company for hampers, her favourite scent, Seychelles, sat in his shopping basket. She sighed and clicked the next tab.

As the last tab filled the screen of Michael's laptop, Ola's initial reaction was bemusement. A clip-art icon of a teacup was perched at the top of the landing page, the words 'All Tea, No Crumpet', written in Brush Script. Naturally, she knew what All Tea was – she followed them on Instagram like everyone else. Like Celie, she claimed she despised it as a concept and was only across it for journalistic reasons. In truth, it was more to do with keeping up with the latest gossip on YouTube famous interracial 'swirl' couples and reality stars. She hadn't realised they had a chat site, however.

Scrolling down the page, she saw thread after thread dedicated to A–Z-list celebs, macro and micro influencers. With each second that passed, it became more apparent what kind of platform it was. Frankie had once done a feature on a similar site – 'Hot Cross Huns' – where critics (or were they fans?)

wrote scathing commentary on the middle-class mumfluencers they hate-followed. Many *Womxxxn* staff admitted reading it on the sly, snickering at the conclusions drawn on the lives of out-of-touch, white female bloggers only slightly posher than them.

Ola stopped at a conspiracy thread focused on *Womxxxn*'s former cover star Jada Smalls, titled 'JAD@ SM@LLZ – Rachel Dolezal 2.0???'. Her mouse lingered over the hyperlink but before she clicked, she noticed a post titled 'Th3 L1st' just below it.

Chest thudding, Ola braced herself and tapped.

'Pap1 D@nk$ still getting airplay' read the first comment from an account called @Na1ra_Bab£. 'I've @'ed BBC 1Xtra like 4 times already to complain.'

'One Times journalist is suing, apparently,' said an account with the username @Poison_Ivy_Carterrr. 'Claiming The List is libel. He started some crowdfund.'

The next comment made Ola's skin prickle. 'Journalists have been the worst in all of this. Between this guy and Micheal's anorexic accomplice, I'm done' @Na1ra_Bab£ had written back. 'Ol@ is a FRAUD. A full on 419 scammer, cosplaying as a feminist when her man is out here abusing women.'

'Hey, new here!' read the message from @just_preeing. 'I proper loved off Ol@'s writing. Used to follow CumTheFckThru and was so happy to see her shining at Womxxxn. But I am sooo disappointed in her, omds! She has to speak up.'

It was as if Ola had been physically slapped across both cheeks; the heat that radiated off her skin, the stinging sensation the words had left. It was hard for her to comprehend that they were talking about her.

@Poison_Ivy_Carterrr: She's been PIM! Yet when it was Gully TV, she was chatting bareee. Tbh there was always something off with her. She never used to post pics of M!cheal on Insta – I wonder if she knew? 😵😵😵

@Na1ra_Bab£: Of course she knew! Some couples do this shit together … Ian Brady and Myra Hindley. Fred and Rose West. It's common! I've listened to enough crime podcasts to know my shit lol

@cicely_bye_son: Michael went my girls sixth form and everyone knew he used to do women dirty. He boasted about being a dickhead on Caught Slippin all the time 😵 #TheNorthLondonRemembers

@Poison_Ivy_Carterrr: Ready to boycott Womxxxn idc. We need to holla them next

An account named @incog_negro posted a gif of Beyoncé dancing at her 2009 I AM world tour, captioned 'Somebody's getting fired.' 17 thumbs up, 9 LOLs.

Ola shut the laptop and tried to breathe, placing her finger over her left nostril and then right, repeating the breathing exercise she had learned from Fola. Be rational, Ola, she thought. You knew this kind of thing was being said. These people didn't know her. They thought her partner was an abuser and that she was protecting him. Was she being trolled? She felt like it. But in reality, they were not harassing her. In fact, just as they had with the title of the thread, they had intentionally obscured her name specifically so she wouldn't find it. When they remembered, they spelt it 'Ol@'; perhaps out of cowardice or a protection that went both ways? She couldn't help but feel a troll was still a troll whether it stayed beneath the bridge or not, but how different would it have been if the conversation had taken place on WhatsApp where she couldn't find it? She'd certainly been vicious about strangers in group chats. Was it merely an issue of etiquette?

Ola was second-guessing herself again, something she had become increasingly prone to. It felt like more than etiquette. She felt violated, humiliated. They wanted her to be 'accountable' but what did that mean? Losing her job? Being endlessly dragged? As she clicked back to the homepage, the urgent red dot of a notification cropped up in the bottom corner. It startled her – people sent private messages on this thing? Shakily, she opened it and let out an audible gasp that cut through the still air of the empty flat. A message from @mirrorissa92 expanded onto the page.

Michael had written to them first.

I know who you are. I know you put Michael Koranteng on The List. Why are you doing this?

The response turned the skin on her arms to braille.

Because I can, Mikey x

Ola staggered backwards out of her seat in dizzy horror, desperately trying to put as much distance as possible between her and what she'd just read on the screen. Michael knew who'd put him on The List. He knew who @mirrorissa92 was. It was an exchange she wouldn't have believed if she hadn't seen it with her own eyes. She couldn't quite take it in. But there it was, in his own words.

Through the haze of shock, only one thing was clear. Ola couldn't marry Michael. She had to call off the wedding. And she had to do it right now.

———————

Ahmaud the Uber driver flinched in the car mirror as Ola sprayed spit, shouting expletives in the seat behind him. Still no answer from Michael; Fola wasn't picking up either. Ola must have left more than eleven voicemails between them, and the deluge of messages that she'd sent had failed to deliver. She considered calling Ruth, even Celie at one point, but decided that if she didn't think this situation could get any worse, her friends would surely prove her wrong.

She frantically eyed the ETA on Ahmaud's Uber app from the backseat. Only nine minutes till they arrived, but the rehearsal started in four. Half an hour ago she had sprinted Bambi-legged to the gunmetal-grey Prius after much back and forth surrounding his location, deserting the order of ceremony booklets on Michael's kitchen counter. As Ahmaud pulled into the car park she practically fell out of the car, barrelling her way towards the venue. Even in her rush, the beauty of the church struck her as she got closer and the details that had once drawn her to it again came into focus. How exquisite the bright white steeple looked with the bright cloudless sky behind it, how majestic the cross-topped spire was above it. The high, ornate, moss-lined windows and manicured hedges that surrounded the approach. A grand archway formed the entrance, with a delicately carved, mildew-covered frieze depicting Jesus on a hillside, mid-Beatitude, encircled by disciples. Fola stood outside it taking a long, pronounced drag from a joint, moonstone adorning her forefinger, turquoise on her thumb.

'Forgot my CBD oil,' she said as Ola approached, blowing smoke over her shoulder. 'And Celie says to tell you she's sick, but she'll be here tomorrow for sure, so don't panic.'

She must be severely ill, Ola thought, or her absence was about something else. When they had been at school, Celie was so renowned for her punctuality and attendance that at the end of each term, she was given a laminated certificate to commemorate it. In Year 8, she went back to school a day after having her tonsils out because she didn't want to spoil her record.

'Why didn't you answer your fucking phone?' Ola said, panting with exhaustion.

'Hey!' Fola snapped back. 'Don't yell at me, okay? Pastor made us leave 'em in our bags because *some* people were on Snapchat during the opening prayer. Some people being Ruth.' Fola surveyed her sister, putting the blunt back to her lips. 'What's wrong? Ola, you're shaking?'

'I need to speak to Michael.'

'He's inside, with everyone else. Hey, is everything—'

'I need to speak to him, Fola. Right now.'

Her sister hurriedly took one last inhale then flicked the joint to the ground, stubbing it out with her Birkenstock. 'I'll go get him.'

She began to push at the front door, but Ola pulled her back.

'Is there somewhere we'd be able to talk? Alone? My mum can't know I'm here. No one can.'

'There's the office on the left where we dropped our bags. I can tell him to meet you there.' Fola gave another worried glance. 'Sis, what's happening? Is everything okay?'

'I'll explain, I promise,' Ola said. 'But I need to speak to Michael.'

A small wooden crucifix hung above the door of the church office, and Ola did her best to dodge the pile of handbags beneath it. Next to the window was a large maple desk with a clunky Dell computer and a tattered leather swivel chair behind it. The other two chairs in the room were plastic, low and red, the kind that she hadn't seen since primary school. She lowered herself onto one, her eye catching a wooden placard right at the back of the room, engraved with the words 'In All Things, Give Thanks'.

Michael was already flustered when he walked in a few minutes later.

'Yo, Fola said you needed me? You got the booklets?'

The legs of the red chair scraped as he pulled it towards him; he looked comically colossal when he sat. As he adjusted himself in the seat, he looked at her properly for the first time since he'd entered. He lifted his eyebrows.

'Rah. You look amazing.'

Ola absentmindedly touched the end of her ponytail with her fingertips. She'd thought the same about him; he looked skinnier and more tired than normal but it was impressive what a trim and a shape-up could do. His compliment took her aback for a moment. The rare conversation they had these days oscillated wildly between dispassionate information dumps via text or explosive emotional showdowns. They'd last seen each other just a week ago but it felt like it had been years, like he was someone from whom she grew more distant daily.

'We need to talk.'

Michael groaned, dropping his head.

'Every time you say that, some shit's happened. What is it now?'

A shaking began in Ola's right leg – it was her vibrating phone. She pulled it from her pocket. A message from Luke.

Call me ASAP

Not this, not now. Luke's timing couldn't have been worse than if he'd sent it when she was at the altar. If it was so urgent, she thought, maybe he'd text her whatever it was he had to say. With a silent prayer, she placed it on the desk in her eyeline and realised her hands were moist with perspiration. She wiped them against her T-shirt and swore she could feel the pounding of her heart against her chest as she did. If there was a God, the time to hear her was now and surely her odds were better in a church.

'Okay,' Ola said, shoring herself up. 'I'll just say it. Michael, I know you know who put you on The List. I saw the message you sent on All Tea to mirrorissa92.'

Horror crossed Michael's face, his mouth dropping open.

'Before you start – yes, I went through your laptop,' she continued. 'I needed to know that I'd done everything I could before tomorrow, left no stone unturned. And this is exactly why. So, I need you to tell me right now. Who—'

The tremors from the table stopped her in her tracks. Her phone was ringing now, Luke's name filling the screen. What had he found that he couldn't put in a message? She tried to speak over the noise.

'Who is mirrorissa92?' Ola pushed on. 'What did you do? Their response to your message – "Because I can, Mikey" – what does that mean? Are you being blackmailed? Tell me the truth, for once.'

Michael frowned. 'Mikey?'

'Just answer the question!'

Ola took a moment to try and regulate her tone. Before all of this they'd had their issues, no doubt, but they had never been one of those couples who couldn't get their point across without raised voices or below the belt jabs. They'd been better than that.

'Tell me, Michael.'

He turned his palms skyward. 'I – I don't get what you think you've found,' Michael sputtered. 'Yeah, I messaged some account on All Tea, to try and see if they knew anything about the allegations—'

'Some account? Or an account that just happens to be using the exact same name as whoever put you on The List?'

'What do you mean?' His confusion was genuine, she could see that. 'Who told you that?'

Ola adjusted the neckline of her top, ignoring the frantic vibrating of her iPhone as Luke's calls began anew.

'The woman who made The List told me,' she said. 'The journalist behind the Google Doc. Kiran put me in touch with her and we met up.'

His eyes widened at this. 'Wow. So you met the person who helped ruin my life and said nothing to me about it?' He let out a short, sharp laugh in shock.

'Yeah, well.' Ola pushed her shoulders back, defiant. 'It's not like she put you on there. And one of us had to do something, since you basically gave me no reassurance whatsoever. But I think you lying about not knowing who put you on there is the bigger issue right now.'

Michael's eyes travelled towards her mobile as it quivered and he watched until the call rang out. He looked back at Ola, eyes narrowed.

'Someone with the username mirrorissa92 has been harassing me in the *Tasted* comments section for weeks,' he said. 'Saying I'm abusive and shit. I saw them saying the same stuff on All Tea under the same name, so I tried to see if I could catch them out. I thought maybe they'd give something away or get shook about the police and stop. I didn't even know they replied.'

Now he said it, it sounded almost reasonable. Plausible, that he'd been provoking the account into providing some sort of intel, without knowing anything other than their username. Ola began blinking rapidly.

'B-but you never told me. Why didn't you tell me if there was nothing to hide?'

He couldn't answer before the phone started to vibrate noisily again. They both stared at it.

'Aren't you gonna answer that?' Michael said.

Ola looked up at him. 'We're in the middle of something quite important, don't you think?'

'It sounds like that's pretty important.'

Before she could stop him, Michael lunged at it. Once he'd pulled it towards him, her frenzied attempts to claw it back were in vain; he was already examining the unlocked screen. He turned it towards her.

'Who's Luke?'

Ola continued grasping as Michael held it to his chest. His eyes were ablaze. 'Give me my phone back!'

'Tell me who Luke is. Is he why you're constantly on your phone, why you're moving so shifty?'

The chair fell from under her as Ola strained towards the phone, stretching cat-like across the table. The terror and desperation in her eyes only seemed to encourage Michael to hold on to the phone more tightly.

'Are you cheating on me, Ola?'

She stopped to let out a sardonic laugh. '*Pardon?*'

'Are you cheating on me, yes or no?'

'Am *I* cheating on *you?*' Even in her panic she found the space to be offended. 'How dare you even ask me that?'

'I'm asking you one last time. Who is Luke?'

She made one last dive across the table, attempting to prise it from his fingers. Michael stood and started to scroll as she watched helplessly, heartbeat in her ears. His face remained unchanged as he continued tapping and reading, unblinking.

'Ola,' he said, still studying the phone. 'What is this?'

'Michael …'

'There's pictures of me at lunch. On my way back from work. What's going on?'

'If you let me—'

'Why does this guy have a copy of my DBS? Screenshots of my Instagram … Ola?'

She studied the table, unable to bear the thought of the devastation on his face.

'I can explain if you just let me.' Ola opened her mouth and then closed it, along with her eyes. 'Luke is a private investigator. I've been having you followed.'

Michael's brows drew together with gradual realisation, his face a picture of pure heartbreak.

'Followed?'

She nodded, head still down. 'I found him a month ago. I paid him to follow you, get access to stuff on public record. Things that are already out there, you know? And then to do background checks and stuff, because The List said there was a restraining order against you and … Anyway, he'd update me every day – nothing came back. But I had to keep it going,

Michael, so I could know for sure. I couldn't just leave it, could I? I didn't know what to do. I just didn't know what else to do.'

The chair creaked under Michael's weight as he sat back down very slowly and passed Ola back her iPhone. The church office was entirely still, though Ola could hear Pastor Oyedepo's voice from the hall, loudly proclaiming something to their friends and family. Michael hung his head.

'Why are we even doing this?' he said in time, audibly choked. 'We can't make this work, can we? I hate that you had to do this, man. I hate that I've brought us here. I don't want to lose you but you don't deserve this.' His shoulders began to shake as he tried to suppress his oncoming sobs.

The iPhone vibrated. Michael didn't move as Ola steadily drew it towards her and opened the text from Luke.

Tried calling you. Have to terminate your job from today. Been one month with no progress and I've had another gig come through. Gd luck with wedding

Ola knew the chances of him finding anything were slim, whether Michael was innocent or not. The majority of these kinds of offences simply went undocumented. It's not like *she* had any evidence regarding the times she'd been sexually harassed or intimidated. Did that mean her experience during the internship had never happened? Every time she'd been felt up at a club, a mere figment of her imagination? Make-believe, since she'd failed to file a police report against the faceless man who'd pressed his crotch against her on a packed train. Every wife threatened by their husband, every woman who had cried out for her date to stop and he'd continued; ghosts. Authenticated, time-stamped records had been improbable but at the very least she wanted to know if her assessment of this man, the only man she'd ever loved, was entirely wrong. If she knew him at all.

As Michael wiped at his damp eyes, Ola did the same. Throughout their relationship, she had only seen him cry one other time — when he received the news of his grandfather's death — and like then, his pain throbbed within her own chest. Her love for him couldn't simply vanish, despite her best efforts. It had taken a beating these past few weeks but it was bone deep, instinctual. For a moment, nothing else in the room mattered other than reminding him of that, as he had so many times before when she was hurting.

Ola placed her phone back on the table and enclosed her fiancé in her arms, resting her head on his shuddering shoulder. He placed an unsteady hand over hers and they held each other, weeping silent tears.

17

The Wedding

The bed at the Marriott remained untouched the entire night, as crisp and pristine as when Michael first checked in. The room was nice, though lacking in character; an identikit interior with an inoffensive beige and brown colourway. He hadn't slept a wink, not even napped – just paced the room and intermittently flopped into the armchair when it all became too much. Adjusting the boutonniere in his lapel, he glimpsed the minibar tucked underneath the widescreen television and felt an aching tug. His first morning in weeks without any alcohol was making him nervy, but he couldn't risk it. He was already so tired, running on pure adrenaline. That morning, he had shaved in a zombie-like state, tied his laces entirely on autopilot and was now clumsily trying to fasten his cufflinks – mother of pearl with a white gold trim.

Kwabz would be here soon to take the rings and accompany him to the church. He supposed the reason his breathing had slowed was because this moment simply didn't feel real. It felt more like he was watching himself apply oud behind his ears from outside the hotel window, looking in with mild interest. Every so often, he'd realise he was clenching his fists, digging his nails into the skin of his palms to ground himself. How could he focus on the rest of the day, the rest of his life, when he was still wrapping his head around yesterday?

The rehearsal had, somehow, gone ahead, tense and robotic from start to finish. Whether their friends and family had explained the atmosphere away as 'cold feet', he didn't know. The details were fuzzy around the edges, thanks to several drags on Fola's zoot. He had arrived at the church already bent out of shape by Lewis's proposal: a joint statement from them both, accompanied by £15k in separate donations to four different charities. He even planned to offer Ola an exclusive comment on the move for an article. The suggestion had set off a choir of screeching alarm bells and a flurry of red flags, flooding Michael's senses with a red-hot panic. His concern was for his own sake as much as Lewis's. Aside from feeling certain it would backfire, Michael feared it would bring more attention to him, too.

'I knew you'd be like this!' Lewis had scoffed at his scepticism. 'Bloody knew you'd shoot it down before I even got started! But 'ear me out; every other day someone's apologisin' for or denying something through some statement done on their iPhone, right? Then what happens? Few write-ups churned out by wankers at the *Sun*, the *Daily Mail*. But that's it. Then it's been responded to and everyone moves on to the next thing, don't they, like the fackin' pack of vultures they are. When you leave it, it just grows and grows.'

It was the only way, Lewis said, to take back control of the narrative. 'I'll make the donations, obviously – don't worry about all that,' Lewis went on. 'Bit of positive PR can't hurt, after all of the shit that's being said about us. Nice bit of tax relief, too!'

A statement was something Michael had briefly considered himself. And although his boys unanimously agreeing on something usually meant he should do the opposite, for once he was sure they were right that it was a bad idea. When he and Lewis parted ways, he hoped Lewis would sober up and see the flaws in his plan more clearly. Their conversation had unnerved him; Michael couldn't pretend that for Lewis Hale, of all people, coming out would be straightforward, but there was nothing to stop it happening at the hands of Cris's sister anyway. He had thought that would be all the excitement for the day, but then Ola had finally arrived at the rehearsal. As soon as Michael entered that church office, she was at him without warning. All guns blazing, with bombshell after bombshell, any of which would have been the headline on a normal day. Going through his computer, meeting with the person behind The List and not telling him – he was trying to process it all. Then she revealed she'd also had him tailed by a private investigator. You couldn't make it up; it was like something off *Jeremy Kyle*, or out of those trashy women's magazines. He should have felt relieved she hadn't found out about Jackie, but in all honesty, he wished she had.

Michael couldn't find solace on the high horse that usually comes with being wronged; yes, he felt betrayed, but he also knew she'd had no other choice. Now, he was doubly ashamed, since Ola had at least admitted to her wrongs. Yesterday was the closest he'd ever come to doing so himself. At one point, she'd asked him point-blank why he hadn't told her about @mirror-issa92. The moment to come clean had been right there, his for the taking. Would he have confessed if the call from the PI hadn't intervened? Either way, the moment had passed and the truth was left unsaid.

That was why he was stood in a tux today, looking through his own reflection. Last night, Michael and Ola had not so much reconciled as come to an unspoken decision. After the revelations and subsequent tears, he had asked her outright what she wanted to do. She'd sniffled in silence for a while, head still resting lightly on his shoulder. Then she'd eventually released her arms from around him and reached for the iPhone on the table.

'We should get to the rehearsal,' she'd said, looking into its camera to check her face for post-crying puffiness. She shook herself as she stood, took a long, deep breath and nodded, seemingly satisfied with her composure. Her expression was calm, resolved, like a statesman. 'Let's go.'

And that had been that. It had taken him by surprise but Michael didn't push for further clarity. She'd said it without saying it; they were getting married. They were going to try to move forwards, despite it all: the lies that had been exposed and those that hadn't, the mutually shared paranoia and distrust. But he hadn't come to terms with everything that had come out yesterday, such as whether it had been worse that the 'other man' in question had been a private investigator. Luke hadn't even been last night's biggest revelation. What had Michael reeling was the response to his message, which he hadn't known about until yesterday.

Because I can, Mikey x

Mikey. There it was. No further questions, no debate. It had to be her. @Mirrorissa92 was Jackie. No one else called him that cloying, cringe-worthy nickname except her. She was taunting him. That was probably why his name had been spelt wrong on The List in the first place – Jackie hardly ever referred to him as Michael. Would that hold up as evidence? In court, with the police? Surely this online harassment would warrant some sort of investigation, an attempt to track down the IP address. Knowing his luck, it probably wouldn't be enough.

There'd been times through this ordeal that he'd wished he would bump into her somewhere, so he could confront her in person. Her behaviour made so little sense to him. Once upon a time, Jackie had seemed to want him no matter what. He was her Ola; someone she wanted to be with whatever it took. How could she do this to him? And where would she end this? There was nothing stopping her messaging Ola one day with the truth about what had gone on between them. This could hang over him for the rest of their lives. He would forever worry about what might set Jackie off: the wedding pictures? Their first child? His and Ola's relationship was on borrowed time, either way, he knew that. But he couldn't help but hope that if he made up for it, proved himself in the meantime, then they might be able to at least start with a clean slate. That would give them a slim chance of happiness, for a while.

A knock on the door brought him back into the room. Kwabz shuffled inside, locs pulled back into a low pony and wearing a colourful, geometric-patterned kente cloth draped around the shoulders of his tux. He peered over his aviators. 'It's the man of the hour,' he said, a hint of trepidation in his voice. 'All good, yeah?'

'All good.'

'Yeah?' He placed a hand on Michael's shoulder and moved it gently to and fro in a reassuring pat. 'You ready?'

Michael rubbed his mouth against the back of his hand. 'As

I'll ever be, man.' He retrieved a small navy box from his pocket and passed it to Kwabz.

His best man took it carefully. 'And you got everything? Wallet, phone?'

Michael patted down his pockets and nodded. They waited a moment, exchanging something unspoken in their look, at which Kwabz pulled him into a one-armed hug.

'All right, bro,' he said, rubbing his hands together as he stepped back. 'Let's do this.'

Some time ago, an internet wormhole had led to Michael reading about phobias and he briefly became interested in looking up the most niche ones on Wikipedia. One that had stuck with him was ecclesiophobia, the fear of churches, which might sound strange to some but had made sense to him. Today was no different: the chapel was undeniably magnificent, but imposing in its grandeur. There was something inherently damning about the columns and came glasswork windows that stood twenty feet tall, letting sunlight through in psychedelic slices. The creaking oak of the choir pews. All of it, solemn. Sobering.

He could hear the tuneless warbling of guests inside from the foyer and see a sea of colours, comprised of African clothing. A rainbow of geles, ankara prints and adinkra-adorned outfits. A smattering of pink aso-ebi uniforms, striped smocks made of gonja cloth. It was as though everyone he'd ever met was packed into the church; Aunty Abena had flown in for the occasion, sat towards the back with his cousin Gifty. He could see Seun's sometimes-partner Rachel on the right, fussing with her fascinator. Then suddenly, the hymn quieted, the crowd began to murmur, and 'Ave Maria' began to play.

As he started his uneasy walk down the aisle, a galaxy of phone lights greeted him from the church pews. He felt insecure; about his weight loss, about the candids that would populate #TheKorantengs19, a wedding hashtag Ruth and Celie had insisted on. As he got closer to the altar, he was comforted by the sight of his grandmother, his mother and father sat by her – the women both in fishtail dresses made of kente, his father in a kente toga that went across one shoulder and around his body. All wore colourful beads about their necks and wrists.

Michael reached the front of the church, where Pastor Oyedepo (looking more like an accountant, in his shiny grey suit) acknowledged him with a nod. His white hair was bright against his dark skin, and his heavily lined face became even more so as it crumpled with solemnity. Michael looked back as the bridesmaids and groomsmen entered next, Celie, Ruth and Fola in differently shaped dresses in the same shade of emerald. Amani, Seun and Kwabz, like bodyguards with black shades perched on their heads. Celie was arm in arm with Amani and looking less than thrilled about it. Fola was linking arms with Seun, every bit the odd couple. And Ruth was using one hand to tug at the front of her dress and the other to grip the bicep of a smug-looking Kwabz. Michael laughed to himself, certain Kwabz would be tensing, and watched as they all took their places. There was a lull, as the room waited for the main event. Then Ola's mother turned the corner.

She sauntered in, hips swinging in an intricately beaded, blush-coloured dress with a matching bag and heels. The Ipele scarf on her left shoulder and gele tied around her head were bedazzled and embroidered. Smiling serenely, she escorted her daughter towards the altar. Ola was walking gracefully, white silk gown grazing the floor, with a long veil attached to a diamante tiara. With each step forward she took, he became certain this was the most beautiful she'd ever looked. Even from behind the lace of her veil, he could see her dark, heavy lashes and the way the highlighter seemed to make her skin sparkle. Her ponytail undulated as she approached and he noticed her nose ring had been swapped out for a tiny diamond stud. Michael rubbed his eye with his sleeve, blinking back the tears triggered by over-whelming emotion. His love for her cut through the distress and anxiety like a knife.

When they got to him, her mother gently took Ola's right hand and placed it in his left. Their palms felt clammy in each other's grasp. Celie avoided Michael's gaze as she teetered towards the bride, arms outstretched and Ola passed the bouquet to her. Ola faced him now, holding both his hands and in that moment, it was as if no one else were in the room but them. Gingerly, he lifted the veil, revealing gleaming eyes.

Pastor Oyedepo cleared his throat. 'Hallelujah,' he began, his Lagosian accent strong. 'We stand together in the presence of our heavenly father, to witness and celebrate the marriage of these his two children, Olaide and Michael. Today, we share their joy and ask for the Lord our God to bestow his everlasting blessings and mercies unto them. Oh, Father God, what you have joined together, let no man put asunder.' He gestured to the congregation. 'Can we please stand to our feet, as we commit today's ceremony into His hands.'

The guests slowly stood, a low hum through the church. Pastor Oyedepo shut his eyes tightly and raised a theatrical hand to the sky.

'Father Almighty,' he said, spraying flecks of spit. 'In your everlasting mercy, I pray you will continue to make your face to shine upon this couple. Lord, as we have started, start with us. At the end of this union of your faithful servants, we will give you praise and glory. Now: let us pray.'

Michael had thought his speech *had* been the prayer, but there was plenty more where that came from. There was the grunting and trilling of tongues. Then, a blessing that sounded like one of his mother's prayerful birthday messages, peppered with thinly disguised pleas for grandkids masked in words like 'fruitfulness' and 'bountiful' and 'multiply'. He wondered what a largely agnostic Ola was making of it all. Turning his head towards her, he saw she was looking at him, her mouth twitching a little. He couldn't tell if she was trying not to laugh or cry.

'In the name of Jesus Christ, Amen,' Pastor Oyedepo eventually concluded, mopping sweat from his brow after a particularly fitful benediction.

'And now, for a short reading from 1 Corinthians 13: 4–8 from Michael's oldest friend and groomsman, Amani Best.'

Attention turned towards his friend who swaggered into the spot next to where the pastor stood, like he was accepting an award. Affection for him pierced through Michael's anxious thoughts. Amani had maintained the same scampish charm since school, the kid in class that made you laugh at the most inappropriate times. He gave a small introductory cough.

'Love is patient, love is kind,' he started. Michael could feel Ola stirring in front of him.

'It does not envy, it does not boast, it is not proud. It does not dishonour others, it is not self-seeking, it is not easily angered, it keeps no record of wrongs. Love does not delight in evil but rejoices with the truth.' Michael too began to feel restless, stood in front of the murmuring agreement of the crowd. God's taking the piss, he thought. It reminded him that the other thing he hated about churches was their ability to make him feel exposed, like his secrets, his soul was being displayed on a plinth for all to see.

'It always protects, always trusts, always hopes, always perseveres.'

Amani gave a small but grand bow, beaming benevolently across the guests in the pews. He made his way back into position and Pastor Oyedepo stepped forward.

'Everybody say Amen?'

'Amen,' the crowd chanted in unison.

A few torturous moments passed and then his lips parted once more.

'*Oya* – the moment we've been waiting for.' Pastor Oyedepo cocked his head towards him. 'Michael, do you take Olaide Deborah Adebimpe Olajide to be your lawful wedded wife? Do you promise to love her, comfort her, honour and keep her for better or worse, for richer or poorer, in sickness and health, and forsaking all others, for as long as you both shall live?'

Whatever it took, whatever they faced: better or worse, richer or poorer, in sickness, in health, in anything else. During their three years together, he had faltered in forsaking all others but for as long as he lived, however long that may be, he wanted to love, comfort, honour, keep her. Through it all, there had only ever been one answer. He ran his thumb along hers.

'I do.'

Pastor Oyedepo nodded with a broad smile and turned his attention to a trembling Ola. The bride, a picture of pure disorientation, her eyes frantic. The shine of her make-up now had the added sheen of perspiration. She stared down the pastor as Michael attempted pleading eye contact with her one last time. He was becoming so visibly stressed that he felt sure the congregation couldn't possibly be reading his demeanour as simple wedding nerves. He gripped her hands tighter in silent prayer.

'And Olaide,' Pastor Oyedepo said. 'Do you take Michael Kweku Koranteng to be your lawful wedded husband?'

18

The Wedding

Taking caution not to unravel her gele, Ola gently rested her forehead against the car window as they drove away from the church. It felt cool against her temple; the car's lavish red leather interior was making the hot day unbearable. A steely silence sat with them in the backseat as she wondered what their chauffeur made of it all. Her, roasting in a pink, rhinestoned iro and buba and Ipele, cooling herself with an ostrich feather fan. Michael, every inch the African prince in an abeti aja hat and agbada in the same colour. Their bodies turned away from each other, as they stared out at their respective passing views.

Hours earlier, she'd dared to feel optimistic. She and Michael had made it through the rehearsal the night before with no questions asked by anyone other than Fola, who kept her promise to withhold judgement when Ola tearfully recounted what had happened. The laptop snooping. The cheating allegations. Michael's agonised face when Ola revealed hiring Luke. The crushing remorse she'd felt watching him weep in that church office was difficult to withstand. When he'd looked up at her and asked 'What do you want to do?', she knew he meant 'about our future'. But she hadn't known the answer to a question as sweeping as that. In that moment, all they could manage was to carry on with the rehearsal as planned. The faff of going into the church, gathering their nearest and dearest only to tell them they were in two minds about getting married was too much drama for an already eventful day. Besides, how could Ola possibly be the one to call things off, when it was her who'd so royally fucked up? Luke had only succeeded in revealing Ola's own dishonesty in her hiring of him. Michael seemed to understand her reasoning, but it didn't stop her feeling terrible. Especially since her trump card, the message from @mirrorissa92, didn't prove anything either. It only made things less clear. In hindsight it read as mocking, but Ola still couldn't say what the motivation was. Something wasn't right. Regardless, she'd snuck around and lied to Michael for weeks, proving nothing in the process.

Ola had checked in to the nearby Hilton hotel the same evening, still uncertain of what she should do – what she *would* do – the next day. Before bed, she absentmindedly rubbed the azurite stone Fola had slipped into her hand as her 'something blue' at the rehearsal. Her shoes, a pair of white Manolo Blahniks from a sustainable fashion rental app were her 'something borrowed', and the vintage Rolls-Royce they would be sweltering in on their way to the reception, her 'something old'. Everything else they'd broken the bank to buy constituted the 'something new', she had decided. Ola lay down on the plush bed, weighing up these superstitious wedding preparations as she drifted off, hoping they might help her in some way. She needed all the luck she could get.

That morning she found herself enjoying something resembling what she'd hoped her wedding day would be like. The hamper Michael ordered arrived, sans a note (what was there to say?), and she sprayed the Seychelles home spray all around the hotel room. As Ruth touched up the make-up the MUA had just finished on Ola, she enjoyed a glass of prosecco or three with her sister and best friends. They'd giggled like schoolgirls in their matching silk dressing gowns, the room a flurry of toiletries and misquoted song lyrics shouted at the top of their lungs. Fola, attempting to look as slick and wet as possible, applying lipgloss and baby-oiling her appendages. Ruth, blaring her 'AFROPOP BOPS' playlist on Spotify while Celie eye-rolled at each extended 'Ayyyyyyyy' Ruth made at the start of her 'favourite song' (always whatever was playing).

'I can't wait for the reception,' Ruth said, bobbing rhythmically to 'Options' by NSG. 'I need to whine the night away on somebody's son. These apps ain't it – I'm tired of saving niggas in my phone with the surname "Tinder", like the world's most toxic family tree! You don't know how lucky you are to be leaving the jungle, Ola.' She gave a lopsided grin. 'Did you see my baby daddy at rehearsal? He's been hitting gym.'

'Kwabz?' Ola asked, the corners of her mouth turning upwards.

Ruth nodded. 'I'm trying to jump on the Ghanaian wave like you.'

'I thought he was too short for you?'

'Can't lie: body's making up for it. Plus, what am I supposed to do, since all the height in Ghana went to Michael?'

'Is that why you're a walking pair of titties today?' Fola gestured at her breasts with cupped hands. Under the dressing gown, Ruth's chest was heaving in her bridesmaid's dress, a green ruched bodycon without straps. It was hard not to look.

'Not even!' she huffed, adjusting the front. 'The girls are out because of the high street's little titty agenda. Everything backless, strapless, undercut, plunge. Keyhole at the front, criss-cross at the back *and* front or mesh ... even the Pretty Little Thing plus-size section don't have shit that doesn't expect you to go bra free. And not all of us can, *Fola*,' she said, eyeing her small bosom. 'And *Ola*.'

Ola giggled as she took another sip from her flute glass.

'How's that scripture go again, Celie?' Fola smirked in her direction. '"The small-breasted shall inherit the earth", or whatever Psalms said.'

They all cackled. The hotel room then began shaking with the bassline of 'Sweet Like Puff Puff' by Papi Danks, Ruth squealing with delight at the inaugural beat drops.

'Ayyyyyyy!' She took a sip of prosecco through her straw, so her lipstick didn't smudge. 'This is my fucking *song*!'

Celie had twisted out her hair into large springy coils for the occasion but abruptly stopped fluffing her afro. Her reflection froze in the dressing-table mirror.

'Why are we listening to this?'

'Shhhh, my other baby daddy's verse is coming!' Ruth said, turning up the volume for Danks. 'Oi, didn't you go same college as him?'

'Sunday school,' Celie corrected. 'I don't know why you think it's okay to put this on? He was on The List and accused of really serious stuff.'

'Er, didn't we all agree that it's innocent until proven guilty?' Ruth had stopped dancing now and her words lingered in the air. Ola felt herself shrink, bubble well and truly burst. She couldn't exactly intervene with Ruth, could she?

Celie twitched. 'That's what *you* guys decided. Not me. Look, I've been meaning to say, Ola.' She spun around to face her. 'I know it's your big day. But I hope you don't expect too much from me when it comes to Michael. Like, I'm not going to be chatting to him or anything.'

'Can we not do this?' Ola groaned. 'Right now?' She'd suspected that her maid of honour hadn't missed yesterday's rehearsal because she was sick and this confirmed it. It was the wedding that was turning her stomach.

Celie turned back to the mirror and continued fussing with her curls. The upbeat music was still blaring but it was killing the mood and Ola had gone slightly overboard with the room spray, making the space feel claustrophobic. 'I'm just saying,' Celie said. 'I'm happy to celebrate you, Ola, but I'm not going to talk to him.'

'Ladies,' Fola said, sharply. 'Good vibes only today, okay? Don't make me get the sage.'

'Exactly,' Ruth said into her hand mirror. 'Let's leave the mess for one day, abeg.'

Celie glowered. 'I'm not being funny, Ruth, but I wasn't talking to you?'

'Okay,' Ruth said, lowering her mirror and sitting up. 'But I'm talking to *you*, Celie, so what now?'

This was how it had been since school: Ruth vs Celie, sometimes Ruth vs Ola, but rarely Ola vs Celie, her best friend since Year 7. The basis of their grouping at St Augustine's girls' school alongside half a dozen others had simply started out as 'The Africans'. Though the two Nigerians would unite against Mozambican Celie during playful, playground diaspora wars, Ruth was the odd one out in their splinter group. Usually defending some problematic viewpoint or person. But these days, the 'problematic person' Ruth was batting for was almost exclusively Ola.

Ola felt her husband's hand on her knee.

'You all right?'

She turned to him in the backseat of the car and gave an insipid smile. The ceremony that morning had been a fever dream starring almost every family member, friend and acquaintance she had. It had been so surreal that when walking down the aisle, all she could think was that this must be the most glamorous plank walk in history. Clinging to her elated mother's arm, Ola felt like a child. She tried not to think of her father, knowing it would set her off crying. As if her mother sensed this, she'd squeezed her arm tightly just in time to stop Ola's eyes brimming over. Ola was glad to have her by her side, even with their differences. They were so unalike, in temperament and appearance. Her mother's shapeliness was accentuated by her pink peplum dress and the congregation murmured about the beauty of both of them when they entered the church. Ola had more of a striking, catwalk appeal compared to her mother's commercial catalogue good looks and her pleasant, heart-shaped face. She was quietly spoken and meek, probably even more so when she had first met Ola's older, worldly father as a naive university graduate. It was clearly a bittersweet moment for her mum, walking her daughter down the aisle, but she looked prouder of her than Ola had ever seen. Her smile wider than when Ola had got into uni, graduated or landed her job at *Womxxxn*. Walking next to her mother, the mix of emotions flowing through Ola was overwhelming. No one could have known how much willpower it took to put one foot in front of the other, to not crumble under the glare of camera phones as the crowd turned into paparazzi. She kept it together, despite the goading from God. He had trolled her, Amani's Bible reading stopping just short of a personal attack: 'Love always trusts.'

Until Pastor Oyedepo asked if 'she took Michael Kweku Koranteng to be her lawful wedded husband', Ola hadn't known what she was going to do. Naively, she thought she might draw strength from Michael when they eventually locked eyes at the altar, but he looked equally queasy. Still: he said 'I do.' She couldn't truly say what she had planned when, after what felt like a life-time, 'I do' fell from her lips too. Despite how life-altering those two short words were, saying yes felt less like blowing up her world than the opposite. The rest of the ceremony was over in a blink of an eye, but the day itself just beginning.

Ola wasn't sure what she thought would change afterwards. Whether she hoped that 'I do' were the magic words that would cause some curse to break or protective spell to activate. But when the confetti fell around her on the steps of the church, she felt the same as before. Except now, she might be 'married to a monster', the bride of Frankenstein. And yet, no one in the wedding party, bar Celie, seemed to mind. They were all suspended in the past, celebrating a long-gone version of her and Michael. People often said things like 'the internet isn't real life' and within the church's walls it seemed like it wasn't. She felt like she was a messenger from the future, the only one with any real understanding of what had been and what was coming.

Everyone else was caught up in the theatre of it all, the costumes and pomp that came with African weddings. Outside the church, guests gathered on the grass in the heat, catching up and waiting for an opportunity to take pictures with the newly-weds. Her bridesmaids were more organised than ever, as the photographer directed them to hold their bouquets at the same height. The groomsmen clasped their hands at their backs in unison. Ola's and Michael's mothers held each other for the camera, looking pleased with themselves. Ola should have revelled in everything being picture perfect, before the day and her make-up began to smudge and blur. But the shoot was excruciating, Michael's hands hovering at her sides while they posed, as if he was afraid of breaking her.

The assembled wedding party either didn't catch the discomfort or ignored it. And she should probably do the same. It's done now, she thought. She'd made her bed and had to lie in it; complaining wasn't about to improve things.

Michael gave her knee another light tap in the backseat of the car, in response to her inscrutable expression. She closed her hand over his.

'I'm fine, sorry,' she said, stroking the stone in her purse with the other. It was supposed to help with intuition, but she just needed something to hold on to.

Ola tried to avoid spiralling by reminding herself of the facts. She had married the love of her life. There was no evidence he'd done anything wrong. She was starting a new chapter. She was going to try to start that chapter as she meant to go on.

———————

They pulled up to the reception venue – a stately neo-Palladian villa in a several acres park in Bromley – and Ola could see it was already pushing its 400-person capacity, guests sprawling from the grand hall into the marquee. It was breathtaking; twinkling tendrils of lights dripped like liquid from the ceiling. Pink, white and gold balloon arches crowded corners and flower arrangements of peonies, white roses and baby's breath lined the space. Well-wishers pouted in front of a large flower wall emblazoned with #TheKorantengs19 in looping gold letters, while a projector magnified images from the hashtag onto a huge screen in real time. Inside the entrance of the marquee, Ola could spy the cake: a mammoth six-tiered salted caramel sponge with sugar lace and edible pink foliate bursting from each rung.

'Wowww,' she heard Michael say. 'The decorators went in.'

Ola nodded; she was dumbfounded by how well it had all come together. Her heart swelled at the thought of her maid of honour and chief bridesmaid, how much effort they'd put in to helping her sort it all out. They weren't there when she and Michael entered the hallway; only the groomsmen stood in a tight circle.

'Perfect timing,' Kwabz said, as they approached. He was now in a white kaftan, his locs sticking out of a pink kufi hat.

'Your parents just did their entrance – I'll get the girls and tell David you're ready.'

He jogged into the throng and Seun took his place, slapping Michael on the back.

'Big Mike! Congratulations again, brudda! Man nearly shed a tear in the church, you know.'

'Yeah well, I'm ready for yours, bro,' Michael said, grinning. 'Soon come.'

Seun backed away. 'Nah, I was about to start crying from stress, fam! I know Rachel was preeing and getting ideas.'

Amani sidled over to Ola and placed his arm around her shoulders.

'Mrs Koranteng! Is that you, yeah?'

She hoped her smile was convincing. Ola wasn't a huge fan of Michael's friends, more because of what they represented as a unit rather than as individuals. Kwabz seemed sensible enough, but she couldn't un-hear the things Amani and Seun had said on their podcast. They had seemed more excited for Michael's stag do than he had, originally wanting to travel to Miami 'on a madting'. In the end they spent the weekend club-hopping in

Birmingham, but she still struggled to sleep that night worrying about what Michael was doing.

'How does it feel, finally being wifey? Best day of your life?'

She wished everyone would stop asking her that.

'Sure.'

From the hall, a succession of 'Amen's marked the end of the opening prayer. As the crowd quietened, Kwabz came back to the group, followed by the bridesmaids who were now in matching pink aso-ebi dresses and waving at her excitedly.

'It's starting,' he mouthed.

The voice of David Aidoo filled the hall, comedian, former Choice FM presenter and for the right price, wedding emcee. These days, he was best known for viral skits on Instagram, donning wigs and puffa jackets as he impersonated a number of inner-city stereotypes: roadmen, south London girls, 'facety' women working the tills at Jamaican pattie shops.

David shouted something incoherent, sparking applause, and then 'Able God' by Chinko Ekun began to play. On cue, Ola and Michael's friends dance-walked into the hall in their procession pairs, to the delighted whoops of the wedding guests waiting to greet them. Seun and Amani bobbed and weaved with their arms outstretched, gun-fingers raised, sunglasses on. Kwabz meanwhile kept his own pair dangling from the neck of his kaftan, eyes fixed on Ruth's impressive hip isolation. Celie's coy two-step looked conservative next to Fola's frenetic twerking.

'Give it to dem!' David could be heard ad-libbing, every other word punctuated with an 'eii' of encouragement. 'The friends of the bride and groom, ladies and gentlemen,' he said into the mic once they had taken their seats, gesturing to the DJ to fade the music. The room came to a standstill.

'Now, those of you who are not standing, chale abeg you stand to your feet.' He was putting on a Ghanaian accent as he said this, talking with the same affectation he did in his popular 'African parents' sketch. 'Presenting the newest couple of 2019, Black excellence squared – Mr and Mrs Koranteng!'

The DJ fiddled with his laptop and soon came the opening chords of 'Yori Yori'. Ola grew rigid: she was back up the aisle again, round two of her death march. Helplessly, she looked at Michael, who gave her shoulder a consoling rub and motioned them towards the hall.

He led and Ola walked behind him, swaying slightly, the noise and camera flashes drowning out her thoughts.

'Oya, shake body!' David demanded from somewhere in front of them, as the party-goers began to close in. She was struggling in her heavy garment, so hitched her iro up to her thighs, freeing her knees to dip lower. It had been a while since she'd done this; at Afro Bar and Brunch for her hen do, a blur of inflatable palm trees, cut-off shorts and sips from bottomless red cups. Ola had tried to keep up with Ruth, who whined till her knees clicked with guys who bought them all drinks on the promise of a faked number. She couldn't contain her smile as she watched her friend push up against Kwabz.

A hand grasped hers and Ola was swung backward. Now she was before Michael, rolling her hips against his like she used to when they went raving. They hadn't been this close in a long time.

'Eii! Love is sweet oo,' David cried. 'See the way they're dancing? They wan make baby before the honeymoon, maame close your eyes!'

The crowd erupted. At that moment, an aunty in aso-ebi shimmied towards them with her open purse and placed a crumpled ten pound note against Ola's dripping forehead. She continued to place money wherever it would stick; cheeks, collarbone, chest. Another followed suit, holding red and purple money to Michael's glistening neck. The 'spraying' continued until money blanketed the floor, Fola and Seun crouching at their ankles to gather notes being trampled by dancing feet.

At long last 'Yori Yori' stopped and 'Assurance' by Davido began, signalling the end of their processional entrance and the beginning of a free for all on the dance floor.

'I wanna see everybody on their feet oo,' David barked, gesticulating to the few remaining seated guests for good measure. The aunty from before wrenched Ola towards her with surprising strength.

'Olaide! How far? You remember me? Your Aunty Korede?'

'Yes, Aunty,' Ola lied, dipping into a curtsey.

'Ehen! Last time I saw you, you were in pushchair!' Aunty Korede called over her shoulder into the crowd. 'Emmanuel! Shebi you remember your cousin Olaide? Come and greet her! Kai!' she said, turning back to her. 'See how you favour your father!'

Ola was pulled into cuddles from cousins she hadn't seen since primary school and cornered for congratulations from friends she hadn't seen since sixth form. She was asked about her pregnancy timeline by elders she'd never met and accosted by complete strangers who had flown in for the occasion. They were all brandishing branded party favours with her and Michael's faces on them: fans, tupperware, clocks, power banks, and Ola felt surrounded. Each felt like a Wanted poster; it was impossible to hide at your own wedding.

She thought she'd never escape, until David announced the buffet was open, and the crowd dispersed with clacking heels and screeching chairs. Soon, three quarters of the guest list were queuing, standing next to trays teeming with kelewele and bofrot, jollof and plantain, 'swallow' accompanied by thick, spicy soups.

Her moist skin cooled as she stepped out from the hall, into the brisk air of the marquee. By its opening, Fola and Ruth stood gossiping; Ruth with a drink in each hand, Fola swaying to the sounds of a Sarkodie song.

'Okayyyy, African queen,' Ruth greeted her. 'That's my best friend, that's my best friend!'

Fola ran her fingers along Ola's sleeve, admiring the lace's fine bead embellishments. 'Did I tell you how incredible you look? God is a black woman for real!'

'You did, about fifty-eight times,' Ola simpered. 'And I'm not complaining!'

Ruth cheersed the air with the glass in her left hand. 'I'm gassed for the next look. Can't wait to see you doing up, *ohemaa!*'

'Right?' Fola agreed. 'When you blessing us with the grand finale fit?'

The last outfit was her favourite: a kente gown made of handwoven silk with a traditional headdress, Michael in a matching toga. They'd opted for traditional outfits, instead of a traditional wedding. Two weddings, as was common with second generation Ghanaians and Nigerians, meant more planning, more money they didn't have. Plus she'd never liked the idea of a dowry, as was custom in traditional ceremonies – even a symbolic one. Taking his surname had already felt traitorous enough.

'Well, I've not been in this half an hour,' Ola said, gesturing at her clothes. 'But soon, if it means I can hide out in the back for a bit.'

Ruth wordlessly passed her the glass from her right hand and Ola downed it in one greedy gulp.

'Thanks. I needed that. Don't know how much longer I can talk about children I don't have with aunties I don't know.'

Fola shook her head. 'They stay so pressed about everyone's pussies but their own!'

'I thought there would at least be a grace period, now you've "found huzzband",' Ruth said, sounding like something out of a David Aidoo skit. 'But you're enjoying, yeah? You're happy? Cos this is a fucking vibe!'

'You and Celie know how to throw a party,' Ola said, eyes scanning the marquee. 'Oi, do you know where she is?'

'Celie? Nah, not even. Probably at an extracurricular Bible study with pastor.'

Ola laughed but reached for her phone regardless and tapped Celie's name into WhatsApp.

Yo where you at?

She and Celie had spoken less and less since the news of The List. Ola knew this was partly her fault, since she'd stopped responding to messages from almost everyone. But as the wedding drew nearer, Celie had stopped checking in. She had updated Ola regarding wedding admin, but she had been distant. Celie was busy, it was true; her publisher had just won a hotly contested auction for *Dot dot dot*, an anthology of essays featuring prominent writers with freckles ('Welcome to diversity in publishing,' she'd scoffed in their group chat). But today was Ola's wedding day and she'd hardly seen her maid of honour outside of the ceremony. As she placed her phone back in her purse, Ola felt the subtle shift in the atmosphere amongst her girls before she saw its cause. Kwabz had made his way over, picking at a plate of fried rice with a side of grilled fish. He pulled Ola into a hug.

'Mrs Michael! Congrats!'

Ruth quickly hoisted up the sides of her dress and patted down the top of her wig as if putting out a small fire. He turned to her.

'*Fine gehl*,' he said, affecting a Nigerian accent. She bit back a smile.

'Hello, Kwabena.' Ruth sounded bored, despite having spent much of the morning describing in needlessly graphic detail what she planned to do to him and for how long.

'I like the dress,' Kwabz said, eyeing her for slightly too long and making Fola and Ola physically cringe in the process. Ruth and Kwabz's focus on one another was so intense, however, it was clear they hadn't noticed. 'Trad suits you, you know.'

Ruth raised an immaculately threaded eyebrow, but her grin had already escaped. 'I prefer you with your hair down,' she said, flicking hers over her shoulder.

'That's all you've got for me?' Kwabz turned back to Ola, his hands placed theatrically over his chest as if Ruth's words had physically wounded him. 'See how wicked you Nigerian babes are? I swear down, this is the year I quit you lot.'

Fola's head yo-yoed back and forth between them, like she was watching a tennis match. 'They always like this?' she asked her sister.

Ola nodded. This dance would likely conclude in one of their beds, as usual.

Ruth was readying herself for her retort when suddenly she jerked her head towards the back of the marquee.

'Wait — who's the *oyinbo*? She looks lost.'

Ola followed her sightline over to an agitated brunette by the gift table, convinced she must be seeing things. She craned her neck forward as she peered through the heaving wedding crowd, trying to get a better look. There hadn't been time for breakfast, so she wagered it might be a mirage on account of her wooziness.

'Is — is that *Frankie*?'

Sure enough, there she was, nursing a prosecco next to a deeply disgruntled-looking Kiran, eyes darting around in confusion. Frankie's brows had shot the furthest up her face — so usually limited in expression — Ola had ever seen. She was impossible to miss among a sea of brown faces, in a short blazer dress showing off a lean athleticism crafted by years of pilates and intermittent veganism.

'Who?' Ruth squinted. 'Wait, wait, wait: is that your *boss*? The Waitrose warrior herself? Nahhhh, I NEED to meet the white woman that's had you on ropes for three years!'

Just when it had looked like she might make it through today relatively unscathed. What could be worse than Frankie at her wedding? As Ola made her way, heavy-footed, towards her, Kiran mouthed apologies behind their boss's head.

'Ola!' Frankie said, standing to hug her. They'd never been this close; she could smell the prosecco mingling with tobacco on her breath.

'Don't you look *fabulous*? Hope you don't mind me doing a bit of wedding crashing, but Kiran and I were brainstorming about the next issue today. She told me she was off to your reception afterwards and, well, I just *had* to give my best wishes in person!'

'I did say it was invite only,' Kiran murmured, facing Ola.

Frankie wasn't paying attention, examining the table of presents instead. 'So who wins out of you two then? I thought Indian weddings were huge, but talk about "My big fat Nigerian wedding"! It's getting a lot of love on that hashtag – won't try to pronounce it, for all our sakes.'

Ola had seen Frankie inebriated enough times to know when to change the subject and began shouting intros over the music.

'This is my chief bridesmaid Ruth and my sister Fola,' she said. 'Ruth, Fola – this is Kiran and Frankie from *Womxxxn*.'

Ruth pulled Frankie into a rocky embrace. 'I've heard *so* much about you!'

'Really?' said Frankie. 'I've never heard *a thing* about you. Ola tells us absolutely nothing about her life!'

Quickly, Kiran guided Ola towards her by the crook of her arm, stylish as ever in a loose silk kurta with cigarette trousers and stilettos.

'I am so, SO sorry!' she hissed. 'I thought I'd lost her on the tube, but when I arrived she was already here! I only mentioned in passing what area you were having it in. She probably went home, got changed then googled every local reception venue and cross-referenced it with guests Insta stories.' She shook her head. 'Colonisation is alive and kicking!'

'It's fine, seriously. I'm glad you're here. I wasn't sure you'd make it …' Ola's eyes said what she didn't.

'Well, it's *your* big day,' Kiran said, shuffling. She gave a lopsided half-smile. 'It's all about the bride, innit?'

Ola gave a non-committal nod and then hesitated. 'Does Frankie … you know? About Michael?'

'She knows you and Michael have just had the wedding of the year. That's it.'

Ola breathed a sigh of relief.

'It's been a nightmare,' Kiran winced. 'I've been babysitting since we arrived so haven't been able to pull once! She's such a shag-snag.'

Ola raised a sceptical brow. 'Kiran. What the fuck is a "shag-snag"?'

'You like it?' Her friend smirked. 'It's my gender neutral alternative to 'cock-block'. But seriously, she's a liability! She thought that girl over there was FKA Twigs, and was trying to get her for our next cover.' She nodded towards a mixed-race woman whose similarities with FKA Twigs began and ended there.

'I did NOT.' Frankie's head bobbed between them like a meerkat, mortification rouging her cheeks in a way that confirmed she had. 'I said she *looked* a *bit* like FKA Twigs, from where we were sitting and *could* be a cover girl! It's too loud in here,' she huffed. She looked on the precipice of a strop, but then her eyes turned to saucers over Ola's shoulder, cheeks shooting so far up her face Ola feared she'd hear a rip.

'Is that who I think it is?'

Michael made his way through the marquee, his special-occasion oud wafting between them. Ola held her breath.

'Mrs Koranteng.' He strode towards her, holding up a red velvet cupcake decorated with their faces. 'Looking good enough to eat.' She groaned as he took an exaggerated bite and leaned in for a kiss, one she ensured stopped short at a peck. Their second since the altar and since this whole ordeal started. It had been so long, she had almost forgotten how fond she was of his lips.

'How long have you been waiting to say that?'

'Thought of it in the car.'

They'd been sent the cupcakes by a brand in exchange for promo on social media, and saved money on wedding finishing touches through similar deals. Ola wondered how legally binding an Instagram DM was, since neither of them were going to be posting. They'd probably have to pay now instead, another cost incurred. Despite herself, she wondered how Michael felt knowing that he couldn't post his most Instagrammable images to date. It was without question that their wedding snaps would have gone viral. But even if The List hadn't happened, Ola couldn't say for certain she'd have put them up on her own account. Not after the commotion their engagement picture had caused. For Michael, the validation from strangers online had made him feel seen, provided him with proof that he was really there. It was sort of like that saying about the tree: did you even get married if you didn't have the viral post to show for it? After everything social media had put them through, how it revealed the swiftness with which admirers can become enemies, where did he stand on it now?

'You must be hubby!' Frankie said, stretching out her hand. Her head tilted from Michael's hat to the bottom of his agbada as he shook it.

'Well, I can see why Ola hid you from the *Womxxxn* girls! Where did you guys meet, a dating app specifically for models?'

Michael laughed awkwardly. 'Thanks …'

'Ola never mentioned of course, but—'

'But I never mention *anything* about my life at work,' Ola cut in. 'Sorry I didn't raise how hot he is during morning catch-up; I wasn't sure it was relevant?'

Michael smiled broadly at that, while Frankie pouted. Ola never would understand this visceral need from her colleagues to feel as though they were friends with her.

'Well, you don't,' Frankie said, curtly. 'But my *God*, you two! I mean, can you imagine your kids? Child models! That's not offensive, is it?' she said, facing Michael again. 'You see, I once said that mixed-race babies were the cutest – a compliment to both white *and* black people, I might add – and Ola got very cross at me. Then again, she gets cross at me for most things.'

Michael offered a tepid smile and interlaced his fingers with Ola's. 'Can you excuse us for a sec? I need a word with my wife.'

'Oh, don't mind me.' Frankie took another sip of her drink. 'You're newlyweds! Love's young dream! Enjoy it! I bloody didn't. So when you do throw that bouquet, keep it away from me, thanks!'

They made their way to the front, batting away the grasping hands of guests like leads in a zombie film. As he guided her through the mob, Ola remembered one of the reasons she loved him so much. Michael made her feel taken care of, protected. Constantly trying his best to make sure she was okay, whether it was by whisking her away from the madness of her boss or overeager wedding guests. For the first time in a month, it was as if they were back on the same team.

Michael perched on an empty table by the entrance and exhaled.

'Listen,' he said, eyes huge with disbelief. 'I know you said your boss was mad but fam?'

'Fam! *Now* do you see what I've been saying? I didn't even invite her!'

He laughed, placing his hand on the small of her back as if bringing her in for another kiss, but over her shoulder he spotted something that made his face split into a grin so wide, you could see the pink of his gum between his gap.

'Ruth and Kwabz are back on their bullshit, then.' He nodded towards them gyrating in a corner to Runtown's 'Mad Over You'.

'Yep.' Ola gestured to the right, where Seun had now cornered her boss.

'And "Sean" is getting to know Frankie. Poor Rachel.'

'She's one of the only white women here,' he sighed. 'It was gonna happen.'

'Who's gonna tell him?'

Michael cast his eyes in their direction and observed them. 'What, is she the gay one? Ain't everyone at *Womxxxn* gay though?'

'Kiran's pan, Sophie's a lesbian,' Ola said, crossing her arms. 'Frankie is a walking microaggression.'

'I wish I could say that would stop him.'

Michael looked about the marquee. Most guests were on their second plates of food and a few drinks in. Children ran past tables in fancy, frilly formalwear now stained or frayed by roughhousing. 'Ay, where's Celie by the way? I wanted to see if I could chat to her. Clear the air.'

'I'm not sure.' Ola paused. 'You guys should probably talk another time, though. When it's not our wedding day?'

'Okay, but do you think I should holla your friend Kiran, though?'

She looked over his shoulder. Kiran was watching them intently, next to Frankie and Seun observing a trio of girls dancing Zanku so aggressively, it looked like they were fighting invisible assailants. She was certain her boss would never pester her for an invite to anything again.

'Let's leave all that for tonight, yeah?' Ola said, wrapping her arm around his middle and bringing him closer to her.

'Cool,' Michael smiled but it didn't reach his eyes. He took a step back and squeezed her hand.

'Listen, it's speeches in a minute. I just wanted to say, before I do to everyone else … I know I haven't always been the man you deserve. But I love you, Ola. So, so much. You'll never know how grateful I am that you're letting me show you how much I do, for the rest of our lives.'

He inched closer to kiss her on the cheek, and in that moment she felt overcome. The sincerity in his face, the pain of the last month, all crashing in on her at once. For all they might lack – individually, as a unit – there was no loss of love between them. That was one thing The List hadn't taken.

Fighting back tears, she inhaled deeply as Ruth and Kwabz stumbled towards them, holding up a fistful of fives earned from dancing.

'I take it back,' Kwabz said, his other hand around Ruth's waist. 'I love Nigerians, small small.' He turned to Michael. 'Yo, speeches in ten, yeah?'

'Calm,' he replied, taking Ola by the hand. They made their way back through the party. The weather was cooler, the light breeze refreshing and welcome. Once they reached the top of the marquee, she hung back.

'I'll be one sec. I just wanna check something real quick, okay?' Michael nodded and kissed her cheek again, walking over to the tulle-covered high table where his parents, his grand-mother and her mother sat on throne-like chairs.

Rooting around her bag at the marquee's entrance, she found her phone and ignored the accumulating message notifications. She'd deal with everyone's well wishes later, but in the mean-time she went straight to her conversation with Celie to read her friend's reply to her text.

Had to run, have a headache. Enjoy rest of the night x

Ola studied it, trying to work out what Celie's words really meant. Fola and Ruth had at least been warm towards Michael, made small talk. Celie hadn't acknowledged him all day; he was the only person she was more standoffish with than Ola. Not today, she thought, putting her phone away. Start as you mean to go on. She couldn't get bogged down with that on today of all days. This was supposed to be a fresh start. Making her way inside, she could see Michael and the groomsmen prostrating at her mother's feet – placing their full bodies on the ground, chests touching the floor. A Yoruba custom she'd told him he was welcome to skip, but he'd insisted on.

Classic Michael. Ola was so busy beaming dopily at him, she almost didn't notice Frankie approaching. She was now practically camouflaged by the ivory marquee, her skin ghostly white. Her boss jumped when she saw her, like she was surprised to see Ola at her own wedding.

'Ola?' she said. 'Are you okay? I'm so sorry, darling.'

'Sorry? For what?'

Ola was exasperated, preparing herself for the worst. She had been right to suspect her boss's presence at the wedding would cause effortless havoc. She wished she would get to it. What had Frankie broken? Who had she mistaken for John Boyega?

'Oh.' Frankie pushed a lock of hair from her face. 'I – I just assumed you'd seen, because you were on your phone and – well, you looked like—'

'Frankie, what is it?' Ola huffed. She was trying not to be short with her boss, but she didn't have time for this. 'Speeches are literally about to start.'

Frankie looked towards a mobile in her hand. Panic shot through Ola instantly, alarm bells muffling all else. No, she thought. Please God, no. I'm begging you. Not today. She saw her boss's face fall even further at the dropping of her own. Somehow Ola managed to speak.

'Show me.'

Frankie passed her phone to Ola, her movement slow with reluctance. Her boss's Instagram was open to the #TheKorantengs19 hashtag. Underneath it, there were no guest selfies courtesy of the hired photobooth, no slo-mo, panoramic videos from the 360 camera. Footage of her and Michael's entrance, photos of her wedding dress, all nowhere to be seen. Those posts had been pushed down, by row after row, square after square of the same image: their engagement photo with thick black text across it:

Michael Koranteng = Abuser
Ola Olajide = Apologist
#TheKorantengs19
#CoupleGoals
#TheList

Ola scrolled and scrolled and scrolled: no matter how far she got, it was all she could see. Looking up from the phone at the whispering guests surrounding her, it became clear the images were all anyone could see. Before her eyes began to lose focus, she saw the slack-jawed party-goers studying their mobile phones in shock. A horrified crowd formed around the projector in the hall as the images from the hashtag began dominating the feed on the 120-inch screen. She saw the back of her mother's head-tie as she watched, looking up at the feed, her cousin Emmanuel's hands covering his mouth in unison with Aunty Korede. The entire room was witnessing the hashtag takeover unfold.

Ola felt herself violently retch, the bitter taste of bile and prosecco at the back of her throat. She fell to her knees. And then there were hands and feet and noises all around her, but for a moment she couldn't hear or feel anything. It was as though she had blacked out yet remained conscious. Like her body and mind had shut down, useless in the moment, but she could see the scene around her. She was numb. What a fool she had been, thinking she was out of the woods. The reason she hadn't thought of anything worse than Frankie at her wedding was simply because she lacked imagination.

PART THREE

19

It was some time before Ola realised she was having a panic attack, the buzzing in her ears and tunnel vision new to her. She felt she couldn't breathe – not even when Fola had shown up moments after she hit the floor, cradling her and coaching her through it. Fola and Ruth near-carried her through the marquee as the guests watched in gobsmacked astonishment. After managing to drag her close enough to a main road to hail a black cab, they bundled her into the back of it.

'What kind of Red Wedding shit is this?' she heard Ruth say. 'What the fuck do we do?'

'I don't know,' said Fola, opening the door and getting in next to Ola in the backseat. She placed an arm around her dishevelled sister. 'Half the guests have already seen the hashtag by the looks of things. Just say Ola's got food poisoning or something, get them out of there.'

Ruth placed her hands on top of the rolled-down window, her long talons against the glass. 'Nah man, don't make me say that!' she shouted into the car. 'God forbid bad ting. Everyone's gonna think they've been poisoned too! Aunties that brought food are gonna start beefing and if they try it, you know I won't hesitate to—'

'RUTH! Just think of something, okay?'

Ola's breathing worsened as the car started to move. She was lightheaded and woozy, so she rolled the window down as far as she could, gulping the air that rushed in. She tried removing her head-tie, loosening the restricting wrapper around her waist but she could still feel her lungs straining. It was as though the past few months' stress was sitting on her chest, winding tightly around her ribcage. The car felt too small, too crowded to contain the world ending in its backseat. The more she tried to catch her breath the less she felt able to and eventually she started gasping for air so loudly that Fola made the driver pull into the car park of a nearby Ibis hotel and called 999. By the time the ambulance arrived, Ola's breathing was settling back to normal, though everything else was in disarray.

It was debilitating, the sense of déjà vu. The same terror and bewilderment as when she'd first read The List that day at work. Her hands were sweaty and cold, numb and tingling. Her head pounding as she was dealt yet another emotional blow she could not handle. Fola wrestled her phone away from her once more so she couldn't read the stream of malicious comments as she quietly came apart at the seams. Her mum and Michael's rang her mobile non-stop, mystified by Fola's mention of 'Instagram' and 'trolls' when she tried to help them make sense of what was happening. They ordered her to put Ola on the phone, so she could tell them who these people were, explain why they were doing this, but Ola didn't know where to begin.

When they got into Ola's flat, her sister ushered her to her bed, where she collapsed into a heap that she didn't leave for days. That short period her sister tended to her was a tearful blur of painkillers and pitch-black, Ola drifting in and out of disturbed sleep. Fola was due to fly back the next evening, but postponed her flight by two days, lying alongside Ola as she cried herself to sleep, spoon-feeding her. She'd begged to stay longer, terrified of leaving her alone. Ola was visibly weak from the stress. But knowing Fola had lost nearly a grand by missing her flight to Panama – and was set to lose more by missing work – only made Ola feel lower. To convince her sister, she had sworn on their father's grave that once Fola went back, she'd stay with Ruth or Celie, her mum if not. Maybe even Michael.

When Fola left, Ola began to truly come to terms with the extent of the damage wreaked. Her sister never gave her back access to her social media accounts, but the fact she'd deactivated them all gave Ola an indication of how bad things must be online. The backlash was even more extreme than she expected due to All Tea posting about the #TheKorantengs19 on their Instagram page, with its following just above the population of the Bahamas. They had shared the edited engagement image in an upload with likes that now surpassed the original she had posted last year. Alongside it in the carousel post was a screengrab of The List, both watermarked with their teacup logo and a large block text headline across the top:

POPULAR INSTA POWER COUPLE MICHAEL AND OLA DRAGGED VIA WEDDING HASHTAG

Sippers and spillers! It looks like Michael Koranteng of
Caught Slippin fame has been caught slippin 👀 He and
his now wife, journalist Ola Koranteng (née Olajide),
are under fire after Michael was named on a widely
shared list of abusive men in the media. He was

accused of physical assault, harassment and threatening behaviour – his victim even took out a RESTRAINING ORDER! 👳👳👳

Despite being a feminist journalist, Ola stood by her man and said YES to the stress, in a lavish wedding ceremony attended by hundreds. But activists organised a takeover of their wedding hashtag #TheKorantengs19, clogging up feeds with the allegations! Looks like we've lost our very own Black Beckham's 😶

What would you do if this happened on your wedding day? Comment below!

And comment they did, in their droves. With the wider reach of the account came much worse attention. Unlike the forums on the All Tea website, their Instagram platform wasn't the preserve of disaffected 'keyboard warriors', hiding behind witty usernames and avatars. It was difficult to write off people with accounts that showed their actual faces – and some faces you *recognised* – as 'trolls'. The abusive comments were public and apparently socially acceptable. No cloak of anonymity was worn by them to spew hate and pass the harshest judgements. The feeling was that if you made it onto the page, you deserved it.

Noooo not Michael and Ola? FFS we can't have anything, I've given up on love bmt

This is why you lot need to stop idolising insta couples. Behind closed doors Ola's moving like Maxine Carr 😂😂😂

LMAO dirty yutes got drawn out on their own hashtag,
look at God 🙏

Is this your king? And your queen?

Ola hated reading the comments, but it was a part of her day
now, like a horrible medicine she had no choice but to swallow.
Under the post, users pointed out things about herself she'd
never noticed. Alongside being an 'abuse enabler', Ola was a
terrible public speaker with a grating voice, who used 'um'
excessively. They roasted her for her *Megamind* forehead and the
most liked comments almost always called her 'bony' or 'breast-
less'. Her hypocrisy, her self-proclaimed feminist status, made
them seem angrier at her than at Michael at times. Michael
meanwhile deserved his head kicked in and many offered to do
so. He was pathetic, 'thirsty for clout': their relationship was all
that made him relevant and he pandered to his predominantly
Black female following with his excessive posting of it.

When Fola had been looking after her, she had repeatedly
insisted that it was 'just the internet'. It wasn't 'real life'. Well, it
felt pretty fucking real. These people *really* hated her. Frankie
really was going to fire her. The internet had *really* landed her –
and come to think of it, Michael – their respective jobs in the
first place. As much as she'd never asked for her following, she
knew it hadn't hurt when she was negotiating real-life speaker
fees.

Who would she be without it? Feminism would have probably found her eventually, but the internet had sped up the
process. She'd discovered Tumblr at university and through it
Audre and Gloria and Angela and bell, as per the viral T-shirt
that then dominated her feed. Pithy shareables piqued her inter-

est, and she read more. Before they inspired her to start her own, blogs showed her images of Black beauty and #BlackGirlMagic that validated her. Though with her newfound feminism, she hadn't been sure if her looks should be the source of her self-worth any more.

Did the benefits of the internet outweigh the harm of it when the harm could be as horrendous as this? She'd been powerless, reading the jubilant messages on All Tea after the wedding, them dancing on her digital grave. The anonymous users on the forum took responsibility for the hashtag takeover as if they were a terrorist organisation, celebrating their victory with champagne emojis. Could they know what this was doing to her? That while it was some sort of sick online game to them, her life had been ruined. Her relationship lay in tatters. Her job in limbo. Her mental health had been in free fall almost as soon as The List went up. Of all the hundreds of questions that continued to haunt her thoughts, day in, day out, one in particular cropped up more than others. Just what, in this life or any other, had she done to deserve all of this?

———————

Ola frowned at her phone screen, crowded with images of angry-looking, oozing lesions. She was lying on her side, sifting through the search results for 'How long does it take for bedsores to form', wondering if she was developing one on her inner thigh. It had begun feeling tender some time ago and the NHS website said 1–2 hours; 2–3 according to WebMD. She didn't have the energy to sit up, peel back the covers and inspect it, but it would be just her luck.

It had been five days since the wedding, three since Fola had gone. At least Ola had stopped crying; at one point she questioned if she ever would. She'd gone a while without weeping yesterday only for a large, beautifully gift-wrapped wedding present to arrive belatedly. She broke down right there at the door, in front of the red-faced delivery man. Today, under the watchful eye of Maya Angelou, Ola lay on her bed, a dry-eyed deadweight, bingeing on her own horror-film montage of her wedding in her mind, replaying it over and over.

The doorbell rang and she groaned in response. She'd been in the same position for so long that she was sure her body had left an indentation in the mattress. She wasn't going to answer, not immediately. Despite assuring her mum that she was okay, she had come around at least twice in the evenings. Ola had texted her saying she'd been staying late at work both times, when in reality she'd been lying in the foetal position in her bedroom. Ruth and Celie, both separately and together, had checked in intermittently since Fola had left; they'd camped outside her door for nearly an hour once. Initially pretending she wasn't in again, she eventually texted to say that she wasn't up to visitors and now whenever the door went, Ola would wait at least half an hour before going down, to put off whoever was there. Ruth took the hint but Celie popped over twice more, leaving chilli chicken noodle pots from Itsu on her doorstep like her personal Deliveroo. They hadn't discussed what had happened, despite all the missed calls and messages. She knew her friends thought they were helping, but this was what self-preservation looked like for Ola: solitary confinement. Being holed up in her room without contact was the only conceivable way to survive this.

Dragging herself up half an hour later, it was only with the movement that Ola smelt herself, her room. Sweat compounded by two-day-old tikka masala had commingled to make a potent, sour, onion-smelling brew. She took the opportunity to check the inside of her thigh for the bedsore she thought had developed; its absence gave her no relief whatsoever. She plodded downstairs in a discoloured, bobbly, XL *Womxxxn* T-shirt. When she opened the door, no one was there. There was, however, a large wicker basket with lavender lining, a card addressed in fancy handwriting placed neatly on top. She opened it gingerly in her bedroom, half expecting something nasty from a troll who'd somehow found out where she lived. Instead, it was a care package: Twinings tea, a sparkly hot water bottle and matching sleep mask, lavender pillow spray and a huge Galaxy chocolate bar. When she read the note, her heart filled.

> *'Rejoice in hope, be patient in tribulation,*
> *be constant in prayer.'*
> Romans 12:12

> *One day at a time*
> *— Celie x*

She must have dropped it off on her way to work. Ola made a mental note to send a thank-you text, overemphasising how much better it had made her feel. She'd felt so alone since the wedding and Celie's kind gesture couldn't have come at a better time. But she also realised with sadness that she'd hoped it was from Michael. She told Fola to pass on the message that he should not contact her, a judgement she was conflicted about, but hoped would be the best for them both. She felt that speaking to him would only further muddy her feelings. Pushing thoughts of Michael to the corner of her cluttered bedroom, she decided to get back into bed, slotting herself into the grooves left by her shape. Her very own chalk outline.

In less than an hour, she'd have to heave herself upright again and venture beyond her front door for the first time in days to face Frankie. Surprisingly, her boss had let some time pass before emailing her for a 'catch-up'. Ola had opted to work from home (meaning lying unwashed in crisps debris) but Frankie had asked to see her face to face that afternoon. No doubt to unpack the events of the wedding, which Ola hadn't yet processed, and formally sack her for what could only be described as gross misconduct. Losing her job had felt like a given in light of all the lies she'd told. She wanted this to be done with, for Frankie to tell her how much she'd fucked up so she could close this chapter. *She'll be wasting her breath,* Ola thought. *Tell me something I don't know.*

Hauling herself out of bed with the remainder of her life force forty minutes later, Ola made her way to the bathroom for her first shower in five days. Her lashes were still sticky with hardened glue, each hand missing two false nails. She avoided the mirror and turned on the tap. The cold water made her jolt. She let it run, hoping the shock of it might help ener-gise her.

Her colleagues stared when she entered the *Womxxxn* offices that afternoon. As if they'd been watching the door, waiting for her to come through it with bated breath; the room had fallen silent in the way it only does when the object of discussion appears.

Ola didn't know where else to look, so simply stared back at them. Some gawped nakedly with concern, others with mouths ajar, forgetting themselves. Ola eventually had to break eye contact, her face warming with shame. The humiliation felt all the more acute because she had spent so much time trying to keep *Womxxxn* staff out of her private life. She stuffed her hands in the pockets of her tracksuit bottoms as she caught Kiran's eye. She hadn't told her friend about the meeting with Frankie, and Kiran watched her pass through the office moon-eyed, like she was looking at a ghost. Once she realised Ola was really there, Kiran mouthed something frantically at her.

Closing the glass office door behind her, Ola could feel dozens of eyes at the nape of her neck. She steadied herself, refusing to give them a show.

'Oh, Ola, darling,' Frankie said on her entry. 'Please, do sit down. How are you holding up? Can I get you a glass of water?'

Ola shook her head. 'No. Thanks, but no. I just want to get this over with, if that's okay?'

'Of course.'

Frankie tossed a 'get back to work' glare over Ola's shoulder. When she looked back at her, her face was on the brink of an unreadable emotion. Like it was in a silent battle with the Botox, so it could also express the same concern as her body language.

'Ola,' she said finally. Frankie was speaking in a voice Ola had only ever heard through the crack of her office door. On the phone to her ex-husband, when the shouting had subsided. It was sad and sincere, gentle. It wasn't the tone she had been expecting.

'Am I that *ghastly* a boss?'

Ola shook her head. 'Not at all,' she said in a tiny voice.

'So why didn't you tell me? I'm trying to understand, but you don't give me much to work with …'

Ola glanced upwards at the ceiling and breathed out. This felt like the very definition of 'being kicked while down'. As much as the idea of being vulnerable with her boss appalled her, she didn't have the energy to lie any more. She had already lost everything; what did she have to lose by being honest with Frankie for once?

'I panicked, Frankie,' she said. 'I saw Michael's name on The List, had a meltdown in the toilets, tried to hold it together but then five minutes later you asked me to write about it. I was scared. But I wasn't trying to stop the article altogether; I promise. I just wanted some time. That's why I asked Kiran to speak to you about holding off. I didn't know what else to do. I really am sorry.'

'You do realise, had you told me, I would have immediately pulled you off it?' Frankie said. 'Aside from the obvious conflict of interest, no one in their right mind would have expected you to write it. We could have talked about it.'

'To be honest, I was trying to hold off on us writing anything at all. You wanted a long read, something in-depth. That involves names, identities. I needed everything to slow down for a second.'

'Yes, but Ola,' said Frankie, with a light shake of her head, 'perhaps I would have been better placed with helping slow things down if I'd known what was happening in the first place?'

At that moment, Ola felt very stupid indeed. As if The List hadn't been bad enough, she had clearly made the situation worse with the way she'd gone about things. All that time ago, speaking to Frankie about it seemed like the worst possible scenario. But not much could be worse than this conversation, in the aftermath of all her poor decisions. She gnawed the inside of her cheek.

'I understand,' Ola said. 'Please know that Kiran was completely against holding off – she only wanted to help me. I put her in a very difficult position, so I hope she won't be fired too.'

Frankie blinked rapidly at this, looking mildly stunned. 'When did I mention anything about firing anyone?' she said. 'I know you seem to think I'm some sort of monster, but I at least *speak* human being. They've not been ideal, your choices. But they've been understandable.'

'Oh,' said a flabbergasted Ola. Now she felt really taken aback. She had gone into work today prepared to apologise and to pick up her P45. Instead, she was presented with yet more evidence that perhaps she had been judging Frankie too harshly. While welcome, it only emphasised how thoughtless she had been these past few weeks.

'Wow. Okay. I don't really know what to say. Thank you, Frankie.'

'You're welcome,' her boss said with a self-satisfied smile. 'Frankly, sacking you would be shooting myself in the foot. I can't think of anywhere better for you to tell your story than at *Womxxxn*.'

Ola froze like she had been cast in marble, unable to move. '… My story?'

'Yes!' Frankie chirped. 'What it's like to wake up to see your other half on The List. As a feminist, too – a feminist *journalist* no less – with one month to go till your wedding. How did you decide you were going to stay with him? When? Why? I'm assuming he's innocent, or you wouldn't have. Unless …' Frankie let out a little gasp. 'You weren't *forced*, were you?'

'No!' Ola shrieked. The shift in their conversation had happened at breakneck speed and she was scrambling to wrap her head around what Frankie was saying. 'No, no. But Frankie. I – I don't think I can … I mean, I wouldn't be able to …'

Frankie leaned back in her chair, calmly watching Ola stumble over her words.

'Well, Ola,' she said coolly. 'You do owe me an article. And while I understand why straight reporting didn't work, a confessional, first-hand piece would be incredibly powerful. It would also very much make up for the past month. Plus, you saw the hashtag – it's all already out in the public domain now, isn't it? Our readers are certainly going to want some sort of explanation – you're one of *Womxxxn*'s founding writers. Look,' she said, leaning forward again, a glint in her green eyes. 'Whatever entry point you feel comfortable with is fine with me.'

Ola's body sank in the chair, the energy leaving her limbs. 'But I thought …' she started.

'You thought what?' Frankie sounded exasperated. 'Reporting on serious allegations about your own husband is one thing, but if anything, I'm asking you to do the opposite! This is a chance to get your side of the story out there, rebuild your reputation.' She pressed her lips together momentarily. 'I mean, you must have seen what people are saying, Ola.'

There she was. This was the Frankie Ola knew and often loathed. When it came to *Womxxxn*, she was ruthless. In truth, it was what made her great at her job, why the brand had flourished. How could Ola have thought this chat was leading anywhere but here? She believed she had been stupid for underestimating Frankie a month ago, but in the last five minutes Frankie had reminded her exactly who she was. Ola felt winded as she stared at her smiling boss, dumbstruck.

'Don't you care?' she managed at last, her voice hoarse from weariness. 'About anything other than clicks and traffic and views?'

Frankie forced a hollow laugh, shaking her head as she did. She pointed a neatly filed peach nail in Ola's direction. 'Do *you* care, is the question,' she said. 'Do you pay for your news, Ola?

Do you even *have* a *Womxxxn* subscription? It's not like I don't pay you enough for one. We would all love to write about moon cups all day, but the fact is, it doesn't keep the lights on. Of this place, or my flat. Yours either. Without the "clicks and traffic and views", we'd both be out of a job. None of this would exist.' She swept her arm upwards, gesturing at the office around them. Ola suddenly became freshly aware of her colleagues watching beyond the glass walls of this fishbowl.

'I'm running a business, Ola,' Frankie went on. 'And I've never once pretended to be doing anything else. So the answer to your question is no. No, I don't.'

She tapped her desk with her knuckles to signify a point well made.

'Now, I'm not expecting it immediately, of course. I'll give you some time to think about your approach and – oh! Wait a sec, what's this?' Her phone buzzed. She studied the screen for a few seconds and then gasped into her hand.

'Well, well, well; it's your lucky day! Remember Morgan Briggs? Pictures of her in Blackface at uni have resurfaced.' She waved the phone under Ola's nose: Morgan, donning a considerably darker skin tone and a pink wig as part of what she could only assume was a Nicki Minaj Halloween costume. Frankie's pupils were dilated to the point where her eyes were nearly black.

'What a fall from grace,' she tutted. 'She was one of our ones to watch last year! But now she's cancelled again, that buys you a few days on The List piece. What do you reckon?' Frankie said, the corners of her mouth hitching upwards. 'You could write an article on Morgan using the "*Womxxxn* staff writer" byline, while we wait for your piece addressing your situation. Does Monday sound good?'

Getting to her feet, Ola looked the office over once more. The pastels seemed even more off-putting today, sickly sweet. This was the place where she'd established herself as a journalist, to which she'd given the last three years of her life. A place where she had without a doubt done work that had changed lives. A place where she had given all she could.

'Frankie,' she said, making her way towards the door and then turning sharply around. 'I quit.' She then walked straight towards the door of the *Womxxxn* office, without looking back, disregarding all of the eyes watching her go.

———————

Ola would have preferred to have been sacked, when she thought about it. To have been pushed as opposed to jumping. Then it would have felt more out of her hands. Walking away from *Womxxxn* with no job or back-up plan felt rash, but the alternative was unthinkable. It was like this nightmare would never end – if she wasn't reading about herself on forums, it was on Instagram. If it wasn't on Instagram, it would be in her own column. Of course, quitting wouldn't stop the story rolling on and on. This was her life now, she supposed. She was the girl who married that abuser. The girl whose wedding went viral because of it. When she eventually started interviewing for jobs again, magazines would probably try to hire her on the basis she would write about it.

As usual, her head felt like it was pulsating with more thoughts than her brain had room for. Who was she, now that she wasn't the Current Affairs Editor at *Womxxxn*? When she'd walked out that office door, Ola had felt far more fearful than free. She tried to focus on the comfort and seclusion of her bed as she made her way home. As she moved listlessly through the barriers of Tooting Broadway Station half an hour later, Ola took her phone from her bag and opened the All Tea forum homepage. She stopped in the street to read the last post on Th3 L1st thread. It was posted by the user @cicely_bye_son, a link to something they'd prefixed solely with 'Yaaaaassssss!'.

When Ola tapped the link, it took her to a tweet from her colleague Sophie Chambers, sent just six minutes ago.

> Thrilled to announce that from tomorrow I will be starting my new role as current affairs editor at Womxxxn magazine! 👯‍♀️🎉

Congratulations were already stacking up thick and fast beneath it from fellow journalists.

Ola minimised the Twitter tab and refreshed the forum, where @incog_negro had followed up with a comment:

> Well done, ladies. M!chael K next.

20

Michael's living room had been shrouded in darkness for days, the thick curtains tightly drawn and the lamps off. The only light emitted was from his TV screen, on which he was 'watching' the series *Billions*. Or rather, he was simply looking at it vacantly; he couldn't concentrate. It was late at night and Michael couldn't sleep. It was hard to say how long he had been lying there, as he'd been splayed across his couch in a faded pair of black boxers since it was bright outside, like he had the best part of the week. The lack of moonlight coming through the curtains made his surroundings all the more ominous.

As his phone vibrated for the umpteenth time, Michael ignored it. It shook almost without pause with messages from 'The List Eleven' group chat, the men hastily giving their two pence on the madness that had taken place earlier in the day. He couldn't believe they were still going. That morning, Lewis had posted a statement online regarding The List and several hours later, the subsequent fallout was all anyone could talk about. Michael couldn't get involved – he already had too much on his mind. Onscreen the vengeance plot of the redheaded, mean-faced protagonist was concluding but Michael could only see himself in his mind's eye. Standing there, helpless at his wedding as his world crashed around him. Ola collapsing and being dragged away. He scrunched his eyes shut in anguished recollection and thought of his wife in her room, doing the same; watching the tragedy of their big day unfold again and again in her mind, humiliated afresh each time.

As the news of the hashtag ambush rippled through the wedding reception hall that day, he was sure he had heard the thud of David Aidoo's literal mic drop in the deathly silence before the murmuring started. It hadn't been long before the whispers turned into a full-blown panicked rumble. Ola was carried to the exit by Ruth and Fola, he remembered that. The next thing he knew, he was outside on the main road too, watching her speed off in a black cab. He wasn't entirely sure how he got out of there, but once he had, he kept walking until he reached a back road where he ordered an Uber. Thankfully it came in a few minutes, though they were the longest and most painful of his life. Michael's phone had started to overheat. It was buzzing non-stop: messages from his mum he couldn't bear to read, the boys' group chat alight already. Calls from +44 numbers he didn't recognise. He used the remaining sliver of his battery to send two hurried texts, to Kwabz and his mother saying he had to leave the function but was okay. Before his phone gave out, he rang Ola, but wasn't surprised when she didn't answer.

On the way home, his battery died in the flood of notifications. He didn't bother to charge it when he got in – what could he say? What could anyone say to him? Instead, he doubled over and, for the first time since his ordeal had started, properly cried until he coughed sorely. His towering frame was racked by body-shaking sobs he had learned to suppress since childhood. In the celebration of the wedding, he had almost forgotten the hell of it all. Not entirely, of course. But his grandmother's smiling face, his friends' tomfoolery, Ola being Ola for the first time in a month; for some of the reception, The List hadn't been the only thing filling his head. For once, he had hoped it might not stop him from sleeping that night.

He left his phone off for the rest of that evening. There had been no alcohol in the house, so he found the remainder of some weed and smoked till he knocked himself out and was woken up again the next day, woolly-headed at a quarter to eleven. Ideally, he wouldn't have turned it back on ever again, if his sleep hadn't been interrupted by a loud banging at the front door, courtesy of a shamefaced Kwabz.

'Sorry, bro,' he muttered when Michael answered. 'Your mum said she was gonna come with the police if she didn't hear from you this morning. Can't even be mad at Aunty, with everything that went down at the reception.' Kwabz had seen him in a bad way like this at university. Michael noted the same alarm on his friend's face and he hated it. He didn't let him in, said the flat was in a state, which was true. Kwabz eventually left on the promise that Michael would send his mum a text every morning until he could manage a call. Michael knew this promise was as much for his friend as it was for his mother. When she came later that week it was without the police, thankfully, but she still struggled to grasp the full extent of what had happened, brushing off the 'internet bullies'. 'Don't mind them,' she'd said, fussing around his kitchen to make food he wouldn't eat. 'They're just jealous.'

He flinched out of his daydream as his phone shuddered into life loudly in front of him. Messages from 'The List Eleven' group chat were coming in such quick succession, it was impossible for anyone to actually digest what was written before they responded. He'd initially muted 'The List Eleven' chat since he'd been added by Lewis the day after the wedding, but whenever he glanced at his phone, the multiplying notifications still made him anxious. With a heavy sigh he sat up, grabbed his mobile and opened the conversation, bathing his face in the ghostly blue glow of its light.

'Fuck these SJWs,' Ben Abbassi, a prominent YouTube personality, had written in one of the few messages Michael caught. 'Try cancel Lewis Hale? This is why you don't apologise to these lot. Can't negotiate with them LGBTerrorists.'

'Them flag bandits aren't oppressed, they're mad powerful,' someone else wrote in response to something else. 'Everyone has to bow to the gay agenda, but see how quick they are to tear down a Black man?'

'It's "Black lives matter" till it's a Black life that aint a sheep,' came another. 'We're living in end times bro. Jesus needs to come spin the block, real talk.'

Michael wondered how Lewis felt, reading what was being said in his name. He guessed he must be used to it by now. There were over fifty men in 'The List Eleven' WhatsApp group and growing. It had begun as a motley crew of eleven men, athletes, writers, podcasters, musicians, actors; all of whom were on The List, all of whom professed their innocence. Since the group was made up of Black men who had been listed, the first members had named it in reference to 'The Central Park Five', which only made Michael more uncomfortable. Largely because lots of them were guilty without question. One man, who Ola had referenced in #MCsToo, was in the middle of a court case defending an aggravated assault charge.

As time went on, it was infiltrated by a number of supporters. Friends and fans from the UK and beyond who helped pool legal advice, when they weren't bemoaning the 'propaganda' of one minority group or another. Despite Lewis's misgivings about the chat, he had thought Michael could do with the support after the wedding went viral. Although the group predated the wedding hashtag takeover, it had served as a catalyst for its expansion these past few days. Admittedly, the messages of support were comforting at first. Then they became nauseating, as Michael would see the same men go on victim-blaming rants littered with rape apologia. He'd often thought of leaving but part of him felt compelled to give the group a chance.

After all, he wasn't guilty, and Lewis's situation wasn't all it seemed. Maybe there were more men like them? Plus, as much as he hated to admit it, he preferred it to the alternative. Michael felt more isolated after the wedding than he had throughout this whole ordeal. Ola had been avoiding him since the reception; the one time she had communicated with him had been through Fola, and it was specifically to tell him to leave her alone. She wouldn't pick up his calls, answer his texts. After #TheKorantengs19 debacle, they were back at square one.

The flashing of the screen in the dark room continued as the onslaught of messages poured into WhatsApp. Someone was now complaining about the 'double standard' for Black men versus the gay community, forgetting (or more likely, ignoring) that gay Black men exist. Men like Lewis, who of course said nothing in response. Lewis hadn't posted anything in the chat since that morning. Michael hoped he was doing okay, after what had happened. They had spoken on the phone a few hours ago and he hadn't sounded good at all. As bad as he felt for him though, Michael was angry at him. This could have all been avoided if Lewis had listened. If Michael had stopped him.

Lewis had given Michael one final chance to join him in making a statement before he posted it today. #TheKorantengs19 scandal had The List on people's lips again in the days after the wedding and pushed it out to a wider audience. Lewis was getting impatient about addressing it. Michael told him for the last time he didn't think it was a good idea. In fact, it sounded worse the more he thought about it.

'All right son, fair enough,' Lewis had written back, dismissing Michael's concerns. 'Good luck with whatever you do or don't do. Either way, we'll be alright :)'

That message, intended to comfort him, made his stomach foam like his whole body was being violently shaken. The sickening, twisting sensation was only temporarily eased when it looked like the plan had been thwarted. Lewis was due to release his statement at 7.30 a.m. but another had pipped him to the post. At 7.00 a.m., a blog was published on Medium by a woman named Nour El Masri, a social anthropology and linguistics student at SOAS. It was titled 'What I Wish I Said Then' and Ben had posted it in the chat, grumbling about the traction it was already gaining.

'No fact-checking obviously,' he'd said. 'This girl can post anything and watch; everyone's gonna jump on her side.' The men backed and forthed on its contents and picked away at its author, many offering up their thoughts right after declaring they wouldn't read it. Michael knew doing so was likely to make him feel worse, but he opened the link anyway:

[TW: SA] You were my first kiss. A 43-year-old man, who didn't care whether or not I consented. You stole it from me in 2014.

In my final year at school, I went to a pitching masterclass for students trying to break into journalism. I wanted to learn from you. I hoped you might mentor me. And so after the panel, when you singled me out of the swarm, I felt seen. You told me to come outside, gripping me around my waist and ushering me into the empty smoking area. Asked for my number under the guise of 'connecting'. As naive as it sounds, nothing untoward immediately came to mind – I saw things in a childlike way, because well, I was still a child.

We chatted; you, pawing at me at any opportunity. Me, wondering if I was immature for my growing discomfort. When you said goodbye, I put my hand out to shake yours and you pulled me into a hug, putting your hand on my behind to place your card into the back pocket of my jeans. You leaned in for a kiss; I did my best to make it the double air kiss kind I'd seen so many media people do and jutted out the side of my cheek for your mouth to catch. You swerved and kissed me on the lips. You insisted on another hug goodbye, and pushed me against the wall, making sure I felt your erection pressed against my thigh. I couldn't move, couldn't speak. I was 15 years old.

I came home and felt disgusted, worried about what I'd done to give you the wrong impression. You'd already found me on Facebook. You messaged me to say how you couldn't believe I was only 15, how dangerous it was for you to be around a girl like me. I

didn't reply, so you texted me a picture of your penis
and I blocked you. And for years, when an internship
application was rejected, I wondered if it was because of
my rejection of you. If I should have just gone to the pub
with you. Ignored the hand on my knee from the man
old enough to be my dad. I felt like a fool for not going.

But there is only one fool in this story. And your name
is Matthew Plummer: a consistent and unrepentant
predator. I didn't speak up in 2014 because I couldn't.
But today I'm saying what I wish I'd said then. I want to
thank the women that have been speaking truth to
power so I can do the same. Through their words, their
writing, their work. And to those who haven't yet found
their voices; we will raise ours for you.

If he was honest with himself, reading Nour's letter was the first time that Michael had properly thought about what it must be like to be a woman who had put a man on The List or a woman who had recognised her abuser on it. How must they have felt every single day, seeing men who assaulted them going scot free? Invalidating the stories that were already hard enough to tell?

By the final line Nour, and all the women she and Ola talked of, were real to Michael. He had only conceived of them in abstract terms before, a faceless, endless mass who wanted him to pay for the crimes of other men. But Nour had a face, a baby face, too. The accompanying picture of her and Matthew at the event made the post even more harrowing. Bush-baby eyes framed by thick, frizzy hair, sticky-out ears protruding from the sides of her face that she hadn't yet grown into. Meanwhile Plummer's greying hair was grown out as if affecting the scruffiness of an ageing rocker. He could have been her father, were it not for the queasy hand placement; lower than it needed to be, fingers pressed into her side.

Nour's post had been up less than ten minutes and already had ninety-four claps of approval from readers. That would be approaching over a few thousand by lunchtime. Surely, Michael had thought, even Lewis would see that the timing was all wrong for his planned statement. It would be tone deaf to publish a denial on the same day, an abject failure to read the room. But Lewis, Michael later realised, had all the self-assuredness of a bona fide national treasure who'd scored fourteen hat-tricks for Crystal Palace.

Lewis posted his statement that morning. Two short paragraphs screenshotted from the Notes app. He sent the group chat a link to his Instagram as soon as it was live and when Michael opened it, he physically winced.

Hi everyone,
I write this statement to address some disturbing, hurtful and untrue allegations that have been spread through social media about me. On May 13th, an anonymous list accused me of being 'violently homophobic and abusive'. Violence and homophobia are not things I condone, and though I am still not sure why I have been accused of this, I believe in accountability.

I am addressing this not just because I have for some reason had my name attached to the bad behaviour of other men, but because as a role model, a husband and a father, I have a duty of care and a duty to listen. I would like to make it abundantly clear that I have no ill will towards the gay community, and that I have never been a violent man in any way, shape or form. To anyone who may feel that I have been either of these things, I apologise. But it is important to stop the fake news.

I hope that off the back of these baseless allegations and my donations to Refuge, CALM, Cybersmile and Stonewall of £15,000 each, we can make space for civilised conversation regarding these issues that affect us all #StopTheHate #AllInThisTogether

L.H.

It was clear Lewis had learned a bit about statement-writing over the years from his team. The post wasn't as bad as Michael had thought it would be without a publicist. The timing, on the other hand, was horrendous. Michael cautiously swiped through the pictures Lewis had uploaded alongside it, genuinely worried about what he might see. His worst fears were confirmed: after the statement was a low-quality selfie of him holding a pair of cleats with rainbow-coloured laces and grinning, every last tooth on his blinding veneers on show. Next were screenshots showcasing the receipts from each of his £15,000 donations. Michael gulped and expanded the comments section underneath.

If you were innocent, why would you apologise for something you didn't do? 😔

This guy really just #AllLivesMattered his apology 😳😵😑? On the same day as Nour El Masri's statement?

This should have stayed in the drafts chief …

How do we know the donation screenshots are even
real? Streets saying he's been broke for years 👀

#StopTheHate? You first Lewis! @bbcsport @bbcone
@bbctheoneshow – Not paying my licence fee to watch
a homophobe!

To make matters worse, Lewis couldn't even take comfort from
his defenders. Football fans in their droves rushed to his defence,
decrying the 'snowflakes', 'melts', 'cucks' and 'faggots' comment-
ing, asking them to get off his page if they were so triggered.
With each refresh came a barrage. His team must have been
playing Whac-A-Mole with his mentions, deleting comment
after comment, only for another thirty to crop up. By the time
Michael called Lewis that afternoon, he'd already been spat at
on his way to Waitrose.

'It's just spit,' he'd said, with unconvincing cheer. 'The bellend
only got me on the sleeve and ran off before I could knock him
out. Seen much worse on the pitch, trust me. Fabien Barthez
got me in the eye once, the fackin' mug!'

He joked about how his publicist and manager and agent
would probably be next, leaving faeces on his doorstep for not
running the statement by them. Some outlets, more than Lewis
had expected, had run stories detailing how he'd 'slammed
homophobia and violence accusations in an online row' and
'sparked backlash with his apology'. Lewis seemed to shrug it
off as the news of the day.

By early evening, any pretence Lewis was fine had swiftly
faded when he rang Michael to tell him he had been doxxed.
His mobile number had leaked somehow and now the death
threats his team were hurriedly deleting from his comments

section were being sent directly to Lewis's personal phone, then his doorstep. It wasn't too hard to find where he lived apparently, since the papers would still run stories on his £3.2-million mansion when speculating about his finances. The online harassment of his daughters – who he'd diligently kept out of the press, off his social media – had him petrified. Someone had messaged Melanie on Snapchat saying that her dad's throat would be slit that night, and they'd had to call the police.

Lewis was no stranger to attention, as well as negative attention that came in the form of lies and half-truths, gossip and rumour. But he hadn't seen anything like this in all his years. He felt like an alien in a world where his apology could lead to this.

'Haven't been this shaken up in a while, I'll be honest,' he'd said to Michael on the phone, the fear rattling in his voice. 'I've got thick skin. They can do what they like to me, but the girls? The things they're sending 'em. I've always tried my best to make sure shit aimed at me never got to 'em and now look. They're traumatised. And Sam blames me, of course. Says there are worse things to be accused of, that I should have just ignored it. But I'm tired, Michael. I just need this to stop.'

'I'm really sorry, bro,' Michael said. He felt awful for the man and knew nothing he said would be likely to provide Lewis any comfort.

Comparatively, Michael had got off lightly. No one had spat at him. His address hadn't been leaked. Again the lack of the 'real fame' he had aspired to came in handy. Although he still felt the judgement swirling around him, the shame. A dark corner of him wanted someone to pick a fight when he next left his house. Just so he could punch someone, and be punched. Hurt and be hurt. He wanted release to lie in someone else's hands and be certain.

Lewis had been trying not to bawl down the phone, starting and stopping sentences when his voice began to crack. Michael listened to his miserable bewilderment as to why his attempts to do the right thing had gone so wrong. He was devastated by the prospect of losing the mother of his children, then recounted the loss of his own mother in February. Leukaemia. It had been a rough year, he told him. He didn't need all of this right now. He couldn't handle it. All Michael could think was how Lewis should avoid public mention of that loss at all costs. At best, he'd be accused of deflection. At worst, they'd use it as a stick to beat him with.

Lewis told him he wouldn't be returning to the group chat. On the advice of his agent, he was 'staying offline' until it calmed down, lying low like they'd originally asked him to. He'd find no sanctuary in hiding, no matter what his people said; Michael was sure of that. He knew that disappearing offline was like being on the run. It didn't mean the police weren't still looking for you. You could never relax. You only waited for them to catch up.

21

'Down in two secs!'

Ola shouted vaguely into the hallway, hoping her voice and its affected cheeriness would carry downstairs. She'd been sat on the toilet when she heard the doorbell go, followed by a series of loud, rapid knocks. It was Celie. She knew because she was expecting her, and because she was the only person aside from delivery men who still rang the bell instead of her phone when outside.

She got up, wiped, washed her hands and took one last look in the mirror. Never in her twenty-year-plus friendship with Celie had she worried about what she looked like in front of her, but today, she needed to convince her friend that she was holding up. Ola hadn't seen her since the reception, though she had glimpsed her silhouette through the Taffeta-glass pane of her front door a few times when she was dropping off food. She hoped Celie bought her act.

Seeing Celie meant she could spread the word that Ola was surviving, even if that was barely true. She'd managed a shower that morning, changed into clean pyjamas. Bit into a pear and managed to swallow. The flat was tidied, but not too neat, as that itself would raise suspicion. The windows had been kept open all morning to let out the funk of fast food, and she'd Febrezed any fumes still trapped in her bedding.

She'd agreed to see Celie yesterday, after days spent gradually easing back into the group chat. Ruth was supposed to come too, but couldn't make it since she had come down with a nasty case of food poisoning.

'Tell your sister I said she's a witch,' she'd grumbled over voice note. 'I try tell her at the reception; the power of the tongue ain't no joke.'

'I'll pass it on, but she's only going to get more gassed about her "abilities",' Ola had replied, hoping her friends noted her timely response and attempted humour. Slowly, she was getting better at communicating with her loved ones. She kept more frequent contact with Fola, graduating from texts to Skype. She'd had a few mutually reassuring phone calls with her mother in the past few days, and when she'd stopped by unannounced the other evening, Ola had let her inside. As soon as she opened the door, Ola could tell from her mum's face that she had been crying. This morning, she caved and had her first call with Kiran since she'd left *Womxxxn*. Her friend promised in several voicemails to swear off wedding talk in favour of bitching about her old workplace and curiosity got the better of Ola. When she eventually picked up, Kiran told her all about who Frankie was eyeing as their next cover girl.

'I'm not sure if you've seen but that girl we met at the Iwosan Group event, Nour? She wrote a viral open letter about what happened with Matthew Plummer. It's everywhere.'

Of course Ola had seen it, right before Lewis Hale's self-centred non-apology for his homophobia and abuse. Despite avoiding social media, she had come across it, because as Kiran had said, Nour's letter was being shared everywhere. She hadn't read it, though; she couldn't bring herself to.

'Frankie's desperate for me to interview her,' Kiran had said. 'You should have seen her when I told her I'd already met her.'

She launched into a hauntingly accurate impersonation of Ola's ex-boss. '"What does she look like? Is she worth shooting? Oh, don't look at me like *that*, Kiran — I don't mean if she's pretty or not, it would actually be preferable if she were a bit overweight, unconventional. Would definitely feel like a more radical cover story. Does she have any visible disabilities, do you know?" ... Verbatim, what she said, Aunty. I wish I was exaggerating.'

Another knock. Ola could sense the irritation behind it and ran down. When she opened the door, Celie was stood exactly as Ola knew she would be: arms crossed, shoulders hunched, shivering theatrically, carrier bags at her ankles. She was in a red polka-dot wrap dress with opaque black tights underneath, a denim jacket and her black ballet flats. Her shoulder-length, tightly coiled hair was scraped back into two enormous bunches at the top of her head, baby hairs gelled downward neatly to the tops of her ears, where they gave way to full, lush hair wisps. It was the only thing she was vain about. Her afro was better fed than most people, with its diet of luxurious coconut oil, the finest shea butter and yet 90 per cent of the time, worn up in a simple halo braid around her head. For special occasions, she'd wear it out and be quietly proud of the mania her mane caused, but avoided it at work, already mentally batting away curious fingers.

Ola smiled. Celie looked like a pint-sized, pissed-off Minnie Mouse. She frowned and stayed rooted to the welcome mat outside.

'It's about to rain, you know.'

'And yet it isn't raining,' Ola said, pleased with her persuasive performance of good spirits. 'Look at God!'

'I've been standing here for seven minutes.' Celie pulled the sides of her jacket towards her as she stepped inside.

'I mean, you really should have come here ten minutes later.' Ola was relieved. Her friend's usual fussiness signalled a degree of normality she hadn't been expecting. 'You know I'm always late.'

'Mmm,' Celie murmured, leaning forward for a reluctant hug. 'Even to your own house.'

Celie made her way to the kitchen and began to unpack two Tesco bags. In them were two packets of Maryland Cookies, three Pink Lady Apple & Grape Pots, a litre bottle of Evian, a box of Ryvita, a six-pack of BBQ Hula Hoops, and a tupperware of what looked like mac and cheese. All of Ola's favourite snacks.

'Brought these in case you didn't pick up food,' she said, putting the drinks, tupperware and fruit pots in the fridge. Ola watched her friend, her most annoying and her closest, as she pottered about the kitchen and began to feel overcome with emotion. Celie's care grated sometimes – it was why her and Ruth so often butted heads. But it was she who planned Ruth's surprise thirtieth, who created a playlist of healing Neo Soul and UK R 'n' B to console Ola the last time Michael had messed up. Music so often said what Celie herself couldn't. That's why in church – whether it was during praise and worship or as the choir soprano – she seemed to come alive in a way Ola rarely witnessed.

She felt a lump forming in her throat and coughed. 'Thanks, Celie.'

'Mmm,' Celie repeated, making her way upstairs. She clearly wasn't going to pretend she wasn't annoyed at Ola for the fright she had given everyone over the last week.

They sat down to watch *Friends* stiffly. Ola sat cross-legged on her bed, Celie perched as primly as she could on the green beanbag in front of her, watching with an almost student-like intensity, as though it would be followed by a pop quiz. They'd seen every episode, so it essentially served as a soundtrack to their conversations these days. But where did they start? It was as if Celie wasn't sure what might send her friend over the edge and felt it was safer not to say anything at all.

Then Celie hesitantly asked her about work, a question Ola knew would serve as the gateway to everything else.

She answered anyway.

'I quit,' she said blithely, eyes still on the screen.

'You quit?'

She nodded, envisaging the disapproving look Celie's face was no doubt now set in. 'Yep. Frankie was trying some fuckery and I just had enough. Sophie was made the new Current Affairs Editor the day I went.'

Celie turned around now, scowling as expected. 'Sophie? The heterophobe?'

'Well, she's the girl behind the #CastrateTheStraights hashtag,' Ola said. Normally she'd have reminded her that heterophobia wasn't real, but the atmosphere was already tense. Ola wondered if this was how Celie saw her too; like Sophie, a dye-job millennial caricature who was more than ready to sharpen her pixelated pitchfork until it pointed back at her.

'Right,' Celie said. 'And Michael still has his job?'

From the look on Celie's face, Ola could tell she knew the answer to that. It was quite something; though Frankie hadn't fired her, she'd still ended up out of a job before him. She too had wondered what it would take to get Michael sacked. It wasn't that Ola wanted him to be, but the fact that neither he nor anyone else she knew of on The List had been fired ultimately shattered the claims of List-related job losses.

Ola watched the screen behind Celie, focusing on Monica Geller instead.

'He's off work.'

Celie nodded slowly and turned back to face the TV. 'Have you spoken to him?'

'No, not yet.'

Not seeing her now-husband since their wedding felt bizarre. Perhaps that was why she was avoiding his calls. It didn't feel real, and she hoped what had happened would turn out to be an exhaustion-fuelled hallucination. But the tug at her heartstrings whenever she thought about him betrayed her. He was the last person she wanted to speak to, but the one person she felt she could. Not simply because he was experiencing what she was, but because she loved him. She was worried about him. And Michael knew how to comfort her like no one else did, make her feel as though somehow, inexplicably, things might be okay.

She was in two minds as to whether she should continue but decided to say what she'd wanted to say to Celie since the wedding. 'I married him because a larger part of me thinks he's innocent,' said Ola. 'But it's like, I have all this hurt and pain and nowhere to put it, so I end up directing it at him. Avoiding him, punishing him.'

They were supposed to be in Barbados in six days, enjoying their honeymoon. In some ways the idea of it felt even more ridiculous than the wedding. Towel swans and rose petals at a time like this. Sitting in a spa when she'd come entirely undone.

'I need to stop acting like I didn't make a choice though,' Ola went on. 'I didn't have to say I do.'

'You really didn't,' Celie muttered.

Ola shifted on the bed uncomfortably. 'Celie. Come on.'

'Well, I'm sorry, but it's true.'

She drew a sharp breath. Why would Celie do this, right now? When it was clear Ola was only just keeping it together? It felt uncharacteristically cold, as strident as she was.

'Celie, please, I appreciate you coming but I can't get into this right now.'

'I can't believe it,' Celie said, her voice unusually shaky.

'So that's why you're here? To make me feel worse than I already do?' The friction had started earlier than she'd hoped. She didn't know why she'd bothered trying. Talking to Celie about Michael – about any romantic relationship – was never easy. Her advice rarely went beyond 'leave him, sis' and Ola felt it was partly due to a lack of experience. Celie herself used to joke that she was often 'sister zoned' by men. She noted the three types of 'sister zones' and said she hit the trifecta. The Sistah ★raised fist★ zone, where men talked non-stop about how much they loved her natural hair, called her a 'queen' and went on to exclusively date white women. The 'Sister in Christ' zone saw men from church suffering from the Madonna/Whore complex desexualise her entirely. And, of course, the 'you look like my sister' zone – where men told her she reminded them of a relative. Since Ola had known her, Celie had never had a serious boyfriend and Ola felt the complexities of relationships were somewhat lost on her.

Celie turned around in the seat of the beanbag to face Ola, the disappointment on her face unmistakable. 'I'm trying to make you see sense,' she said. 'The Ola I thought I knew wouldn't just shrug at allegations as serious as the ones against Michael.'

Ola knew Celie's stance on things but was astonished to hear her spell it out so bluntly. She felt herself becoming flustered. 'How can you say I "just shrugged"? I've done everything I can, Celie. You have no idea.'

She didn't want the situation to escalate but anger had already settled in her chest, her heart thumping against her ribcage.

'Oh really? So what have you *actually* done about it?'

'I hired a fucking private investigator to look into him!' Ola said, her voice raised. 'Is it my fault he didn't find anything?'

Her mouth clamped shut after she said it, as if she hoped to swallow what she'd said. She hadn't wanted to tell her, but she needed Celie to understand. Ola watched Celie hold her breath for a moment and then shake her head solemnly.

'Look at yourself, Ola,' she said. 'Michael has you pretending to be Miss Marple yet again, because of his lies. A private investigator? Really? Do you think that's normal?'

Ola's stomach clenched with embarrassment. Some time ago, at her most insecure, she'd had Ruth and Celie take it in turns to spy on Michael's Instagram likes from one of the many joint burner accounts Ruth had created. They'd been a weave bundle vendor, a catering company; they even used pictures from a former friend at St Augustine's to front one.

She tried to calm herself. How had they got here? Celie had only come over to support her and now they were fighting.

Her friend leaned forward slightly, so she was closer to Ola. 'You can never really know someone,' she carried on. 'Michael has lied to you before and he's probably lying again, otherwise he wouldn't be on there.'

'Like you know anything,' said Ola, exasperated. 'None of us can say what is or isn't true on The List!'

'Well, I can!' her friend said. The crack in her voice was faint, but Ola caught it and froze.

She sloped forward on the bed. 'What's that supposed to mean?'

Celie said nothing. She slowly turned herself back around again, looking away from Ola, her eyes fixed on the screen, unmoving.

'Celie. Seriously.' Ola uncrossed her legs and kicked her leg out from underneath her. She lightly nudged the dip in Celie's back with her big toe, prompting her friend to face her. 'What's going on?'

Celie looked at her lap and didn't respond. Ola felt her throat close up. 'Okay, you're scaring me. What happened?'

'Just forget it,' Celie said over her shoulder.

'So, something did happen?'

Silence.

Ola fell back onto the bed, defeated. 'I don't know what you want me to do,' she said, voice soft. 'You want me to hear you, but you won't speak to me. You know I would take your word over anyone's, but what exactly are you saying? You're telling me not to trust someone I've been with for years, but won't—'

'I was assaulted,' Celie said quietly.

Though on her back, Ola felt like she was going to fall when she heard it.

'You were … Celie, what?'

She could hear Celie's rapid breathing before she spoke again. 'It happened two years ago.'

Celie was holding on to the sides of the beanbag as if she needed it to keep herself upright.

Ola shook her head. It simply didn't compute. She sat up and watched as Celie's body shook, feeling sick as the weight of what she had said started to sink in.

'Oh my God – Celie. I – I'm so sorry.' Ola sprang from the bed and rushed forward towards her friend but felt her flinch, so stopped short of a hug and squeezed her arm instead. Overwhelmed by guilt, remorse flooding her, she could think of nothing to say. There were no fitting words.

'I'm so, so fucking sorry,' was all she could repeat. 'I don't even know what to say. Fuck. I'm a fucking idiot. I'm sorry.' Turning her face from Celie's, Ola tried to stave off her tears. Her friend's expression remained blank and it wouldn't be right of her to be the one sobbing.

'No. I didn't tell you – that's on me,' Celie said, her voice controlled. 'That's my fault; I was never going to, really. But that's why I … The List. I've been trying to—'

'You don't have to explain,' Ola interjected. 'I can't even imagine how triggering this must be—'

'You don't get it, Ola.' Celie shook her head as she stared forward. 'I'm trying to say, the guy who did it … He's … Haven't you ever wondered why I'm so sure the men on The List are animals? Why I couldn't give Michael the benefit of the doubt?'

Ola's head was swimming with what felt like hot lava. Her sorrow gave way to dread at the mention of his name. Her tongue felt thick in her mouth as she tried to wrap it around her words.

'Oh my God.' She couldn't bring herself to finish the sentence. 'Celie, no. No no no no no no no. Michael didn't—'

'No. NO. Michael did not do anything to me,' Celie said, enunciating each word as clearly as possible. Ola's body immediately flooded with short-lived relief.

'Duro did. Or "Danks" to you lot. You know we've known each other since we were kids. Went same Sunday school, pre his "Sweet Like Puff Puff" days,' she said with a joyless laugh. 'I know for a fact what's being said about Duro is true. So when I saw Michael's name ...'

Ola hardly dared to breathe.

'It happened on the night we went to that label party, in that bar on Old Street,' said Celie. She was fidgeting with her fingers now, focusing on them instead of the TV screen. Ola remembered the event – the type of thing she only went to for the freebie-filled tote bags.

'You didn't want to go,' Ola said, more to herself. She'd promised Celie the drinks would be on her ('Ola, it's an open bar. And I barely drink?' 'Okay, so there's even less for either of us to worry about!'). Eventually she'd worn her down.

'I don't know if you remember, but towards the end of the night some guys from the label asked if we wanted to go to the afterparty.' Celie's eyes were back on the TV. She was looking at anything she could that wasn't Ola. 'It was only a few streets away, and they offered to give us a lift.'

Of course Ola didn't remember; she'd drunk far too much that night. She had no recollection of a car journey to the afterparty, either. Drunken teleportation was her superpower: like a witch in a cheesy 1960s sitcom, she'd blink for just too long and find herself with an entirely new backdrop, surrounded by different people. She knew that Celie would only have accompanied her to make sure she was safe. Whenever they went out and Celie wanted to call it a night, Ola begged her to go home without her. Celie would insist they both leave, then give up and stay with Ola as she was in no fit state to be left alone.

Ola did remember that when they arrived, the walls had been vibrating with the sounds of an Afroswing song that had dominated that summer: Papi Danks's 'Sweet Like Puff Puff', which compared a woman's breasts to the Nigerian dessert. 'Gyal, you sweet like puff puff, you know Danks is into the rough stuff'. It went on to say something about Balenciagas, rhymed 'penger' with 'Arsène Wenger'. She remembered thinking how silly the lyrics were, and now could not help but think of how sinister they sounded. She only vaguely remembered Danks approaching them. She didn't remember her drunken relief at being freed from her chaperone Celie by her old family friend.

'When we got there, I bumped into Duro,' Celie still looked through the TV screen as she spoke. 'You saw some people you knew, and we made small talk while you were gone.'

A sharpness started in her stomach. Ola – in her drunken selfishness – had left her.

'He asked me where I was working, how my brother was doing,' Celie said. 'It had been a long time.' She exhaled slowly.

'He said he wanted to give my brother a mixtape – you know he does music too – so he told me to come outside, to his car. I followed him to the car park and he asked me to sit with him while he found it, because it was freezing, remember? He kept going on about it being a brand-new G wagon, the heated seats. I said I was fine, we'd only be a few minutes. But he kept pushing and pushing.' She was speaking quickly now, the fear in her voice distinct. Ola had never seen her like this.

'I didn't think anything of it, Ola, I swear. I hadn't seen him in years and, yeah, he used to misbehave a bit at church and we'd been drinking, but I didn't …' She caught her breath before she began to hyperventilate. Once she had calmed herself, she continued, her voice even. The adrenaline seemed to have drained from her.

'When I got in, his whole demeanour changed. His body language, everything. He started touching me and saying all this stuff. We were never like that, me and Duro,' Celie was saying. 'Ever. I tried to get out, but he was restraining my arms. Talking about how he's "never lacking", always carrying something for protection in case someone tries to start on him. And basically ... basically he said he'd hurt me if I didn't ... if I didn't give him ... He forced me to give him oral sex.' It took her some time to get the words out but when she did she was devoid of emotion, sounding flat and clinical.

'When it was over, I begged him not to hurt me and he said he didn't even have a weapon on him. That he'd been joking. He acted like I was crazy for taking it seriously. But the look in his eyes when he said it, Ola ...'

The women sat without speaking for a moment, the canned laughter from *Friends* jarring amid their silence. Everything Ola thought she knew about her friend was shattered. She was nauseated by sheer disbelief. They'd hardly ever talked about sex during their friendship, let alone something like this. Celie never spoke about her experiences and she and Ruth had simply assumed that she was waiting until she got married.

'I didn't even think it counted as real rape, first. It was only after I went to the police that they told me that the definition included ... you know ... forced ...' She took a sharp intake of breath. 'Forced penetration of the mouth.'

'Y-you went to the police?' Ola managed.

Celie nodded. 'It took me half a year. And they were fine, really. They didn't ask why I went to his car or what I was wearing or anything. But they were useless, Ola. Absolutely useless. When they were writing it down, it felt like they were just writing stuff down for the sake of it. It felt more like a confession – even as I said it, I knew nothing would come of it.'

She closed her eyes tightly, as if ensuring any tears were unable to fall.

'Three months later, they said the case wouldn't be taken further. It "failed the evidential test". I'll never forget that. "Failed." You'll think I'm crazy for saying this – but I was relieved. I didn't want to go through it all again, relive it. With someone like Duro as well. What if the trial went public? Sometimes I find myself thanking God it ended there.'

She looked at Ola for the first time, her eyes large and moist with tears. 'You must think I'm mad, I know. I don't expect anyone to understand.'

Through the chaos of her mind, Ola began to sift through the pieces. When Celie had stopped going to church weeks after the party, something that had once been so integral to her life, Ola had been too wrapped up in her own life to question why. The morning of her wedding, Ruth had been playing a Danks song and Celie had tensed up, made a fuss. Her turning her back so firmly on Michael – the picture clicked into place. At the time, Ola hadn't read deeper into it. Instead, she'd felt abandoned by her. Unsupported. Been upset at what she had seen as Celie's failure to understand the nuances of her situation. But Celie had been a quiet martyr, grappling with her trauma all over again just so she could be there for her friend. Never once did Celie make it about herself. She'd listened as Ola worried about her wedding, her marriage, her reputation. She'd watched as Ola repeatedly questioned the validity of the allegations and those who made them. Knowing all the while that someone who had abused her was effectively being exonerated by those same words. When Celie had texted her that fateful day The List went live, asking if she was okay, it was right after seeing her own abuser named.

'I left you with him,' Ola said weakly.

'No.' Celie's tone was almost scolding. 'Ola, don't you dare do that. It wasn't your fault.'

'But I did, Celie. I left you with him that night. And you've been listening to me cry about Michael. You've brought me food, man. But I left you with him. You didn't even want to come, Celie. You didn't even want to come.'

She was desperately trying to not let everything she was feeling spill over. How could she, when Celie was sitting there, eyes glistening but without tears falling. What made it even harder not to break down was knowing that if she did, her friend would not hesitate to comfort her.

22

Ben's penthouse looked strange with so many men in it. It was as infamous as he was Insta-famous, doubling as the set for his YouTube show and therefore usually seen swarming with scantily clad women. You could see why he filmed there: south London's very own modern-day Playboy Mansion. Lots of other influencers and content creators lived in the same block, but Ben's place was certainly the most lavish. Everything inside it was flat and shiny and new, all LED ceiling lights and sleek white surfaces. Michael was standing in the spacious open plan reception room slash kitchen, which opened out to a private roof terrace. To the left, you could make out the London Eye if you squinted and on the right, the greenery of Dulwich Wood. A view of London's skyline was visible from each room, of which there were many. A large skylight took up most of the ceiling on the landing.

There were about fifteen or twenty people there. The air was thick with smoke, Paco Rabanne 1 Million and testosterone. After the fallout from Lewis's statement, Ben, the group's self-appointed spokesperson, had decided to take action and gather them in person.

'We're in a war with no game plan,' he'd announced over text. 'We gotta pattern up. Organise. How else are we supposed to defeat these feminazis??'

That afternoon, he handpicked a few from 'The List Eleven' group to come around to his and 'strategise', Michael and Lewis among them. Michael couldn't think why; he never said anything in the chat. In any case he wasn't planning on going. Lewis was still off grid, and he had little desire to leave his house to shop for groceries, let alone to 'strategise'. But Amani wouldn't drop it. He'd been in the group, now at over a hundred members, for three days at this point, added by another podcaster who had been accused. At first, Michael felt almost reassured by his presence in the chat. Then Michael received the invitation to this evening, and Amani demanded to come with him. Amani was convinced it would be useful, knowing the plan of action. Good to get out of the house. Powerful men would be there. Guys with money for lawyers, guys who *were* lawyers.

'I don't know why you think these man are your enemies bro,' Amani had written on WhatsApp. 'They're not the ones posting fuckery about you online.'

So here they were. Michael had anticipated a sit-down meeting. What he ended up at was a drink-up; Ciroc and Hennessy in ice buckets, balloons with laughing gas being passed around. Amani made breezy small talk while Michael drank cognac straight and avoided eye contact with anyone. His wedding day sobriety had been short-lived; he'd picked up the bottle right where he left off as soon as he was able. As the men chatted, the mood felt jarringly jovial, when you considered what had brought them all there. He hadn't expected a funeral, but instead it felt as though he was at a house party with little reason to celebrate.

Ben was holding court in a mint-green Aries Arise tracksuit and white Yeezys, looking a great deal shorter than he did on YouTube. Now Michael thought about it, he'd never seen him shot straight on; the camera was always tilted upwards at a slight incline. Ben's show, like him, was both popular and problematic. Billed as YouTube's 'XXX Factor', female influencers competed in a series of X-rated challenges in the hopes of winning a £18,000 Birkin bag. It had survived accusations of misogyny for years, but its host had found himself in hot water after The List had labelled him 'handsy'.

'We're in the OnlyFans era,' he was saying, from the centre of the semicircle they stood in. 'These gyal are leaking their own nudes in the name of empowerment. How can it be "politically incorrect" to do the same thing, but on my channel?'

He was relatively pale, his dark-brown hair blackened by gel and swept back in a sequence of waves. Fans who knew him first by his distinctively nasal voice on his streetwear podcast often commented with surprise on YouTube when they saw Ben was white. Or at least, as he fiercely reminded anyone with ears, simply looked it. Just yesterday he'd referenced his Iranian heritage via his mum's dad three times in the group, when yet another member asked him why he thought the term 'men of colour' included him.

'The empowerment chat makes me sick, I swear.' A man with a thick beard, thick glasses and grey beanie hat was shaking his head at Ben.

'Like, no disrespect to your hustle, but these instahoes are tapped. They're dividing the Black community, the Black nuclear family.'

As the drink seeped into Michael's system, so did the realisation that he'd get nothing but aggro out of this evening. How loosely the word 'strategise' had been used. Since he'd been there, all each man had done was list their individual grievances with women, which were virtually identical to the man before him. This wasn't about his innocence or anyone else's, and the fact this was the only invitation he'd received in weeks depressed him further. He shouldn't have come. But somehow drowning his sorrows with strangers felt less sad than doing so at home, alone. Drinking too much went from tragic to 'laddish' when the context was right: at a BBQ, at a mate's, in a club.

Michael thought of his dad suddenly. For the first time in his life, he felt bad for him. He was useless, granted, but he wondered what demons drove him to the bar. Maybe like Michael, he was a good-for-nothing despite his efforts to the contrary. Had he only ever come up short, too? Michael was continuing to try to make things right, despite knowing it wouldn't be enough. It had been a week since he'd spoken to Ola and yet he called her every day, texted her. Likely pissing her off. He knew she didn't want to speak to him, but not speaking to her was making an already horrendous situation unbearable. They didn't have to talk about any of it: the wedding, the reception, The List. He just wanted to hear her voice. He missed her.

Amani tapped his shoulder and motioned towards the sofa unit with his head.

'Danks is here you know,' he said, unable to hide his excitement. 'Madting.'

Michael looked over. He knew it was him immediately, not only from his entourage – his face wasn't easy to forget. Thick lips darkened by smoking copious amounts of weed, the top one in particular protruding. Large nostrils, inky near-black eyes with whites that were a milky yellow. He looked as Michael had only ever seen him look: high fade, freshly trimmed, in a tracksuit with extravagant jewellery. Today's was a white Balmain hoodie with a black trim, with joggers in the inverse colourway. A chunky diamond-encrusted bracelet on his left wrist, a Rolex on his right. Every time he spoke, a gold tooth caught the light, and the same bejewelled chain was around his neck as always, a pendant reading 'DANKS' taking up half his chest. The same three or four guys flanked him whether it was a music or Instagram video. Michael wouldn't recognise them if he passed them on the street individually, but when they were all together, he could identify them by disparate details. The one with the messy cornrows, the one with the big teeth, the one who without fail had shades on. They were passing a blunt between them, watching one of Danks's videos play on the flatscreen.

'He's doing bits, you know,' Amani added. 'Mixtape made top forty last week.'

Michael had heard more about him since the allegations were published than before. Papi Danks was a one-hit wonder, usually only mentioned in his friends' group chat in relation to some Twitter beef that had made it to the gossip pages. But last week he had been longlisted for the BBC's Sound of 2019. Michael felt all wrong about it, about him. He'd been accused of terrifying things on The List — rape, kidnap, sexual battery — and it made Michael feel unwell, the swiftness with which it had been swept under the carpet.

He couldn't raise his concerns to Amani without inviting the obvious rebuttal, however. Because on paper, what was the difference between the two of them? He had as much proof of Danks's guilt as he did of his own. Ola said several times that life would continue as normal for most of the men named, whether guilty or not. He'd never understood how she could say that, seeing everything it was doing to him and others named. One

Olympic runner in attendance tonight had a deal with a sports brand disintegrate. Another man, a freelance film critic, simply stopped receiving responses from the editors of publications he wrote for. But in truth, they were a minority. Most of the men's careers were unaffected. And Michael could see that in some cases, like Danks's, things hadn't continued as normal. They'd got better.

'I don't rate, to be honest,' Michael said dismissively. 'That one hit he had was mad corny. And he's always getting into passa online like some wasteman.'

'Fam, if you don't rate man who get into passa online, then I'm taking it you don't rate a single UK artist.'

Michael faked a smile and turned back to the wider group. All eyes were on Beanie Hat now, who seemed to have commandeered the conversation while Ben sulked by the kitchen unit.

'It's mad out here,' Beanie Hat was saying to the group, large forearms crossed. 'Shit has me looking over my shoulder like, is that DM gonna be pulled up in a police station?'

'Alie?' Amani responded. 'Man ain't trying to get tried in court for thirsting. And I've been reading about what you were talking about, bro.' He indicated towards Beanie Hat.

'The Central Park Five? It's wild. Five yutes put in jail for like six, seven years in the 90s after some white woman said they raped her.'

'Yeah man, yeah,' Beanie Hat said. 'And don't forget the Cardiff Five. Five Black men charged with a white woman's murder in the 80s. No evidence. Here, in Britain. Don't get it twisted; that shit just mutates with time and location. See how they try do Bill Cosby? I don't care what anyone says, that was some modern-day lynch mob.'

Michael felt his jaw clench. He looked around; no one seemed to be fazed by the comparison.

'Why did all those women come out after a whole lifetime, bro?' Beanie Hat went on. 'At the same time? Even with R. Kelly … I don't give a fuck, any time a Black man is successful, reaches a certain level, you know they ain't gonna let him stay there.'

Should he say something? Most of these men had proven themselves to be rotten, but surely he couldn't be the only one who noticed how fucked up the conflation was. How could they make wrongly imprisoned Black men interchangeable with serial sex offenders who happened to be Black? But the conversation had already moved on.

'It's all part of the emasculation of Black men, you feel me?' he continued. 'Our feminisation. Man and woman are built different. A king needs a queen. Females should use their grace and femininity to command a room. But let a man be the man.' The other men were nodding their heads at this sagely.

'You're speaking facts!' Amani shouted. Michael felt the knot in his stomach grow as he watched his friend. 'Instead of doing that though, these gyal are carrying on reckless, getting run through by how many man. Then, body count in the double digits, they'll say they deserve a "high value man". Can you even boil water?'

The room shook with stampeding feet as the men ran to separate corners laughing, and then reconvened to slap each other's backs.

'Am I lying though?' Amani said with a snigger. 'Like what are you bringing to the table, rude gyal? When I was younger, my mum was working two jobs and *still* had food on that table before my dad touched down.'

Michael winced. It was more venomous in nature but all they needed were mics and it could have been an episode of *Caught Slippin*, the red solo cups and casual misogyny already there. Is this how he and his boys had sounded when discussing women on the show? So backward and contradictory? The men were repulsed by what they perceived as female traits but abhorred women who 'acted like men'. They bemoaned gold-diggers, but simultaneously argued that a man's role was as breadwinner. It made no sense.

Amani hadn't said anything Michael hadn't heard before. From him, from Seun, at the barbershop, at football, online. For as long as he'd known him, Amani had thought like this but today Michael burned with shame for both himself and his friend.

Amani stopped talking thankfully, eyes now fixed across the room. Michael tracked his eyeline to Danks, who had stepped away from his boys and was headed through the large sliding patio doors.

'I'm gonna holla him,' Amani said, power-walking in the same direction. 'See if I can get him down the gym for some promo.' Michael had stopped listening. His phone was pulsing in his pocket and when he checked the screen, he saw what he'd been waiting for all week.

OH LA LA calling …

'Cool, I'm coming out with you, yeah,' he said, making his way behind him. 'Gotta take this.'

'Is that Ola?' said Amani. 'Tell her I don't like how she's moving. This ain't the 90s; men don't beg in the rain no more.'

Michael shushed him and answered as they stepped into the cool night air. He steadied himself.

'Yo, you all right?'

'Sorry for calling so late.' Her voice was hoarse, as if she'd been crying. His momentary relief at hearing from her was quickly replaced with worry.

'I meant to ring earlier but …' Ola paused. 'Are you out?' she said, her tone becoming more pointed. 'I can't hear you properly.'

The music blaring from the living room was still audible outside. Michael cupped his hand over his left ear to try to drown out the noise. The last thing he needed was her thinking he was out partying while the future of their relationship hung in the balance.

'I am. But I'm leaving, so I can holla you when I'm back? Is everything all right?'

'Where?'

'I'm with Amani.'

'But where are you guys?' she said. He could hear her frowning. 'It sounds like you're at a rave.'

Michael mouthed 'Fuck' and pinched the bridge of his nose in frustration. She'd probably prefer he was at a rave than here. This was not how he wanted their first conversation since the wedding to pan out. 'I'll explain later when I bell you. But you good?'

'Why can't you explain now?' Ola said, her voice tinged with aggravation.

Michael raised his eyes to the night sky. 'Because it's complicated.'

He knew what he said next would likely lead to several more days of silence from her. It wouldn't be easy, maintaining this clean slate he'd promised, but he had to at least try. He rubbed his forehead.

'I never mentioned cos shit's been mad, but … I got talking to Lewis Hale a while back, all right. He's on The List, innit.'

All he could think to do was speak quickly so that he didn't lose his nerve. He pushed on, before she could admonish him.

'And I know what you're thinking but his ting ain't what it looks like at all. I can't really explain on the phone but when I do, you'll see how The List was manipulated. At least, with me and Lewis anyway. He introduced me to some other guys on there and a few of us got together. Amani's here too.'

Michael exhaled once he'd finished. He would have told her about Lewis eventually, the group chat, all of it. But the drama of the rehearsal, the mess of the wedding … there hadn't been time. It was too late now, anyway. He waited for her scolding and was met with her quickening breath on the end of the line instead.

'Is Papi Danks there?' Ola was speaking in hushed tones, making her harder to hear over the music. The annoyance he heard earlier in her voice now sounded like alarm. 'The rapper?'

He looked to his left, where Amani was guffawing at something Danks had said, slapping him enthusiastically on the back.

'Yeah he is,' he said, puzzled. 'Why?'

'Michael. If Papi Danks is there, you need to leave. Now.'

She sounded jumpy, panicked. He was startled but tried to calm her down. 'Listen, I know what you're gonna say and I hear it. I'm leaving, I promise. I know what The List says about him. I'm not chilling with him, trust me—'

Ola let out an impatient groan. 'You're not listening to me. It isn't some rumour, Michael. He hurt someone I know.'

His heart skipped a beat. Why did Ola sound so afraid? So worked up? He didn't like where his mind was going. 'What do you mean?'

'Can you just get out of there? Please?'

Michael had already turned to face Danks. His face felt as hot as a furnace suddenly, his hand balled into a fist. It was like both his chest and throat were constricting in tandem.

'D-did he do something to you?' he said through gritted teeth.

'Me? Michael, no!' Ola near-shouted.

'Ola, if he fucking touched you, I swear—'

'He didn't!'

But Michael wasn't listening. He was fuelled entirely by fury and booze. 'I'm going to fuck him up,' he said, charging across the patio.

'Michael, it wasn't me!' Ola's distant voice shrieked down the line. She paused. 'Swear to me you won't repeat what I'm about to say. Swear it.'

'Ola, I swear. What's going on?'

Ola took another moment before she spoke again. 'It was Celie, okay?'

Michael stopped dead in his pacing on the balcony. It was as if someone had turned off the music.

'I can't go into it,' Ola said abruptly. 'But the allegations about him on The List are true. You just need to leave, all right?'

He stood stunned for a moment, before The List he'd studied religiously every day for the past month appeared to him with the allegations against Danks's name: rape, kidnap, sexual battery.

'Once you're out of there, call me,' Ola said in response to his silence.

Michael stood there, phone still to his ear after she'd dropped the call. Eventually he pulled it away from his face and turned to Danks and Amani laughing across the terrace. He felt disorientated, like he needed something to help prop him up. But the shock of the news had sobered him. The fuzzy edges of the evening were now replaced with a sharp shooting pain in his head. As if his legs were possessed, they walked him towards Danks with no clue of what he was going to do once he got there.

Danks was busying his fingers rolling a spliff when Michael gave him a tap on the shoulder that was closer to a shove. He lost balance momentarily, but heat radiated from his glare, like laser beams scanning Michael, as he regained it.

'Fam, mind how you're moving me, you know,' he snarled, with a step towards him. Danks turned to Amani. 'What's your boy on?'

'You know my friend,' Michael heard himself saying, before Amani could answer.

Papi Danks's face relaxed with the recognition of what he mistook to be another overzealous fan.

'Ah yeah?' he said, licking the edge of the Rizla. 'What's his name?' His voice was so deep that it sounded faked on his records, but he spoke with the same low growl in person.

'My girl's friend,' Michael said, forcing out the words that were sticking in his throat. 'Celie.'

Danks lit the zoot and took a nonchalant drag. 'Nah, not ringing a bell,' he said after an exhale.

'Celestina?'

Danks's nostrils flared and his jaw tightened. Despite his stealth, even in his inebriation Michael clocked his eyes scanning the patio to see who might be in earshot. With only them and Amani outside, he smiled and stepped closer towards him.

'Rah, Celestina?' he said. 'Yeah, I know her still. We go way back.' He shook his head as he sniggered. 'Gyal like Celestina, you know. How is she? She stopped with her lying, yeah?'

'Lying?' Amani said, sounding relieved that the tension had seemingly passed. 'Real talk?'

'Yeah, yeah. We used to go same Sunday School as yutes, innit. Celestina's known for chatting shit. Twisting things.' He gave a knowing smirk. 'She still on that?'

Though he remained outwardly composed, Michael could see a vein throbbing in Danks's neck.

'Boy. I never had her down as the type,' Amani said. 'I thought she was mad Christian, "on fire for Christ" and shit.'

'They're the worst ones, bruv,' Papi Danks said with a hearty laugh. 'Last time I saw her, at some industry ting a few years ago, she was acting like one reckless pastor's daughter during freshers' week. She was on man,' he said smiling, his gold tooth glinting in the dark cloud of the terrace. Michael's ears began to hum.

'Rahhhhtid. *Celie?*' Amani coughed into his hand. 'No *way* you beat, bro!'

'Not even. Gave me head in the car park though, lightwork. But obviously when shit goes down and you're tryna avoid that hellfire, you say anything to make it out like it was something it wasn't.'

Sweat was making Michael's hands damp. He couldn't stand this much longer, but he also couldn't interject if he wanted to. He was lost for words, dumbstruck at how casual Danks was about the assault, at how easily his friend swallowed his lies.

'Swear down Celie's a freak?' Amani spluttered into his fist again. 'That's spun me, I can't lie. It's always the quiet ones!' He turned to Michael. 'And there was me thinking Ruth would be the one on crud. Kwabz is checking for the wrong girl!'

Danks flicked the remainder of his spliff over the balcony. 'These girls move loose then start capping about it the next day,' he said. 'When the Gully TV madness was happening, couple groupies and ex links try drag me into all that, accusing me of all sorts. Obviously, man buss case though. Why would man have to force himself on anyone? I'm that guy, bro. I'm fucking rich.'

Amani put his fist out for Danks to touch with his and he turned to Michael again. 'They try get you out of here too, innit, saying you're some woman beater? Don't watch nothin', man. You know how these hoes be.' His grinning teeth were luminous.

Michael had reached boiling point, irrepressible rage rolling through his body. 'You're a rapist, fam,' he said.

In a blink, Danks leapt towards him, away from the balcony railing as if it had suddenly caught fire. They were nearly nose to nose.

'Fuck you say?'

'I said you're a fucking rapist,' Michael spat, taking another step towards him. Before he could think, he was lashing out at Danks, fists trying to connect with whatever part of his body they could. Amani was between them with his arms out before he was able to land the first blow.

'Ay, Michael, chill chill chill. Allow it, man,' Amani turned to Danks, palm outstretched, dodging his swinging arms. 'He's waved, he don't mean it.' He pushed Michael towards the door. 'Oi, come man, let's go.'

'Are you dumb?' Danks was feeling for something around the band of his trousers, bobbing and weaving as he tried to get to Michael. 'You think I won't wet a man up? 'Cause man will kill you, right fucking now, cuz!'

'Aight, go on den!' Michael shouted, nearly striking Amani's head as he aimed for Danks's jaw. He didn't care if he hurt his friend in the process. He didn't care if he hurt himself. All he wanted to do was knock Danks out cold. 'You fucking rapist!'

By now Ben was outside too and a few of the other men had also got in the middle, the rest trying to hold off Danks's boys. Michael was hawking up phlegm to spit in his direction before he was dragged away by a panting Amani.

'I'm gonna find him and fuck him up bruv,' he heard Danks scream from behind. 'You think you're bad, yeah? Me and you ain't finished, rudeboy. Next time I see you it's on sight, fucking pussio!'

Michael was still swinging as he was pulled along the corridor, down the stairwell, towards the fire escape. His friend practically choking him wasn't enough to stop him writhing like a bagged animal. Danks meant what he said, he knew that. He was going to get him jumped. But the fear hadn't yet risen to the surface. By the time they made it outside, Michael had tired himself and Amani out, both wheezing breathlessly with hands on their thighs. It was then he saw the blood on his shirt; he touched his lip, and his fingertips came away looking like they'd been dipped in wine. He hadn't even realised Danks had got him.

'Bro, what the fuck are you tryna do!' Amani said, still hunched over and catching his breath. 'All that smoke for Danks? When he's rolling with man as well? You know they're never caught lacking. Half his bars are about stabbing guys up, it's in the fucking chorus of his last tune!'

'Ay, shut up man,' Michael barked. He was panting and pacing now, working himself up. 'That dickhead is a fucking lowlife.'

'What you mean?'

Michael stared at Amani in utter disbelief. 'What you mean "what you mean"? He's been accused of fucking rape.'

'Accused?' Amani's face contorted with confusion. 'What, like you? And half the man here?'

Michael didn't have an immediate response that made sense, so he simply shook his head.

'Bro. You're not listening to me,' he said, breathing heavily. 'He did that shit.' He stopped for a moment, tried to gather his thoughts. 'You have to believe me. He's a fucking rapist, bro.'

'I can't lie,' Amani said, standing straight now that he was able. 'I don't know about all dem tings dere.'

'Are you sick, fam? Did you not hear what I said?'

'Michael,' said Amani curtly. 'Mind your tone, bruv. I heard you. You're telling me The List is legit except where it says you're boxing up women?'

'So that's what we're doing now, yeah?' He couldn't believe what he was hearing. Hot angry tears began to build behind his eyes, but he knew better than to let them fall. He blinked hard. 'Amani, you've been my boy since I was eleven. How can you even compare it?'

'I ain't comparing nothing. But how can you violate man because of the same shit that's happening to you? Makes no sense.'

Michael stopped pacing, still gasping for air. 'Whatever, man.'

He began to walk away from his oldest friend, without turning back. He couldn't look at him, stand to be around him. He was livid that Amani didn't understand what should have been clear.

'Fuck this shit,' he said. 'Fuck all you lot. I'm out.'

'Fuck me, yeah?' Amani shouted after him. 'Me that just saved your life, yeah? All right cool, say nothing. Fucking wasteman.'

Michael walked to clear his head. He knew what he had to do. It was over. From the moment Ola had hung up the phone tonight, he understood that the next time he picked it up, it would be to detonate his life. Time had run out long ago; his lies had caught up with him and he had to stop running. There was nowhere left to go. This past month had all been in avoidance of this moment, and yet it still came to this.

Michael took his phone from his pocket. He opened WhatsApp and sent Ola the message he'd hoped he'd never have to.

I need to speak to you in person. It's about why I'm on The List.

23

It was hard for Ola to envisage what would happen once he said it. She might shatter like glass or spontaneously combust. There wasn't a sufficient reaction available in the wheel of human emotion. Though she wasn't one for melodrama, a part of her truly believed she might drop dead on the spot once the words left his lips. Her heart couldn't take it; the hammering in her chest was already pulsing in her neck, her wrists, down her arms. It was only going to get worse. If there was one thing she had learned over the past month, it was that no matter how dreadful she felt presently, she could and eventually would feel worse.

She'd imagined how it would go in her head repeatedly, but knew it wouldn't feel real until she saw him. Last night she'd texted back immediately asking Michael to call her, come to her flat – she didn't give a fuck if it was 2 a.m. But he said he needed to be sober. Selfish as ever. Dropping something like that on her in the middle of the night, with no regard for how she'd cope in the meantime.

It was nearly 9 a.m. now and he'd be here soon. Ola couldn't think what to do with herself. How could she pass the last few minutes before the end of the world? Reliving the past month, fretting about an inconceivable future. She would never trust anyone again, never move on from it. How could she? She had been stupid enough to stay with Michael. Married the man. For weeks, she had stood by him – in front of him rather, shielding him from bullets that he had assured her were misdirected, only for him to confess he deserved them.

Except he'd never admit that, the self-pitying narcissist that he was. Not completely. He'd explain it away somehow. Claim The List's definition of harassment was wrong. That a restraining order was pending but that didn't mean it should be. Her stomach convulsed at the thought of his victim, @mirrorissa92, whoever they were. Then the faces of Celie, then Nour, then Rhian, then Kiran all flashed through her mind. The scores of faceless women she'd silenced. However he said it, he would confirm the unthinkable. Like Danks, Matthew Plummer and all the other pieces of shit on The List, Michael was guilty.

The doorbell rang. Ola was standing by the door and as she opened it, saw Michael hurriedly rubbing at his eyes. They were red and veiny. She could have slapped him then and there, for having the nerve to cry. Only Michael could make himself the victim in this. How did he have the audacity to stand there, wounded and whimpering?

She walked wordlessly into the living room with him trailing her, making sure not to sit down – she didn't want this to take any longer than it had to. He had already wasted so much of her time. She just wanted to hear him say it: no equivocations, no pleas. The truth, then he could get out of her flat and her life forever. They both stood there for a moment, Ola with her arms crossed, unable to look at him, Michael with his drooping by his sides, shoulders stooped. His bottom lip was split, blood set in the crease.

'Before I start, I just want to say I'm really sorry about what happened at the reception,' he croaked. 'I'm sorry about Celie. I'm sorry for everything, Ola. I really am.'

Something curdled within her. She didn't say a word and he didn't wait for her to speak. At least he knew her well enough to get on with it. Michael closed his eyes tight and sighed, as if for pain relief. Each word seemed to cause physical anguish as it left him. He was using all the strength he had to get them out.

'I told you repeatedly that I didn't know who put me on The List. It's not fair to you to continue saying that when it's not true.'

Silent tears rolled down Ola's cheeks. Now he was actually here, she didn't think she could cope with hearing the words.

Michael wiped his brow with the back of his hand.

'I don't really know how to say this,' he said. Michael was glued to the spot, unmoving. 'But before we got engaged … For some time … we were going through it. You remember we had problems when I wasn't working.'

She almost laughed. He wasn't even five minutes in before he was placing the blame at her doorstep. Excuses, excuses, as expected. Accountability cast off before it had even been taken. What was he trying to say? That because they'd had relationship problems, he'd been compelled to assault another woman?

'We weren't really communicating,' he continued. 'And that's on me. I own that. I own all of this.'

Ola suppressed an eye roll. Did he want a pat on the back for finally accepting responsibility for something? She was tempted to walk out, but she knew she needed to hear this to accept she'd been so wrong about him.

'But during that period …' Michael lowered his gaze and his voice. 'Me and Jackie started talking again.'

Instantly, Ola felt her knees buckle. Her whole body rippled at the mention of that name. She would never forget the moment she understood what he was saying. What he was *actually* admitting. It hadn't occurred to her that Michael would be confessing to anything else other than the allegations being true. But of course. Of fucking course.

'We didn't sleep together,' he said, level returning to his voice. He wiped his running nose and eyes with his T-shirt like a primary school kid.

'Never met up. Nothing like that. But it was a complete disrespect. Before I proposed, I locked it off, for good. I dropped her out completely, no contact. But Jackie was upset about it. You've had your own shit with her. You know how she moves. And I think …' He shook his head and started again with more conviction.

'Ola, I *know* she put me on The List. I know she did. I never threatened her, never hit her, nothing. I promise you. But I know she put me on it as some sort of payback, because …'

Ola could literally see him fighting to say the words. He looked like he might be sick.

'… because she threatened me. She warned me she was gonna do something, after I deaded it. I wasn't sure what – she said all sorts. But I guess this was what she decided to do.'

Of course. The whole time, Luke had been looking for the wrong thing. Michael was lying about something, but that was the thing about her husband: he was full of surprises. So predictable yet so unpredictable. She hadn't even suspected infidelity this time. Like an idiot, she'd thought she'd never hear that name again.

'I know you'll probably never forgive me,' he went on, feebly. 'And I'm not asking you to. I don't deserve your forgiveness. I just wanted to explain everything. I told the police when I went to the station that it's her. She made sure I knew it was her. She's been trolling me on that mirrorissa92 account. That's why I sent that message on All Tea.'

A second penny dropped in the silence.

'Because I can, *Mikey*', @mirrorissa92 had written in response to him. Ola's mind went back to the screenshots she'd been sent by Jackie all those years ago, of messages between her and Michael. His number saved under 'Mikey' next to a red heart emoji and a monkey with its paws covering its eyes. It all flooded back to her. How she'd shuddered at that nickname. How painful everything had been to read.

On the day she'd first found out about Jackie and Michael years ago, Ola hadn't planned to go through his phone. She'd had no reason not to trust him. But she decided to after seeing the name 'Jackie' repeatedly in notifications on his lock screen, a name she recognised from his Instagram comment section. '@ jackie_ayyx' was hard to forget. Plain in the face (something that caused Ola relief and rage in equal parts), but her body looked like a plastic surgeon's boastful 'after' pic of a Brazilian Butt Lift procedure. All au naturel however, which Jackie was quick to remind her followers of via various hashtags.

He'd left his mobile on her bed while in her bathroom, and the niggling feeling she felt whenever she saw Jackie's name on his page pinched at her until she picked it up. Soon, Ola was scrolling through their Instagram DMs. She read the same missives that had made her stomach light with butterflies during their first weeks of dating, and now they were tying it up in knots. The DMs were flirtatious, but not over the line to the untrained eye, hard to gauge without the context of in-jokes from prior conversations. However, the nudes she found on

WhatsApp left no room for doubt. The last had been sent mere hours before.

She would never forget his offended face when she confronted him, as if he expected her to be the one offering an apology for going through his phone. His first tactic was flat-out denial; he claimed he and Jackie were just friends, that Ola had been overreacting. After further grilling he eventually came clean, but denied wrongdoing. When Jackie and Michael were first hooking up, Ola and Michael hadn't been 'official-official'. That was the line. They'd been seeing each other for six months 'exclusively' although each clearly had different definitions of what that meant. Ola hadn't been with anyone else, but Michael claimed that theoretically she could have been. From the start he'd told Ola he'd been seeing her only, which he later claimed had meant 'seeing only her seriously'. Semantics aside, his flippancy when confronted was what had really hurt her. As if the feelings they'd built up to that point were only ratified by a boyfriend stamp. As if he hadn't told her he'd fallen in love with her within their first month, and introduced her to his mum.

Michael reassured her by claiming what he and Jackie were doing was minor, 'just casual'. It was 'different' to what they had; he loved Ola after all. Plus, Ola had never asked him if he was sleeping with anyone else. Which was technically true, but she'd been under the impression Michael wasn't having sex with anyone except her. This was why she hadn't used protection when sleeping with him. Ola, normally cautious, careful, took the same advice she doled out on her blog. She asked him then and there if he and Jackie also had unprotected sex and he answered with his eyes, directing them at the floor.

After some grovelling via Kwabz and some time, they got over it. It's not a mistake he would have made if they had been official, Michael maintained, and so they made it so the second they reunited. Ola's walls never quite came back down, however. Her chest would tighten whenever his phone vibrated. Late at night when she couldn't sleep, she'd wonder what else she might have found, a few weeks further into the relationship. Would he have ended it with Jackie if she hadn't found the messages? The possible answers worried her.

Since vagueness had been his get-out clause, she was crystal clear with him moving forward. He responded to female attention in a way that knocked her Nigerian pride. She'd offer up hypotheticals, asking him how he'd like it if, say, a man had made a suggestive comment about her body as some woman had under his gym selfie. Would he be okay if she, as he had, replied with a bashful smiley and a kiss? Because she wasn't, and she didn't care if it made her look possessive and insecure. Because maybe that was who she was now. He'd counter that he'd never react the way she did. And Ola could never conjure any proof to the contrary; Michael had one up on her eternally, because she'd never put him in a position to find out.

She knew her inability to trust him left Michael feeling permanently punished. She knew he missed the old Ola, but it was his fault she no longer existed. It was hard for Celie and Ruth to shake the memory of their strongest friend's self-esteem shrinking back to teenage lows because of a man they never rated. After 'the incident', Ola made sure even in her worst bursts of anger to never divulge the full extent of his wrongdoings to her friends ever again. To provide only the outline but never details, no colour. They used her own words to lay into him whenever he fucked up and that echoed in her ears each time they reconciled. If Celie and Ruth hadn't seen The List before her, she might have initially tried to deal with it without them.

That was 2016, and here she was again three years later. Michael was consistent, she'd give him that.

'So you came here to tell me that you cheated on me.' Ola said it as clearly as she could, her shoulders rolled back and her face stormy. Michael stared at his shoes.

'You didn't harass or hit Jackie, or anyone, but she's accused you of these things as revenge. And you never told me this. You told me you had no idea who would put you on there and allowed me to go ahead with the wedding. Knowing what you were hiding, how guilty I've been feeling about everything …' Spelling out his betrayal felt like being stabbed as she listed each charge, but after weeks of deceit and confusion, Ola needed total transparency. He seemed to grow smaller with every sentence, drawing back from the sheer ugliness of his actions now plain to see.

'I'm so sorry,' he croaked.

'You lied to me. About everything. Again, Michael.'

'I just want you to know that I—'

'You fucking accused *me*,' Ola bellowed, so loudly that Michael pulled back. 'Looked me dead in the eye and asked if *I* was cheating on *you*.'

'Ola,' Michael said, his knees bent and his hands touched together in beseechment. He looked like he was begging for his life. 'I know there's nothing I can say to make this right—'

'After everything, you went back to Jackie,' Ola went on. She was consumed by unadulterated anger, arms flailing. 'Of all people. Jackie. The one person I begged you to stay away from. The one person you promised me you would never speak to again.'

Michael took his hands and clasped them behind his back, as if ready to be physically flogged.

'I'm so sorry, Ola.'

Ola could feel herself losing her grip. She tried to breathe deeply for a moment, to quieten her rage. She still had questions. She needed answers. 'What did you do?' she asked after a few long inhales.

A puzzled crease appeared in Michael's forehead. 'What do you mean?'

'Well, you said you weren't fucking,' said Ola, sharply. 'So what were you guys doing?'

Michael's face somehow sank further.

'Mainly texts. Facetimes. Nudes. Nothing physical.'

'How kind of you both,' Ola said, voice thick with sarcasm. She looked away from him. She would not allow him to see her cry. 'How long?'

'N-nearly two months,' he stammered. 'It started around Christmas and I stopped it last February.'

'And you were sexting?' she said, feeling the bile rise within her throat.

Michael pushed the heels of his hands into his eyes and groaned. 'Sometimes it went there, yeah,' he said eventually. 'But we never acted on anything in real life. It was bad enough as it was, but I didn't want to disrespect—'

Ola marched up to him then, and shoved him with such force he nearly fell.

'Don't you FUCKING dare, Michael,' she thundered. 'Respect? Really?'

For a minute, she could hear nothing in the room other than the ringing in her ears. He stared at the floor again, eyes pooling.

'So what did you talk about?' He was silent and she laughed dryly. 'Oh, *now* you're shy. Go on, Michael. You said you wanted to tell me the truth!'

'I said me and you were having issues,' Michael said quietly. 'That I wasn't sure if we were gonna work out. I wasn't sure if … if we were right for each other.'

Ola felt the shock catch in her throat. Even her anger couldn't mask the piercing impact of that statement. In an instant she imagined Michael and Jackie in bed, in each other's arms, giggling. Dissecting her flaws and their relationships as part of their pillow talk. She had to compose herself before she went on. 'Did you mean it?'

'No,' Michael said immediately, locking eyes with her. 'Not like that … I mean, sometimes I did, when things were bad. I don't know. Ola, sometimes I think you're better off withou—'

'What else?'

Michael placed his hands over his eyes again, visibly crushed by what he was having to say. As he dragged them downward, he revealed a face contorted with agony. 'I just said stuff in the moment,' he said. 'Ola, I'm so sorry—'

'Show me the messages.'

She could tell from the way his shoulders sagged that he had deleted them. 'Of course,' Ola said to herself.

Suddenly the room was red as she picked up the remote and threw it at his chest. He remained unmoving, silent. She was hurling insults into the air as he looked on and she wanted to break him physically, mentally, spiritually. The less he responded, the angrier she got, and the angrier she got, the less he reacted.

'How can I even be sure it's her who put you on there?' she said, hoping it would make him say or do something.

'Or that you didn't do what she said? Since you only ever lie and hurt women. Maybe you did harass her. Hit her, or someone else. How do I know?'

It wasn't an unreasonable question, even if she didn't mean it. Of course, Michael could have done everything Jackie accused him of. Him admitting to the affair didn't prove anything, but for it being with Jackie. Jackie, whose worrying infatuation with Michael she'd witnessed first-hand. When she and Michael began working things out after their initial split, Jackie became intense. What Ola hadn't come across the day she went through Michael's phone, she'd later seen in screenshots. Jackie sent them to Ola repeatedly in several tirades over DM. It had been horrible, reading everything Michael had said to Jackie, everything they'd done. Charting the timeline and working out the dates he'd been with both of them on the same day. But she'd also seen flashes of what Jackie herself might be capable of in message after message telling her she was a dickhead, a doormat, a hoe, a bitch. That she and Michael were embarrassing and deserved each other. That she hoped for Ola's own sake she knew how to fight. Jackie was always the first to watch her Instagram stories, and when she eventually blocked her (and the accounts of her friends who also started cropping up) Ola then had the task of locating and blocking the many burner accounts that no doubt belonged to her too.

Ola cringed at the memory. She had been trapped in a petty 'The Boy Is Mine' back and forth, over a man who wasn't even a 1990s Mekhi Phifer. Women didn't simply sprout from the ground mad, raging and vengeful as in Greek myths. Ola knew that. But given their history, Jackie harassing Michael felt less of a stretch of the imagination than vice versa. She wished she had drawn the conclusion of his innocence because she trusted him. In reality, it had been because she trusted herself, her gut.

Michael lifted his head slightly and held her gaze. 'I just want to be honest.'

'And then what?' Ola said. 'You expect me to believe anything you say, ever again? What was this supposed to achieve? We're separating, obviously. So what was the point?'

She honestly couldn't tell if she would have preferred not knowing.

'I know you'll never want anything to do with me again,' he sniffed. 'And I will never forgive myself for hurting you. I don't know what's wrong with me. I don't know why I can't be the man you deserve, when I love you more than I can tell you. But I need you to know that … me and Jackie, we didn't … it's not like we …' He caught himself.

Ola's head shot up, searching for the end of his sentence in the hush. 'It's not like what?'

Michael drew back slightly.

'You were going to say it's not like you and Jackie fucked, innit.'

'We didn't,' Michael bleated. 'And I'm not trying to upset you by saying that, but I want to be clear.'

Anger was now howling in her ears. Ola raised her hand to slap him, but before she knew it, he had her by the wrists. She freed herself and pounced on him a second time, so he wrapped himself around her, squashing her arms against her chest as she gnashed from left to right.

'Fuck OFF!' Ola shouted. She kicked him in the shin, and he let her go. Maybe Michael deserved it, every horrific thing that had happened over the past month. Perhaps karma was a bitch named Jackie Asare.

'You're worried you're not good enough for me, because you fucking aren't,' she said, straightening out her jumper. 'You never have been, and you never will be. Just leave.'

Michael walked towards her front door. With his head

lowered, he looked even smaller than when he'd entered. He pulled it open and as his foot hit the mat outside, Ola slammed the door behind him with all the strength left in her body.

Though she publicly swore marriage was little more than a formality to her, she'd had the nerve to feel proud when she told her loved ones she was getting married. Silently smug that she was the first of her lot to end up engaged to her *king*. Her mum would say that those vows were still all that mattered. That Ola was overreacting, because whatever the fuck Michael had been doing with Jackie wasn't as bad as him sleeping with her. At least Ola hadn't endured what she had and even then she made it work with Dad.

But how different was Ola from her mother? Even as a kid, the anger that should have been reserved for her cheating father was aimed at her mum. And now, the anger that should have been reserved for her own cheating husband, she aimed at herself. As Michael had stood in her living room, stooped and snivelling, she felt the undercurrents of pity rising to the surface. Love made her, a clever and capable woman, thick as pig-shit. She imagined him now, recounting his version of events to his mates, who would say she was 'doing the most' as always. He'd blame it on his issues that he never spoke about unless to excuse his shortcomings. Ola was the bad guy for not realising how bad he'd been when he was made redundant.

A part of Ola wished he'd fucked Jackie. Because Michael thought not going all the way with a wrong made him honourable somehow, as opposed to a coward. This meant he got to say he 'wasn't like other guys'. He thought he was a catch because he remembered their anniversary. He was physically 'faithful' to her, which was more than could be said of some men. He was a 'good' partner generally, which was easy to achieve when honesty was placed on the backburner.

This was what she had always known being with a man to be. Suffering, offset by the pride of having one. She'd seen it with her mother, how all the slights and secrets were deemed worth it for the title of 'wife'. She vowed that would never be her. And yet. And yet here she was penalised for trusting Michael, again. Relieved that he wasn't assaulting or intimidating women, only cheating with them. And even when he'd been accused of those offences, she'd stayed, hadn't she?

'I want to spend the rest of my life making you happy,' he'd once said, overly earnest on an early date.

'You want to make me happy?' she'd repeated, mulling the words over. 'That's easy. Just don't embarrass me.'

He'd laughed. 'Man can't be held responsible for what he does when he's had some Wray and Nephew and "Pow!" comes on.'

'Seriously.' She twisted her mouth to the left. 'Don't have me looking stupid in these streets.'

He took her hand and kissed it gently. 'Why would I do that?'

Why *would* he do that? Why *did* he do that? Because she felt stupid often. The List was not the first time she'd suspected whispers behind her back. She should be used to it, acclimatised to the inevitable dull ache of betrayal that Michael had inflicted on her many times before. But each time felt as fresh as the last, tore through her body like a debilitating sickness; robbing her of her appetite, her concentration. She was, for the first time, as sure as she could be of his innocence. '*Michael better be telling the truth,*' Kiran had said. '*And he better be able to prove it.*' He'd proven it, all right.

Her phone, heavy against her leg, started to vibrate and she felt fresh fury rise inside her. How did Michael have the temerity to ring minutes after he'd left, pathetic and mewling? She pulled it hastily from her pocket but it wasn't him. It was Kiran.

Ola looked at the time on the screen. It was after ten and Kiran would be at work, so she couldn't have been after a quick lunchtime gossip. Maybe it was something important. But like Michael, *Womxxxn* wasn't Ola's problem any more. Besides, nothing good came from answering her phone these days. She placed it on the kitchen counter and traipsed upstairs. Whatever Kiran wanted, it would have to wait.

24

By the time Michael stood at the Elephant and Castle round-about later that day, it was rush hour. He stumbled approaching the kerb, passers-by only half interested in his scattered steps and the sullen swigs from his bottle.

That was one thing he hated about London. That specifically metropolitan, cool disinterest in the fate of others, laced with disdain. The way Londoners could so easily avert their rolling eyes from the outstretched hand of a homeless person on a packed train, tut as though *they* were the ones inconvenienced. Once, he'd seen a woman in a tube carriage bawling, eyes and cheeks red and blotchy from tears. He was the only person to ask if she was okay. It wasn't that he wanted anyone to approach him as he stood wet-faced and shaking by the traffic lights, but the disregard of the commuters around him had a tinge of annoyance to it, like he was in their way. Holding their coats and *Evening Standard*s tightly against themselves, bodies tensed with wariness.

He watched as buses and cars whizzed past, gripping the cold post to steady himself. His hands shook as he brought the rim of the bottle to his lips and swallowed another burning mouthful, waiting for the world to blur. What was below rock-bottom? Hell? Hell-bottom, that's where he was likely headed. It didn't sound right, and the whiskey made him laugh out loud at the thought.

How many times had Michael felt like this in the last month? When The List had first been released, it seemed the whole world knew. Then on their wedding day, #TheKorantengs19 hashtag made it clear that there was more pain to come. Lewis's post brought it to a brand-new audience. And now he had lost Ola for good. This was a fresh low. It felt like things were only getting worse each week.

Soon after Michael had left Ola's that morning, he received his first message about the piece. He was less in the loop after leaving 'The List Eleven' group chat, but Lewis, who he hadn't heard from in days, sent the link followed non-ironically with ':('. *Womxxxn* magazine had published its definitive long read. 'The Men Amongst Us: UK Media's #MeToo Moment' was the headline, the name 'Sophie Chambers' in the byline. Michael could only bring himself to skim it to see if he was mentioned by name, which he wasn't. They had, however, mentioned the wedding hashtag takeover, referring to the groom as a 'former podcaster who had been hired by CuRated after a well-publicised race row'. That description, as well as the inclusion of the allegations made him entirely identifiable. The exclusive in-depth quotes from Nour it included had put The List right back on everyone's radar by the afternoon.

Ola must have given up on holding off her boss, then. Served him right. He'd hurt her again and again and she'd finally snapped. Got fed up with protecting him, tired of the chasm between them. He was forever on the back foot in their relationship, constantly compensating, trying to make it up to her.

Then he'd fuck up again and the divide would widen. He didn't know how many mistakes she'd have to make for it to be a level playing field.

The piece wasn't the most devastating thing to happen to him that morning. The ramifications of the *Womxxxn* article were felt quickly. It had referenced allegations that were widespread but could still be written off as petty online gossip and made them into a bona fide, legitimate news story reported by a credible source. By the time he reached his front door, it was dripping with egg yolk, the welcome mat coated with the shrapnel of shells. When the abusive texts started, he checked All Tea and among the celebratory posts, he saw his phone number and address published alongside a few dozen others. Within the hour, Beth had emailed for an emergency meeting and roughly forty mins from then he was standing in front of her and Seb in Curated's Camden office.

'Michael,' his boss said. 'Please sit down.' It was disarming how terse Sebastian sounded when his sentences were stripped of their 'mate's and 'pal's. Today he was the spitting image of the first policeman Michael had spoken to about The List, wearing the same worn expression. The interior of Seb's office was generic and unremarkable, far more pared back than the rest of CuRated. There were none of the bright neon signs, no posters and few personal effects. It was as if the decorators had stopped once they'd reached it. The only thing of note was a ceiling high shelf that stood behind him, lined with Netty Award after Netty Award.

'Thanks for coming in at such short notice,' he went on. 'We thought after this morning's developments it would be good to chat face to face.' He picked a bit of invisible lint from his navy blazer.

'We've been doing some thinking during your time away, trying to find a way forward with your … situation. One that would still result in a safe working environment for everyone at CuRated.' Michael shrivelled at the word 'safe'.

'Unfortunately, after the publication of an article outlining serious allegations concerning your conduct at other workplaces, a number of colleagues have reiterated their discomfort. Between that and your absence for the majority of your first month—'

'Absence?' Michael cut in, knowing it was futile. 'I was signed off. Beth's the one who suggested it.' He looked at Beth then, who turned her eyes towards her lap.

Sebastian paused, waiting for Michael to finish. '—we feel your position has become untenable,' he continued, jerking back to life as if an invisible hand had nudged a 'play' button and Michael hadn't said anything at all. 'Regretfully, we'll be terminating your contract, effective immediately.'

'But the restraining order doesn't even exist,' Michael pleaded. 'You know this. I haven't done anything wrong.'

'We're sorry, Mike,' Beth said under her breath. Her cheeks had turned rosy with discomfort, rivalling today's cherry red lipstick shade.

'So let me get this straight,' Michael said. 'You lot are firing me to protect your reputation? As if that's not why I was hired in the first place?'

Sebastian surreptitiously eyed his watch and then Beth. 'I'll let you take it from here, yah?' he said, not even looking in Michael's direction.

'I tried my best,' Beth said as the door shut behind them, her voice newly desperate in her boss's absence. 'I know it doesn't help hearing that, but it's true.'

Michael rubbed at his temples. 'It helps you feel better for fucking me over,' he said.

'I'm sorry.' Beth looked up at him. 'Michael, we're still trying to claw our way back after the "Not Rated" fiasco. We just can't afford to be thought of as sexists as well as racists.'

Michael could think of nothing else to do other than shake his head.

'It will be quiet,' she went on. 'No statement from PR, no twisting the knife. We won't announce it, I'll make sure of that.'

The white sands of CuRated's white guilt had finally reached the other end of the hourglass. It had been fine when he'd helped them mop up their PR crisis. Now he had his own, he was a liability. It shouldn't have come as a surprise, but the care with which Beth had sent him on leave, the commitment she'd showed to helping – it had lured him into a false sense of security. Getting a job he actually wanted had been an uphill, years-long struggle. Michael didn't have parents that worked in the media like so many others did, couldn't afford to take the unpaid internships. His hiring at CuRated had been a huge deal. Something that he'd worked towards forever, gone in an instant. And now he was back to square one. Back to the broke boy that Ola loved but didn't respect. Except, now he had lost her too.

After the meeting that morning, he stopped at a newsagent to buy a bottle of Jack Daniel's before making his way through the warm summer air to Camden Town Station. As he staggered into the encroaching rush-hour commotion, through turnstiles and down escalators, a breathless hijabi tapped his shoulder and passed Michael his house keys – he hadn't heard them drop from his pocket. He drank the entirety of the journey, immune to the scowls of commuters. When he made his way out of the station, he lost his footing slightly and tripped before realising he couldn't find his card, so trudged back down to the tube platform in case he'd dropped that, too. Rummaging through his rucksack on the escalator, he found it at its bottom.

Michael arrived at Elephant and Castle sweaty, drunk and certain he was covered in a thin film of underground grime. He'd always liked the area; in the old days he and Ola used to visit Mercato Metropolitano every week, buying different food from a different vendor each time. How carefree they were then, eating cannoli and kebab meat off each other's forks. He imagined a young Lewis walking these streets too and considered texting him but thought better of it. The only person he wanted to talk to hated him. Saw him as a stranger. He hadn't expected forgiveness, but he could tell by the way Ola had looked at him that morning, that he made her skin crawl.

Michael understood, felt the same even. Ola seemed to think he'd texted Jackie back because he had wanted to be with her however. It was as if only he had any recollection of how things had been between them. They barely spoke in those dark days, when he struggled to get out of bed, couldn't make the walk to the Job Centre. At first, Ola had said she hadn't minded that he was still in the process of getting his shit together. She got it; she'd gone to the better uni, because she'd got the better grades, for the better degree, which led to the better job with the better salary, after all. But when he was made redundant – from work he hadn't wanted, a role she'd never rated – her support at times felt like derision similar to that of his sharp-tongued parents. 'What can you actually do with a business management degree?' Ola would tut as they trawled job sites.

He'd felt thin-skinned and silly when her digs upset him. But he couldn't remember a time in their relationship that he hadn't felt emasculated, somewhere deep down. The things he liked about her – that she was educated, that she was successful, that she was sexual – didn't necessarily make him feel good about himself. When she told him how many people she'd slept with, he never let his face betray his horror that it was only slightly below his own colossal number. It was complicated to articulate without sounding like an idiot, which is why he gave up trying. In any case, he'd disrespected her, lied to her, hurt her. He loved her in a way that was of no use to her, in a way she was better off without. Telling her that he loved her more than life itself meant little as he didn't love life. But he loved Ola in a way that gave his meaning. That made him believe it was worth living. It wasn't, of course, but that wasn't her fault. It was his.

His vision was becoming unfocused now as he surveyed the large brutalist structure at the roundabout's centre, a shiny, stainless steel cube. Ola had once told him it was some kind of memorial. He'd never paid it much mind, but today he couldn't help but think it looked like a spaceship. Michael watched as the lights from the traffic refracted off its mirrored surface, imagining where flowers would be left for him when he died. I could end this, Michael thought, right now. There was nothing stopping him. He could toss back the rest of this bottle, shut his eyes tight and step into the oncoming traffic. It probably wouldn't even hurt. The Jack Daniel's had numbed his body; he could hardly feel his limbs.

His mind drifted to his funeral. All the people he had disappointed and let down in his life, who would be forced to pretend he was a better man in their mourning. His mother, who he didn't visit nearly as much as he should, would be debilitated by grief. Wailing uncontrollably. He was sorry she hadn't been able to have more children, or any grandchildren. How could he do this to her, after everything she had gone through to have him? Her only child, outlived by both his parents and his grandmother? He wished he could carry on, if only for her sake.

Kwabz would try his best to comfort her as she cried in his arms. The most stand-up guy of his boys, the best of them, though they made fun of him for it. That said it all, really. He was the brother that Michael had always wanted and needed. When all was said and done, his friends had been good to him. The mandem had his back, when it came down to it. Although Seun had his faults, hadn't Michael? It would always be love; that went for Amani, too.

Then there was Ola. Would she go to his funeral? He loved her so much that in this moment the only reason he feared death was because it meant he would no longer be able to see her, make her laugh. But she never wanted to see him again, so what did he have to lose?

The intensity of his thoughts made him shake his head, as if trying to dislodge them. Michael brought his bottle to eye level and studied it; he was three quarters down. He shoved it into the pocket of his jacket and pulled out his phone, on which he started shakily drafting a message to Ola. Even in his drunken stupor he was careful to try to correct spelling mistakes, the screen blurring and coming back into focus. He wanted to be clear.

Theres so much I want to say to you but dont know how. Youre the one with all the words. I do want to tell you tho that I am so sorry for the pain Ive caused you. You of all people dont deserve it.

I wish I could explain how sorry I am, Ola. For everythin.
I know its hard to believe but I promise, all I ever wanted
was to make you happy. Deep down I knew I never
could. I wasnt happy myself. But I didnt want to lose you
and because of that I was willing to lose everythin. Thats
what Ive done, through no one elses fault but my own.

I want whats best for you and we can both agree that
isnt me. But I will always love you.

Michael read it back once before sending and pulled his bottle
from his pocket. Draining it, he peered over the road at the
shimmering box-shaped construction again. It was so large and
peculiar — he wondered if there might be an engraving on it or
something, a plaque that explained its presence. He wiped his
streaming eyes with the back of his sleeve and began to cross the
road haphazardly, making his way over as cars and Deliveroo
bikes sped past. Michael didn't flinch as they beeped their horns
at him, a calmness overcoming him as he realised he didn't mind
if he was hit. A few more slow, sluggish steps towards the soft red
blob of the traffic light.

What came next happened fast. He heard the car horn and
screams before he saw the headlights. He saw the buildings
across the street turn to sky. And then he saw nothing.

———————

Michael couldn't remember the moment of impact and when
he tried to picture it, only pitch-black appeared to him. The last
memory he recalled after stepping into the road was trying to
lift himself up from the asphalt, then a faraway voice telling him
not to stand, that the ambulance wouldn't be long.

The next moment he woke up in a hospital bed, with a brace on his neck, a drip in his arm and a tube down his throat. What the doctors told him as he lay unconscious had infiltrated his mind and weaved memories; he felt like he could see the swerving car, remember the bumper hammering into his side and flinging him airborne into the next lane. The driver behind the wheel rubbing his neck from the whiplash, an injury which could have been more severe according to the paramedics. That verdict applied to them both; Michael sustained a punctured lung, a fractured jaw, a dislocated shoulder and eight broken ribs.

When his eyes flickered open the first face he saw was Ola's, leaning over his broken body like he was a baby in a cot. His mother was behind her, hastily wiping her eyes as he stirred awake. She squeezed his calf from the foot of his bed, looking tired and relieved. The two women he loved most, fretting at his feet like the biblical Marys.

'Don't try to talk,' Ola said, brushing his hand lightly with hers.

He was grateful for the feeding tube; he didn't know what to say. After all he'd put her through, she was picking up the pieces yet again. Of course he hadn't expected her to be there in the hospital room; *he* hadn't expected to be there himself. But she was. The guilt from their last conversation was now replaced by the guilt of this. All in turn eclipsed by the acute shame he felt.

What if Ola thought Michael had done this as some desperate ploy for attention, to manipulate her into speaking to him? Though he remembered very little of what had happened at the roundabout, he was as sure as he could be that it was an accident. Yes, he'd been very drunk and very low, suicide weighing heavily on his mind. But he hadn't walked into the road with the intention of getting hurt. Had he? It felt more like he had simply stopped caring what happened to him. Like he was willing to let nature take whatever course it saw fit.

He wouldn't have put Ola, his mother, through this if he was thinking straight. Not after everything. He needed her to know that. He tried to lift his arm to tug at the tube but it felt anchored. When she saw his anguished effort to move, Ola placed her hand just above the cannula to stop him. And then she cleared her throat.

'Michael,' she said softly. Ola parted and pursed her lips a few times before she spoke again. Her eyebrows were knitted at the middle, like a doctor at his bedside about to give terrible news.

'Michael,' she repeated. 'Something has happened.'

PART FOUR

25

A cocktail of alcohol, cocaine and antidepressants was found in Lewis Hale's bloodstream, the toxicology report said. In a statement, Orpington Police confirmed that officers were called to an address in Keston Park, Kent, shortly before 5.30 p.m. on 14 June 2019. Lewis was found unresponsive in his bedroom. The coroner gave a provisional medical cause of death as suspension by ligature. Although the press were banned from going into too much detail about his actual suicide, it was reported that he had been taking sertraline for some time and was in the process of filing for bankruptcy.

The next morning, the papers ran stories about his mother's death, his marital issues and his suicide note, in which he wrote at length about it all, including his struggles with his sexuality. His last social media post was an Instagram story, featuring lyrics from Adele's 'Million Years Ago' in which she reminisced about her friends and her mother.

The outpouring was immediate and overwhelming. His last upload was flooded with prayer hands, hearts and dove emojis. Accounts that had previously told him to 'off himself' commented with their condolences on Samantha's post announcing his death. Celebrities uploaded greyscale pictures with their arms around him, penning page-long tributes in Instagram captions.

'I keep thinking about our last drink, Lewis,' one sports presenter had written underneath a Getty watermarked image of them embracing on a red carpet. 'You were such a class act, a total gent and an absolute legend. This can't be real.' That morning, he had shared the *Womxxxn* article on The List which had alluded to the allegations against Lewis, in a since-deleted upload. Hundreds of posts like this went up, reminiscing about him, speaking to him directly as if he would respond. Michael wondered what these people had said to Lewis, if anything, when he needed them.

A mural of him in his Crystal Palace kit was spray-painted on the side of the Elephant and Castle shopping centre, but you could hardly see it for all the flowers, rainbow flags and football shirts. A silent vigil was held at Selhurst Park and the Michael Faraday Memorial was inundated with placards and Post-it notes. Mourners watched the funeral procession sobbing from the sidelines, holding candles and balloons. The #RememberLewis hashtag immediately went viral, warning users to think of his untimely demise before posting negative comments online. It spawned a campaign called #ThinkFirst which was soon emblazoned across T-shirts and Twitter headers. Within a week, a crowdfunder to set up a foundation supporting homeless Black LGBTQ+ youth in his name had surpassed its £250,000 target four times over.

Then MPs jumped on the issue. The day after his death, a petition to pass 'Lewis's Law' combating online defamation reached over 100,000 signatures, meaning it would be considered for debate in Parliament. The next week it was mentioned in Prime Minister's Questions by Paul Moore, the Conservative MP for Orpington.

'Mr Speaker,' he said, adjusting his glasses as he read from his notes. 'My constituent Lewis Hale was a national treasure, a Member of the Order of the British Empire, a footballing icon. A father, a husband and a son. He also, like too many men in Britain, was a casualty of suicide. Suicide is currently the number one killer of men under the age of forty-five in the United Kingdom. Lewis was forty-two years old when he took his life, after the publication of unfounded allegations made anonymously online. Will the Prime Minister join me in demanding urgent action on this matter, by backing the proposed "Lewis's Law"?'

By the time Michael had been instructed he could eat solid food again by his doctor, the bill was already the subject of a fervent free speech row. It was impossible for him to avoid the discourse surrounding Lewis's death; it was in every paper, on every channel. Nurses and doctors made small talk about it when taking his vitals. Tutting and sighing and shaking their heads in concern. 'Social media can be such a terrible place,' they'd say, as the blood pressure monitor constricted around his upper arm.

It still didn't feel real to him, even days later: Lewis's passing, the aftermath, his own near-death experience. When Ola had first told him, it didn't quite sink in. Both the shock of the accident and the fentanyl had made him tired and off-kilter. Everything had a slight, dream-like quality about it when he had woken up in the hospital. He had fallen back asleep immediately afterwards and almost forgotten what she'd said until he watched the news the next morning at breakfast. He turned the TV on to a blonde, bouffant *Sky News* anchor dispassionately reading a headline about Lewis's suicide, and his body jolted in recollection. The room began to swim, his peripheral vision became shadowy. He'd been grateful his mother was asleep. That she hadn't had to comfort him during that moment of realisation. His heart sinking to the pit of his stomach, the quiet tears.

The news cycle moved past the eulogies and soon culture war debates swarmed around Lewis's death and The List. These were televised on *Loose Women*, then raged on LBC when the nurse turned on the radio. *Good Morning Britain* argued about it in the morning, *Question Time* in the evening. When Michael was able to use his phone again, he was recommended YouTube videos with headlines like 'Did feminists KILL Lewis Hale?' and podcast episodes with titles like 'Modern Day Salem Witch Trials: How Lewis Hale Was Sentenced to Hanging by Twitter'. Once, in what he had initially thought was a hallucinatory side effect from the pain medication, he heard Ben Abbassi's nasal, disembodied voice autoplaying on one such show, a well-known libertarian podcast called 'Wokeflake Pod'.

'How many other girls were lying, bruv?' he was saying, as the presenter mm-hmed in agreement. 'How many other man are being lied about? Lewis was an active member of our movement, "The List Eleven", and we're not gonna rest until we get justice. For him and every other man on there.'

Just as before with 'The List Eleven' group chat, Michael wondered what Lewis would have made of all that was being said and done in his name. Michael imagined what they would have made his own dead body ventriloquise, if he hadn't survived the accident. Lewis had become a political football, batted back and forth between sides. A saint, a martyr, an effigy, a hashtag, as opposed to the living, breathing human he was. Or had been. Every day, Michael thought about how much he wished he'd sent that text to Lewis when it crossed his mind that day at the Elephant and Castle roundabout. When they had spoken at his house, his situation had seemed so impossible; Michael had barely been convinced by his own assurances that the world was more understanding, more progressive. He was sickened by the sudden outpouring of empathy for Lewis, empathy he had needed so desperately while alive. But Michael felt he wasn't so different from the hypocrites. He too could have said something, checked in. Reached out to Lewis as Lewis had to him, all those weeks ago. When everyone else had written him off, Lewis had tried to help Michael. The crushing remorse for his own inaction made it difficult for him to eat. He blamed it on the God-awful hospital food, ignoring the guilt that ate him from the inside out. Lying alone, he felt tears sliding down the sides of his face, soaking his pillow.

For three weeks Michael stayed in Guy's Hospital, his mother and Ola at his bedside every day without fail. They took turns reading to him, talking at him, while he stared distractedly out of the window. Once he was able to sit upright, Ola told him that Kwabz, Seun and Amani had visited, his dad too. The idea of the men of his life circling his unconscious body, the doctor's account of events swirling in their ears, had made him feel uneasy. As soon as the tube was removed, he told the nurse to hold off further visitors. For a near-month, it was only him, his mother and his recently estranged wife, day in, day out. He'd watch Ola as she dozed off in a chair beside him and couldn't believe that he'd ever thought she'd sold him out. Had Lewis thought Samantha would have abandoned him if she'd found out the truth? Every time Michael heard her in hysterics on the radio, he'd wince. The pain in Samantha's voice was visceral. She was devastated, not because of Lewis's sexuality or even infidelity. But because she'd lost her best friend. The father of her children.

On the day he was discharged, Ola and his mother picked him up to take him to his parents' house. As Ola approached the boot with his bag, she gave his hand a small squeeze. One that told him everything else could wait, for now. That none of it – the wedding, the lies, the hurt – mattered in this moment. That they had time for all of that later. Using all the little strength he had regained, Michael squeezed hers back. He felt comforted but mournful. If only Lewis were still here to feel the reassuring grip of Samantha's hand, he thought as he got into the cab; the comforting weight of his daughters' heads against his chest. He knew Lewis's family, like his, would have given anything to be able to assure him that everything else could wait, for now.

26

'So,' said Ola, 'how are you feeling?'

Michael raised his shoulder. 'I don't know. You?'

They walked slowly side by side through the light autumn breeze, Ola with her arms hugging her chest, Michael's hands in his pockets. She wasn't close enough but could smell the phantom scent of his Tom Ford in the wind.

'I feel like a bit of a failure,' she said.

He stopped in his tracks. 'A failure?'

Ola continued walking, hoping he'd take the hint. She didn't want to hear it, his assurances that it wasn't her fault, that there was nothing she could've done. Words she knew were true in a way but still rang hollow. He must have understood because she soon heard him padding behind her again.

There was a quick intake of breath before Michael switched gears. 'I'm feeling your *Lemonade* era, you know,' he said after a few silent strides, nodding towards her honey-blonde braids. 'Looks good on you.'

She loved the way the gold popped against her skin. Ola almost felt bad for how good she looked, though she'd spent the morning meticulously making sure this was the case. The outfit was among her most flattering; a form-fitting sweater dress with a high split, from which a thigh-high boot extended. She thought it best not to overthink whether she'd worn it out of spite or because of that same feeling that still made her stomach flip when she was around Michael.

'Well, blondes have more fun, right? And after the last year …' she trailed off.

Michael nodded. 'Just don't come at my shit with a baseball bat, yeah?'

'So you finally learned to drive?' she said, too sweetly for it to be anything other than sarcastic. 'Because if I recall correctly, Beyoncé was bussing car windows.'

He groaned. 'You're still a savage, man.'

They laughed as if no time had passed at all. The tension between them when they'd first seen each other, attempting to navigate their new boundaries, hadn't taken long to dissipate. It was just over a year since Guy's Hospital had called Ola in as Michael's emergency contact. She'd last seen him a few weeks after he was discharged. The swiftness with which she had gone from raging to wracked with fear the day of the accident had given her emotional whiplash. It wasn't as though it had made her realise she loved him – she already knew that. Rather, seeing him lying there made her realise she didn't want him dead, which she couldn't have said for certain earlier that same morning, in the heat of their argument. The weeks she spent by his bedside with her mother-in-law, taking shifts in making cups of tea and breaking down out of sight in the corridor, made her certain that she would love Michael for the rest of her life. But also certain that that wasn't a good enough reason to spend it with him.

The day that Michael had told her about him and Jackie, Ola had known there was no coming back from that knowledge. At least, not as who they had been then. Not as the newlywed Mr and Mrs Koranteng, the poster children of Black love that had become an unwitting cautionary tale. Their home built on a bedrock of mutual distrust. With time she had come to believe that Michael wasn't a bad person. She knew that, despite his strange way of showing it, he did love her. But love alone simply wasn't enough; certainly not a love that made her question how much she loved herself. She had forgiven him, but they couldn't make it through Jackie after everything else that had since come to pass. And that was okay. Ola felt like a quitter, a failure at times, but she refused for love to be something that she endured. Something that took from her and made her smaller. She had come to realise that in an alternative world where The List hadn't happened, they would still have separated, eventually. Maybe it would have been a few more months, even years before she'd found out about Michael and Jackie. They'd have enjoyed each other for slightly longer before the inevitable. But ultimately, they would always have ended up in another lawyer's office.

'Michael – you'll have eight days to respond,' the lawyer had explained that afternoon. 'Provided you agree, the next step will be an application for a decree nisi, confirming the court is also in support of your annulment.'

The whole process would take about six months. The wedding had cost over £30,000 and yet to undo it all, £550.

'Still can't believe we never smashed,' Michael joked when they left. Ola had filed on the grounds that the marriage wasn't consummated. 'Married sex is fully the only type of sex we didn't have.'

It was a shared coping mechanism, the banter. They fell into it effortlessly; the more serious the subject, the more likely they were to make light of it. Today had been difficult, but Michael's commitment to stealing begrudging snickers and disapproving frowns from her made it less so. Ola was surprised that she was rather enjoying their stroll through the chill of Battersea Park, bathed in a deceptive amount of sunlight, slim shafts sneaking through the leaves. She'd missed him. She was ready to talk. Since Michael had become sober, the plan was to make their way to a cafe where they'd attempt to process the beginning of their annulment and the year that had led to it.

A year that she was still only just making sense of, in terms of its effects on both her and Michael. Before the collision, she had tried to stifle pangs of sympathy in case they were for a man who was abusive. Then when the truth came to light, any compassion had been throttled by her fury at his lies. Only when she'd received the call from the hospital was she forced to comprehend its toll on him too, and in the worst way imaginable. There were so many things she'd wanted to say that she'd never had the chance to, that hadn't felt right until now. Ola turned her body towards him. 'But how are you, though? You still training?'

She wasn't sure, because Michael was no longer on social media; even his old inactive Facebook had gone as part of the cull. This was partly why she couldn't stop looking at him in the park today – it had been a long time since she'd seen her soon to be ex-husband. Right now, he looked every bit the college tutor, with his smart casual jacket and chinos, his hair grown out and clumped together into thick textured curls, neatly sponged at the top of his low fade. There were a few streaks of stress-induced grey, but he was as handsome as ever.

She'd nearly come offline altogether herself, deleting both her Instagram and Twitter profiles permanently. Most of her followers were off the back of a relationship that no longer existed, so it seemed logical the accounts should go too. Eventually, she started a new, private Instagram where she only followed and was followed by those she knew personally, finding comfort in the padlock symbol that kept the rest of the world at bay. Sometimes, when she received a request from a stranger, she'd click on her own profile and try to imagine what it would look like through their eyes. How she was perceived when she wasn't defined by her relationship with Michael, for better or worse.

'I switched to part time, so I've got a year and a bit left now,' he answered. 'It was proper intense and Marcia said I've got to chill, take my time with everything.'

Ola gave an approving nod. Marcia, a woman's name that actually brought her relief when Michael mentioned it. The hospital had referred him to her for therapy for post-traumatic stress disorder after the accident, but for the first few weeks, she'd mainly addressed his trauma from The List. It had been his therapist who'd told him to put his business management degree to use, encouraged him to do his PGCE like Kwabz. He reminded her of her youngest, apparently, and those nights when he felt the walls closing in, worrying about his new colleagues discovering a damning article or tweet, he told Ola she took his calls after hours.

Neither of them could believe how straightforward it had been for him to get a placement at a sixth form. She couldn't help but think about the guilty men that could move on with their lives at the same pace, into similar positions of trust. Michael had left presenting behind because he knew he'd struggle to find work. Most men named on The List had kept their jobs, however, so didn't have to worry. The YouTuber

'That Guy Abe' simply rebranded his channel. A lot of men who had initially been vocal supporters of The List quietly backtracked, others more loudly. The swiftness of their U-turns convinced Ola that they had hoped their condemnation of the accused would automatically make them one of the 'good guys', protect them against any potential claims. And they weren't the only ones to have had a change of heart. When Ola realised Th3 L1st page from All Tea was gone, instead of relief, she felt robbed. Everyone else got to move on with their lives once they'd scrubbed their servers. But a few people – Lewis, his family, Michael – bore the scars of it all.

In the weeks after the collision, Michael couldn't bring himself to talk about Lewis, but whenever she glimpsed his phone, he'd be reading the commentary surrounding his passing. Ola couldn't stop reading about him either. She felt blameworthy; she couldn't help it. Despite her lack of surety around Michael, she'd quickly assumed Lewis's guilt and only questioned his treatment when it was too late. She felt worse for the fact that even with all the headlines, the pledges and promises, his death had changed nothing. Every other week, Ola would see a clumsily worded tweet or distasteful video turn into a pile-on online lasting days. She'd see a rumour ruin a life before the facts had been ascertained. And what got her, what she couldn't stomach, was that there was no difference between the people calling for the harshest punishments and those insisting that more grace was needed on the internet. They were one and the same, considering themselves righteous in each scenario, finger pointing at anyone and everyone but themselves. The thought of accounts that harassed Lewis using the same Wifi to mourn him made her blood boil. She saw red each time she thought of those using the #ThinkFirst hashtag right after they'd driven someone offline for good. The internet never forgets, until it does.

Out of habit, she still scrolled All Tea from time to time, half expecting the thread to show up again. It never did, but it was only a matter of time before some other tragedy struck; trolls continued to use the site in the same way. Sometimes she wished she could falsely accuse a user on there herself. Pick an account at random and then blow their life to pieces, just to show how easy it was. How like them, she and Michael had been real people, assumed powerful because of visibility and an arbitrarily acquired blue tick.

Ola crushed a browning leaf underneath her heel with a satisfying crunch. 'That's great, Michael,' she said, taking care not to refer to him as 'babe'. 'Good for you.'

'And you?' he asked. 'What's freelancing saying?'

'It's good. I had a meeting with an agent yesterday, actually. She liked my book proposal – you know the one I wanted to do on the rise of female rappers? Think I'm going to sign with her.'

Ola's only regret was not leaving *Womxxxn* sooner; she earned more now and worried less, wrote about whatever she wanted. Plus, she was never late since her desk was in her bedroom.

'Oh shit! Ola, that's sick. Proud of you, man.' Michael scratched at his beard. 'I guess you'll be writing under "Ola Olajide" now?'

'Well, yeah, I was never going to change my pen name anyway. "Olaide Olajide" bangs. My dad really didn't have to go as hard as he did when he named me.'

'You know what, I'm here for it. Means no other man's gonna give you their surname either. Silver linings.'

Ola held a bubblegum-pink-tipped middle finger up at him.

'You know Ruth and Kwabz are fully dating now?' she said, swiftly changing topic.

'He told me. Man took her to Hakkasan on the first date,' Michael tutted teasingly. 'What changed her mind? He's still the same height last time I checked.'

'Fola read his birth chart and apparently it's fine that he's a Virgo, because his moon is in Aries. Or Aquarius? I don't know.'

'Rah, is it?' he laughed. 'We're compatible though, right? Pisces and Taurus?'

'Oh *now* you believe in star signs?' Ola said, wrapping a rope-like braid playfully around the end of her finger. 'Because you used to say it was juju …'

'Yeah, well, I keep telling you. I've changed, innit.' Michael let out another abrupt laugh before turning away. 'And Celie? How is she doing?'

The truth was, Celie was as she had ever been. Stoic, keeping calm and carrying on. Refusing to risk their friendship a second time, Ola didn't push when Celie said she didn't want to go to a counsellor, but was relieved that she had started attending a women's Bible study group again. Ola was glad her friend had something to help her through those initial months, after having her assault resurfaced so traumatically by The List. It was unbearable to hear Papi Danks use Lewis's death as evidence that it was a 'hoax', his girlfriend even taking to Snapchat to attack the 'clout chasers' and 'thots'. How painful it was when the 'Sweet Like Puff Puff' remix went to number 11 in the Top 40 and became even more ubiquitous than the original, dominating shop floors and dance floors for months. New life was breathed into it by the insufferable viral 'Puff Puff challenge' dance on

TikTok by nimble-limbed teens, making it virtually inescapable. But Celie didn't want to talk about it, so they didn't.

Ola tried to find solace in the silver-lining sacking and black-listing of Matthew Plummer. After an internal investigation, he was one of a handful of men to lose their job. But his crowd-funder put a damper on any sense of victory, launched to raise money to sue Nour El Masri. Her legal fee fund far surpassed his (Ola had donated, but felt less compelled to make it public this time) and yet the fact he had donations at all struck her as galling. That was the irony; men feared false accusations, but survivors were the ones being wrongly smeared. No matter how much evidence there was to support an allegation, for months afterwards accusers were demanded to #ThinkFirst and #RememberLewis.

'Celie's cool,' said Ola. 'Busy with work, church stuff. We're flying to Brussels in November for her birthday. Ruth's already asking why we're not going to Dubai.'

Michael smiled. 'Cool, cool. Sounds fun.' He slowed his pace a touch and drove his hands further into his pockets. 'So … are you dating?'

She responded with a spluttered cough; he'd caught her off guard. She wasn't, much to Kiran's dismay. She had created profile after profile for Ola on app after app, singing the virtues of pansexuality and polyamory like she had shares in them.

'I'm a Je-hoe-vah's witness, spreading the good news', she'd texted her just yesterday. 'Omg! Should I tell Soph that's my religion??!! 😂😂'

Currently, Kiran was in a throuple with an emotionally distant actor she'd met on Hinge and his graphic designer girl-friend, who she much preferred.

KIRAN: as a connoisseur of pretty much every gender
going, i'm telling you aunty: date women. you'll be a
catch amongst catches. with guys? yeah, there's plenty
of fish in the sea but you're way more likely to just end
up catching feelings for a dickhead.

KIRAN: or herpes.

KIRAN: and I actually think herpes might be less painful.

Ola gave Michael the same reply as she had her friend. 'I'm just focusing on myself right now, really, working on the book.' She tried to make her voice sound as nonchalant as possible. 'Are you?'

He shook his head and Ola realised she'd been holding her breath.

'Nah. The List still comes up if you go far down enough on the Google results. Not the greatest dating app icebreaker. "One of these is true: I'm allergic to cheese, I was born in Scotland, I was once falsely accused of harassment and physical assault."'

He wasn't wrong; the UK was small. It would be harder to find someone who hadn't come across The List than had.

'Besides,' he added, eyeing Ola. 'If I couldn't make it work with you, I probably can't make it work with anyone.'

He continued to gaze at her until Ola scrunched up her nose, looking sceptical.

'Ay,' Michael chuckled. 'It was worth a shot!'

They walked further, laughing and catching up. Then, as they turned and made their way past the children's zoo, Ola saw her. The hairs on the back of her neck stood up and her mouth swung open. She recognised her instantly: there was no mistaking that prominent jaw, the side profile she'd studied so many times on Instagram. Deep-set eyes, plump mouth. In the distance she could see her hair was different − a blunt-cut black bob − and she was holding the hand of a fudge-coloured girl who hopped up and down as she skipped along the pathway. Her other hand was pushing a grey and silver stroller.

As she got closer, the orb of her stomach became more pronounced, protruding in an oat-coloured ribbed dress, rivalling the rotundness of her backside. Ola had never thought she was pretty, but today she was radiant with that undeniable, otherworldly pregnancy glow. Watching her, she suddenly felt very intensely like something had been stolen from her.

She couldn't help but gasp. For so long, Jackie Asare had been an onscreen assailant, the final boss in a video game. And there she was, in the flesh, flanked by a brood of kids like a fertility goddess. But there were no horns, no hooves, no trident adorning her. She looked like anybody else.

It happened as quickly as she spotted her: Ola marched towards Jackie. By the time Michael cottoned on and realised who she had her sights on, she was way ahead of him while he stood stunned. Ola could hear him calling after her in the background, trying his best to stop her. But she powered through the throng of dog walkers and office workers on their breaks, a woman on a mission that she hadn't yet worked out. What would she say to her? What might she do to her? What would Jackie have to say? Would she flat out deny it? Catch Ola off guard with a tearful apology? Ola was running now, the wind rushing in her ears. 'Oi!' she shouted in Jackie's direction. 'Oi!' She swore Jackie caught her eye. As Ola gained pace, eyes still on her, she careened into an adolescent on an electric scooter, knocking him clean off and halting her stride. Onlookers slowed down, craning their necks to watch the commotion. Ola looked down to see the unharmed teen dusting himself off before she looked back over to Jackie. She was gone.

Ola stood stupefied for a moment, searching vainly from left to right. Before long, Michael was beside her, caught up and saying things she couldn't quite catch. He pulled her towards a bench, so she gripped its arm and his as she sat, trying to breathe. Perched next to her, he radiated heat.

'Did you see her?' Ola panted.

Michael nodded. 'I mean, it looked like her. Might not have been though,' he added without conviction. She considered it for a moment. That her rage and hatred had created a convincing mirage. That Jackie had an eerily identical doppelganger and Ola had fixed on her manically.

'It was her,' Ola said, finally.

'Yeah. Maybe,' Michael said, the doubt clear in his tone. He pressed his shoulder into hers lightly. 'Are you all right?'

'No. No, I'm fucking not.'

'Yeah. Me either.'

'That woman fucked our marriage before it even started, Michael,' Ola said, her voice breaking. She felt queasy at this feeling she knew too well. It was as if she was back in 2019 and her life was falling to pieces yet again.

'The cheating – yeah, that was both of you. I know that. But all her lies, her bullshit on All Tea … it nearly killed you. I still have nightmares about our wedding day.'

'I hear you.'

'She fucked everything, fucked off, and then went on with her life. No consequences, no charges. Not even an apology. And we're supposed to just what, move on?'

'I know.'

'It's fucked up!' Ola bellowed. Her shouting startled an Irish setter who barked loudly in response. 'She can't get away with it. She can't.' Ola waited for Michael's concurrence, but he continued to sit quietly.

'Michael?'

He slumped backwards and sighed. 'I don't know, man. I guess I've kind of got used to the idea that she will. Marcia warned me I might not ever get closure. If you went up to her today, she probably wouldn't admit it. And that would only make things worse. You'd just be seen boxing up a pregnant woman in Battersea Park. And I know you ain't trying to go out like that. Plus—'

'Plus *what?*'

'*Plus* she's already taken so much from us, Ola.' He sighed again. 'She took my job, my health. She fucked things up with the only woman I've ever loved. The only woman I ever *will* love.' Ola felt her heart skip.

'Don't get me wrong – I know I did dirt. But I can't let her take the small peace I've finally got. You can't either. You get me?'

She fell back onto the bench beside him, dog-tired, and sighed. 'Kind of.'

They sat there for some time, listening to the leaves rustling in the breeze, their chests rising and falling as they caught their breath.

'That was kind of sexy though, you running to go and knock her out,' Michael said eventually.

Ola chewed at the inside of her cheek to suppress a laugh. 'Not funny.'

'Who said I was joking?' He edged closer to her. 'What is it with south London girls, man? You were coming like Suge Knight!'

'Marcia still has work to do, I see.'

'Nah but seriously. You were about to square up to the baby bump. Maybe you're not as bougie as I thought – that was some *Love and Hip Hop* shit.'

'Yeah yeah, keep chatting shit, innit. You think I won't find that baseball bat?'

'See? Always choosing violence!' Michael laughed, then rubbed the back of his neck. 'We still good to get coffee? I get it if you'd rather not, no pressure.'

Ola kept her eyes on the ground as she considered Michael's words. They lingered in the air, as the cooing of pigeons passing by their feet filled the silence between them. With a huff, she raised herself up from the bench and dusted the front of her dress with her palms.

'I have time for one turmeric latte,' she said, unable to conceal her smile at Michael's own that stretched from ear to ear.

27

When Jackie got inside, she locked and bolted the door behind her. She tried her best to stay composed – she didn't want to worry an already agitated Amiyah – but her hands were shaking as she leaned against the banister of the staircase to steady herself. It kept her standing, at least.

Aaron came out into the hallway when he heard the bang of the front door, a kitchen towel slung over his shoulder. One look at Jackie's face and he knew something wasn't right.

'Babe?' he asked, concern in his voice. 'What's wrong?'

She trembled as she fell into his arms. Jackie gave him that look that communicated she couldn't speak while her step-daughter was in earshot: 'Not in front of the kids.' Amiyah was four now, at that age where no conversation could happen without her repeating it shrilly like a parrot.

'Amiyah, sweetheart,' Aaron called out to his daughter. 'Go to your room and put on *Peppa Pig*, yeah?' Amiyah bowled up the stairs happily. He turned back to Jackie.

'I'll put Danielle to bed and then we'll talk, okay?'

She nodded, her face covered by her hands and he carried their sleeping baby from the pram to the bedroom upstairs.

When he came into the living room, Jackie was sitting on the couch hugging one of the cushions on her lap, staring forward, mind occupied. Aaron sat and slid his hand behind her neck, massaging it as he did.

'What's up?'

'I just saw Michael and Ola,' she said quietly. 'In Battersea Park.'

Aaron hated hearing Jackie say his name, hated thinking about her anywhere near that man. His jaw and fist clenched in unison but he tried to maintain his characteristically chipper exterior. His anger was overshadowed by eagerness to hear what she was telling him. 'Oh rah,' he said. 'They're still together?'

Jackie shrugged. 'I don't know. But it was crazy. Ola clocked me and the next thing I know, she's running at me from across the park like some madwoman, shouting shit. Michael was behind her, coming at me too. I'm still shaken up.'

Heat flashed through Aaron, who was now so livid that he had to stand and pace. He covered his mouth with his hand.

'Did he touch you?' he rasped. 'Amiyah? I swear to God, if either of them—'

'No, no, no,' Jackie said, standing to hold his arms. They dropped at her touch. 'I managed to get out of there before anything could pop off. It was just a shock and … so weird?' She shuddered. 'After all this time, after everything that came out about Michael last year, all that shit with their wedding, it's *me* she's coming for? I've moved on. I thought they would have by now.' She squeezed Aaron's shoulder, as if for emphasis. 'I haven't spoken to him in more than two years. I've made no contact since it ended. With either of them.'

Aaron looked away from her, nodding stiffly. The atmosphere in the room shifted.

'I know I moved mad in the past, but that was the past.' Jackie shook her head. 'God only knows what he's said to her, to have her going on like that.'

Jackie lowered her hands and bit her lip, taking a step closer towards him. Aaron took her in his arms and stroked her hair, feeling his chest becoming wet with her tears.

'I'm so sorry that this is still affecting us,' she sobbed. 'I only wanted to take the girls for a nice day out, but it's like I can't put that shit behind me.'

Aaron sighed and shushed her. 'Don't be silly, babe. We all make mistakes. You're not that person any more. Now,' he wiped beneath her eyes gently with his thumbs, 'try not to stress. It's not good for Jordan.'

She sniffed. 'I love you so much, baby,' she said, burrowing back into his chest, words muffled by his embrace.

He smiled and cupped her chin, tilting her head up towards him before kissing her lightly. 'I love you too.' Then he stepped back, spreading his fingers wide as he placed his palms on the curve of her belly. 'And you too, little man.'

Jackie fell asleep on the couch soon after. As she dozed, Aaron crept back into the kitchen to put the kettle on. He'd make her a mug of hot water for when she got up. It was the least strange of her pregnancy cravings – lemons and ice among them – and he hoped it might calm her nerves. He watched her chest and stomach rise and fall as she slept and felt an overwhelming urge to bundle her and the bump in his arms, smother them with kisses. He loved them so much. What a terrible day his poor girlfriend had endured. She was so shaken when she got in, had clung to him for dear life. He'd be lying if he said he didn't feel some guilt as he watched her rest. Jackie was the last person he intended to hurt. He'd done it for her, after all.

It had been impulsive, putting Michael's name on The List. It's not as though Aaron went out of his way to find a spread-sheet of abusers to add Michael's name to – he wasn't crazy. He merely saw an opportunity and he took it, exactly like Michael had with his girlfriend. The List had been sent to him by his sister who worked as an A&R and wasn't shocked at the pres-ence of her former client Papi Danks on it. When Aaron realised what it was, he saw what a list like that could do to a person's life. In his hands, it was an anonymous, immediate way of settling a score. Addressing a wrong that had long eaten at him. As he typed Michael's name into the spreadsheet, Aaron accepted that he might never get over Jackie's affair. He thought about the sleepless nights. The humiliation. Coming across Michael's smug, self-congratulatory post about his new job the week before. The engagement post before that, crown-ing him and his none-the-wiser fiancée as the king and queen of #BlackLove. And the day before that, when the living-room Bluetooth speaker synced with Jackie's Spotify and showed she had been listening to old episodes of *Caught Slippin*. He'd seethed internally.

Aaron had never understood what Jackie saw in Michael. What it was about him that made her want him so badly. He was charismatic, he could grant him that, on that podcast she obsessed over. She'd had the nerve to take Aaron along to a few live shows. Said it was 'good research' for his own flailing podcast that never took off. In hindsight, he knew it was to make Michael jealous. He'd seen him around a few times before and after that; at workshops, events put on by mutual friends. Tall, dark and handsome, just like Jackie liked them – she'd initially curved Aaron because she didn't like 'lighties'. Still, how she'd continued to vie for the love of a man who so obviously didn't respect her, he could never understand. But perhaps they were the same; Aaron had loved her since college, even though she was the type of girl most guys didn't take seriously. He'd seen everything in her that Michael was blind to. Jackie was the kindest person he knew; her energy was contagious. It was a cliché to say, but her smile really did light up any room she walked into. When they finally crossed a line in spring 2016, and Aaron moved his luggage in from the friend zone, he felt like he could fly. Until Jackie hooked up with Michael and ghosted him. Of course, he'd been there to pick up the pieces when Michael discarded her, just like the rest. Wiping her tears as he did today.

They had got back on track, or so he'd thought. But a year later she was suddenly sullen again, monosyllabic. It had been around Christmas. He knew it was Michael straight away and as soon as he was able, he went through her phone as she slept. She'd changed his name in her phone from 'Mikey' to 'Nail Shop' but lo and behold there appeared message after hysterical message that Michael hadn't even bothered to reply to. He scrolled up and was greeted by explicit sexts, pictures of Michael's erect penis. Transparent bullshit about him missing her, thinking about her. Then, most painfully, nude pictures of the body he lay next to each night. He couldn't believe Jackie had gone back there after how easily Michael had ditched her the first time. It was as if she preferred his cruel indifference to Aaron's love, his decency. He felt like a fool, alone, reading her passionate declarations to a man he would never be.

The content of those messages made him retch. Outlining vile, repulsive acts that she claimed to want done to her, pleaded for. But Aaron and Jackie never had sex like that, so where did it come from? She must have been pressured, coerced. Her dignity so thoroughly degraded by this man that she wanted him to choke and spit on her. There was a power dynamic at play, surely; an imbalanced one. He wasn't naive enough to suggest Jackie had been forced to cheat, but there must have been an element of pressure.

Aaron acted on his first instinct. Using Jackie's phone, he called Michael to tell him in no uncertain terms to leave her alone. But Michael didn't pick up the late-night call, in what Aaron began to realise was his good fortune. As she lay sleeping, he wrote everything he wanted to say to Michael in messages from her number. He wished death on him, his mum, said he knew where he lived and would fuck up that pretty face of his with acid. Promised to ruin his life. A bit out there, but perfectly plausible given Jackie's past behaviour. Her self-destructive tendencies, her lack of self-worth, her recklessness. Michael would never be tempted to reach out to her, never reply if she messaged him again, which she likely would in her weakness. When he pressed send, he marvelled at the magic of modern technology, deleting any evidence of what he'd written, all wiped clean from her phone.

Initially, when he confronted Jackie about Michael, she downplayed it, saying they'd only exchanged casual texts. When Aaron told her he'd read that she planned on leaving him, she claimed Michael had been the initiator, which was of course debunked by the messages. She squirmed pathetically for an excuse, landing on having been starstruck, dazzled by Michael, that he had some kind of hold over her. A 'soul tie', she called it. After a night of fighting, he'd relented and they adopted the idea that Michael had wielded his status like some sort of intoxicating cult leader, which finally made forgiveness possible. That, and the fact she blurted out that she was three weeks pregnant.

The baby was definitely his, since she promised she and Michael hadn't slept together in their recent rekindling of contact, like that somehow made any of this better. So, there was the truth: she'd been taken advantage of. Not her exact words, but Aaron knew her better than anyone. He could read between the lines. Michael was famous, powerful, and Jackie was vulnerable, weak. Men had taken advantage of her in the past – he'd seen it first-hand. Her previous relationships, a pattern of co-dependency and self-sabotage.

Aaron knew he'd got carried away protecting Jackie. He hadn't wanted to destroy anyone's life: everything he did was to protect his own. They had their first kid on the way, Jackie was a great stepmum to Amiyah. And she *had* been abused. Sort of. Okay, so he'd employed a little poetic licence. But who could say whether abuse had taken place? It was likely at some point, wasn't it, with someone like Michael? The way he'd treated Jackie, leaving her sobbing every night. The toll it had taken on her self-esteem: that had been real. Michael was a menace. He needed to be taken off the streets, stopped from hurting some-one else. Stopped from hurting Jackie, again. Aaron was keeping her safe from a man who would never love her, not like he did.

'Mirrorissa92' was supposed to start and stop with The List, plus a few trolling comments here and there to freak Michael out. When Aaron joined All Tea, it had been less to progress an agenda and more to vent. In truth, he'd got a thrill out of letting Michael know exactly why he'd done what he'd done, when he messaged him: 'Because I can, Mikey'. Still, he forgot about The List after a while, when no outlets picked it up. But beneath the surface, the allegations took on a life of their own, grew larger in all those chat rooms and forums online. The endless harass-ment, the doxxing. The wedding hashtag takeover – even he knew that was a step too far. Ola was collateral damage, and the forum didn't seem to care. These women on All Tea were so angry at these men, so ready to fight.

He said women, but they could be anyone, really. 'What do girls like?' Aaron remembered thinking as he searched for a screen name for his account. Jackie loved *Insecure*. Issa Rae. Before landing on 'mirrorissa', he'd toyed with 'ChampagneMami_' and 'Beyonces_Tethered', wracking his brain for the pop cultural references his sister and Jackie made. '92' was simply the year he was born. He was careful never to post from his own laptop or phone; instead, he used one of the open computers at the coworking space where he hot-desked.

If anything, Aaron had been merciful. He could have accused Michael of rape. But he left it vague, intentionally. Harassment: but of what kind? Assault: to what degree? He laced it with just enough detail to make Jackie and the rest of the world wake up to the fact that Michael Koranteng wasn't all he was cracked up to be. He hadn't been convinced anyone would take it that seriously. He hadn't even spelt Michael's name right. But it got deadly serious, fast. It worked like a charm. Aaron didn't consider himself particularly clever or cunning, really. He'd simply lied on the internet, as people did every day.

And got away with it. That didn't mean he hadn't been surprised by how far it had gone. There was nothing he could do to pull it back, slow it all down. Some days he'd scroll the forum in muted shock, as the All Tea army planned their next line of attack. When he heard through the grapevine that Michael had ended up in hospital after a collision with a car, it kept him awake that night. Rumours swirled that it had been a suicide attempt, like Lewis. That wasn't what he'd planned. But

Aaron had promised Michael that he'd ruin his life, just as he had done his. And unlike Michael, he made good on his promises.

As the kettle came to the boil with a whistle, he heard Jackie stirring awake on the couch. 'Babe?' she called sleepily, into the emptiness of the room.

In the kitchen, Aaron closed his eyes until he heard the bubbling water in the kettle still. He stared into space as he poured the water into Jackie's favourite mug, letting the rising steam envelop his face for a moment. Once he felt the tension release from his neck, he took a deep, calming breath. 'Coming, baby,' he shouted, as he made his way back into the living room.

Acknowledgements

The List is a book I very nearly didn't write. It would have never come to fruition if it wasn't for a number of amazing people I am incredibly blessed to have known over the years, who have inspired, encouraged, edited, championed, supported and loved me. Sometimes all of these things, sometimes all at once.

Yem and Yinks; my two favourite people on the planet and biggest inspirations. Whenever things have felt impossible, it is you guys that have kept me going. I love you more than I can ever express, so I will just keep dedicating books to you both.

Mum and Dad; thank you for always allowing me to be myself, for better or worse, whatever that looked like (and boy, did it look strange sometimes!) Mum, thank you for being the most reliable, selfless person I know. Dad, thank you for the gift of imagination – the stories on the walk to school, a journey that has ended up right here. I love you guys. I love you too, Nana; thank you for all the love, encouragement and prayers.

Michelle Blackman-Asante and Pamela Chinwe Nnajiuba; my first readers of what was a confused mess of a book. But you both still believed in it, and in me. Meech, my day one G and OG bestie. You have been putting up with me for over twenty years! Thank you for doing so. Pam, I have been putting up with you for over ten. You're welcome! Seriously though, you both inspire me and I'm so proud to call you my friends.

Elizabeth Uviebinene and Philippa Mensah; Polly, without you, I wouldn't have this book, let alone four others. I already got so lucky with my sisters and then God threw in an extra one for good measure. Pip, thank you for your realness, your prayers and your you-ness. Whenever people meet my loved ones, they comment on how great everyone is and you guys are such a clear example of why.

Bosun Lewis and Nels Abbey; my mandem whisperers! Thank you Boss for the legalese and ensuring I didn't disgrace myself with the football references. You are solid as a rock and I appreciate you. Nelson, thank you for being the older brother I was certain I did not want or need. Thank you for sitting through the countless tearful phone calls about any and everything. You are both wonderful adverts for the male of the species.

Clarissa Pabi and Trim Lamba; Ola's inadvertent wardrobe inspiration, all black everything gang. I still hope I can absorb just a fraction of your smarts by osmosis. There isn't a more iconic duo – thank you for always being honest with me and having my best interests at heart.

Jochebed Fening, Amanda Regan and Sasha Bello; Joch, thank you for saying I was 'lexically gifted' in that politics class in college. I very much took it to heart! Mandy, thank you for still cheerleading my every move from overseas and your endless, unwavering backing of me. Sash, for always checking in and sending your love, no matter how long it's been or how busy you are.

Silé Edwards, Helen Garnons-Williams, Alison May, the 'Devon Firestarters' and Debbie Flint; thank you all for, in numerous ways, helping me change and shape this book for the better, whether it was by reading it at its worst, giving me words of encouragement at my most fraught or providing a well-catered, idyllic backdrop to write it in (and wine! Lots of wine!)

Thomas Mensah, Leticia Mensah, Peter Asante; Aunty, Uncles, thank you for helping me with the Twi in this book and ensuring I did not insult my Ghanaian brethren!

Hayley Steed – all I had was 30,000 words and a dream. Thank you for helping me make it into so much more. Thank you for having the courage I was at times lacking in telling this story. Thank you for changing my life. Kishani Widyaratna and Jessica Williams; you made something that was a billion half-formed, frantic thoughts into an actual book. You made me think deeply about the ways I could tell this story, ensured I did it justice and were at the core of creating something I am so proud of. There aren't words for how grateful I am! Queen Naomi Mantin, Niriksha Bharadia, Matt Clacher, Liv Marsden, Jessica Thompson, Katy Archer, Nicole Jashapara, Essie Cousins, Martin Bryant, Amber Burlinson, Paul Erdpresser, Natasha Lanigan, Rochelle Dowden-Lord, Anna Derkacz, Bethan Moore, Michelle Kane, David Roth-Ey, Chris Gurney, Graham Holmes, Arthur Heard, Josie Freedman, Hannah Ladds, Jacqui Siu, Neil McSteen, Glenn Miller, Micheal Foster, Deborah Frances White, Amy Reed, moukies: thank you, thank you, thank you.

And everyone else; Tawanda Mhindurwa – you have been rooting for me from the second I showed up on your Twitter timeline nearly a decade ago. Thank you for being there during the high-highs and low-lows. Bernardine Evaristo, for being the kindest soul in a business that can break ones, and as cool as everyone thinks you are. Tonica Hunter, because I don't think

I've ever properly thanked you for pushing me to make something of my year out of university with writing; here are your deserved flowers. Adjoa Kwarteng, because I wouldn't have made it through the second year at aforementioned university without you and therefore wouldn't have written this book. Tom Northover, because you randomly implored me to take writing seriously over Facebook Messenger some ten years ago and I never did (and never will!) forget it!

Last but by no means least: to you, reader, for taking the time to read my first novel (and these long winded acknowledgements).

Book Club Questions

1. What did you think when you first read that Michael's name was on The List?

2. Did you feel more sympathetic to Ola or to Michael? Did that change as the book went on?

3. How did reading their alternating perspectives shape how you saw the story?

4. Were you familiar with lists like the one Michael's name appears on before reading the book? What do you think of the discussion of them in the novel?

5. Do you think the ability to be anonymous online is a good or bad thing?

6. How did you feel about the portrayal of Michael and Ola's relationship in the novel?

7. Do you consider Michael guilty of any wrongdoing? Why, or why not?

8. Ola identifies as a feminist, but in the wake of Michael's name appearing on The List, she begins to doubt herself. What did you think of her navigation of that dilemma?

9. If someone close to you was subject to anonymous accusations, how do you think you would handle it?

10. What did you think of the way Celie responds to The List and how did that change as the novel went on?

11. Discuss the portrayal of the mental health challenges faced by Michael, Lewis and other characters in the novel.

12. The novel explores the relationship between the online and offline lives of its characters. Do you think the two worlds can be separated?

13. How did *The List* make you consider the possible routes to justice available for survivors of sexual assault?

14. How much did you sympathise with Lewis, and to what extent is his fate a product of the internet?

15. How did you feel when you read the ending?